A FORGOTTEN MAN

S.p.i. BOOKS

A division of Shapolsky Publishers, Inc.

A NOVEL
Carl Bancoff

S.P.I. BOOKS

A division of Shapolsky Publishers, Inc.

Copyright © 1987, 1992 by Carl Bancoff

Reprinted from the 1987 Seth Press hardcover edition.

All rights reserved under International and Pan American
Copyright Conventions. Published in the U.S.A. by
Shapolsky Publishers, Inc. No parts of this book may be used
or reproduced in any manner whatsoever without written
permission of Shapolsky Publishers, Inc., except in the case
of brief quotations embodied in critical articles or reviews.

For any additional information, contact:
S.P.I. BOOKS/Shapolsky Publishers, Inc.
136 West 22nd Street
New York, NY 10011
(212) 633-2022
FAX (212) 633-2123

ISBN: 1-56171-095-4

10 9 8 7 6 5 4 3 2 1

Printed and bound in the U.S.A.
by Ringier America, Dresden, TN

PART I

1

FOCUSING

Another hot, humid day. Later in the afternoon, the usual heavy rainfall would help drive the temperature down; no matter, Saigon, in the Fall of 1963, was a city never too far removed from the boiling point.

On a quiet, downtown street, three youngsters played a languid game of tag. A barber plied his trade as two squatting customers awaited their turn. On an old woman's back lay a pole with buckets of water at each end. She paused to spit betel nut juice and then continued on her way. The shops were closed and the surrounding streets had no cars, bikes, food carts, or the notorious Honda cowboys. The temperature was rising.

The inactivity was disconcerting to a young man standing alone near the itinerant sidewalk barber. Chac Duo Trang wiped his brow with a trembling hand and took a deep breath. Professor Ling had been delayed. Chac questioned his judgment, his mettle—his ability to survive without his mentor. Time was no longer an ally. The frightened university student had an urge to run, but self-preservation yielded to curiosity.

A small group walked towards him from a park a block away, at a brisk but controlled pace. The Westerners who had been milling about also saw them and now approached the street corner. They all wore PRESS badges, two toted still cameras, another held a large movie camera on his shoulder.

Vietnamese, mostly young men, quietly strolled towards Chac from every direction, except from the street leading to the park—it bore no pedestrian traffic.

It was an orderly crowd that waited at the main intersection. There was no conversation from the attentive audience, its collective eye riveted on the barren street.

A barely audible sound grew in strength, clearly approaching the corner, but from a distance. At first, many strained in anticipation, but then there was the unmistakably dull clang of cymbals. The faint sound of chanting could soon be heard. Voices clear and strong were singing a deep but soothing melody.

The source of the music came into view at last. The chanters, a column of Buddhist monks—bonzes—surged from the park into the empty street, clean-shaven and bald, their brown robes moving ever so lightly over frail frames, their sandals silently gliding to the same beat.

The men were of various ages, though elders dominated the front rows except for a young man squarely in the center. Their faces were taut with anguish and commitment as they continued to chant their droning litany in unison. Each stride heightened the tension; the effect on the crowd was hypnotic. Chac turned away from the procession and noticed the semi-circle of altars in an open area.

The robed men had reached their destination. They sat on the ground in the lotus position. The chanting and the prayers resumed, but now they were not as one; it was a loud confused chorus, each man going in a different direction and pleading with forces unseen.

Their prayers were answered. Many screamed, a few whispered, some sobbed, others openly cried and the tears streamed down proud and knowing faces. Then they were one again, and they harmonized the sweetness of a shared revelation.

A slight shuffling of sandals. Two robed men positioned themselves at an altar near the Western reporters; a third, in his early twenties, and the young man who had earlier caught Chac's attention sat alone in the center.

The youth's hands cupped his knees, the back arched forward, puckered lips tightened an already small mouth, large and starry eyes reached out to survey the universe. Though the mood was somber and serene, he appeared content and joyful. No longer part of this world, his senses and spiritual being had already departed, only the flesh remained.

An elder quickly poured gasoline in a circle around the youth, and then directly on him. Chac heard the clicks of a still camera and the hum of motion pictures. A monk stood and shouted into a bullhorn, "A Buddhist priest willingly sacrifices his life for the principles of his religion!" The bonzes began to recite their prayers. Another elder approached the young bonze with a match and threw it quickly into a puddle of fuel.

The monks were in a frenzy, they renewed their supplications to Buddha and the joy of martyrdom. "A Buddhist priest willingly sacrifices his life for the principles of his religion!" was repeated in Vietnamese and then in English by a screaming, hysterical bonze.

A numbed Chac, only a few feet away, watched the jumping flames consume the bonze. His dreamy eyes remained fixed, his mouth did not quiver—not the slightest movement to indicate that anything out of the ordinary was happening. Finally, like a great tree that has received the axe's final blow, the bonze's body keeled over and struck the ground.

Above the roar of the fire, a middle-aged priest left the altar and quietly awaited his turn. This bonze sat more erect; the body slanted backward and the neck flexed skyward; eyes peered at the heavens from behind thin-framed glasses. Though Chac could only see his profile, he thought he detected a grin. The gasoline was poured in exactly the same way. The bullhorn blared the same refrain and the priests remained in their frenzy. The smell of burning flesh sickened Chac and he turned away, clutching his abdomen. The second bonze was already engulfed in flames.

Chac looked toward the park and saw an open-bed truck with white-helmeted soldiers turn onto the street. Almost instantly the other streets were blocked with police trucks and army jeeps. The Buddhist priests could no longer be heard, loudspeakers mounted atop police vans blasted American rock-and-roll music.

The anti-government rally was in total disarray, the screaming crowd dispersed in all directions. Chac ran into a burly Western photographer who was grappling with two men over possession of his camera. Helmeted soldiers with swinging truncheons were nearby, above the music he could hear the thud of a club as it struck bone. Chac would have to act quickly to avoid arrest. He assumed the two men in civilian clothes confiscating the film were undercover police agents. Could he pass himself off as one of them?

Some priests gathered around the altars, others were running and looking for an escape route. Chac tackled a passing bonze from behind and wrestled him to the ground. No resistance was offered, but it was not enough to arrest the priest without signs of a struggle. He punched the bonze with solid blows to the nose and mouth. The priest, now bleeding profusely, was brought roughly to his feet; Chac held his wrist, applied a strangle hold to the neck and sought a police van.

They walked past other soldiers and police who gave them little notice. The bonze limply let himself be dragged along. Chac could see trucks filled with prisoners. He was slowing down to gain precious time as they approached a shop. Chac noticed a door slightly ajar and a little boy looking directly at him. He pushed the bonze towards the opening before the child had time to act and both men tumbled into the shop. Chac quickly closed the door and looked out a window. The priest staggered to a chair and collapsed into it. Chac was convinced that in the confusion, no one had seen their escape. The fires continued, but a water truck was approaching the site. The altars were no longer upright and no priest or newsman could be seen. Two boys ran past the window, clutching their heads.

A young woman entered the shop from a back door. She was startled to see two strangers, but smiled with relief when a boy darted from behind a counter and rushed to her side, crying, "Mama, Mama." Chac bowed politely and asked for her help. She moved quickly, tearing pieces of cloth into bandages and applying them to the bonze's wounds.

Suddenly the rock music stopped. Chac peered out of the thin crack of the front door. The government troops were gone. Chac turned quickly and bowed to the bonze. As he helped the woman attend to the priest, he tried to explain his aggressive behavior and apologize. After the bleeding had stopped and the dressings were removed, the priest thanked the woman and embraced her son. He bowed humbly to the university student and said, "Your motives were honorable. Please accept my gratitude."

"You were next," Chac said. "I saw you sitting at the altar. You were waiting to have your body drenched with gasoline and set ablaze."

"Yes," he said proudly, and for the first time, the bonze smiled.

The young woman offered them food and drink, but they both refused. She praised both men for their courage as she wiped her boy's forehead. She then clutched his hand (no sense waiting for trouble to return) and left the store front to an adjoining room.

"Why did you come to the demonstration?" the monk asked, a cigarette dangling from his swollen lips.

"It was not my idea. Professor Ling, my history teacher and a long time family friend, was supposed to meet me, but he never came. I've had some reservations about our leaders and he suggested I try to understand the opposition's viewpoint. This rally was to be the first phase of my re-education process." The bonze looked at him squarely, an opportunity not to be missed.

"What is your view of the government?"

"I see the corruption and the terror in Saigon," Chac answered calmly. "Some of it is unnecessary. But there must be stability before we can grow and develop as a nation. You priests must return to your pagodas, stop the play acting and find ways of reconciling your differences with Saigon. The struggle against the National Liberation Front will be strengthened. Catholic and Buddhist must live in harmony, or our future is doomed."

"We view today's threat as greater than tomorrow's uncertainty," the priest said with a smile. "Dialogue was tried and it failed. You think this is play acting? Do you doubt our sincerity?"

"No. Only your methods. I had always believed the bonzes renounced violence, whether to others or self-inflicted. Now you lead the protests and openly defy the government. How can they fight the enemy when their own house is not in order?" a hint of anger creeping into Chac's voice.

The bonze surveyed the shop, rose from the chair and walked to the window. He made no effort to conceal his identity from anyone who might be lingering in the street. He turned around after a period of reflection and walked across the floor to where the young man stood. He faced Chac again. "Who is the enemy?" he asked. The bonze had a paternal, benevolent look Chac recognized. He had often seen it on the face of his parish priest. It always suggested that Chac was misguided.

"Maybe it is you and the other bonzes! The burnings and the protests only stiffen the government's resolve. Look at the reprisals! Innocent people suffer . . . those of us who try to understand the issues and have remained silent," he said bitterly.

"In this country," the bonze replied firmly but with no displeasure, "someone like yourself who chooses not to speak, has perhaps the loudest voice."

An agitated Chac shouted, "Your actions will lead to more conflict and weaken the cause of peace. I saw that bonze burn, and the look on his face. It was the world of the Absolute! The need to be part of the realm of Nirvana! If you think dying in those flames benefits me, is in my welfare, then you are wrong. This whole crazy demonstration is a grab for political power, it has nothing to do with religious freedom. The new leadership you want may be worse than the present. Does that mean more burning? Soon there will be no more Buddhist monks. Go back to the pagoda and forget about politics. There is no Nirvana in a gasoline can."

The bonze strolled to the door. He was neither resentful nor in a mood to argue with the ill-tempered Chac. He chose to weigh his words carefully; not to offend, yet be true to his own ideals. "To speak of such things can only mean you cannot understand. Please thank the woman again for her kindness. I am in debt to you for saving me from the soldiers. You have permitted me the privilege of fulfilling a great duty."

Chac shook his head in disbelief. The anger was still there, and the frustration. The monk stood serenely at the wide open door and looked out into the brilliantly sunny street.

"I have a good source for petrol!" Chac called after him. "Let me know if you run short."

The bonze was not disturbed by Chac's remark. As he proceeded into the vacant street, his thoughts focussed on the fastest way to find the other monks. Another demonstration should be organized quickly, there mustn't be any changes and, he would remind the elders, it was his turn.

The shuffling of sandals became rapid. The brown robed priest broke into a trot. Speed was important, time precious. There was much work to be done.

* * *

2

THE stately Georgian mansion on Pine Street had a noble and prominent role to play in Colonial Philadelphia. It was built by Lars Swenson, a well known and prestigious attorney in the latter part of the eighteenth century. Mr. Swenson was a friend and supporter of Samuel Powell, Philadelphia's first mayor after Independence. The home Lars built for his family was a jewel in a city known for its beauty and magnificent architecture.

The dinner parties at the Swenson home were exquisite, an invitation assured one of meeting the important and influential people in the arts and government. John Todd and his wife Dolly were frequent guests and good friends. After John's death, the widow Todd would meet and marry President James Madison. Lars Swenson left Philadelphia to live in the new city of Washington and serve his country in the Madison Administration.

His home would be occupied by the Right Reverend Harrison Keller of the Protestant Church of St. George. The Reverend Keller and his clergyman father were celebrated for their militant positions in the struggle for independence, when many other church figures advocated peaceful accommodation with the British. The Keller family lived in the Swenson House (already designated a landmark site, commissioned and named by the Philadelphia Historical Society) for forty years.

There were many occupants over the course of the next sixty years, but no one lived in the house for more than a decade. It remained a single dwelling until the early part of the twentieth century, when the Sisters of Mercy bought the Swenson House and the adjacent property to create a much needed orphanage. The good Sisters needed a much larger orphanage after World War II, and so sold the Swenson House—the mansion in disrepair and the neighborhood in a marked state of decline—to its current owners at a ridiculously low price.

The Historical Society and other agencies reversed the trend in the early 1950s and the Society Hill section would become the desirable area the Swenson's had known in the Republic's early days. Progress did not come easily and the new owners of the Georgian mansion were forced to make certain improvements to the exterior to maintain the original architectural style.

Indeed, Ben Franklin himself would have felt at ease walking the cobblestones of Pine St. in modern Philadelphia. If he stopped at the Swenson House, Ben would note a wrought iron hitchingpost at the curb; next to the steps was an original footscraper; an iron firemark of an early insurance company contrasted with the fine masonry of old and refurbished brick. The fanlight above the ornate door was original, as was the parapet on the balcony. A shed dormer was a recent renovation, but in keeping with the original style. The small belfry was no longer present, a reluctant but necessary move made by the good Sisters after an orphan boy had fallen from the turret. Old Ben would have had difficulty understanding the interior of the Swenson House, for it retained little of its Georgian grandeur. But to its present occupants, the brothers of Beta Signa Tau, the only fraternity house of the Osler Medial School, style and design make way for functional requirements.

Located in one of the City of Brotherly Love's finest residential communities and in the heart of America's historical shrineland, the Beta Sig house was clearly a rocky ship amid a sea of tranquility. The noise level, beer stench and rowdiness of medical students and their guests had been brought to the attention of the police on many occasions over the years. To the utter amazement of the many neighbors who had registered complaints, there had been no arrests or any decline in the blatant disorder of Swenson House. The officers certainly knew of Swenson House and its activities, but were also well aware of the Osler General Hospital's Police and Fireman's Clinic; Beta Sigma Tau brothers of today would be the physicians who tomorrow would write the medical excuses and determine who was fit for duty. It seemed only natural for a symbiotic relationship to develop, and such had been the case since 1947 when the fraternity first settled on Pine St.

A neighbor need only walk into the frat house during a Saturday evening party—at least one policeman and his date would be there to greet him. The law enforcers' generosity extended beyond security and permitting the brothers to establish their own social order. Contributions were made to special events like the pledge party and meeting in the fall of 1964. An officer had stopped a drunk and abusive driver, a search of the car followed and six reels of eight millimeter film were confiscated, and were soon the subject of an intense review by the brothers and alumni of Beta Sigma Tau.

The Right Reverend Keller had burnt many a midnight candle pondering religious and philosophical questions in the library at Swenson House. The adjoining sitting room was Mrs. Keller's favorite; a fine spinet occupied the front window side, two elegant Chippendale chairs were in another corner, the ceiling was reminiscent of French rococo. The wall separating the library and sitting area had long ago been torn down, replaced by one larger meeting room for the Beta Sig brothers. Where the massive bookshelves once occupied an entire wall, there hung a white sheet in lieu of a screen, a table with a Bell and Howell projector had replaced the piano.

The brothers and alumni had greeted the pledges on a cold, windy autumn evening. Their introduction to Beta Sigma Tau was a traditional warm affair, not even the poor quality of the sixth and final reel, straining both vision and the viewer's imagination, could distract young eager minds in pursuit of cinematic excellence.

"Now that's what I call a high rider!"

"Look at those moves! Real textbook stuff. Is that Cheryl in disguise, Willy?"

"It's Maria, wise-ass. This is what you might get if she's crazy enough to marry you. You're good at begging."

"Enough! No family quarrels allowed. Does anyone have a road map?"

"No problem old chap. One fellow is hitting her from the rear and the other is up front. The maid is providing the hand and mouth action."

"Bullshit! It's the butler on Lady Sidney and the guy with the big nose and glasses . . . the chauffeur . . . is doing a number on the maid."

"Idiot! How could it be the maid when you see high heels? It has to be Lady Sidney."

"Why don't we stop before we all become blind? Projectionist! Somebody get the lights. Before this classic is returned to the

Smithsonian film archives, I would like to take advantage of our perfect attendance and call upon distinguished alumni to help sort things out," said Herb Klein, president of Beta Sigma Tau. He sat at a small table reserved for fraternity officers, puffed silently on a white meerschaum pipe as he waited for the brothers to cease their in-depth film analysis and quarreling. The gavel was pounded twice more and finally the chatter subsided. "I'd like to call on Joe Ripley, Class of '62, and now an ENT resident. During the last scene, the camera focused on a mouth. Who does it belong to?"

Joe stroked his chin. "Tough call, Mr. President. The shape and morphology of the oral cavity and the configuration of the tongue's papillae" . . . the sound of guzzled beer and exaggerated grunts punctuated his words . . . "lead me to only one sensible conclusion. The mouth belongs to a male, and the shape of the nose would eliminate the chauffeur. It has to be the butler."

There was a spontaneous crescendo of hissing sounds clearly rejecting Dr. Ripley's interpretation. Chancellor Klein called for a vote and the brothers unanimously voted for the maid.

"Joe," Herb paused to relight his pipe, "Your fixation on male tongues tells us something about your sexual preference. The Brotherhood suggests you look into alternative careers like wine tasting and politics where you can utilize your oral skills and not subject the public to unorthodox medical theories."

After the applause, the Chancellor added, "I would like to submit a two part question. I will assume the maid is in the prone position. What orifice is being entered and who is the enteree? Would you handle this Ashley? For the benefit of our pledges, Ashley Burton, Class of '60, is a fellow in gastroenterology with a special interest in proctology. Ashley's father, the Honorable Terrance Burton, is president of the Society Hill Bank and a friend of this fraternal organization for many years." . . . applause . . . "The Burtons play a prominent role on the Main Line. Christian, Ashley's sister, took a second over-all at last year's Devon Horse show." . . . applause.

"Thank you Herb," replied the eminent Dr. Burton. "Your interest and genuine affection for my family is truly heartwarming . . . like a wet fart on a crowded elevator." The bespectacled scholar put his bottle of beer on the floor and strolled to the front of the room. "Fellow Beta Sigs! I want to suggest a daring and radical approach to your president's inquiry. To begin with, this fine work of art . . . What was the name of this provocative masterpiece?"

"'Lady Sidney's Surprise'," yelled an attentive pledge.

"Yes," nodded Ashley. "In the beginning of this ne plus ultra, Lord Sidney leaves his estate to go on a hunt. I have personally participated in many hunting parties and this man was not wearing the proper attire. I'm proposing that Lord Sidney returned to the manor house surreptitiously and disguised himself as the chauffeur . . . remember the glasses and fake nose. The enteree was none other than the master of Trent House, the Right Honorable Lord Sidney. The second part is elementary. The thrust and position of the pelvic structures, the difficult entry, a look of pain and anguish by both partners and the subsequent tenderness of both lovers point to only one logical conclusion: the orifice must be anal."

Ashley Burton returned to his chair. The brothers appeared stunned, there were neither signs of affirmation or rejection. One hand did raise and was acknowledged by the president. He was the only one in the audience who wore the standard green garb of the hospital operating room.

"Stu Levin, Class of '64. I'm a surgical intern and I start an OB-GYN residency this June in my home town of Boston. It pains me to argue with my distinguished brother, but it's even more painful when men of great intellect and reason are subjected to Ashley's absurd analysis. Firstly, the hair on Lord Sidney's scalp, eyebrows and pubis is black; the chauffeur's auburn. Secondly, there was a small mole on Lord Sidney's left cheek and none on the chauffeur. The other part is madness. You could see the entry—mons pubis, labia. It had to be vaginal. Gentlemen, sometimes the obvious is just that, obvious." . . . applause. . . "I would also like to add, Ashley is not the same man we have known in the past. I first saw the change after he started doing all of those procto exams and I believe he suffers from an anal fixation. But what really concerns me, and I don't want to sound panicky, but what about Eileen Burton, Ashley's wife of six months? I propose to send a delegation headed by Warren Whitson, a former brother and psychiatry resident, to see Eileen and find out if Ashley's confusion has interfered with his marital obligations."

A chorus of ayes and catcalls followed Stu's remarks. Herb tried to maintain order by pounding the gavel. The noise subsided and Ashley responded: "I would simply like to say that tonight while all the Beta Sigs are having visions of Lady Sidney and self-manipulating themselves into a state of ecstasy, yours truly will be connected to Lady Eileen."

Ashley mechanically fixed his glasses and made short, sniffling nasal sounds; he had spoken with the reserve and aplomb of a Main Line Burton. The goodbye wave to the Brotherhood was flamboyantly performed, the middle finger sought the heavens even as he reached for the door. Herb swung the gavel. "All right, let's start the official meeting."

To the Chancellor's right sat Larry Lewis, vice president, and on the other side was treasurer Sam Stein. As Larry whispered into Herb's ear, several in the audience prepared to leave. "I would like to thank our departing alumni for sharing this momentous evening and our projectionist, Joe Stuckle. . ."

"Snuckler! Joe Snuckler," said the middle aged man putting on a Navy peabody jacket.

"Sorry. I'd like to thank Lieutenant Snuckler of the Homicide Division for his technical assistance," said Herb.

Larry led the polite applause as the policeman smiled and left Swenson House with the six cans of film in a shopping bag.

"Nice guy!" said Herb approvingly. "Will the treasurer, Sam Stein, please give his report."

Sam opened two large accounting books, scanned a yellow legal pad and memorandum sheets, organized his thoughts, jotted some reminders on a scrap sheet and spoke: "Shared in-house costs for September are $75 and. . ."

"Thank you Sam. Do we have a surplus or a deficit?" asked the President.

"Surplus," answered the treasurer.

"Sam, you're doing a great job," beamed Herb. "I move the Treasurer's report be approved and made part of the minutes."

"I second," shouted a brother and a chorus of ayes followed.

Treasurer Stein nodded, puckered his lips, stacked the papers in a common pile and like Brother Ashley, swept his hand skyward with the same gusto but without the smooth, straight, vertical extension. Sam's middle finger was slightly bent.

"Next is the report on the beverage committee by its illustrious chairman, John McFadden. Let's give him a big hand."

Before anyone could clap, a tall, muscular fellow with flaming red hair arose and angrily thundered, "Cut the shit, Herb. The other two chairmen quit and presently, I'm the committee. If you can't find two other assholes like myself to help in one week, than its BYO from here on in."

"Thank you Brother John. We appreciate the job you're doing and I can assure you assistance is on the way. Gentlemen," Herb paused to relight his pipe, "this concludes the business and formal phase of Beta Sigma's combined meeting of brothers and pledges. . ."

"I think the formal phase is too time-consuming. Can't you find a way to cut out all the bullshit?" cried a voice near the front window.

"Your elected officers will take that suggestion under advisement, but right now I'd like to introduce Connie Strickland who chairs the committee on the Reverend Harrison Keller Report."

"Thank you, Mr. President," said a tall, handsome chap with blond hair and blue eyes, who stood with an open pad in his hand. "For the record, I want everyone to know I have reluctantly taken this position. Frank Tomaso, my predecessor, told me that, with the exception of beverage chairmanship, this is the most unrewarding job in the house. The Keller Report, as your know, has always been a covert operation, only the brothers and pledges are privy to its contents. Along with the size of your hard-on, the information I give you will be one of the great secrets of your life. Due to the lateness of the hour, I will give a few examples in each category. I know this is unusual; some of our meetings are totally consumed by the Keller Report. The first category is 'Possible.' Heading the list is Sheila Keiser: nurse, Pediatrics, day shift, age 21. She's been at Osler General for a few months. A midwesterner and an avid Iowa Hawkeye fan. Favorite singing group: Beach Boys. Loved Ian Fleming's *Dr. No*. A Protestant with no religious hangups. Sheila gives a great hand job and is ambidextrous. This girl is a real beauty and deserves your attention . . . Next is Diane Kyzant. . ."

"Would you spell that please?" implored a diligent pledge, pencil and notebook in hand.

"K . . . y . . . z . . . a . . . n . . . t. Great potential. An absolute knockout. She's a receptionist for Dr. Englin in Urology, third floor in the Morris Weinstein Pavillion. Age 19, loves folk music and Bob Dylan in particular, read *Fanny Hill* over the summer, ecstatic about the Phillies, but hates Gene Mauch. Likes to be held tightly and a guaranteed fabulous dry hump. Adequate hand job. Should be ready for the big leagues by the end of the school year. Let me go to the next category: 'Probable'. . ."

"Connie," Herb frowned, "don't feel rushed. I'd like to encourage the pledges to ask questions and please give your name and college. Bill?"

"Bill Hyatt, Dartmouth. What happens when two or more brothers are pursuing the same girl?"

"I can understand your anxiety," Connie nodded his approval, "Dartmouth is the kind of place where a best friend will stick a shotgun up your ass to kiss your girlfriend's cheek, but we do things in a democratic way around here. We ask the brothers to try and resolve the problem. If not, then the Keller Committee will intervene and make the final decision."

"How about asking the young lady if she has a preference?" suggested pledge Hyatt.

"A daring and radical approach! No one has ever made that proposal, but the committee will consider it. . . Let me proceed with 'Probable'. Sonia Stein, age 22. A physical therapist, her career choice is predicated on meeting a Jewish doctor. If you're a Gentile, we suggest you raise subtle hints about conversion. A definite winner who knows all the tricks. Likes restaurants with candles. Mention Sandy Koufax's name and she goes into heat. Sonia spent a summer in Israel, so be prepared for a lengthy discussion on the rigors and joys of a kibbutz. Anything you want to add about your cousin, Sam?"

The treasurer leaned forward, "Connie, you are a typical Princetonian: a thinking man, a theologian, a philosopher . . . and you talk and act like a putz."

"Brother Sam is pissed off about the financial report," resumed Connie, "but let me assure the pledges, he's an asshole even when not angry. The next delight is Jessica Jennings, 20 and a junior at the University of Pennsylvania. A former debutante and winner of the Cotillion Ball at the Bellevue Stratford Hotel as 'most promising newcomer'. Read the *New York Times* book review section and have some general knowledge of the top ten sellers in hardcover fiction. Jessica is one of these girls always swimming against the current . . . needs to think she is doing the unconventional. A great body and will give you a sample when you least expect it. Likes to give a quick feel in crowded places. Act surprised. What say we leave Probable and move on to 'Confirmed'."

"Drew Potter, Duke. How can we be sure the category is valid? Isn't it possible that a possible is not really a possible but a confirmed, and a probable may in fact be a possible?"

"We're not out to fool you, Drew, or any of the other pledges. This is meant to be a guide based on available information, but we are relying on the integrity of our informants."

"Kevin Farrell, Notre Dame. Any weirdos or druggies on your lists?"

"We share your concern, and if someone is known to have a significant problem she will not make the Keller Report," declared Connie with solemn conviction. "Let's move on to 'Confirmed'. Myra Lear, 27, a social worker located on third north, Main Building at Osler General. Loves to ski and a great cook. Specializes in Chinese, Szechuan style, but also comfortable with Greek. Myra read *The Feminine Mystique* and has made this book her bible. Create the illusion of sexual parity and she's all yours. Highly recommended. Next is Fay Haskett, 22, an OR nurse who works weekends and crazy hours. Has a 'live for today' ethic. A real knockout. There's lots of competition for this one. Favorite expression in bed: 'Oh babsypoo! Work hard Daddy, you can do it!' A nasty rumor is circulating around Osler about Fay becoming an airline stewardess, so haste may be in order. We also consider Miss Haskett a 'fantasy special'. Masturbators please take note. That concludes this abbreviated version of your Keller Report. Any questions? . . . Herb."

"Thanks Connie. There is an adjunct to the Keller Report, the Sisters of Mercy Proclamation. Joe Cinone is in charge of this operation . . . Joey!"

"Thank you, Mr. President," said Chairman Cinone, not bothering to move from his position atop a table. "I want to echo Connie's remarks about secrecy. I think you'll understand after I'm finished, but first let me give you background on the Sisters' of Mercy orphanage here at Swenson House. For many of the boys who came here, it represented a last chance for compassion and love. The orphans were deprived of the kind of things you and I take for granted. They were victims of circumstances beyond their control. The Brotherhood has always been cognizant that similar problems involving its members could arise. The idea of a 'last resort' was the impetus behind Sisters of Mercy Proclamation. No questions, gentlemen. I'll read the list and the rest is up to you. . .

"Nancy Dryer is a housewife, 28, and has two children: Jennifer, 3; and Mary Elizabeth, 1. Her husband Terrance works for Sidney's Sporting Goods as a sales representative. His hours are 8 to 4:30 with occasional out-of-town business, but always home on weekends. Residence is 738 Spruce St., Apt. 5B. . .

"Florence Stiller. A housewife and a hospital volunteer with a crazy schedule. In addition to candystriping, she is a guide in the Wallace

Museum of Fine Arts and Design. Her husband, Cyrus, is in his 60s, a retired stockbroker and a former executive in the Morgan Fund. She's 30 and there are no children . . . 16th and Chestnut, Wellington Arms, Penthouse B. . .

"Theresa Stagnone is a 26 year old housewife with three children: Anthony, 8; Peter, 7; Ann Maria, 5. Her husband, Nick, is a brick contractor who works long hours during the week and occasional weekends. Nick's evenings are sometimes spent in the company of Sharon Bleck, who knows him as one Angelo Pagano . . . 323 Shelster St. . . .

"Judy Lowenstein, 32, is a housewife and attends Hadassah meetings on Monday and Thursday mornings. One daughter—Melanie Stacy, 9. Husband's name is Morton, nickname Ziggie. He is the owner of Soul Brother's Chicken and Rib Restaurant on Lombard St. His hours are variable, but many . . . 1422 Delancy St. and a summer home at 127 Charles Place, Margate, New Jersey. . .

"Beverly Styzanski . . . a teacher at the Blessed Virgin Elementary School . . . 25 and no children. Husband Stanley, known as 'Stash', is a third year Neurosurgery resident at Osler General. They live at Galen Hall, married house staff residence, 9th and Pine.

"Adele Snuckler . . . housewife . . . 42. Children are John, 22 and Mary, 20. A grandchild, Joseph Jr. is 1. Husband Joe is a Homicide Lieutenant in the Police Department . . . 2668 Posner St.

"Gentlemen, the last two entries were submitted by the subject's husband. In the case of Mrs. Styzanski, Stash happens to be a former Beta Sig, Class of '59."

Joe Cinone closed the notebook, scratched his chin and nodded to Herb. The brothers sat quietly, but the pledges were not sure how to react to The Sisters of Mercy Proclamation. A no-question policy spoke for itself, but it also added to the mystique. An idea firmly planted, Beta Sig's president sought new ground: "I want to talk about something which is painful, but necessary. Next month is our faculty get-together. Last year's attendance was an absolute disgrace. This year, Dr. Raggio will give a lecture on electron microscopy of stomach parietal cells of mice exposed to excess acid loads. In addition, Dr. Conrad has graciously consented to tell us about his recent visit to New Guinea and the medicine practiced by primitive tribes. We know how excited you are to meet faculty members and their wives and to listen to these special lectures. Dinner starts at 5:30 and the faculty members will leave no later than 9. If you attend the buffet and the lectures, then you will be extended an invitation to a dance recital performed by Miss Jackie LaRue starting at 9:30. Let me assure you, this will not be a repetition of the immortal Betsy Brite. You will remember, after she had stripped and was in her bump-and-grind, we were forced to hand out emergency clothes pins. Miss LaRue's recital is arranged and guaranteed by Sergeant Ron Whitsky of the Vice Squad. We are also in conversation with a lovely lady about one-on-one encounters in the back guest room. Your officers are most appreciative to Brother Irving Insulman of the Dermatology Department, Class of 1954, for his assistance in the successful treatment of Sergeant Whitsky's psoriasis. The Sarge also permitted us to give him a new enema bag and a year's supply of suppositories for an imaginary constipation problem. Security will be tight and you can be certain only those brothers and alumni concerned with maintaining our excellent relationship with the faculty will be allowed to remain for the cultural phase of the evening's festivities. . . Because of the hour, I'm going to dispense with the House creed and song. . . " The brothers were already racing to the door, when Herb swung the gavel, " . . . Meeting adjourned."

* * *

3

THE obstetrics-gynecology ward consumed the whole of the fourth floor in the Main Building of the Osler General Hospital. A young man stepped out of the elevator, veered to the right and stopped at the nurses' station. He wore a short white lab coat, a stethoscope was in one pocket and a black looseleaf notebook protruded out of the other.

"How is she?" he asked.

"She's fine. You look like shit," said the nurse, who then resumed writing a note in a patient's chart. "Have a seat, Herb."

"I'm sorry, Jane. This is the worst part of my day. I guess it really shows. I saw Danny the other day. He looks good. Have you set a date?"

"Sometime in the spring, if he's able to walk down the aisle. A medical internship at Osler is brutal. My shift conflicts with his and when we do spend a few hours, Danny is too tired to go anywhere or . . . do anything. Except for the Beta Sig Cinema," she added with a wink. "He's always up for that."

"There's nothing wrong with being a movie afficionado. Our last feature was a DeMille epic," smiled Herb.

"Sure! I spent the evening in Galen Hall at Martha Cameron's apartment along with Jill Ripley. Dan and Sheldon left for Swenson House to greet the new pledges and 'discuss important matters.' They looked so dignified and professional! And then Jill told me the truth. A stag party, French movies! What a disgrace!"

"It's a way to let off steam. Beta Sig has nothing to do with the real world, Jane. Let Danny have his fun."

"At least he could be honest."

"Danny has you in mind. He doesn't want you to feel inadequate, or give the impression you're marrying an oversexed, horny pervert."

"Maybe. Listen, Herb, can you keep a secret?" He nodded and Jane continued. "Martha told me this story. It happened last spring, a day after one of your bashes. Sheldon returned from the hospital and wanted Martha to change into her best clothes for a night on the town. He asked her to arrange for a babysitter and check on Tom, their one year old toddler. Martha returned from the nursery to get dressed in the bedroom. She was in her high heels, bra and stockings, hooking on her garter belt, when out of the closet jumps the eminent thoracic surgeon, Dr. Sheldon Cameron, wearing his birthday suit and holding his . . . thing. 'Whore,' he yells, 'I know what you want.' Martha is a real prude, 'Hell' is a dirty word in her vocabulary. Sheldon carried her to the bathroom shouting, 'You need Long John, you need Long John.' He made love to Martha on the toilet seat, demanded she keep the high heels on and positioned her so he could watch the whole scene in the mirror. Christ, this jerk is a heart surgeon!" 'A familiar plot,' Herb thought, and then recalled the controversy at last spring's stag party over the film, 'The Plumber and the Socialite'.

". . . Would you let this man operate on your heart? Sheldon apologized to her, but I want you to know, Herb, Martha is a nervous wreck every time Beta Sig has a special session. Jill Ripley said it takes about four or five days before her husband returns to normal. Two years ago, right after another smoker, Joe forced Jill to make love in the back seat of a car parked in her father's garage while her parents watched TV. How's that for an ear, nose and throat specialist?"

'The Chauffeur's Revenge,' recalled Herb, fondly.

"Not a word, Herb. Not a word," implored Jane, her hand on his. "I'm not worried and I trust my fiance, but men are sometimes hard to figure out. I'm a very giving person and believe me, Danny is not deprived of affection."

He smiled, "Jane, don't take it personally. Beta Sig will continue to be a big plus in your life. Give us a chance."

She nodded reluctantly. "Let me check on your patient." She walked into a room directly across from the nurses' station, but quickly returned. "There's been a little accident and I'm going to change the sheets. A few other odds and ends; I need about fifteen minutes. She wants everything just right for you. There's fresh coffee by the drug cabinet. Why don't you go to the on-call room and I'll call you when I'm finished."

The intern's quarters had spartan furnishings. An old wooden table with a telephone was squeezed between the bed and wall, in another corner stood a bureau. Herb Klein rested his back against two upright pillows, closed his eyes and smelled the rich aroma of the beans; he liked his coffee with a little cream and a teaspoon of sugar . . .

Sophie Klein loved tea. She would never drink from a cup, but always out of a glass atop a saucer. Regardless of the season, weather, time of day, or occasion, Sophie's pleasure was sipping hot tea from a spoon just barely immersed in a glass.

Six years ago he had just started his sophomore year at Cornell University when his father called: Sophie was seriously ill and the prognosis wasn't promising. Could he come home?

The ride from Ithaca to Philly aboard the Lehigh Valley train was thirteen hours. It was a time to remember, reflect and pray. Herb proposed a pact. If God would help his mother recover, Herb would do his share: attend Sabbath services; adhere to the dietary rules; never date, let alone marry, a shiksa. There were so many things they could do together, but she would have to get well.

The instant he saw his father on the Reading Terminal platform it was obvious there would be no deal. Sophie had died before their telephone conversation. A well meaning Ben simply wanted to make his son's trip less painful.

His mother had never been ill or in a hospital, he could only recall an occasional cold. A tireless worker, Sophie always had to be doing something useful around the house. She had told Ben, 'I don't feel well,' and in a few minutes it was all over. Later, after the autopsy, the Doctor would say the cause of death was a ruptured cerebral aneurysm. No symptoms were common with congenital aneurysms; she was a walking time-bomb, and Sophie's had ticked for forty-nine years.

Herb never had a close relationship with his father. He was aloof and never openly affectionate like his mother. Herb offered to transfer from Cornell to a college in the Philadelphia area. Pity and guilt guided him, but the main reason was that he believed his mother would have wanted it. Ben said no, because he thought Sophie would not have approved. Six years passed; father and son continued to look at their mutual problems through Sophie Klein's eyes, such was her influence.

Three years after his mother's death, he was admitted to Osler Medical School in Philadelphia and soon became a pledge at Beta Sigma Tau. Herb lived at home, but it was evident that his father treasured his solitude. A room soon became available at Swenson House, and Herb accepted—it was an opportunity to honor Ben's need for privacy.

The only fraternity house at Osler, Beta Sigma Tau was in theory an academic and not a social club. No one really believed the myth of Beta Sig as a center of scholarship, least of all the medical school administrators, who looked away as long as the brothers made no waves.

Herb was not treated poorly, though he was the only pledge then living at the Swenson House. There was an occasional errand or a plea to help out in the kitchen, but the brothers' requests were minimal, never at the expense of his studies and more like an appeal than an order.

The kitchen was a real sore spot, as it is for all fraternities. Karl Werner was an excellent chef who had emmigrated from Germany after World War II. He had quit on two previous occasions, and this was his third time around at Beta Sig. Herb was told of the long succession of cooks over the years, and how important it was to keep Karl at any cost, despite his eccentricities.

It meant if the pancakes rattled your back fillings, or you could not understand why one second after the clock struck eight, the chef would leave the kitchen for his constitutional, then you were to discuss the problem with the food chairman and not Herr Werner. He once quit the house because a brother had chided him for watery eggs.

Karl was a big man; he would have made a perfect Santa Claus. His short, glistening hair was parted in the middle, the cheeks had a ruddy 'beer hall' look. He had spiced his English with a strong German dialect and relied solely on his mother tongue when angry. He ran a tight ship, providing the brothers with excellent food at modest prices. The fraternity reluctantly indulged the chef's whims, and so Herr Werner—also known as Mein Fuehrer, SS Karl, Hauptsturm-fuehrer—remained the undisputed king of the kitchen.

"Mr. Werner, I'm Herb Klein, and . . . ," sputtered the pledge, eager to please and make a favorable first impression.

"I know who you are, Herr Klein. You help me, and ven you finish potatoes, I give you more verk."

Herb volunteered to work in the kitchen, and tried hard to nourish a friendship with Karl. The cook stood firm, but one day the assistant chef was ill and Herb served as a substitute.

The waiters (also brothers) loaded their trays with platters Herb had delicately prepared. Suddenly, there was a loud bang, sounding like a gun shot. One waiter dropped his partially filled tray and fell to the floor. Another used his tray as a protective shield. Even Herb ducked under the counter top. Herr Werner remained standing and continued to cook his steaks as if nothing had happened. A distinctive smell followed, which left no doubt about the origin of the noise. All eyes turned to the chef. He bowed in the noblest European tradition, and with a modesty not in keeping with his image, said humbly, "Excuse please . . . entshuldigen sie, bitte. . ."

The waiters laughed, and Herb, a broad grin on his face, put his arm around Herr Werner's shoulder. He couldn't be certain, but Herb thought Karl's lips quivered in preparation for a smile. 'Der Fuehrer' recovered and shouted, "Ve're late, yu shtinkers. Get vurking!"

Two days later, right after breakfast, the German cook approached his helper; he was busy and needed a prescription filled. Could Herr Klein help?

"It would be my pleasure," replied Herb to the soft spoken chef.

Herb joined an elite group when he gained Karl Werner's trust; it was comprised of himself and Amanda Williams, the housekeeper. She had been the chef's sole confidante before pledge Klein joined the triumvirate.

Herb first met Amanda Williams during his second week at Swenson House. He had left the anatomy lab early and was standing in the fraternity foyer when Stan Henry asked him to find Amanda and have her help rearrange furniture and do a better clean-up in the living room. Unexpectedly, two professors and their wives would be dinner guests and VIP measures were in order. Herb found Amanda in a third floor room changing bed sheets. She was a graying, middle-aged black woman of medium height and had a well-developed healthy look and prominent, high set cheekbones. The pledge, short of breath from the rapid climb up the stairs, asked Amanda to stop what she was doing and come down to the first floor immediately.

"What's your name?" she asked in a thick Southern accent, not pausing a beat as she tightened the sheet to avoid crease marks, and then tucked the edge under the mattress.

"Herb Klein."

"An' who sent ya?"

"Stan Henry."

"Now you go back to Doc Henry and tell 'em he can kiss Amanda's big, black ass."

"Are you serious?"

"Yes'm," answered the housekeeper now pounding a pillow, "and you can tell Doc Henry dat dis Nigger ain't nobody's slave, an' if he don't like it, then let him find another Nigger."

Herb's verbatim report to Stan Henry was received with a shake of the head. "Doesn't anybody know how to take a joke around here?" he muttered.

Like Karl, Amanda was secretive about her past. She was born in the South, and migrated to the North during World War II. Her first several months in Philadelphia were spent with the Father Divine Peace Mission on Broad St.. Her only child, Franklin Roosevelt Williams, was born in 1947. In the early fifties, she became active in a small, storefront church on South Street—the Open Love Baptist Church, the Reverend John Tucker presiding. Since the first semester that Beta Sig Tau occupied the Swenson House, Amanda Williams had been its only housekeeper.

A tireless worker (she seemed to thrive on it), yet her importance was far greater than any housekeeper's. The house officers consulted with Amanda on any physical change within the fraternity and many personal matters as well. Despite her strong influence, she was not one to misuse power; criticism of the housekeeper always dealt with style, not substance.

She usually stopped at the kitchen before going home. Herb would see her sitting in the corner near the big oven reading the Bible, a finger pointing to each word, and the lips moving slightly and echoing each syllable. Often, Karl would give her leftover food and she would depart.

One day, a black teenager entered the kitchen, sat in Amanda's chair and wrote in a notebook. After a few minutes, he appeared disturbed. Herb asked, "Can I help?"

"How are you in Math?" After Herb helped the boy through the problem, he said, "You have a nice way of explainin' things. My name is Franklin Roosevelt Williams."

Amanda stood nearby holding two large shopping bags, and quietly observed her son introduce himself to his new friend. At their next meeting, the housekeeper thanked Herb and soon Amanda was recounting to him Beta Sig's illustrious history: a pet monkey living in the basement during the late forties, two robberies in '56, the terrible snowstorm of '61. And not much later came the day when Herb talked of Sophie.

The visit to Amanda's apartment was unexpected. Franklin had stopped by Swenson House to help, but there was more food and supplies than mother and son could carry; Herb offered to help. He wondered why it was not obvious before, but it was apparent that none of the kitchen leftovers ever reached Amanda's table. They carried the bags to the Open Love Baptist Church for distribution among the needy. It was at the church when Amanda invited Herb up.

The second floor apartment on Bainbridge St. consisted of two rooms and a bathroom. One large room was for eating and living; it also served as Franklin's sleeping quarters. Amanda had her own bedroom. A wooden divider effectively screened the small kitchen, nearby was a small sofa and two easy chairs centered around a console TV. In the other corner of the room was Franklin's desk, above it two shelves of books. Opposite the desk was a small table with religious objects and a rollout bed. The walls were stark except for framed photographs of Jesus, Reverend King, FDR and JFK. The flat was spotless; the wall and rug were worn, but the colors blended nicely with the furniture.

Herb walked over to Franklin's desk while Amanda made some coffee. He thumbed through some of the notebooks and then browsed through the other books in the small library. Amanda watched Herb through the corner of her eye not missing a movement; she seldom did. Her son was preoccupied with the television.

It was during the second cup of coffee, while seated at the kitchen table, when Herb turned to Franklin and said, "You know, the best years of my life were in high school. I would love to relive some of those enlightening moments. Why don't you come over to Beta Sig and we can review the subjects you're taking."

Amanda gave Herb a knowing glance, but a puzzled Franklin put down his glass of milk, scratched his forehead, and then fumbled an acceptance. "I guess so. If that's what you want . . . if it will make you happy."

It was time to leave and they stood at the door while Franklin visited the bathroom. She put her strong arms squarely on his shoulders, and said with tears streaming down her cheeks, "Lord have mercy! Doc Klein, you is some kinda man."

The hours spent tutoring Franklin developed into a major undertaking, beyond anything Herb had contemplated. This high school sophomore had been pushed along by teachers who were more impressed with his gentlemanly behavior than with his learning skills. Basic fundamentals, presumably the province of elementary education, had to be relearned, reviewed, and mastered. It was a painstaking process, progress came slowly and not without struggle. Herb marvelled at the student's resourcefulness. It took some time for Herb to become convinced Franklin was not a basket case, but he still had little faith in the boy's future. In a discreet way, he raised the possibility of Franklin taking vocational courses and dropping the academic curriculum. Unlike his mother, Franklin was not good at detecting disguised signals. Herb would drop the issue and continue the lessons.

He lied to Amanda and gave her glowing reports on Franklin's accomplishments and intellectual skills. She listened intently and sometimes her lips would quiver, a little sign Herb would interpret as pride in her son's progress; on other occasions, it was simply a 'Lordee,' or a 'Thank you, Jesus.'

In the early fall of '62, Herb and Amanda had their first serious disagreement. The Jewish High Holy Days were approaching, and he had said to her as a joke, "I love this time of year, it gives me a chance to sleep late." She asked him to elaborate, and Herb casually explained how God no longer played a role in his life. He had not attended a synagogue since Sophie's death, and he never intended to go again.

She listened, showing no signs of resentment or displeasure, and said nothing. After Amanda left, he realized how stupid his comments were. Amanda had strong religious feelings, covered by the thinnest veneer. The misunderstanding would have to be straightened out at their next meeting, he decided, but he never got the chance.

The following day, before he could apologize, Amanda let loose a blistering barrage: "Doc Klein, yu listn' . . . de good Lord is everywhere but his home is in the church and the sinagod . . . ain't a blessed thing yu can do abou' your Mama except give Mama to the Lord for saf' keepin' . . . let Jesus take you to the sinagod. Yum Keper is your holee day, its dis day yu meet de Lord an' yer Mama . . . ain't a good thing can happen to yu unless yu walk with de Lord . . . de Bible, Reverend John Tucker, and de Rabby will show you de way." At the door, she turned and sobbed, "Bless your name, Jesus."

Herb just stood there, confused and speechless. He was moved by her suffering over his heresy and by the intensity of her spiritual commitment. He ran after her and pleaded for her forgiveness. All right, he would attend the Synagogue on Yom Kippur, and thank you, thank you, Amanda for helping me get back on the right track. The fences mended, Herb wondered (but without much worry) whether she believed his lies. A few months later, he found out.

Amanda would ask the brothers to donate clothes for the needy parishioners of the Open Love Baptist Church. One Saturday morning, a bundle in hand, Herb met the Reverend John Tucker at the Sanctuary door. After the usual civilities, he asked, "Reverend, is Amanda here?"

The Pastor looked puzzled. His answer, "It's Saturday! She's at your Synagogue," froze him in his tracks.

Some investigative work, and Herb was able to piece together the puzzle. 'His' congregation, he discovered, was an old synagogue on Lombard Street. The building was in a rapid state of decline, needing more money for even the most basic maintenance than the dwindling membership could provide. Almost all of the members had listened to decades of sermons and departed for the 'Promised Land', but suburbia was not what the Rabbi had in mind. Congregation Ohel Zadek now stood as a proud reminder of better days, tenaciously hanging on, but just barely. Nothing came easy; even trying to find a minyan of ten men to pray would often send the faithful combing the streets for help. The few who attended High Holiday services huddled in one small section near the pulpit, a screen separating the men and women. A far cry from the standing-room-only days, when the major problem was crowd control.

Herb visited the synagogue and met Morris Sipkoff, an elderly man who claimed to be the *shamos*. Morris proudly showed him the recent improvements, discussed past glories and outlined the promise of a bright future. Thinking Herb was a prospective member, he arranged for a meeting with the wise and revered Rabbi. Herb graciously accepted the appointment and cancelled the next day.

Along came Amanda Williams asking the 'Rabby' whether she, and other members of the Open Love Baptist Church, could help to revive an ailing, if not already terminal, Congregation Ohel Zadek. The thought of the Rabbi and Amanda joining forces was too much for Herb to comprehend.

'Lordee,' he imagined Amanda saying to the Rabbi, 'I thank de Rabby for lettin' us into the Lord's house. Jesus be with you forever.'

'Amanda, Bubbeleh,' the Rabbi would respond, 'Hob mazel, und kein tsuris nicht dein gantze leben. . .'

Whatever the relationship, Herb was convinced their shared objective, the revival of Ohel Zadek, was a pipe dream, akin to making Franklin Roosevelt Williams a Rhodes scholar. He thought it best to feign ignorance, but he had always looked upon Amanda's actions as a form of retribution on his behalf.

He reached for the telephone and heard Jane's voice: "Everything's in order, Herb."

She sat in a chair reading her bible, unaware of his presence. The other bed in the hospital room was empty. There were cards and flowers everywhere. The largest bouquet of a dozen yellow roses was on a reading table next to her chair. "From The Brothers of Beta Sigma Tau With Deep Affection," read the huge get-well card dangling from the flower vase. On a large poinsettia plant resting on the bureau: "Open Love Baptist Church . . . Jesus Is With You." He watched as her lips danced to a rhythmic beat. She was bent over, holding the Bible firmly in both hands as she eagerly absorbed each word.

"Hi Amanda! How are you feeling today?" he asked.

She heard him, but he knew the paragraph must first be completed. Herb moved a chair to her side and sat down as she placed the Bible on the table next to the roses. "Laundree," Amanda said drily, not bothering to look at Herb.

He took out the month's laundry bill from his pocket and handed it to the housekeeper. Since he had become fraternity president, she constantly looked over his shoulder making sure he made all the right moves. It had become her obsession, no problem was too small for serious discussion.

"Where de pillow cases?" asked Amanda, at last turning to look at Herb.

"I told Emma Mae to separate the linen, and the laundry man took only the one bag. The pillow bag was near the cellar door and he missed it."

"Boy, yer a stupid ass. Can yer tie yur shues right? Yu tell Emma Mae to call me everee mornin', yu understand?"

Herb nodded, and they went on to more important questions: wall color of a second floor bathroom; how many dining room chairs were needed; should they buy the more expensive wooden hangers for the cloak room? He was always mentally exhausted after a session with Amanda and tonight was no exception.

Karl Werner entered the room holding a small bouquet of flowers. Even Amanda smiled as she saw the huge German cook with his bulging belly, in a jacket a size too small and ready to pop the one button holding it together. Herb stood and gave his seat to Karl, and then stood next to the dressing bureau. He noted the get-well card from Ohel Zadek and recalled that depressing day three years ago he spent in the dilapidated synagogue. He opened the card. "Eight names! It probably represents all the dues-paying members of the entire congregation."

Amanda and Karl were laughing as they shared another story of the infamous Jim Barry, Class of '53. It was a tale Herb had heard many times before but which never failed to amuse Amanda and Karl. Brother Jim had a great propensity for sleep, but another flake, Vinnie Vacaro, Class of '52, changed his alarm clock, and the unsuspecting Jim missed classes and showed up for lunch in a robe expecting breakfast.

Herb said goodbye; neither of them heard, they were lost in their memories. "You should have seen der look on Herr Barry's face!" Karl said as he held Amanda's frail hands in his own.

At the nurses' station, Herb picked up Amanda's chart and looked through pages he had already committed to memory. Once again, he plowed through progress reports, lab results, biopsy analysis, consult-ant recommendations, nurses' notes, and even the social service comments. There were no surprises, nor had there been since that hot, humid day in July when Amanda underwent exploratory surgery.

Harvey Leider, Class of '55, had been the surgeon. Stu Levin, who was on the gynecology service at the time, assisted. They met in the recovery room and the look on Stu's face told the whole story. "It's Big Charlie, Herb. A real mess. Big Charlie's everywhere. Harvey took a good look, sampled a few tissues and got out real quick." Stu then spelled out the particulars, reviewed the options, and finished with the mandatory upbeat approach about a 'similar case' of Harvey's where the patient lived for 'a whole three years.'

Herb entered the waiting room as Harvey Leider was leaving. Karl stared at the floor and shook his head in disbelief. A tearful Franklin asked, "I don't understand Dr. Klein! Does this mean my Momma's going to die?"

"Listen!" Herb's hands reached for Franklin's, "Dr. Leider is telling you your mother has cancer of the ovaries and it's spread to other parts of the body. It may not be operable, but that doesn't mean the disease is not treatable. There's chemotherapy and x-rays. . .I was just talking to a friend of mine, and he was telling me of another case just like this one where the woman lived twenty years and is still going strong."

Franklin and Karl smiled. They both believed a fourth year medical student over a skilled surgeon, because Herb had told them what they wanted to hear. He was never put in the situation of having to give these phony explanations to Amanda. She understood the problem full well with all its ramifications. Any discussion of her illness with him was off limits.

The ritual chart review was nearly finished. He heard laughter and then the strong, stentorian voice of Karl belt out a familiar name. 'A Sid Levy story,' thought Herb. He turned quickly to the entry on the chart's last page.

Nurses Note—Vital Signs . . . 104/72,60 and regular, respirations 16, temp. 99 . . . Lab: CBC, Electrolytes, U/C, Chest x-ray-completed . . . Dr. Leider and Dr. Sedgman saw at 4 . . . Incontinent of urine x 2 . . . Mrs. Williams offered no complaints, and was her usual pleasant self throughout my shift. Her mood continues to be good, she shows a positive attitude with no signs of depression . . . Jane Murray, RN.

Herb put the chart in the rack, reached for his tobacco pouch, and slowly walked to the elevator. He would return tomorrow and bring along a big surprise. The gas and electric bills had arrived and they showed a sharp decline since the new conservation measures. Amanda would be pleased.

* * *

4

"IT's a statue of Pegasus, the winged horse in Greek mythology. When I was a little boy, my mother would say, 'Herby, how would you like to take a ride in the sky? Wouldn't it be fun!' I remember telling her, 'Yes, but you would have to come with me.' I had dreams of flying horses, but she never made the trip. I was up there in the heavens trying to find my way among the stars and planets. Do you know how difficult that is without your Mom?"

She giggled, while playfully tucking leaves underneath his shirt: "Hey, if you want someone to accompany you to the heavens, let's find a quiet place and I'll see what I can do."

Herb wrapped his arms around her lithe body. Together they slowly blended until a position was found which halted their wriggling, and kept them still like the surrounding trees. Herb watched the leaves, swirls of fall color yield to a fickle wind. A nearby patch of flowers had only a few remaining petals, their twisted stems turned toward the ground. The chill of a brisk autumn day yielded to the warmth of an embrace.

"Can I be honest with you?" asked Herb as they disengaged.

"No!" she replied firmly.

"Do you want me to lie? You're a tough nut to crack. Everything's a joke. I can't figure you out."

She fell to the ground, both hands covered her chest, a resentful scowl and then a cry of anguish: "The pain of rejection hath no equal. Take me away, Pegasus!"

Herb slid to her side, brushed a hand through her long auburn hair, carved his fingers over her long sensuous neck, touched sparkling hazel eyes, and sought her yielding lips with his own. It was a lingering kiss, and then wrapped in each other's arms, they rolled over and over using their bodies, leaves, and grass to cushion the earth's hardness. Lying on their backs, short of breath from a playful joust, they both became engrossed with the sky tones of blue and the spectacle of a flock of birds performing a precision flying exercise.

"I can't get angry or serious with you. I'm in a trance." Herb was sitting, legs crossed, and filling his pipe bowl with tobacco.

"I have a thing about people being 'honest with me,' or saying 'can I be frank'. . . I hear that, and a neon sign in my brain flashes, 'Bullshit! Bullshit!'" She paused to light a cigarette, "You know, Herb, in the short time we've been together, I find you're much too hard on yourself. It's one thing to learn from the past and remember the good times, but why give the heartaches first place! You know where I came from. Neschaunk is a dreary and depressing coal town where most of the men have 'black lung,' and the women work in mills to support their families. The only time my father leaves his house and the oxygen bottle, is to drink booze with the coalcrackers at the neighborhood tank. Still, the people in Neschaunk are content and happy with their lives because they've learned to accept what they can't change."

"You don't really believe that," sighed a skeptical Herb.

"Can't I be honest with you?"

Herb first met Christina Loreski in the Osler General Hospital cafeteria. Christie was the new girl in town, a recent graduate, it was her first week as a pediatrics nurse. Of their first encounter, she would tell him, "I looked into those starry, expressive eyes of yours . . . and saw a horny guy on the make." The old lines and some new ones just didn't work with Christie. The unpredictable became routine, he was constantly thrown off balance in her presence.

"I really have the hots for you, even if you are the biggest chain jerker I've ever met," he said affectionately.

"Strong language for a pure-bred sheeksa," said Christie.

"Shiksa, not sheeksa," corrected Herb.

Swirls of leaves were rejuvenated by a sudden, brisk wind. She snuggled against his chest. "I know so little about Fairmount Park. How about a rundown."

"The grand tour is later. The Klein house is just a few blocks away. The park has always been my second home. When I was a little kid, the architectural gem behind Pegasus was a museum, but now Memorial Hall is a recreation center."

"Why was it built? It's so isolated."

"Do you know about the 1876 Centennial?"

"Not really."

"Philly was chosen as the official site of America's One Hundreth Birthday Party, and it was the biggest bash this country's seen. Memorial Hall was the site of the Art Museum. It featured many of Europe's greatest artworks, including many nude statues and paintings—daring stuff for the Victorian Age. As a teenager, my great-uncle came to the World's Fair every day. . ."

"You mean Uncle Otto Sachs, the bootlegger and con artist who lived to be almost ninety, and never worked an honest day in his life."

"The same."

"Oh, good! I'm in the mood for more of his shtup."

"That's shtick, Christie. I've been trying to shtup you for two months, but you keep on telling me you're not ready."

"Oy vey! You're right. I mean Uncle Otto's shtick." ·

Herb chuckled. He was always tickled by Christie's flirtations with Yiddish. "My uncle was a tour guide at the Fair. He got a little reward for each customer he brought to certain restaurants, and there were similar deals with the souvenir concessions. My father told me that Otto would induce men to take a tea break with a lovely hostess at one of the whore houses just outside the fair grounds. The madam would pay him, and he was entitled to use one of the peep holes free of charge as part of the solicitation fee. On occasion, he would get an additional bonus by threatening to tell the gentleman's wife."

"How did he get along with the rest of your family?"

"Uncle Otto and Grandpop Jake Klein lived with us at our Wyal Street house, everybody got along real well, but they had a special relationship. My grandfather was a Russian immigrant who never really adjusted to the States. He was a tailor who worked in sweat shops his whole life. My father worked with him for a brief time as an assistant and messenger boy. Grandpop Jake couldn't read or write, signed his name with an X, but boy could he count! In a dress factory, when he'd cut a piece of material into a garment, a ticket was issued. I counted the tickets for the week, and made out the salary slip. If I made a mistake, it was curtains! He would let loose with a barrage of Yiddish curse words, and then apologize the next day. My father was his constant target. Ben wasn't a go-getter, or risk taker. As a shoe salesman, Dad could have doubled his salary by traveling on the road, but family time was always more important. Grandpop Jake liked Uncle Otto, he admired his ambition, honesty. . ."

"Honesty? Oh, come on, Herb! Would you please define fee-splitting, pimping, and black mail for me?" grinned Christie discarding the cigarette.

"Otto never pretended that he was anything other than a crook, but he had a conscience and never tried to hurt the little guy. My uncle used to say, 'I wouldn't know how to make an honest living unless I could do it in a dishonest way.' He loved to talk about rip-off schemes. My mother would try to change the subject to protect her little Herby, but that only stirred him on. Otto would unwind, Dad would translate into Yiddish for my grandfather, and everybody, including Mom, would soon be laughing."

"Alright, I'll bite! Tell me a tale about this Robin Hood in a yarmulka."

"Do you know what an ambulance chaser is, Christie?"

"A shot of Ouzo after a double gin and tonic on the rocks."

"Not quite. Uncle Otto would follow an ambulance to the scene of an accident, and would let the victims know there was a remedy available for pain and suffering called the 'judicial process.' His employer was an attorney by the name of Harry Weldon, Sheister-at-Law. Their service provided a medical consultant as well, one Emanuel Lipson, M.D., who just happened to be our family doctor, and a specialist in phantomology."

"What is fantology?"

"A nurse has never heard of phan-tom-ology!" Herb carefully spelled the word, relit his pipe, and put his arms around her to combat the chill of a strong wind. "Let me give you an example. A phantomologist, like Doctor Lipson, is an expert diagnostician in a variety of muscular and bone disorders. He can always find abnormalities in whip lash injuries and back problems, even when the x-rays are normal. He is coveted and revered by lawyers, like Harry Weldon, and is constantly involved in accident liability litigation because a phantomologist has all the right answers his clients are looking for. Juries are impressed with his wisdom, he makes an excellent expert witness. The key to Doctor Lipson's success rested in those areas where documentation was not necessary, and where scientific data was replaced by his remarkable common sense, astounding intelligence, and unerring judgment."

"I see. So a phantomologist is someone who makes something out of nothing. Another example might be a woman telling a guy about those multiple orgasms she has when they make love," countered Christie playfully.

"Crude, very crude, but I think you get the idea. Let's get back to the car!"

Hand in hand, Christie mumbled, more for her own ear than Herb's, "Uncle Otto the ambulance chaser, a sheister, and a phantomologist!"

"Your medical-legal community is loaded with these types. I remember Dr. Lipson died when I was in high school. He was a respected man in the community, whose name and plaque have an honored place in our Synagogue. To my Mother, he was a role model for me to try to emulate, and somebody who made housecalls. I knew him as the doctor who put a needle in my ass no matter what the problem, and at my Mother's prodding, he would say, 'Now Herb, if you study real hard, you too can be a successful doctor, just like me.' Weldon went the way of all crooked lawyers. He entered politics and did quite well screwing the general public, rather than just the Insurance Companies and his clients. Yep, Uncle Otto had some great friends."

They had reached the parking lot, and Herb announced it was time for the grand tour. It was still early afternoon as Christie's old Ford Falcon turned onto Exposition Drive to nearby Centennial Lake. At the water's edge was a giant oak tree, under its shade, his uncle taught him to fish and shared memories from an old, but still fertile mind.

Herb maneuvered the car over a winding dirt road and stopped at the Ohio House, one of two World's Fair Buildings still intact (the other was Memorial Hall). It had been in the first floor men's room of this magnificent Victorian-Gothic edifice that Herb tried his first and last cigarette; Izzy Gold, a fifth grade classmate, provided the weed and the instruction. At the rear of the Ohio House was a ravine, and the entrance to Otto's favorite amusement, the world's first monorail.

The Ford rambled along another dirt road, and halted at a small fieldstone wall with an opening that funneled cold spring water. Jacob and his grandson made this trek twice weekly. They would fill their jugs to take home on an all steel Olympic Flyer Wagon, with a wooden tongue and a metal handle painted red (except for the white letters 'DELUXE' on one side). As they were leaving, Christie noticed an old, battered sign—DANGER DO NOT DRINK THE WATER. Herb was sure the wagon, now brown and rusty, was still in the basement on Wyal Street.

They paused briefly at the Japanese house, Sophie had loved to explore its beautiful gardens. Herb remembered the day Murray Fein shared those little 'two by four comicbooks' found in his brother's drawer, pictures of nude men and women in unusual and silly positions. They sat in the tea room overlooking the little Zen stone garden, laughing and trying to decipher with their eyes, what youthful minds could not imagine.

Herb found a parking space near an arrangement of Bonsai plants. Christie walked beside him down a short trail through some heavy underbrush. They reached a clearing with a huge weatherbeaten brick floor; steps led to another terrace, and to a solitary stone statue of four young women holding a table in their hands. The Sundial Sculpture had been a fountain, symbolic of the four seasons, it was all that remained of Horticultural Hall, a Centennial structure patterned after the fabulous Crystal Palace in London. The Klein family had spent many hours walking within the Hall, and strolling through the beautifully manicured gardens. Sophie cried the day she learned the building was to be destroyed. Outside of home and family, her happiest moments were spent in the company of things botanical.

They soon approached a Colonial manor, the Rebecca Morris House, one of many authentic 18th century country estates still thriving in Fairmount Park. Located on a hilltop in a pastoral setting overlooking the Schuylkill River, it had stunning floor to ceiling windows, ornate grill and wood work, and classical Chippendale furnishings. It also had a huge cellar where the caretaker and Uncle Otto had stored Southern moonshine and bathtub gin during Prohibition.

The tour continued as the car crawled toward the River Drive. The baseball field near the train tracks had not changed. The rocks and stones remained in the infield, catching a hard hit grounder would still be an act of courage. A nearby stretch of grass was the makeshift football field, and Herb saw the yardmarkers still in place: a railroad switch, a signal pole, a tree, and a trash basket were well known landmarks to the boys of Wyal Street.

At the riverbank they watched a lone oarsman sprint toward Boat House Row. The sculler crossed an imaginary finish line; fatigued and gasping for air, he waved a victory signal to an observer on the deck of the old aquarium.

"My mother and I would take long strolls along the riverbank, and sit on that bench near the water . . . "

"Hey, isn't it time for some chow, big fella?" said Christie. She had sensed Herb's melancholy and, moving close to his side, she cupped his hands between hers.

"No thanks." His mood changed, he asked smilingly, "This car is in great shape, considering it has well over a hundred thousand miles. What's the secret?"

"In a small town like Neschaunk unemployment is the major industry, and you learn the value of friendship and the true meaning of the barter system. And it's understood you help people. Well, about six years ago the Loreskis were in real bad shape. We were living off father's medical disability, my brother Paul was in college, and I was in high school, working as a waitress on weekends. Mother worked part-time jobs, but not very often. Medical expenses wiped out what little savings my parents had. A major storm destroyed the roof, and a few of the rooms needed replastering and painting. That's about the time the Ford died on us. My cousin rebuilt the entire engine, but in the end we had a better automobile."

"What was your cousin's fee?"

"Walt had a great passion for Polish perogi stuffed with lekvar. He struck a hard bargain, but my mother finally submitted."

"I suppose friends repaired the roof and rooms for similar favors," Herb winked.

"Nu. Vatt else?" she replied in her best Jewish accent.

Herb grinned and stared at the lunch baskets. "I've changed my mind. What have you got to eat?"

"For you a ham and cheese sandwich. For me, the shiksa, I'll have a little gefilte fish, and then a bagel and lox."

Herb took a bite of his peanut butter sandwich, and asked, "Okay smarty, how did you know I liked the 'crunchy' rather than the 'smooth'?"

"Remember the other night at my place, when we were on the sofa? You were hot and bothered, and said something like, 'Oh, baby, when are you going to let me put the crunch on you . . . pant . . . pant?' Well, that's what gave me the idea," she answered.

"Tell me Christie, how do you like your peanut butter . . . crunchy or smooth?" His hand caressed her inner thigh.

She met his glance, and scowled at him. "Don't you know when to give up. Isn't it time to leave your adolescent hangups behind, and enter the world of big people. What you see is what you get. I'm very happy with the present arrangement; sorry you're not, but. . ."

"Christie, I'm sorry. I just want to be with you, the location is optional."

She was the clear victor, but it was neither her inclination nor nature to gloat over success: "You're forgiven. But only on the condition that you tell me one more Uncle Otto story."

"Okay, but later over dinner. Why don't we go to Wyal Street? My father should be coming home soon," he said over the roar of the engine.

The steep hill to Exposition Drive was the old Ford's greatest challenge, Herb had to negotiate Parkview Drive in low gear. It was late afternoon and the day had become overcast, the leaves were swirling more now. The car came to a stop just a short distance from Centennial Lake.

"I thought we were going to your house?"

"I changed my mind. Christie, I wanted to tell you something," he said, pointing to a makeshift fence surrounding a small withered bush. "I'm not sure of the details, but when I was a teenager there was a great deal of commotion about that bush. At this site, a young woman said she saw the Blessed Virgin Mary and spoke to the vision."

"What did she say?" A curious Christie was aroused.

"I don't have the slightest idea, but I can tell you a hell of a lotta people believed the story, even if the Church did not. Thousands came to this very spot; many were crippled and in wheelchairs or stretchers. On the bush and the surrounding ground, were crutches, braces, canes . . . you name it!"

"It sounds like Lourdes or Fatima, but what has this to do with my little Jewish prince?"

"Guess who was on the scene as a salesman of religious articles," an embarrassed Herb had both hands on the steering wheel and peered through the windshield.

"You," she said after a hearty chuckle, " . . . you, Herb Klein!"

"I'm sorry I can't share the joke. The memory of it has given me pangs of guilt for a long time. I've always been ashamed of making money on other peoples' religious convictions."

"What exactly did you sell?" she asked, regaining her composure.

"My partner and I sold commemoratives, miraculous medals, rosaries and statues . . . nothing outrageous about the prices, it was the going rate for those kinds of items. We made a small profit on each article, but what volume."

Christie said in a gentle voice, "You did nothing wrong. I'm sure there was no arm turning. You brought happiness to many people who were caught up in the excitement, and pushed a beautiful dream a little further. Believe me, they would be the first to thank you."

"Nice try baby, but I still feel like shit."

She cuddled to his side, and held him tightly. "I forgot to ask about your accomplice. Who was the mastermind? Izzy? Murray? Another maverick Jewish boy gone astray?"

"I had nothing to do with the original idea, or getting the merchandise. Give credit to my partner."

"And his name," she added to the climax, ". . . Ta, da!"

"He was confined to a wheelchair. A few months after the start of this whole business, he died at the tender age of . . ."

Christie put a finger to his lips, and then quickly removed it. "You lied. I thought you said no more of Uncle Otto until dinner. He was your partner."

"You're right. He also would have lied to you," Herb flashed a smile, and kissed Christie on the cheek. "Think of it this way, you just got two Uncle Otto stories for the price of one."

* * *

5

HERB resumed his duties after the intern and resident left the room. He took the pulse and blood pressure, listened for fetal heart sounds, regulated the IV and awaited the next contraction. The patient, now pain free, continued her ranting and raving. He clenched his fist and prepared for the next onslaught. She was right on target: "Where's my obstetrician, Dr. Pringle? Why didn't anyone tell me how painful labor was? Why are men such animals? Would it be possible for the Doctor to tie my tubes after delivery? Why do men think only of sex? Do you know a good lawyer who would help sue the father for child support?"

Herb responded to her questions as politely as he could. He was surprised when she asked, "If you're a doctor, why isn't there an M.D. after your name, or a Dr. before it?"

His explanation that he was a fourth year medical student fell on deaf ears. She called him Nurse Klein for the duration of her labor and the questions changed accordingly: "Is it better to breast feed? Is there a preferable sanitary napkin to use after my hospital stay? Is Mary a good girl's name? Could you suggest a boy's name?"

After she was fully dilated and taken into the operating room, Herb scrubbed and observed the delivery. The attending physician, despite numerous pages and the urgent pleas of the head nurse, had not yet arrived. A frantic resident, assisted by the intern, performed a difficult breech delivery. Dr. Pringle, the missing obstetrician, entered as the baby let loose with its first cry; he surveyed the situation and calmly reached for the forceps, sidled next to his patient, and said, "My dear, you were just terrific. Your son is simply the most exquisite baby I have ever seen. He has your features. Wasn't she great, Dr. Brickton?"

The resident, emotionally drained and speechless, drenched in sweat, overjoyed at the survival of mother and baby (he had strongly considered an emergency Caesarean section), mustered his remaining strength, and nodded approval.

The new mother, awake from anesthesia, recognized a familiar voice; she focused half-shut eyes on the victorious physician holding blood stained forceps, and said weakly, "God bless you Dr. Pringle. I just don't know how to thank you."

A humble obstetrician squeezed her hand and made a few remarks on the merits of teamwork in times of crisis. But his final words were reserved for the nurse, whom he cornered and in a small voice said, "Miss Pechulli, how are you? I just had a fabulous meal at The Venetian House, the pasta was sensational. You must try the green and red pepper lasagna. The Marsala whipped-cream tart dessert with fresh figs is heavenly. . . And by the way, would you make sure the patient signed her insurance form."

Later that day, an exhausted Herb visited the young mother, who unlike him, had been able to sleep during the interim. She looked fresh and well rested, a pink nightgown's huge ribbon at the neck matched the rosy color on her cheeks. They discussed the joys and responsibilities of nurturing a newborn. He rose from his chair, ready to leave, when she asked, "I'm not trying to be nasty, but who are you?"

"I'm Dr. Klein. The drugs and anesthesia can play tricks with your memory. I was with you during much of your labor and in the OR."

"Are you Dr. Pringle's partner?" She continued without waiting for a response, "When can I start to have sexual intercourse?"

"I'm not his partner. I suggest you discuss that question with your obstetrician." He looked for a way to change the subject, "What name did you give your son?"

"It's funny, I really wasn't prepared for a boy. If it was a girl, her name would have been Mary. I was so drugged up. There was this name going round and round in my mind. Tell me, Dr. Klein, how does the name Herbert appeal to you?"

The thirty-six hour obstetrics rotation was over, and Beta Sigma Tau's president sat at his desk ready to tackle fraternity business. Herb stretched weary arms behind his back, yawned, and then collected the yellow and pink slips surrounding the telephone, in order to make a single pile. The prospects of an early evening did not look good as he started to read the messages.

While You Were Out—Stu Levin called . . . Amanda doing well on chemotherapy. Will probably be discharged this weekend. Talked to son Franklin about medical problems, but couldn't make a breakthrough. The guy's in another world and Stu wants you to take a shot.

Dave Garrett

While You Were Out—Sgt. Whitsky of the Vice Squad says dance recital with Miss LaRue still on, but to forget about the other performer. Talk to Larry about this one.

Pete

While You Were Out—Father called. Nothing important.

Connie

While You Were Out—Reverend John Tucker of the Open Love Baptist Church wanted to thank you for the food and clothes. Be reassured, even in Amanda's absence, they are helping Congregation Ohel Zadek . . . painted Sanctuary walls last week.

Larry

While You Were Out—Christie Loreski thinks you're a real asshole. Wants a real man to love, so I gave her my credentials . . . nine inches of pulsating excitement. You're finished Herb!

McFadden

While You Were Out—Franklin Williams wants you to call when you have a moment.

Sid

MEMORANDUM

Need to talk to you about the cost of new dining room chairs. Mr. Burton of the Society Hill Bank called about investing fraternity money in a real estate deal . . . sounds promising.

Sam

MEMORANDUM

Emma Mae is pissed off at Amanda over the frequent telephone calls and the constant criticism of her work. Unless it stops, she told me 'we're gonna need a new darkie to do the housekeepin.' Der Fuhrer said that unless Emma Mae stops badmouthing Amanda, Beta Sig will soon be looking for another shmuck to handle the cooking duties. Karl also wanted me to know that he's making a list of take-out restaurants, out of deference to you, because his exit may be in great haste. . . It's all yours Herb.

Larry

MEMORANDUM

Dr. Winston Collingsworth II, a Brother and Class of '51, Associate Professor of Medicine at Osler, and last year's recipient of our 'Albert Schweitzer Humanitarian Award' submitted the following for the 'Sisters of Mercy Proclamation': Priscilla Collingsworth . . . occupation, ball buster . . . age 34 . . . children—Grace 9 and Henry 7 . . . takes the Wednesday 8 A.M. train to New York for Sachs Fifth Avenue, Bloomingdales and similar places to fulfill shopping needs . . . Friday, 8 to noon—'William and Steven's World of Beauty Salon' . . . husband is Winston (Winnie to friends and all Beta Sigma Tau brothers) . . . Physician with various hours—check either Osler Hospital beeper 94728, or answering service for whereabouts . . . if interested, check out the maid Jennifer, who I can personally guarantee is a 'confirmed' . . . 381 Merry Robin Lane, Gladwynne.

Would you Believe!
Joe Cinone

'I believe,' thought Herb as he rearranged the messages into a preferential order. He arose immediately, walked across the hall, knocked on the door, and entered without waiting for an invitation.

"Did you use Cecil or Harrison on your Medicine rotation?" asked Larry Lewis as Herb walked over to the desk and sat on the edge.

"I have both books, but I probably read more Cecil."

"The consensus seems to be Cecil is better written, but Harrison is more complete. What's your view?"

"It could be, Larry, but I read more Cecil because it's on the shelf next to the toilet."

"Beautiful, Herb. Thanks old chap. . . You've cleared up my confusion."

"What are friends for?" Herb waved two message sheets, "Whitsky. Emma Mae."

"Ah yes. Sergeant Ronald Whitsky. . . I talked to him yesterday. Miss LaRue will be here, but the other performer will not be attending our post-faculty dinner party. Sarge claimed she didn't accept our offer and her figure wasn't worth discussing. Beta Sig's deal was an honorable one. A short time ride for $20 and we offered to pay the same for those brothers desiring hand and oral massage, recognizing the going rate is in the $5 to $10 range. She wanted a guarantee of $200 an hour, no less than three hour's work, and all the money prepaid. It's a real shame Herb, I heard she was a knockout."

"How could she, in good conscience ask for that kind of money," said Herb, angrily.

"She told Whitsky about a friend of her's who worked the Beta Sig House a few years ago, and I was able to confirm her story with Ashley Burton. It seems a few of the married brothers got laid before coming to the dance recital, and then they had a little too much beer. Tradition dictates seniors are entitled to the first dips. The poor girl never got past the third guy. Remember Sol Weinstein . . . a big ox, maybe 250 pounds. . . ."

"Nope," and then Herb recanted, "Weinstein. Sure. . . . He was Kosher. Karl told me about all the problems preparing his food."

"The same," said Larry assuredly. "I think he's doing an orthopedic residency at Yale. Anyway, Sol was in the room with the Queen, when everybody heard a thud and a scream. A few of the brothers rushed in, and Sol was still going at it hot and heavy. He turned around with a big smile, and said, 'Hey, no problem fellas. She's come three times, and she just can't get enough. That scream means number four is on the way.' Ashley happened to notice Sol's hand was over her mouth. It took three brothers to remove the hand, the Queen yelled 'Help' and became hysterical. The story was that Sol couldn't come, and the Queen was utterly exhausted. She told him his time was up. Ol' Sol went whamo."

"Alright! So we've had one bad experience at the Swenson House, and Whitsky's choice is afraid of a repeat, but is this the only fish in the sea?"

"She's the best in her class Herb, and Whitsky samples what he recommends. Whitsky knows."

"Shit, Larry, what the hell are you on? I asked if there was anybody else, not who was the best."

"There is not a respectable whore in Philly, Cherry Hill, the Main Line . . . you name it, who will touch Beta Sig without a lot of upfront money, that we are just not able to pay."

"Whitsky, what about Whitsky? Can't he do anything? Irv Insulman cleared his psoriasis. We supply him with coal tar, Synalar cream, and plastic wrap for the skin. Is this the way he shows his gratitude?"

"He's grateful, Herb. Ron is giving us Jackie LaRue, a great stripper, for a song."

"I don't buy that. Do we know anybody else on the Vice Squad? Stuckle, what about Stuckle?"

"It's Snuckler, Lieutenant Joe Snuckler of Homicide, and he's given us enough already."

"It's been a long day and I'm tired," Herb stood up and stretched, "Let me think about this before we throw in the towel. Now the nonsense about Emma Mae. Tell her you talked to me, and I was upset that she wasn't getting the credit she deserves. Offer her a $5 a week raise, and if she's not receptive then get her medical history and see where we can be of service. I'll handle Amanda and Karl."

Herb darted back to his room and quickly dialed Ben's number, but then remembered his father would not be home because of a weekly pinochle game. Leaning back in a chair, he pinched his abdomen; muscles were still taut, the body lean and supple, but the edge was lost. The time required for the obstetrics-gynecology rotation, Beta Sigma Tau, Christie and friends, had all eaten into his exercise routine. He seriously doubted whether he could last ten minutes at full speed in a half court basketball game. It was so easy to lose that physical and mental edge, it was even easier to find good excuses to justify why it happened.

Ben Klein never made excuses—that was his trademark. Tonight he would play pinochle, and it would not matter whether the cards came his way or every game was a loss. His father's passivity had always been a sore spot with Herb. Even when his mother was alive, Ben was a homebody who needed his wife's prodding to try a new restaurant, see a movie, or even take a walk in the park. He was a gentle and kind man, who, like his own mother, was never critical of other people's shortcomings, and rarely showed his anger. Unlike Sophie, who was effusive and provided Herb with an abundance of warmth, Ben Klein rarely kissed or hugged his son.

Christie and Herb had dinner at the Klein house on Wyal Street, the night of the Fairmount Park tour. Herb knew Ben would be courteous and civil; he suspected a quick house tour, a quiet dinner, and a hasty retreat. His father was always in bed at 10:30 and up at 5:30, and opening Pearson's Shoe Shop at 7:00. This had been the routine six days a week, fifty weeks a year, for as many years as Herb could remember. That night, they stayed until after midnight, and then Herb used an early class the next day as an excuse to leave.

His father sat in a favorite chair, a rocker with a recliner back and a foot rest extension, upholstered in dark brown leather already beginning to fray on the arm rests. Christie sat on a small stool close enough for Ben to whisper and be understood. The evening started slowly, both unsure of themselves, neither wanting to offend. Soon Ben took control of the discussion, his topics restricted to bits of family history. Christie listened, her enchanting smile and sparkling eyes riveted on him. Ben was clearly enthralled.

Herb went to his room to pack a suitcase with winter clothes. He soon returned downstairs, and walked through the living room to prepare a snack in the kitchen.

At the stove, Herb turned around and looked at his father. Ben was talking about Uncle Otto's days as a committeeman and politician. The story he was telling dealt with an old ploy Otto had used many times. It was common practice to arrest young children on petty misdemeanors, and then Uncle Otto would quickly negotiate their release. The parents would be reminded on election day who they could count on in times of need. One day, on a vacant lot with a barely visible "No Trespassing" sign, a group of children were hauled off to the police station. Grandmom Sarah Sachs never forgave her brother for arresting little Sophie, despite Otto's plea of ignorance. It was not the familiar tale, but his father's actions, that startled Herb; Ben was laughing, one hand held Christie's, the other rested on her shoulder.

Ben Klein had always been a gentleman. He brought flowers home for Sophie, pushed her chair in at dinner, opened the door, and this kind of behavior was not restricted to his mother. Ben wore a Bond Street gray hat with a black band and raw edge brim, he always removed it ever so lightly, when passing a woman on the street. True to form, Ben Klein stood in the hallway helping Christie with her jacket as they prepared to leave. She thanked his father for a wonderful evening, and then kissed him on the cheek as her arms encircled his shoulders. They waved goodbye to his father; Herb noticed Ben's tears, a sight that he had not seen since his mother's death.

Ben was not the only one struck by Christie. Herb had introduced his nurse friend to Amanda during her second hospital admission. The conversation never drifted beyond the weather and Amanda's improving health. The meeting was cordial, but neither ever mentioned the other's name after their first encounter. Herb assumed it was their last. A few weeks later, the housekeeper's condition deteriorated and she was readmitted to Osler General Hospital. Amanda had difficulty breathing because of the accumulation of fluid around her lungs and in the abdomen. Herb finished examining a late night admission, and decided to see how Amanda was doing.

The head of the bed was raised and she appeared asleep, Herb counted five tubes protruding from various parts of her body. The private duty nurse sat by the raised side-rails holding Amanda's emaciated, frail hand. He was startled to see it was Christie. When she saw Herb standing at the door, she gently let go of the hand and walked quietly with him into the hallway. "She just fell asleep a few minutes ago. She's much improved."

Herb could only mutter the obvious, "Twelve hours on a pediatric ward is not enough for you?"

They held each other, it was a lingering kiss both would have liked to continue, but for another voice from inside Amanda's room. "Christie . . . Christie." Amanda's voice was filled with a special tenderness that told Herb instantly these two women were not strangers.

"That was a great pick-me-up," Christie smiled, and then she briskly reentered the room to continue her all-night vigil.

Since their first meeting, it turned out, Christie had often visited Amanda, and she also knew Franklin and Karl. Why hadn't Herb been told? Amanda wanted it that way, and no one ever chose to question her wishes or motives.

Herb shifted the desk chair and was thinking about his recent chat with Larry. He would not confront Amanda with Emma Mae's complaints. Any attempt to pull the wool over Amanda's eyes was doomed to failure. She had a way of looking at him, and somehow peeling away the layers. "Dr. Klein," her finger would point skyward, " . . . de Lord don't like bullshit." He would simply tell Karl the new housekeeper was admonished, and would be fired unless she shaped up.

His eyelids grew weary, fatigue had set in, but he knew there was one more telephone call to be made. Herb was about to dial Christie's number, when he heard a knock and a familiar voice, "Pete James here."

"Come in Pete," a surprised Herb, had completely forgotten this scheduled meeting with his friend.

"I know obstetrics rotation is a mess. How about tomorrow?"

"No way. I was waiting for you," a peppy Herb smiled.

Pete sat barefoot on the edge of the bed. He wore tattered blue jeans with holes at the knees. A huge belt buckle, initialed PJ, was partially covered by a plaid shirt. His curly jet black hair blended into a well-groomed full beard and moustache. "How's Christie?"

Herb shrugged his shoulders, "I haven't been in touch for a few days, but I guess she's okay." He picked up a briar pipe shaped like a squat bulldog with a diamond shank and a saddle bit, the bowl's wood was straight-grained. It, along with a pound of Balkan tobacco had been gifts from Christie and were prominently displayed in the center of the desk. Under the cannister was the attached note, still legible: 'Never smoke the cheap stuff you call tobacco in my presence. Enjoy the Balken.'

"What's going on Pete," he asked, while tamping the tobacco evenly in the bowl.

"I got an ultimatum from the Dean's office, and I've decided not to comply. As of tomorrow, I cease being a student at Osler Medical School and a Brother at Beta Sigma Tau. I can reapply next fall, and they'll act favorably on my application if I play by their rules," said Pete with no remorse.

"Pete," Herb leaned over, and extended his arms on the desk, "When you started this campaign about long hair and beards, you were looking for a fight. Why don't you tell the Dean and his friends that a well-groomed beard with a nice white jacket and a correctly placed stethoscope adds to your image as a blooming psychiatrist in the Sigmund Freud mold."

"I don't want to win the battle with a bunch of lies. The dress code is illogical and unfair, and maybe my protest will change things."

A frustrated Herb responded, "You broke your balls here at Osler for two years, not to mention the four at Amherst, and you just have the rest of the third and fourth years left. These are the fun times! All you have to do is not fart or pick your nose in front of a patient or your proctor, wear a tie and clean shirt, keep your whites sparkling, and cut your hair and shave the damn beard and moustache. Play the game, get your MD degree, and then tell the big boys what they can do with their dress code!"

"You sound like my old man, Herb. He told me to graduate med school, get my internship out of the way, and then do whatever I wanted. If that meant jerking off watching the sunset over the Ganges River, he would buy the round-trip ticket to India."

Herb looked at Pete, the former Osler Medical student was relaxed and comfortable with his decision. An endpoint had been reached, it was senseless to persist in an argument his friend had already buried. "Is there anything I can do? Do you know what you're going to do? What's your money situation?"

"I thought about finding a job to earn enough money for a

European trip . . . maybe a swing across the states. I know one thing, I'm not going to my father for a handout."

"So you have no money, and no place to go. Why don't you consider staying at Swenson House?"

"C'mon Herb! You know the rules. Only undergraduates can live at the frat, and I'm no longer an Osler student."

"Yes, but you can be the assistant Chef."

"One person can't make that decision, even if you are the president of Beta Sig."

"I don't make unilateral decisions," Herb relit his pipe, "there was an emergency meeting of the house officers; Karl threatened to quit. Larry, Sam, and I voted unanimously to hire you. The brothers will make it official at the next meeting. I'm sure we'll be able to manage a small salary for your services in addition to room and board."

"Some day I'll pay the house back, every penny and then some," said an appreciative Pete.

Herb was tempted to remind his friend of rule bending, but would raise the issue another time when Pete was not defenseless.

"Leaving Osler was not an easy decision. I'm no martyr. It's just something I have to do."

Herb tamped the pipe's hot ashes, "I don't challenge your sincerity, only your wisdom. Pete, there's somebody I'd like you to meet."

"Sure. What's cooking?"

"You'll see. How about tomorrow morning at eleven, the hospital lobby at the information booth."

"Eleven it is," smiled Pete as he closed the door.

Herb returned to the desk and silently puffed his pipe. The last twenty-four hours had taken its toll, he felt washed out. The obstetrics-gynecology rotation was a drag, a pit stop on the race to get his M.D. degree. An asshole like Pringle was good for a few laughs. He knew how to play the game. However absurd, meet the patient's expectations, cuddle up to the nurses, congratulate the resident on a great job when he does your work, and always make sure the insurance form is signed.

The affairs of the fraternity had him wondering whether he was the right man for the job. Larry Lewis had a laid-back attitude that seemed more in tune with getting things done without a hassle. So what if Whitsky didn't produce a Queen for the party? So what if Der Fuehrer and Emma Mae quit? Beta Sigma Tau would survive.

Amanda's illness weighed heavily; her slow downhill descent taxed his patience, highlighted his impotence, sapped his energy. He was damn angry. It wasn't enough to make the best out of a bad situation.

And Pete, poor Pete. All he had to do was shave and he's back in school. What a putz! As if he's the only one around here with a gripe. One more chance to set him straight tomorrow and if he doesn't bite, than he's on his own.

Herb sought the only person who could restore normalcy back into his life. He dialed the number quickly and spoke softly into the receiver: "Christie! . . . How are you?"

"How am I? I haven't heard from you in so long that I was just about to put on the gas jet, take an overdose of sleeping pills, and hang myself. Otherwise, I'm just great, Doctor Klein," came a stern voice over the telephone.

Together, they laughed.

* * *

6

DR. Sorrel Spatch entered the conference room, and gingerly put a black, leather attache case on the table. He wore a Brooks Brother's striped gray all wool suit, and a bright crimson bowtie. He carefully took off his double breasted jacket, and replaced it with a clean white laboratory coat.

A slender man with a small moustache and dark black hair parted in the middle, Sorrel's elegant appearance and refined manner had been his style since prep school days at the Penn Charter School for young gentlemen. Tasteful fashion, savoir-faire, and aesthetic virtues accounted for his high school nickname: Sorrel, on and off the campus, became known as 'Spiffer.'

He had attended Yale University and the Harvard Medical School, but returned to Philadelphia for post-graduate training in obstetrics and gynecology at Osler General. Faculty members, knowing his credentials and academic achievements, were surprised when Spiffer chose to become a clinician, rather than a researcher and academician.

At age fifty, his dignified attire and correct mannerisms continued to symbolize his breeding. He reached for a gold pocket watch, and declared, "Gentlemen, it's 11:15 . . . shall we proceed? I already know Dr. Brickton, a second year resident. Mel, why don't you make the introductions?"

"Thank you, sir," the two men shook hands and the resident continued, "Dr. Spatch, the intern this month in the GYN clinic is Stu Levin. Stu is looking at OB-GYN residency programs in the Boston area. Next to Stu is our fourth year medical student, Herb Klein. Extern Klein is thinking about a rotating internship here at Osler. To his left is Peter James. Pete is a third year student who has chosen to take a leave of absence this year. We have invited him to listen and participate, if that meets with your approval."

"Dr. James is certainly welcome. What will you be doing before you return next fall?" asked Spiffer.

Pete glanced at Herb, "Right now Dr. Spatch, I'm thinking of becoming a chef."

"Mmm . . . I think Dr. James, this session can be meaningful from two points of view. Gentlemen, please feel free to interrupt, open discourse is to be encouraged. I want you to challenge my ideas." Dr. Spatch sat on a chair and motioned for the others to join him, "When I was a student at the Harvard Medical School, Dr. Lionel Stingley was my proctor, a brilliant diagnostician and meticulous history taker who only rarely needed a physical examination to confirm his conclusions. Even the great Sir William Osler took the same view in his book *The Principles and Practice of Medicine*, published in 1892. History taking was key, physical exams usually not as helpful, and laboratory studies frequently superfluous and too costly. We are so cost conscious in 1964, aren't we, Dr. Brickton?"

"Yes sir," Mel said emphatically. He was recalling the difficult breech delivery and Dr. Pringle's concern with rising medical fees and cost containment.

"Does anyone know Dr. Brian Kramer of the cardiology department? Yes, Dr. Klein?"

"I recently finished my medical rotation and Dr. Kramer was a ward attending. He would examine the patient first with a stethoscope, and from the heart exam would develop the patient's history," Herb said, admiring of the cardiologist's prowess.

Dr. Spatch signalled his approval, "Precisely, Dr. Klein. Dr. Stingley believed in the power of history taking, Dr. Kramer in auscultation, and I gentlemen . . . I believe in the virtues of the olfactory sense. The neuroanatomy and the physiology of smell is poorly understood, less so than the other visceral phenomena. We know the olfactory mucous membrane is the specialized portion of the nasal lining containing the nerve cells which transmit sensations of smell to higher centers in the brain, the so-called limbic system or limbic lobe. The threshold for different substances is highly variable. For example, receptor cells can detect methyl mercaptan, the active component of garlic, at a concentration of less than one millionth of a milligram per liter. Contrast this with the large quantity of ether in a similar area before the odor can be detected. . . Smell and taste are interrelated. Nasal congestion is associated with an alteration of the nasal mucosa, and a concommitant change in the taste of food." Spiffer paused, and turned to the prospective chef, "Dr. James. I too have an interest in gastronomy. I especially enjoy the culinary delights of French cuisine. The epicure not only appreciates the taste and visual aspects of gourmet food, but the aromas as well. Dr. Brickton, will you explain the academic exercise planned for this morning!"

"There are two patients in separate rooms who are on examination tables, and draped in the usual manner. When we enter each room, the nurse will put the patient's feet in stirrups and move her into the usual lithotomy position. I will make the introductions, and Dr. Spatch will take over."

Mel was finished, and the five men left the conference table for a nearby hallway. The gynecology resident knocked on the door, both patient and nurse were smiling as the doctors entered the examination room.

"Miss Marilyn Detch and Nurse Connors, I'd like to introduce you to our attending consultant, Dr. Spatch—also, Doctors Levin, Klein, and James."

"Thank you, Dr. Brickton. Hello, my dear," said a smiling Spiffer to Miss Detch, her legs already artfully draped by a sensitive nurse. "Gentlemen, I think it's important to note the windows are shut, as well as the door. Before we proceed with the examination, I suggest we blow our noses. I carry a handkerchief, but tissues will do."

A box of Kleenex was shared as the young doctors complied with Dr. Spatch's request. Miss Detch, puzzled by Spiffer's remarks but not wanting to be excluded from events related to her person, also cleared her nostrils with a tissue.

"Now if everyone will inhale deeply and relax. Is there a distinctive scent?" As Dr. Spatch spoke, he looked at the doctors around the room to gauge a response. "Good! I agree. There is nothing at this point to suggest a problem, but always first assess your patient from afar before advancing. Nurse Connor, will you push the drape to one side and expose the object of our inquiry. Gentlemen, let us approach the patient and position ourselves between the stirrups. Now bend over and inhale . . . Dr. James! Why are you standing in the corner? Are you feeling well?"

Pete rubbed his upper abdomen, "I'm sorry Sir. I have an upset stomach. I guess it was the pancakes at breakfast."

Herb walked over to his friend, and guided him to the other

doctors. They had formed a huddle; Herb and Pete were closest to the patient, their heads parallel to Miss Detch's knees; Stu and Mel positioned themselves at the stirrup levels; Spiffer was at the rear, and squarely in the middle.

"Now gentlemen, there is a subtle, but distinctive olfactory response. Does anyone want to hazard a guess?" Dr. Spatch waited patiently, but no one responded. He continued, "May I suggest you begin to utilize the sniffing reflex. This helps to direct the air currents superiorly and dorsad to the olfactory nerves in the bulb. Sniff gentlemen, sniff!"

In unison, the doctors tested the hypothesis. Their inhales blending into a loud, mucous harmony. "Miff . . . iff . . . giff . . . iff."

"Am I okay? Did the doctors find anything?" asked an anxious Miss Detch.

"Everything is fine, my dear. The doctors will explain after they are finished," Nurse Connors answered her.

". . . Gentlemen, please stop! Would anyone care to make a diagnosis? . . . No volunteers? Okay, let me share with you my impression." The attending consultant gynecologist stroked his chin and then his pencil thin moustache, "Try to relate the smell to something familiar. To me, this odor is reminiscent of *poelee de cepes et ris de veau*. Does anyone understand French? No, not even our future chef, Dr. James? This exquisite dish is sauteed sweetbread and mushrooms; the smell is characteristic. It has a yeastlike quality. I would now like to suggest a diagnosis."

At this point, Dr. Spatch stood up and the others followed. Mel Brickton was especially grateful; prone to muscle spasms periodically, he gently rubbed his lower back in an attempt to abort another attack. Stu and Herb remained attentive, but expressionless. Pete was bewildered, not quite certain of what to say or do, he looked at the others for guidance.

"I believe the patient has monilia vaginitis," said the erudite Spiffer.

"You're correct, Dr. Spatch. We received laboratory confirmation earlier this morning." Mel turned to the patient, and in a comforting voice added, "You have an infection in your vagina, and we expect good results with the medicine you'll be getting."

Miss Detch was relieved to hear her disease was not serious, and amenable to drug therapy. She expressed her thanks, and as the medical men prepared to leave the room, she politely asked, "It sounds so inviting, Dr. Spatch. Could you share the recipe for the sauteed sweetbread and mushrooms?" Spiffer agreed, Marilyn had been such a nice and cooperative patient.

Mrs. Yolanda Brown was told by Nurse Wilson that a group of doctors would soon be coming, so she was not surprised when Dr. Spatch and his colleagues entered the examination room. Aided into the lithotomy position by the nurse, Yolanda heard the names of the physicians announced by a doctor rubbing his back. One doctor closed the window which was only open a crack. A young man with a full beard and moustache in the far corner of the room was grasping his stomach. All of the physicians blew their noses. They all took deep breaths, and then signaled 'no' with shakes of their heads. They started to congregate between the stirrups at the same time Nurse Wilson was pushing aside the drape. Mrs. Brown also noted that the doctor who had closed the window, took the bearded doctor by the hand and positioned him by her right thigh. They were bent over, and she could only see the crops of their heads. "Mfff . . . hfff . . . ffff . . . fff. . ."

"What you all doin'," asked Yolanda, a bit indignantly.

"Everything is real fine Mrs. Brown. The doctors are trying to determine your problem," reassured Nurse Wilson.

"Shit! That kind of problem my husband can handle," said Mrs. Brown as she watched the huddled doctors, their arms extended over adjoining shoulders.

"*Loup en croute avec sauce choron a la dijon.*"

"Nurse," Mrs. Brown's voice quivered, "Does that mean I have cancer?"

"No, no, not at all. There is nothing to worry about," the nurse said.

"Sea bass in puff pastry with a touch of mustard."

Yolanda noticed the bearded doctor now standing in the corner next to the sink; he continued to hold one hand on his upper abdomen, while waving the other in front of his face like a fan.

"Foreign body, most likely a tampon. . ."

"Mrs. Brown," said the doctor with the bad back, "Your symptoms are due to a tampon you forgot to remove, and is still present in your vagina. I'll see you in a few minutes, and we will resolve the problem."

Dr. Spatch led the doctors back to the conference room. Two patients had been correctly diagnosed, and there was a shared sense of accomplishment in a job well done. There were no further questions. The attending removed his starched white laboratory coat, and put on a jacket and overcoat with Herb's assistance. He picked up the attache case, warmly shook hands with his younger colleagues, waved goodbye, and said fondly as he left, "Bon appetite."

Mel and Stu immediately left for the clinic, Pete remained sitting on the conference table. Mel was nearing the hallway, but Stu had stopped; bent over, legs spread and holding his back side firmly with both hands, the intern let loose with a resounding fart. He took a few steps toward the door, quickly veered around to face Pete and Herb, pointed an accusing finger at both, and shouted at the top of his voice, "Schlachtopf mit Sauerkraut und Klossen!"

"Levin," Peter was flushed and in a state of tearful exultation, "the Spiffer would be proud!"

"You've just met my hero," a jubilant Herb chuckled, "Dr. Sorrel 'Spiffer' Spatch, the 'Snatch Sniffer.'"

They were alone. Pete wiped away the tears, and said in a somber tone, "I know there's a reason for my being here other than to further my cooking career, but I'm not getting the message."

"Fair enough," replied Herb in an equally serious mood. "I'm sure you realize you're not the only one who doesn't like the way things are done around here, and I'm talking across the board. You can start with the first year here at Osler Medical school, and Professor Zucker's Gross Anatomy class. Remember his opening remarks at the first lecture? 'If you don't think by the end of this semester, that I'm not a flaming asshole, then I have not done my job, and I would now like to offer you the only apology these humble lips will utter.' At the end of the day, half the class acknowledged he was a prophet, and after the first week there was not a single non-believer. Yes, sir! Ol' Morty sets the tone. He tells you you're here to learn how to think, memorization is a small part of the process, and then the examinations deal with a plethora of irrelevant minutia. The 'Zucker Factor' continues throughout medical school: exposure to the total body of knowledge of a subject so you never feel shutout, you always gotta be in the ballpark. The lingo has a monotonous strain—main idea, big picture, heart of the matter—and then you are inundated with a barrage of bullshit destined to keep you reeling and prevent you from thinking. By your third year, the word is passed around that the weak sisters have been weeded out and only the strong have survived. People at Osler begin to look at you in a different way, even Morty has been known to smile at an upperclassman. You're almost one of the boys, but not quite. The study stuff is still heavy, but for the most part you deal with clinicians who can relate to real, live people, and for the first time you even feel like a doctor. An attenuated Zucker Factor demands you know a myriad of esoteric diseases to get an A on an exam, or be able to show your stuff in friendly one-upmanship contests at the bedside or in the conference room. The major problem now becomes dealing with other students and doctors who have been stepped on, abused, maligned, and led to believe they are something special. By the time Morty Zucker and his friends are finished, you have a lot of very sick egos. They are ready to live by medicine's golden rule, 'I broke my ass, now somebody is gonna pay for it.' The faculty and attendings, all of whom have been molded from the same cast, walk around Osler with a club in their hand, foaming from the mouth, their pants zippers down, and they want action. Enter, Pete James!"

"Alright, I led with my chin. The deck was stacked. I don't deny I was a marked man, but I made a stand on principle. Are you trying to tell me your hero is a rebel with a cause?"

"You better believe it," said Herb adamantly. "Enter Sorrel 'Spiffer' Spatch. Penn Charter, Yale, Harvard, top grades, a few quality research projects to his credit—the sky's the limit. He comes to Osler General for a clinically oriented residency with the idea of seeing patients and teaching. Spiffer hopes it's not high stakes roulette in Philly, but it turns out to be New Haven and Boston in disguise. Faculty placement and advancement is based on the number of research papers published in respectable periodicals, like the *Journal of Clinical Investigation*, and how many key conferences around the country require your services as a speaker. The knack of acquiring grant money . . . and of course, the ability to kiss ass better than your opposition! Like you, Spiffer sees the hypocrisy and the deception, and rightfully concludes there is no place on a medical faculty for someone interested in just seeing patients and teaching, no matter how skilled. But. . ."

"But," interrupted Peter, "Spiffer's method is not to openly confront, but to out-bullshit the opposition at their own game. How do you know this isn't all a big put on? Maybe the guy is just a screwball. Maybe the other faculty members feel sorry for him, and don't want to hurt his feelings?"

"I think they're afraid of him. Spiffer has the strongest credentials possible, starting with an Ivy League background and now a host of organizations that entitle him to a place in Who's Who In Medicine. Challengers! The Morty Zuckers already have their tenure, and the guys below don't want to jeopardize their chances of becoming

'Mortys' themselves. Dr. Pringle and the other part-timers are making so much money gouging the hospital and the public they neither have the financial incentive or the time to pick a fight. None of them will take on Spiffer because it will draw attention to their own inadequacies, possibly compromise their own aspirations, and of course, there is the distinct possibility they may lose. Pete. . . ," Herb changed to a more subdued voice, "I really am not sure what the Spiffer's motives are, or why he acts the way he does, but let's look at it another way. I would like to believe every time Sorrel Spatch comes to this institution and talks or sniffs, he sends out a message to all the assholes around here with my name on it."

"It's not my way, Herb! I don't go for the backdoor approach, but I can agree with you, Spiffer doesn't follow the Osler protocol."

"Which is?"

"Around here," Pete stood up and followed his friend's lead, "When you get kicked in the nuts, you're supposed to understand it's necessary, in order to make a better disciplined and more compassionate physician. You bow your head, and thank the guy for the favor." As Pete finished, he quickly jerked his leg toward Herb's groin, but intentionally fell short of the mark.

Both men laughed as they walked to the door, but Herb stopped at the bulletin board, and after looking quickly at the many announcements, pointed to the one that attracted his interest—

PELVIC INFLAMMATORY DISEASE—NEW DIAGNOSTIC
   APPROACHES
MAHONEY ROOM JANUARY 25, 8 A.M.
COFFEE AND DANISH TO FOLLOW
GUEST LECTURER—SORREL SPATCH, M.D.

"Wouldn't miss it for the world," Pete said, and then he remembered, "Ah, I'm going to be working with Karl in the kitchen. He'll never let me come."

"Not so," smiled Herb, a hand on his friend's shoulder, "it all depends on how you play the game."

* * *

7

"BE careful, and step lightly . . . the women can hear every step. Come over here by the window and you'll get a better view. Watch out for the junk. I ain't been up here for a while. Used to come here every day when I was feedin' the pigeons. A lotta father-son-and-holy-ghost houses on Kerr Street had pigeon coops. No more, not a one left. That's Pearl Street." The silver haired man with a ruddy complexion pointed to a group of row homes parallel and close to the Delaware River. "My brother lives there. He's a retired longshoreman, just like me. Everything is old in Southwark. This place is where Philadelphia got its start. Swedish people and then the Limeys. They were all seafarin' types. Straight ahead was the dry dock of the Navy yard. My granddaddy worked there after the Civil War."

"Horace! Horace? Horace Flint!" screamed an angry voice from the second floor steps.

"Looks like the old bag o' wind caught us," whispered the old man, who then replied meekly, "Yes dear."

"Don't you yes dear me! You know that floor's in bad shape. You bring down them young fellas right away."

Horace was a huge man, who at sixty-eight looked as if he could do an honest day's work on the docks and warehouses a few short blocks from his home. Almost daily he would walk to the union hall and talk to anyone who would listen, about what it was like to be a longshoreman in the days before the container ships and the big fork lifts, when Philly was the 'King of Ports' and the berths along the Delaware River were occupied with ships from every corner of the world. Despite the long hours and the arduous work, he showed no adverse affects of a lifetime devoted to strenuous physical labor.

The clapboard house on Kerr Street was built by his grandfather before the Civil War, and the Flint family had been its sole residents. Many of the neighbors could tell similar stories, Southwark and the river had become the constants in their lives. The Doherty family of Front and Christian Streets were a part of that tradition.

Molly Doherty, a seaman's daughter, married Horace when she was fifteen, and there was not a day in the intervening forty-seven years when she regretted the decision. Their four children had all been born at home with the help of Mrs. Taylor, a midwife who lived on Catherine Street. The first child died of 'double pneumonia' in her first year. The second was a stillborn, but then came George and Thomas, robust and sturdy lads who possessed the vitality of their Southwark forefathers. Their photographs were atop a TV set in the living room, one son sat next to a young woman with a small baby in her arms, and the other stood alone in an Army uniform.

It had been three years since the Flints had seen Tom, his wife Nancy, and granddaughter Jenny. They lived in a small town near San Diego in Southern California, but their last letter hinted at a possible trip East in the summer.

A reunion with George was out of the question, not that Horace hadn't considered it. For a few years after World War II, Horace planned and schemed to find a way to get to Europe. He had visited the shipping line offices and learned about the freighters calling on European ports, and even obtained a schedule of trains with the capital city of Luxemborg as a destination. To visit George, only a short bus ride remained; Number 18 to the City of Hamm, site of the American military cemetery.

The trip to Europe was never made. The Flints' world was Southwark, and an occasional excursion a few blocks north to Society Hill. On a Sunday, weather permitting, they might walk as far as Elfreth's Alley. Cobblestoned streets, hitching posts, well preserved older homes intrigued and delighted, an automobile had never even been a consideration.

Southwark had provided them with an identity, a sense of community, and neighbors that were extensions of their families. But with their advancing years and limited resources, the Flints had to find a way to supplement Horace's social security check. Their savings had all but been eliminated when Molly's bleeding ulcer required surgery. After a long convalescent period in the hospital, she returned to find a new household member. Horace had built a bedroom on the first floor, from an enclosed back porch, and converted the upstairs into an apartment.

"Be down in a sec," yelled Horace, who then winked at the two young men, and spoke softly, "you see the beautiful wooden eagle, hand carved by S.L. Joiner over at his shop on 2nd and Dock. A master craftsman. . ."

"Horace!"

"No sense arguin' with a mule-headed woman. Let's go fellas. Steps are narrow, so be careful."

The three men were greeted by Molly and the young woman who had leased the second floor apartment. The selection of a tenant had not been an easy task for Horace. One advertisement in the Sunday Bulletin had kept the telephone ringing with a barrage of inquiries. Ten appointments were scheduled, but the last four were cancelled.

Number six greeted him with a smile and a kiss on the cheek. The longshoreman's face was aglow, his earliest instincts had proven correct. In Molly's eyes, number six was a clever ploy conceived by Horace to assure continuity of medical care. Why else rent an apartment to a nurse? Molly was led to believe her initial impressions were correct, but the truth was that in the excitement and pleasantries surrounding their first meeting, Horace had neglected to ask the young woman about her job until after they had agreed to an apartment lease. In a few months, number six had brought joy and happiness to the Flint house that had no parallel since the death of their son in World War II, at the Battle of the Bulge.

A kiss was not enough for Horace; he hugged the nurse affectionately, to Molly's embarrassment. The two young men shook hands with the burly longshoreman, each was grateful for an interesting and informative little tour. The tenant, unaccustomed to failure, tried one more time: "Couldn't you reconsider? I have so much food, won't you have dinner with us?"

Horace reached for her hand, "It's not every day you have your boyfriend and brother together. And besides, we eat up here much too often. You don't need an old gabbermouth like me around." He reached for Molly's hand to help her down the steps, but turned suddenly. "Oh Christina! I have tins of cookies and cakes from Neschaunk on the table next to the refrigerator. Maybe Dr. Klein and Paul would like some."

For the first time since Herb met Paul, they were alone. After a short introduction, Horace had burst on the scene and insisted on a quick survey of his beloved Southwark. In rapid succession, they walked to the docks and strolled along the river promenade; made a pilgrimage to the 17th century Old Swede's Church and the Neziner Synagogue; ascended the winding staircase of the shot tower, a munitions factory in the 1812 War; and visited friends in their homes at Mifflin and Workman's Place, houses occupied exclusively by longshoremen and their families for nearly two hundred years.

It was early winter, crisp and chilly, few people walked the streets of Southwark, but Horace knew them all. For Paul, it reminded him of Neschaunk and the small town feeling he always found missing in the big city. Herb, not a stranger to the old man's circuit, continued to marvel at the dynamics and history of river life.

The house tour had been interrupted by Molly, or they would still be rummaging through relics on the floor above them. Horace's enthusiasm had propelled him to center stage. Herb and Paul had barely spoken, but were keenly aware of each other's presence.

Christie pointed to the living room, "Why don't you two relax. Dinner should be ready soon. Paul, are you okay?"

"What a meat cleaver for a hand! Do I still have all of my fingers?" Paul winced, flexed his wrist and fingers, and then grinned at his sister.

"My fault. I should have told you about Horace's handshakes. Go for the thumb and the upper part of the hand, or you're a gonner," grimaced Herb as they sat on the two chairs straddling the huge bay window overlooking the river. "How was the trip from New York? Jersey Turnpike crowded?"

"No problem once I got out of New York, but I made the mistake of seeing a friend at the Rockefeller Institute on the East side, far removed from Columbia. I overextended my stay and got caught in a traffic jam trying to get back to the Lincoln Tunnel." Paul stopped cleaning his hornrimmed glasses, "Do you know anything about electron microscopy?"

"I had a little exposure during my Freshman year at Osler. What's the relationship to Polish literature and Joseph Conrad," joked Herb, referring to what had become Paul's major interest at the university.

"My friend at Rockefeller has her apartment's walls decorated with huge black and white photomicrographs of 'submicroscopic particles.' A minute part of a small part of a cell, one cell among billions or trillions in a single organism," Paul hesitated and sought help with the total number of cells, but Herb shrugged his shoulders. "She tells me someday there will be a microscope many times more powerful than the present ones, and they will magnify the submicroscopic particles in a similar fashion. The cycle will have repeated itself, and a whole new set of photographs will cover another wall. I like science, it's so rational in the way it goes about its business. If only we humans were more analytical and less emotional."

Paul's uneasiness, and his final remark was a prelude to something else; Herb sensed a set-up. 'Parental problems in Neschaunk loomed nearby,' he thought. Herb continued the sparring, "The idea that science embodies singular answers is a myth. In reality, you start by asking a question, and you end up with more questions. For me, the intrigue of medicine is people, not science."

Paul's laugh reminded him of Christie's—short, hearty, and with full exposure of sparkling, perfectly arranged symmetrical teeth. He had the same high cheek-bone structure, brown hair, and large expressive eyes as his sister. A noticeable scar on the chin was the remains of a childhood accident, otherwise his skin was boyish and smooth in complexion. Herb doubted he had to shave more than every other day; his own beard required a razor daily.

"Christie tells me you're still undecided about your internship next year."

"I'm leaning toward a rotating program at Osler General, though I'm pretty sure I'll do a residency in internal medicine. What are your plans after you get your Ph.D. at Columbia?"

"To teach at a college level. In today's world, that also means obligatory research and an occasional book with the smell of something original."

"Any idea where?"

"I'll either stay in New York, or come to the Philly area. Both places are good college cities, and they have the advantage of being close to Neschaunk. Two to three hours is all it takes by car."

"I understand you visited Neschaunk last weekend to see your parents. I'm sorry to hear your father is doing poorly. . ."

"Damn it!" shouted Christie, "The matzah balls are breaking up. Disaster lurks in the wings. Prepare yourselves for the Horn and Hardart."

Both men smiled, but Paul's was shortlived. "I spoke to Mom last night. Dad still refuses to go to the hospital. How that man has suffered. No more boozin' at the local tavern, the cronies now come to our house. He can't even walk up the steps. The bed is in the living room. Sitting in the chair is a struggle, always short of breath and bringing up that black stuff when he coughs. My father is a stubborn man, it's a trait all the Loreski's share," he turned to the kitchen and grinned. "I know Christie had the chest x-rays reviewed by your friend, and there have been consultations between my father's physician and the Osler pulmonary specialist. . ." Paul's voice tapered to a whisper, ". . . but I know there's no cure."

Herb tried to lighten the load, "Paul, your father's disease is not fully appreciated even today. Just a few years ago, there were knowledgable specialists in the field who felt coal dust was totally innocuous to the lungs. Now we know the silica in the coal causes damage to the lung, and your father has a straightforward case of Anthracosilicosis, or coal miner pneumoconiocosis, meaning simply that the inhaled dust has caused scarring and the fibrosis has replaced the good lung tissue. The tuberculosis and heart failure your Dad has are common complications. The TB is being treated, and presently in remission; the heart failure is also responding to treatment. The fibrosis is a funny animal, and can reverse spontaneously at any time. Once the medications start to work, you'll see a difference," Herb said in his most cheerful bedside manner, though not really believing his own words.

Paul looked at Herb intently, and then turned to the river. Darkness had not yet fallen, a container ship and a tow boat pulling a huge barge were still visible.

"I feel so damn angry. Everytime I go back to Neschaunk and see that old abandoned mine, I get a sick feeling in my stomach. You know, Herb," (the name was mentioned for the first time), "there is not a vindictive bone in his body. An old miner will come to the house and they'll talk about the good old days, and every few minutes he'll be raising black sputum from his lungs and spit into a bottle covered with a towel. It's crazy!"

"He doesn't want to be a burden to anyone. It's his way of protecting his family and friends from feeling the pain."

"I realize that Herb, but it's also a big part of the problem. My father has never thought of himself; he lives through my sister and me. It's a sickness. I sometimes think it would have been better being a neglected child. I've never heard the man complain."

Paul scanned the river upstream, a lone tug boat on the Camden side rounded the bend and headed toward Southwark. "I was a little boy when my father started to take me to the Neschaunk coal mine. I was to know every aspect of how a coal mine works, and his own role. He had no false illusions. The mine was his coffin, and that's what he called it. A secret for father and son to share. He wanted me to be afraid."

"Did it work?"

"In spades. The message is written in indelible ink in the middle of my brain." Paul turned away from the river, leaned forward, and said in disgust, "Do you know my father was eight years old when he started to work in the mines?"

A head shook in disbelief, "You're kidding!"

"I wish I were Herb. My father started out as a 'breaker boy,' sorting out the coal from the slate after it reached the surface. I've seen those breaker boys work—you wouldn't believe the noise and dust, and what picking out those jagged chunks of coals does to a kid's hand. One day, the foreman promoted John Loreski and at the age of nine my father became a 'jig runner.' Jig machines are sliding pans that separated the slate from the coal. The Loreski code calls for excellence, and John's efforts were rewarded. At age ten, he began working on the coal cars as a 'patcher,' a switchman. But this was only in preparation for the final test: a 'spragger boy.' That's where you insert wooden sticks between iron spikes to stop these giant coal cars. He survived without breaking a hand or arm, so in the finest Loreski tradition, he was now ready to enter the 'man's' world of the underground mine at the tender age of twelve. . ."

Herb listened, and couldn't help but think of the similarities with his own father. Ben Klein worked in a tenement sweatshop as a youth. The garment industry also had strange sounding names: sewers, pressers, pullers, basters. 'After fourteen hours, my head pounded, the eyes were ready to explode and fall out of their sockets, but I was too tired to complain,' Ben would say, usually squinting, while recalling the despicable working conditions of his childhood.

". . . His parents were actually proud," continued Paul, "it was as if he graduated college, summa cum laude. More money came into the barely surviving household, and anyway coal mining was the only game in town. There were a few textile mills fifteen miles away near Hazelton, but they hired only women. When my father entered the mine, his parents gave him a gift which he still has today: a Stanley lunch pail with a pint thermos bottle to fill with hot tea. My grandmother believed coal dust—and all other poisons, in fact—could be flushed out of your body with tea."

Herb nodded; he understood about the curative properties of tea. It was his turn to look at the river.

"A mine can be very lonely. Deep down, in the bowels of the earth, my Dad's first job was to stand in the pitch darkness for ten hours a day, six days a week, opening a door from one chamber to another to permit a coal car to pass by. Jesus, what a job! He worked two years as a 'trapper boy.' His final achievement was to hand operate a ventilating fan in the robbing section. That's the deepest part of the mine where the last remaining coal is excavated, and the area is usually loaded with smoke, dust, and suffocating gases. After two years as a fan turner, he was ready to become a fullfledged miner. No giveaways in those days. You had to earn your pick and shovel."

"That's enough Paul," murmured Christie, as she stood at the kitchen doorway, her arms on her hips. She moved to her brother's side and put a hand on his shoulder, "Pop was not a martyr on our behalf. He always said coal mining was in his blood; our feelings changed nothing! Let's eat," she said, and then arm-in-arm escorted the men to the kitchen table. "I'm not fishing for compliments, but I've worked very hard at preparing this meal and it wasn't easy. I want you both to be perfectly candid. Constructive criticism will make me a better cook, and a more complete person. I can handle it, so let loose fellas. . ." She watched Herb start the chicken soup with matzah balls, and Paul excitedly attack the lekvar perogies, ". . . but I hope you're both wearing jock straps with metal cups."

Christie had orchestrated a memorable meal with a little help. The perogies had been frozen, but still had the taste and freshness of Mama Loreski's Neschaunk kitchen. Herb's gefilte fish was compliments of Mrs. Yetta Brodsky. Sheldon, her eight year old grandson, had totally recovered after a long convalescence from a ruptured appendix. Sheldon was famous for his disappearing acts and solitary wanderings throughout Osler Hospital. Even the farewell party Christie had arranged was delayed until the dear boy was found. How could Yetta show appreciation for all that Christie had done for her Shelly?

Paul loved mashed potatoes, and he had to admit Christie's matched his mother's, though less creamy. Horace Flint would have readily detected an Irish touch, no one handled a potato like his Molly. The hallah was freshly baked, and no more than few hours out of Sol's Bakery oven on Bainbridge Street.

Her own efforts were concentrated toward the matzah ball soup, the kasha and bowties, and the stuffed cabbage. Yetta was a good consultant, and even offered to prepare the dishes herself, but Christie insisted on making her own mistakes. Sophie Klein, the creator of Herb's favorite dishes, was a graduate of the "little of this, and a little of that—ah, it tastes right!" cooking school. A telephone call to Ben confirmed the obvious; no oral or written record of her culinary magic existed.

The stuffed cabbage, known to Herb as prakas and to Paul as halupke, was sheer misery to Christie. Three emergency calls to Yetta were required, but if nothing else, the final product had the look and smell like something edible. The crucial taste test would soon prove whether or not she had succeeded.

The dessert was a huge babka cake with sliced almonds, another specialty from Yetta's kitchen. Mrs. Brodsky also added another surprise, homemade damson plum wine.

The meal was a major success, exceeding her wildest expectations. Each course was ravenously devoured, and only a few morsels remained. This raised a serious question in her mind that in the Loreski household would have been unforgiveable: had she made enough?

The food and wine had changed Paul's mood. At ease and relaxed, Paul became very talkative and needed to reminisce. He recalled 'Helena,' the Raggedy-Ann doll that was his sister's security blanket, and how he would hide it only to have the doll reappear when their parents took part in the search. Christie's fear of going to the outhouse alone, and the need to accompany his sister no matter what the weather. The hide-and-seek games on the hillside by their home, and how he would deceive her by crawling from one tree stump to another (the trees had been cut to provide the beams and timber for the mine) even though moving after hiding was against the rules.

Did Christie remember the visit to Dr. Lazio in Stenville for an eye examination? At St. Stanislaus Elementary school, she had always been an excellent student and in the top reading group (Infant Jesus), but a decline in her skills pushed her back a notch to a lower section (Blessed Virgin Mary). A visual checkup was recommended by Sister Mary Margaret, and it was at the doctor's office when she admitted she was deliberately doing poorly so she could be with her best friend, Stella Jeraski. Sister Mary Margaret, Christie recalled, was the same nun who punished rule breakers by making them drink old, sour milk in the cloak room.

Paul insisted that Christie and her mother constantly argued. Anna

Loreski was raised in a strict, traditional Polish Catholic home, and her attempt to inculcate the same values into her children met with mixed success. Paul, always the submissive type, claimed his obedience was strictly lip service. Arguing, he had reasoned, only aggravated the problem and Anna's rage, and removed him from his studies and his beloved books. Christie, always the straight shooter, spoke her mind and was in constant conflict with her authoritarian mother.

Anna had completed one year of high school; John Loreski was a functional illiterate with no formal eduation, but possessed a great gift for story telling. After dinner, the family often assembled in the parlor; Paul on the sofa, Anna knitting in a rocking chair, Christie on her father's lap in his favorite easy chair. John's repertoire included Polish tales passed on to him by his immigrant parents, but dealt mostly with the Loreski Neschaunk experience. And then the tables turned, and Christie would become the narrator.

"And do you remember Korzenowski?" Paul asked as his sister reached for cigarettes.

"How could I forget?" she said, her eyes widening as she moved an ash tray to share with Herb. "This schmuk . . ."

"Christie," mouthed Herb. He stopped filling his pipe with tobacco, and said aloud, "How many times must I tell you not to use that word. Let's go back to the days when you were twelve, and became the family storyteller. And incidentally, the word is not schmulk, it's shmuck. Maintain a little self-respect, and don't use it."

"I want to thank you Doctor Klein for your advice. How gracious of you to correct my language, and your concern about my image is truly heartwarming . . . but you are a schmulk and a shmuck, and a fourteen carat one at that, for talking to me in a subservient tone and manner. And Paul, will you remove the foolish shit-eating grin! It puts you in the same category as this fool with a pipe sticking out of his face."

Paul imbibed his drink quickly and sought yet another refill "Where did you get this great vino?"

"The plum wine comes from the vineyards of Shelly and Yetta Brodsky in the Oxford Circle neighborhood of Northeast Philadelphia," Christie answered. She couldn't mention the Northeast without being amused by the picture of block after block of row homes in this middle class Jewish neighborhood where grass was at a premium.

"Brodsky wine is the greatest," Paul toasted his hosts, neither of whom had more than a few sips. "Please continue my love, you were saying about me, 'This schmuck. . .'"

"This . . . ," Christie sneered at her antagonists, and resumed, "nice brother of mine suggested I read Polish stories to my father, a Josef Nalecz Korzenowski was a highly recommended author. I spent hours at the St. Stanislaus and Hazelton libraries looking for this writer, but no one had ever heard of the man. Paul, this whiz kid and only citizen of Neschaunk ever to attend Harvard, then tells me to try his other name: Joseph Conrad."

"And he loved those sea tales and exotic adventure stories," said Paul between belches.

"My brother had the short stories, and many of the novels in his room. . ."

"He wrote in English and the literary world knew of his English name, but the man was a Pole. Conrad's parents were sent to Siberia, they advocated Polish nationalism, for Christ's sake!"

"Paul, I think you've had enough," Christie reached for the wine bottle now in her brother's hand.

"First a toast to Josef Nalecz Korzenowski, and to the freedom Poland will one day know despite the big, bad Russian bear."

"How about a cup of coffee. . ."

"You see Herb," Paul interrupted his sister, "my sister is free spirited like my father. I'm more in my mother's mold. I attend mass every Sunday, not when the mood moves me, like my father or Christie. I pretend to be a free thinker, but basically the Church and my parents have me by the balls, and they're squeezing. . ."

"Paul really! Let's change this conversation. Any good plays on Broadway?"

"Leave him alone Christie. Go ahead Paul."

"Thanks Herb. You have no idea what I've been through since my sister told my parents about you. It's been sheer Hell," Paul reached for the wine glass and one final surge of encouragement. "Most people in Neschaunk have never met a Jew."

"Come off it, Paul. You have no right. . ."

"Christie! I'm telling you for the last time, let him talk," ordered Herb.

"They are honest, hard working, good people," Paul's voice was shaky, "but like everybody else, they have their hangups. . . Nobody from Neschaunk would be caught dead at a synagogue wedding with Christie as the bride, nor would you be welcome in their homes, including my father's. If you marry in the Catholic Church there will be no problem. If you split up," Paul turned away from Herb, but stared at the table rather than at his enraged sister, ". . . all is forgotten, Christie, and I can assure you no one will ever raise the issue again."

"And what's your view?" asked a calculating Herb.

"I told them you were dating, and not to raise the issue. But the thing is an obsession with my mother. She's afraid her daughter will leave the Church. I personally don't care what the both of you do. It's none of my business. If you married in a synagogue, I would gladly attend, though I wouldn't want to advertise the fact because of my parents."

Herb rested the pipe in an ashtray and sipped the wine. "I appreciate the difficulty of being a messenger boy. It's never an easy task when you don't agree with what you're doing. We hold no grudge against you."

"Speak for yourself. How dare my brother. . ."

"Christie! Will you put away the babka cake and do the dishes. Please let me finish," Herb paused to relight the pipe. "I want you to know that we," he turned to Christie who remained seated, "don't want to cause pain or misery to anyone. I have no idea about our future, but I do know the last five months with your sister have been the happiest in my life. I feel terrible. My presence has caused so much unhappiness, and I know how tight-knit your family is and how much you need each other. But I can't change my ways. After my mother died a few years ago, I stopped going through the motions of being a Jew but I've never been able to cut the umbilical cord. If nothing else, I always intend to hold on to the label. I don't want to marry in a synagogue or a church, but I'll never leave Christie," Herb reached for her hand and squeezed. "Never. She'll have to get rid of me. I need her . . . I love. . ." He could not go on, his head bowed, the puffing became more active, and the smoke between Paul and Herb thickened.

Paul nervously fingered the inside of the empty wine glass, blood-shot eyes began to blink: "I didn't want to come here. I pleaded with them to let things ride. I don't want to hurt you, Herb. I told my mother I make a lousy hit man. The whole affair is more than I can handle. My mother cries and prays all the time, she'll talk to anyone about her misfortune when there is even a remote possibility of earning sympathy points. And my father . . . looking at photographs of his daughter, spitting black stuff up into a bottle, always short of breath . . . the only fresh air in his life is Christie."

"That's it! I have had it with the both of you!" shouted Christie. "No one has bothered to ask me for my opinion. How wonderful it is playing a cameo role in one's own life. Who do I thank? I've got to clean up. Please go into the living room, and if you insist on continuing this conversation, make sure it's out of my range."

Christie's remarks had a solemn affect on both men. Herb returned to the chair overlooking the river, but Paul opted for the couch. A fog had rolled in, lights on the docks and ships were barely visible. Rain drops lightly bounced against the window pane. The deliberate rhythm of Herb's pipe was regular and slow; the strong, sharp flavor of Balken tobacco mingled with the saccharine after taste of Brodsky wine. The rain intensified, water rapped heavily against the huge bay window.

As a young boy, Herb liked to walk in the rain along the river's edge. It was fun to splash through puddles and not around them, especially when he wore sneakers and wasn't burdened with rubbers and rain gear. The rain was always a time to refuel, clean the slate, erase the excesses and demands of a complicated world. Too much homework, an unfair teacher, a friend who turned out not to be a friend . . . rain washed away problems, if only for a short time.

"I hope they're happy thoughts," Christie stood at the side of his chair, her folded arms lifted firm breasts.

"I was just thinking of taking a walk," his arm encircled her waist. Herb turned and saw Paul asleep on the couch. "The travel and the drinking finally caught up with him."

Herb followed her into the kitchen, and was ready to sit down when Christie pointed to another door, "We have some things to discuss. Let's leave. The light may disturb Paul."

Christie's bedroom was stark. It had been the Flint guestroom, arranged with the idea their son's family would always have a comfortable place to stay. A fresh coat of white paint was applied to the walls and ceiling, the oriental rug cleaned, and the hardwood floors polished in expectation of a new tenant. The furniture remained untouched, relics bought at a store on South Street called 'Serendipity.' A roomy chifforobe served as a closet, a full sized dresser with a rotating mirror lie opposite the four poster bed, and a bedroom rocker made of walnut with a burl design occupied one corner. The mattress was soft, but the bed springs annoyed Herb. More than a few of the spring coils were broken, creating a squeaky metallic grating with any change in position. The pillows were filled with goose and duck feathers, he put one of them against the bed board to support his back.

Herb focused on the dresser top and mirror. Next to a tray of perfumes and cosmetics was a family portrait: little Christie sat on her father's lap; Paul stood by his side, Anna draped one arm around her son's shoulder; dressed in their finest apparel, they proudly smiled as St. Stanislaus Church loomed in the background. The recent framed photograph next to it was Herb's personal favorite: Christie playfully pulling on her father's red suspenders and whispering into his ear, John Loreski caught in a genuine fit of laughter. Other small pictures were tucked into the frame of the mirror: Herb as a sixth grader standing in front of Horticultural Hall between Sophie and Ben; a Cornell year book graduation pose; Herb in his white medical jacket and Christie wearing a nurse's uniform embracing in front of Osler General Hospital's entrance.

She entered the bedroom, kicked off her penny loafers, flopped onto the bed, rested her head on his chest, and waited for the spring coils to stop their ring. "A walk in the rain spells trouble. Out with it Herb!"

"I can't believe what I told your brother. I've always renounced religion, and here I'm talking about this mystical bond with Juadism. Marriage is something we have never even discussed. But what really pisses me off . . . and hurts, really, . . . I still can't believe it! The first time in my life I profess love for a woman, I'm not talking to her, but find myself looking into her brother's bloodshot eyes. Talk about timing!"

Christie chuckled before kissing him on the lips. "Nothing said was a surprise. You were feeling sorry for the Loreski family, and yourself."

"Christie! I wanted a French restaurant, a small table with a bouquet of flowers, candlelight. . ."

"It doesn't mean a thing, Herb, because I can say 'I love you,' and you can't. I know how you feel, and the opposite is true, too. Other men have told me they love me, and I recognized it was a polite way of asking for a bedroom partner. I'm happy you feel good about us. The rest is nonsense, and the others are a nuisance."

"Don't talk about your family that way."

"Let me tell you about my family! Paul is a brilliant scholar, a nice guy and a good brother whom I love dearly, but he wears a Congressional Medal of Guilt when it comes to my parents and the whole Neschaunk scene. He was right when he told you he didn't want to be here. He never wants to be put in a situation where he may have to take a stand. He always looks for the comfy middle ground. And that stuff about Joseph Conrad is damnright ludicrous! I'm sure his Ph.D. thesis will be a model of academic excellence—his papers always are—but I guarantee he will have missed the point of Conrad completely. There are times when you just can't hide from a problem. The answer may not be as important as coming to grips with the question. If there is a fight, you can rely on Paul to try and find a way to become a referee. Tell me Herb, if you were a Pole and believed in Polish nationalism, how many Pauls would you like to have on your side?"

"God-al-mighty! Have you ever considered becoming a lawyer, or a writer, or. . ."

"That's another sore point with me. Paul was distressed when I chose nursing and not a fancy girl's college. Medicine, status, and all its dollar rewards was what he had in mind. I like being a nurse, and I don't find cleaning bed pans demeaning."

"If money isn't important, then how come you're so upset with nurses' salaries?" joked Herb.

"The days of sweat shops—children in coal mines, and slave labor—are over," said Christie as she swung an elbow into Herb's belly, "don't you agree?"

"Uhh . . . Those are precisely my thoughts. Are you sure you didn't work in a coal mine," he asked, massaging his stomach.

"I'm glad common sense prevailed. Let me correct some half truths my enebriated brother planted in your mind."

"Paul was in control. He knew exactly what he wanted to say, and alcohol didn't compromise his sincerity."

"Paul had been drinking before he ever took a step into this place. I smelled booze on his breath when he kissed me. My guess is he started last night and continued in the morning. In Neschaunk, if you got a problem you can't handle, a woman prays and a man drinks. Without alcohol, my brother would have needed your help to take a leak."

"He certainly fooled me."

"I can assure you, he doesn't fool me or my father. Mother is another story. Paul knows how to pull the wool over her eyes. Mama's world is the family and the church, and her joy is making everybody believe she serves both in an ideal fashion. Her daughter's happiness and the teachings of the church are now in conflict, so what do you do? The church won't budge, it never does. It makes more sense to crush your daughter with the idea she will be unhappy at first, but in the end will be happier because you cared enough to tell the truth. In the meantime, you create a holding pattern, and try to get as much support and sympathy from people who share your prejudices."

"And your father?" Herb looked straight ahead at the photograph of Christie whispering into his ear.

"Papa will appease others to keep the peace. His real feelings are another story. I have no doubt if we marry in a synagogue, he would come in a wheel chair with his oxygen and expectorant bottle. And the following Sunday, if he was in the mood, he would attend church and his head would be held high. While I'm on the subject, Paul would accept an invitation graciously, but find an excuse not to show up at our wedding. He would spend his time at a bar drinking up a storm, telling anyone who will listen, how he always finds himself in no-win situations."

"I'm not going to walk in the rain. I can use a cup of coffee," said Herb, his spirits buoyed.

"Later. There's something else I want to talk about."

"Sure," he said confidently, convinced his awkward moments were over.

"I want to get laid."

"You what?"

"It's simple. I'm no longer interested in remaining a virgin, and I've chosen tonight for my coming out party. Unless you know another way, Herb, I need your cooperation. Just think, after tonight I'll be a confirmed on the Keller Report."

"You've got to be nuts, Christie. I told you the Keller Report is geared to the pledges. After a few meetings, even they realize it's all a farce. Every woman is a possible, probable, and confirmed. It all depends on her mood, and who she is out with that evening. We get requests from girls to have their names put onto a certain list. How's that for a real clandestine operation! And they lie! One girl who claimed to be a confirmed, had an intact hymen. Lou Wright swore he was propelled off the bed. Another girl claimed to be a possible and Sergeant Whitsky of the Vice Squad knew her as a part-timer who worked the big hotels on weekends when the convention boys are in town."

"You're getting mad. I only said the Keller Report thing as a joke.

What I really need to know is whether you're man enough to handle the job." Christie kissed his neck, and pushed her hand under the shirt to massage his chest.

"For a few months I tried desperately to make it with you. I finally gave up, and filed you in my 'impossible dream' portfolio. I really am content with the making out. It reminds me of the great times I had in high school. You are one hundred percent right, it's best to wait until you get married."

"I was wrong, Herb, and I'm big enough to admit my mistake. Would you please screw me. Pretty please!" her hand moved toward his belt buckle.

"This is ridiculous. Your brother is in the next room. We're lying on the noisiest bed in Southwark . . . the Flints are right below us."

"I love a challenge. Don't you!" she said while pulling at his pants zipper.

"Sure! And of course you are using the rhythm method to prevent an accident. You're better off flipping a coin."

"I agree. I'm on the pill, and I just started my second month with no side effects. My doctor is quite happy with the results."

"Who's your Doctor?" asked Herb, incredulously.

"Stu Levin."

"Stu Levin? He's my friend, a fraternity brother, only a year ahead of me . . . just an intern. Stu knows only a little more than I do, which means he's a phony. You don't want to compromise your health. Let me send you to a real doctor."

Christie put a finger to his lips, moved atop Herb, and then slowly rotated her hips and breasts. "I can tell you like me," she said smilingly. "Let me bring this conversation to a close. I need you, I want you . . . whatever happens for the rest of our lives, I'll always thank you for this moment."

The bed recoiled. Metal rubbed against metal. The clang of spring coils increased, slowly and methodically.

"I told you it's noisy. But who cares!" he said, alert to a new mission.

Paul rubbed his eyes as he walked into the kitchen. "I'm sorry. How long did I sleep?"

"It's almost one . . . about five or six hours," said Christie reaching for the coffee pot to fill her brother's cup.

"Why don't you sleep here, and return to New York in the morning," suggested Herb.

"Thanks, but I really have to get back tonight or tomorrow will be lost. I'm wide awake . . . no cream," Paul pointed to the coffee. "I want you both to know I will do everything possible to make things easier with my parents. Whatever your decision, I support it. If I can help in anyway, just call me."

It was time to leave. He kissed his sister warmly, and shook Herb's hand. The first floor was totally dark, and Paul used the small light from the kitchen to descend the stairs. He opened the front door partially and could sense the dense fog, though it was no longer raining. Paul turned to the second floor landing where he saw the silhouettes of Christie and Herb.

"Be careful," his sister whispered.

He paused, and stared at the motionless black figures above. Paul had an impulse to scream back, 'You, Christina Loreski . . . and you, Herb Klein . . . both of you be careful, very careful.' But he said nothing, and disappeared into the darkness.

* * *

PART II

8

FRAMING

THE applause was not encouraging. Only a few clapped: the din from the bar and the musicians' loud playing masked any sign of appreciation. The singer took the mandatory curtain call, bowed, and waved a meaningless thank-you before leaving the stage to the accompaniment of There's No Business Like Show Business. The bar was two and three deep, many stood behind tables with makeshift seating to accommodate the overflow. The band's next number was rivaled by the conversational hum and the clang of glasses. It was a restless crowd, and the man observing behind the curtain recognized the symptoms. Joe Dolan had seen it all before.

"Negative. No way Stan, not tonight. They'll eat you alive."

"For crying out loud, Joe, this is the third straight show. A magician needs to work in front of live bodies."

"You'll go first next time, and Mickey will follow. Stan, will you tell Maureen to get her butt ready? I gotta see somebody." A bespectacled young man stood nearby listening to the music. Joe grabbed his arm, "Wilson! We have to talk."

"Sure, Mr. Dolan. Great show. The fellas love it."

"Cut the shit, Wilson. The natives are stirring. I want more police protection placed where they can be seen. Center stage if necessary."

"This is a party night, Mr. Dolan. Everybody's a little loose. There won't be any problems. After all, you know where you are, these are respectable. . ."

"Wilson! Understand what I'm going to tell you. I'll say it once," Joe's face was flushed but he kept his voice down to a loud whisper. "This place is ready to explode. The guys out there are no better than wild, hungry animals looking for food, and you can bet they're not going to feed on me or anybody in my group. These boys are first class pricks! Either you get more security guards, or the show is over."

"Yes sir!" Wilson was well aware of who would be blamed, if Dolan followed through on his threat.

Joe Dolan tightened his tie, buttoned a loose jacket, walked to the side of the stage, and signaled to the musicians. The drummer's roll greeted him as he strolled to the microphone.

"May I have your attention gentlemen! May I have your attention . . . Gentlemen! There's been a change in plans. . . Your attention please, Shh!" pleaded Joe, a finger to his lips.

Others in the audience followed; "Shh . . . Shhh," soon became a chorus, then the clamor subsided.

"I regretfull. . ."

"Where the hell is your star performer," yelled a voice from the bar.

"Meow . . . Meow . . . Meow," a few chanted. Many more banged their fists against tables. A drunk shouted, "Wilson! Wherever you are—if there's a screw up, your ass is grass!"

Joe wiped his brow with a handkerchief, "Gentlemen! Miss Feline is here and will be performing shortly. I just . . . ," a standing ovation caused another delay, ". . . wanted to say regretfully, Stan 'Mandrake' Colten, a great magician and illusionist who has delighted audiences in every part of the globe with his unparalleled wizardry, is ill and unable to perform this evening. While we are preparing for the finale, I'd like to share some thoughts with you. It's difficult to be away from your wives, families, and girlfriends . . . your loved ones," a note of desperation crept into his voice, ". . . the loved ones back in the States who can't be replaced, and God willing, all of you will soon be home safe and sound in their care, and their arms. The members of this small troupe want you to know, we share the concern and love of those you left behind. We recognize and appreciate your courage, and the sacrifices all of you are making on our behalf . . . the overwhelming majority of Americans share in this belief. We are happy to be able to bring a little joy and fun to the finest men America has produced. . . "

"Meow, meow," isolated cat-calls were growing in strength.

"Where the hell is Wilson?" he thought, aware that his stalling tactics had been found out. "And now," cried a relieved Joe Dolan, spotting the Air Police as they entered the club and a smiling Wilson waving his arms at the main door, ". . . The Doom Club, the Officer's Open Mess at Da Nang Air Base Vietnam is proud to present its feature performer. The exciting, vivacious, the beautiful . . . everybody's favorite pussycat. . ."

Offstage, Maureen Stanton awaited her cue. "After tonight, a few more dates, and then I'll be leaving this hole . . . And this was to be my fresh start, and introduction to the big time!" she thought, disgustedly.

Joe Dolan's offer a few months before had sounded so inviting. Two months in Indochina and the Far East entertaining the boys. Where else could a second-line stripper clear $750 a week with all expenses paid? Performances took place in the secured areas, so the danger was minimal. A junket to Southeast Asia would not hurt her portfolio; in 1966 patriotism was still in vogue in the show business sector.

Maureen first met Joe Dolan in a private club in Jersey City. He was a comedian who traveled the burlesque circuit when it thrived, and had become a well connected wheeler-dealer with a nose for the dollar action. Joe found work for Maureen at a time when most exotic dancers were waiting tables. Most of her friends had either left stripping, or, like Maureen, were part-timers hoping for a break-through. The burlesque theaters like the Globe in Atlantic City, the Trocadero in Philly, and Newark's Beach, were all marking time awaiting the wrecker's ball. The private party had become the big game in town, and the routine had changed. The appeal was no longer the bump and grind, the tantalizing and calculated tease, which by design always fell short of the mark. "All the way baby" was what they wanted now. Maureen bought the package. What choice did she have? Strippin' was the only trade she knew and enjoyed.

"Show 'em muff," Joe Dolan so eloquently commanded, but muff was not without its dangers. She got busted on the Island, but the arrests didn't disturb her as much as the crowd. Public bars, clubs, or burlesque theaters had restraints; men at private parties felt they had a license to say or touch anything. Joe's new proposition provided an out. Goodbye Knights of Columbus, B'nai B'rith, Alpha Zeta Phi fraternity, Sid Hershel Humanitarian Foundation, O'Toole's Wearers of the Green, Uncle Anthony's 75th birthday, Nevil's bachelor party, Barry's divorce, Central High's 25th reunion, and the Antique dealers' convention. Hello Vietnam, a new start, old style exotic dancing, more money, better credentials for the future, and respectability.

Dolan had other ideas. There was a great deal of money floating around in the Nam, and the military clubs were only the beginning. Nobody gave two shits about a comedian, singer, or a magician, but a long legged, American, big titty stripper with the promise of a hot pussy was worth a gold mine. Maureen was a novelty; a remembrance of things past, yet not forgotten.

The military clubs were the facade, the big money was in the private parties, and to Maureen's dismay, that's exactly what Joe had in mind from day one. Nice, cozy performances for the private contractors, the engineers, press correspondents, the diplomatic corps, and Vietnamese entrepreneurs who relished anything labelled 'Made in America.'

Maureen resisted, but Dolan always had the upper hand. At first, he took a gentle approach, pleaded with her to go through with the private bookings to extend contacts, build a reputation, and further a dancing career on the verge of stardom. More money and gifts were other incentives. Joe always liked to talk about the influential people in the crowd, he provided the exposure, and the rest was up to her. But the only offer she ever got was an invitation to bed, all expenses paid.

At Cam Ranh Bay, she took a stand, and a refusal to obey his orders resulted in a switch blade carving a scar at the hairline above her left ear, a permanent reminder not to rock the boat. Joe had other sources of income. He was heavily involved in the money exchange game. The military was paid in script rather than dollars, but American civilians throughout Vietnam had an abundance of greenbucks that bought Piastras at many times the official rate in the rampant black market. Maureen's many prizes (silk pajamas and robes, costume jewelry, Ao-Dais, music boxes, handicrafts) cost a fraction of their true value. The military personnel directing the clubs were on the take and Joe's usual source of contacts. There were more propositions for private parties than he could handle. Mandrake once told her, "Salary around here is pocket change."

From Nha Trang to Da Nang, including a side trip to Pleiku in the Central Highlands, there had been no further confrontations. She abided by his wishes, and understood that now stardom was a mirage, a fantasy shattered into a billion pieces, never to be reassembled.

Maureen was ready to perform. Everything was in its place, ready to be removed, from the huge robe to the tiny G-string. She took a deep breath, and smelled the aroma of various colognes mixed with perfume applied to parts of her anatomy. The drummer started his roll, and for the first time that evening, a frightened and unhappy Maureen Stanton began to smile.

". . . From New York City . . . the one and only . . . lovely and I mean lovely, the delightful Miss Frankie 'Purr Purr' Feline."

The curtain opened and Maureen was greeted by a thunderous ovation. The lights had been dimmed, and a single spotlight followed her every move. The only prop was a black fur-lined chair in the middle of the stage. Her black cloak enclosed all but her hands and head as she strutted along the edge of the stage.

The music's intensity decreased as the cloak was removed, and a slow tantalizing dance number followed. A tight red dress emphasized every line and curve; long shapely legs with rounded calves, narrow waist, flat belly, and firm breasts bounced ever so lightly with each calculated movement. A long white necklace matched the color and design of the earrings, they swayed gently with her body in this the warming-up stage.

Maureen maneuvered toward center stage in front of the prop, and slowly bent over, supporting her weight on the arm rests. The spotlight narrowed its focus on well proportioned buttocks, making circular movements which followed the direction of her wriggling . . . clockwise . . . counter clockwise . . . clockwise . . . counterclockwise.

She snuggled into the furry seat, smooth and slippery like a cat. Her hem line was just above the knee, showing sheer nylon covered legs, and red high heels with long narrow spikes to full advantage.

Displaying virtuosity embodying the art, each movement performed with care and precision, she slowly crossed her legs, repeatedly exposing the blue straps of a garter belt and the fleshy thighs above her nylons. For the first time, a smile was replaced by the puckering of her lips, "Hmmm, Hmmm . . . Meow, Meow."

"Take it off!"

"Frankie baby . . . Do it!"

"You da one, you da one"

"Swing it me love, swing it!"

Miss Feline raised herself with the support of the arm rests, the dress's hem clung to her wide hips as vertically extended legs performed scissor movements. "Purr, purr, purr . . . ," purred the Cat Girl above the soft music.

"A-One . . . number one"

"I hear yah, Frankie, I hear yah"

"Sock it to me"

The music stopped. The room was pitch black, except for the spotlight featuring a motionless Frankie; darkness began only a few inches beyond the tip of her high heel shoes. "Help me!" cried the Cat Girl assuming a spread eagle position, her hands held shapely calves. "How would one of you big Air Force boys like to take a trip!" Her voice was appealing and strong, "I need somebody to hold and caress me. Anyone interested? Any guy wanna stroke the Cat Girl? . . . meow, meow . . . Oh baby, I need it."

Miss Feline suddenly stood up and faced the audience. "C'mon," inviting all with a sweeping gesture, "C'mon now," she pleaded while raising her dress to garter belt level. "This is a dangerous mission. You'll need a big gun. Any volunteers? Who here wants to make it with this pussy? Take a chance, and slide right in."

The Doom Club erupted. As Joe Dolan requested, Lieutenant Wilson had positioned the Military Police in front of the stage while the lights were dimmed, and their presence had the desired effect. Only the cat-calls reached the stage.

"I'm your man"

"Captain Tompkins reporting for duty"

"Yes ma'am, I'm a-comin'"

"This is a job for an F-4 jockey; Major Lassion here"

The music resumed—piercing, ear splitting sounds of strip-tease harmony. Men clapped, nodded and hummed the well-known refrain.

Frankie reached for the zipper behind her back, and in one swift motion, discarded the red dress. The melody was upbeat as she skimmed the stage front. A sudden pull at the front clasps released her bra, and uncovered huge breasts.

The Cat Girl coyly tugged at her panties, and then removed the black briefs after titillating an excited audience. The exposed G-string matched the color of her nylons.

She stood only a few feet away from the helmeted MPs. Showdown-time had arrived. A restless body met the challenge: rotating pelvis, gyrating hips, wriggling buttocks, and uncontrolled bouncing breasts. The Cat Girl's hands cupped the back of her head, sweat poured out and merged with make-up and heavily scented perfume, a moist tongue rolled across crimson-colored lips. Bordering on the convulsive, Frankie Feline delivered her final message, a bump-and-grind with unrestrained passion.

The show was over. She acknowledged the applause, and returned for a curtain call; on the fourth bow, her eyes met a youthful captain standing in the front row holding a mug of beer. He was light skinned, and his short blond hair sported a crew cut. She could even make out the insignia on his flying suit only a few feet away—349 Air Commando Squadron, Hellcats.

The captain, when it was obvious he had her attention, yelled: "Frankie! Frankie, I got a prick standing at attention with your name on it. Interested in a good fuck, baby?"

She moved closer, squatted, making sure the legs were maximally spread giving the captain a good look, and then extended a hand over the MP's shoulder to seek his sweaty palm. Grinning, she addressed her admirer, "Sweetie! Your mama's name is in big letters on your cock, not mine. Get a microscope and check it out, Honey."

His fellow officers were still laughing at the speechless Hellcat when she met Joe Dolan in the wing preparing to go onstage. He whispered, "Maureen, my Love, a 100% on the jerk-off scale. These sons-of-bitches will never forget yah."

Maureen watched Dolan as he grasped the microphone. The atmosphere changed quickly back to just another crowded bar. Few paid attention to Joe as the men sought their tables and a review of the evening's festivities over another round.

"Gentlemen," said Joe Dolan tenderly, "that concludes our show at the Officers' Mess, the Doom Club at Da Nang Air Force Base. Come home safe and sound . . . our prayers are with you . . . we love you . . . God Bless you all . . . God Bless!"

The Air Police left and a proud Lieutenant Wilson received congratulations from every corner of the Officers' Mess.

"Best show ever"

"What a piece of ass . . . where'd you find her?"

"Hey Wilson, is any of that action for sale?"

"Ol' buddy, let me buy you a drink. I'd like to talk to Frankie if . . ."

The bar area was fighter pilot territory, and the jet-jockeys maintained an exclusive drinking enclave off-limits to all but a few. Heavy drinking, frequent rumbles, and a high decibel level was the rule; tonight was particularly high-spirited. The Air Force boys who flew the F-4 Phantoms, F-100 Supersabres, and F-102s were joined by their Marine A-6 Intruder counterparts. Their conversation did not deal with SAMs, evasive techniques, or the flak at Hanoi, Haiphong, and the Panhandle; nor the merits and maneuverability of their respective aircraft, but with the moves of the Cat Girl.

The tables near the windows and furthest from the stage were occupied by aircraft maintenance and administrative types. Payroll, photo reconnaissance, and the legal officers sat near the door and along the wall opposite the bar.

In the center, groups of tables were arranged by squadron affiliation. The AC-47 crews, affectionately known as 'Spooky' or 'Dragon Lady,' occupied the middle; C-123 and C-130 crews were on one flank; helicopter, sea plane, and rescue personnel congregated on the other side.

Lieutenant Wilson weaved his way through the club till he reached the table closest to the stage, undoubtedly the best seats in the house. He tapped the shoulder of a blond-haired captain drinking beer, previously unaware of his presence. "Doc. Doc Jarden. Did you like the show? What do you think of Frankie?"

"Just great, Lieutenant. And let me speak for the other doctors at the hospital," he waved a hand backwards to his colleagues seated around the table. ". . . we all want to thank you for the fantastic view."

"Any time I can help you Doctors, just say the word," Wilson said cheerfully, then he leaned over and whispered into Captain Mark Jarden's ear, "By the way, Doc, my burning and drip came back. Can I see you tomorrow?"

"My pleasure, Lieutenant. Set it up with Sergeant Lincoln," the doctor said discreetly.

Wilson smiled, and happily returned to the plaudits of the other officers in the packed Doom Club. Mark lifted the beer pitcher and refilled his mug.

"Did the lieutenant get another dose of the clap?" inquired Dr. David Wyatt, General Surgeon at Da Nang's Casualty Staging Hospital.

"Is Vince Lombardi interested in winning? Do the Beatles sing? Does Frankie 'Purr Purr' Feline's pussy smell?"

"Funny thing about that, Mark. I thought it was Frankie, but I wasn't certain," said the Hospital Surgeon.

"I'm sure, but what do you think, long-timer?" Mark asked the man seated next to him.

"Loup en croute avec sauce choron a la dijon. . ."

"What? You're in this country a few weeks, and I think you are beginning to crack. I asked you about Frankie's odor," said Mark.

"That's right. And I said, sea bass in puff pastry with a touch of mustard."

* * *

9

MASTER Sergeant Frank Lincoln examined his uniform: shined black shoes, straight creased tan pants, shirt buttons aligned with a brass belt buckle. The Sarge's wrist watch confirmed that it was 1300 hours, he glanced at the eye level sign on the door—Herbert Klein, Capt. MC USAF FMO—and knocked.

"Come in."

"Sergeant Lincoln, sir!" he saluted smartly and awaited further orders.

"Close the door Sarge, and have a seat. What can I do for you?" Herb sat at his desk reviewing a medical chart.

"Sir, am I interrupting anything important?"

"I'm finished," said the doctor, putting the chart in the 'out box.' "I was ready to go to the PX for some shopping."

"I just wanted to confirm your appointment with the Colonel, Dr. Klein."

"No problem, Sarge. I just hope he's in a good mood."

"He's rough but fair, that's about the best you can hope for in the military. There is something else I'd like to talk to you about, Captain, if you can spare the time."

"Shoot," Herb removed the stethoscope from around his neck and placed it on the desk.

"You know Captain Jarden is a real short-timer. Everybody around here is sure going to miss him. Nothing personal, Captain, but sometimes it's hard to find a doctor who's a regular guy, not stiff or uppity. Somebody who looks at you as a person, and not just a sickness."

"I read you, Sarge."

"The fellas around here, I'm not just talking about patients, need a personal touch. Somebody that can speak their language. Captain Black's a fine General Medical Officer. Captains Parson, Wichel, and Swicker are top flight surgeons, but you know," Sergeant Lincoln leaned forward and put his arm on the desk, "Doc Klein, you are something special."

"What made Captain Jarden special?"

"He's the kind of guy you can ask a little favor of, and not feel embarrassed. The Air Force manual doesn't answer all the questions, sometimes you have to improvise. I've been in the military for sixteen years. . ."

"Were you in the Korean War?" probed Herb.

"Yep, and believe me, Captain, that was no bullshit party."

"And the Nam?"

"I'm here six months, and I still can't figure this place out. But I'll tell you something. Don't ever trust a Geek. A few months ago, there was this old guy who used to sweep up and do little things around the hospital. We all called him Pappysan. He used to smoke a corn cob pipe, just like you. One day, he was caught stealing medical supplies, and was handed over to the good guys as a VC spy. A week later, he returned to the dispensary, and we were told everything was okay. Two weeks went by, and he was arrested again as a *dangerous* spy. I was there when they put him in handcuffs, and Pappysan laughed when they took him away. I'll be a son-of-a-bitch if I didn't see the little sucker scratching his ass and makin' sand bags over at the air field depot about a month ago. You figure it out."

"I'm trying to, but I need your help. If you can't trust the Vietnamese, then who can you depend on?"

"Captain, may I smoke?" mumbled the Sergeant as he lit a cigarette, not waiting for an answer. "Did you enjoy the steaks Friday night? I think you recognize top quality meat, especially compared to the junk you eat in the mess halls. A lotta men prefer Marine jungle boots and fatigues to Air Force handouts. The fresh warm doughnuts we eat before sick call in the morning. . . I notice, Captain, you like the plain ones to dip in your coffee. You can thank a Marine baker who has been real nice to us."

"I hope we returned the favor," smiled Herb, "those doughnuts are great."

"A little whiskey can be very helpful, sir, especially when the Marines don't have access to the stuff. I know it's hard for a professional man like yourself to understand, but wheelin' and dealin' is a way of life. Don't get me wrong, Captain, there's no stealin' or money transactions. We deal in services and exchange products. . ."

"You mean the barter system."

"Yeah, that's what I mean, the barter system. And Captain, there is nobody not on the take, and I mean nobody." Sergeant Lincoln was emphatic as he paused and took a deep drag of his cigarette, "It really comes down to knowin' where to draw the line. Our commander, Colonel Stalley knows all about the things I mentioned. . ."

"He eats the doughnuts?"

"Loves the sugary kind."

"Sarge," Herb shifted in his chair, "What can I do to help the war effort?"

"It's really simple, Captain," said Lincoln as he mashed the cigarette in a huge ashtray that contained two of Herb's partially smoked pipes. "Could you see Captain Jarden's patients? I'm not talking about just the flight personnel, but some others who technically speaking, should not come here. There are a few Vietnamese, but mostly civilian types like engineers, contractors, administrators . . . and there are a few Marines who like our facility. . ."

"Bakers and supply people." Herb guessed.

"Yes," nodded Lincoln, "There is another group. It includes high ranking officers here at the base. Let's say, for example, Chaplain Dalton gets a dose of clap from the toilet seat. . . I understand that's possible. For obvious reasons, he's not going to want that fact advertised on his medical chart. If you can provide good medical care without the embarrassment, the Chaplain would be most apprecia-tive."

"Done."

"What was that, Captain?" asked a startled Sergeant Lincoln.

"I said, Sarge, that I'm your man. I will see Captain Jarden's special patients provided they don't interfere with my regular duties. I'll see them in my free time, or if it's slow, during regular sick call."

"Captain," sighed a relieved Lincoln, "I want to thank you for being so understanding. Sir, if you'll just have a talk with Captain Jarden, he can fill you in on the particulars. . ."

"I already have."

"I don't understand, Captain, he told me to come here and sound you out."

"You were set up, Sarge. Mark Jarden approached me the other day, and I agreed to the whole package. I was supposed to listen to your spiel, act indignant and accuse you of trying to bribe an officer. I angrily fake a call to the Air Police, watch you sweat, and then spill the beans. I agreed . . . but I just can't do it."

Frank Lincoln laughed, and at the same time, hit his knee with a hand. "Damn! I thought something was funny when Captain Jarden insisted I talk with you. I deal with the enlisted men and the NCO's. I should have known he'd try to get even."

"What do you mean?" Herb asked.

"I mean, Captain, that Doc Jarden struck out with Untouchable and he blames me. He didn't make it with the chick, and he thinks I gave her bucks not to go to bed with him. You know what a real lady's man he is. It's probably the first time a Geek ever said no to him since he's been here."

Eighteen year old Lee, known as 'Untouchable,' was employed on the Hospital's housekeeping staff. She always wore a white Ao Dai that was tight fitting, accentuating her narrow waist. Her black hair ended slightly below the shoulder, wide and expressive eyes glittered, sparkling teeth gave rise to an inviting and sensuous smile deceptive in its message. Unlike many women on the staff, she was friendly, but not available; even the best bull-shitters among the military personnel did not claim victory. In the two months that she had worked at the hospital, a parade of officers and enlisted men had been unsuccessful in their advances. Untouchable had withstood all challenges, including Mark Jarden's best shot.

The Officers' medical barracks consisted of twelve contiguous units, each capable of housing two occupants. They were metal, prefabricated structures, 14 by 9 feet, with a small built-in kitchen and bathroom. A huge tent barracks had been occupied by the medical staff, as well as a variety of flight personnel. Two weeks prior to Herb's arrival, the Hospital officers vacated the big tent and moved into their new quarters.

Herb's roommate was Mark Jarden, and the housekeeper had been an elderly, betel-nut chewing, wrinkled, black-toothed mammasan who not only cleaned the room, but also did the laundry. After his first week at Dan Nang, a change in assignments occurred; the new maid was Lee.

"I arranged for Untouchable's transfer to your room, the rest was up to him," Lincoln nodded his head approvingly, "but Captain Jarden doesn't like to admit failure."

"Who does?"

"Nobody, I guess. But I think politicians and lady's men might be the worst offenders," Lincoln theorized.

"You know, Sarge, maybe someday I'll strike out with a woman and I'll be able to test the theory," kidded Herb as he stood up to shake the sergeant's hand.

"Captain Klein, if you like, we have a friend at the PX who can help you with your shopping."

"I'm looking for a good, cheap camera. Any suggestions?"

"Spotmatic Pentax," Lincoln answered without hesitation. "It costs a little more than a hundred, but it's a fantastic piece of workmanship."

"I'm ahead of you, Sarge. I was at the PX the other day and wanted to buy the camera, but there's a waiting list. The clerk at the counter estimated a two month delay. . ."

"Captain, beg your pardon . . . a Pentax camera will be on your desk in one hour. Would you like a roll of black-and-white or color film? Stills or slides?"

"Sarge," chuckled a bemused Herb, "I don't know anyting about cameras. This is for home-front consumption. . ."

"Captain, sir," Sergeant Frank Lincoln was at attention, "excuse the interruption, but Sergeant McNally from photo reconnaissance will be here to instruct you in the use of the camera and any questions you might have."

"Does somebody take my pictures for me!" joked Herb.

"Captain, in the military there are three rules worth remembering: don't piss into the wind, stay away from the commander's wife, and don't fuck with the Medical Corp," said the Sergeant, gingerly closing the door.

"Sit down, Klein," said Lieutenant Colonel Harold Stalley, chief Medical Officer of the 75th Tactical Dispensary and 340th Casualty Staging Hospital.

Colonel Stalley was a tall, thin, balding man with a handlebar moustache, thick and meticulously groomed. He wore flying fatigues, and a bright yellow scarf around his neck, symbolic of pilots who flew in jet fighter aircraft. Head bowed, he continued to work in silence; a folder was finally closed, and an intercom button pushed. "I'm busy."

"Yes sir!" barked the Sergeant in the adjoining office.

"Klein," Stalley's eyes now met Herb's for the first time, "are you happy here?" Before Herb could reply, he resumed, ". . . I have this little note requesting transfer from the 420th Tactical Fighter Squadron. Don't you like to fly in F-4 Phantoms?"

"Colonel, I. . ."

"You know, Klein, most flight surgeons would be honored to take care of these boys. I know I am . . . flew an in-country mission this morning in an F-4. How much time have you logged, Klein?"

"Sir, I. . ."

"Klein, my people tell me you have been complaining about sick call. We try to direct only flying personnel toward the flight surgeons, but we don't have enough general medical officers, so we all have to pitch in and take care of the non-flying types. I know it's not the work of a flight medical officer, but it comes with the territory . . . you know what I mean?"

"Sir, it doesn't bother me to. . ."

"Let me take a little time and review our mission," said Lieutenant Colonel Stalley readjusting his chair and stretching his legs so that the flying boots rested on the desk top. "We provide the best possible medical care for flying types. Secondly, we give non-flying people adequate care. Dave Wyatt runs the Casualty Staging Hospital. He checks out the shot up Marines in stable condition ready for med-evac to either Japan or some stateside hospital. We give backup to Dave, and rotate one guy through his service. If the war heats up and we start taking more casualties, then we'll probably get another full time surgeon. Klein, we are now adding another phase to our mission, and I see you as someone who might be our man." Stalley pushed the intercom button. "Tell Sergeant Dalton to meet me at the back entrance with the jeep in five minutes."

"Yes Sir!" responded the Sergeant in the same shrill voice.

"Klein! I usually don't like to transfer my Docs out of fighter squadrons. I consider the medical needs of our jet jockeys our highest priority. But I'm willing to make an exception in your case. I'm also considering decreasing your sick call to three times a week, and taking you out to Dave Wyatt's rotation. How's that for openers?"

"Thank you, Col. . ."

"I've reviewed your history." The Lieutenant Colonel reached for an open folder, and in no particular order, began to mumble: "Born in Philadelphia . . . only child of Sophie and Benjamin Klein . . . mother died in '58 of a cerebral aneurysm . . . graduated Cornell University with honors . . . president of college fraternity . . .

graduated Osler Medical school with honors . . . President of medical fraternity . . . Rotating Internship at Osler General Hospital . . . In summer of '66, enlisted in Air Force . . . Aerospace Medicine at Brooks, San Antonio . . . Assigned to DaNang Air Base as a flight surgeon in September of '66 . . . married June, '65 . . . wife's name Christina . . . occupation, registered nurse . . . no children. Klein," his voice now loud and distinct, "I'm a good judge of character. I recognize quality and leadership when I see it . . . fella, you got the goods! I think I found a way to utilize your talents. Interested?"

"Yes sir," said Herb, who felt a queasy feeling in the stomach as he rubbed the moisture of sweaty palms with his fingers.

"I received a directive from Saigon a few days ago. We are to try and add to our mission, a program designed to win the hearts and minds of the Vietnamese people. I would like you to set up, organize, and implement a Civic Action program at the village level to provide medical care for the natives. It's a pilot program, and because it deals with the care of non-military types, I will only accept volunteers. We'll start with the hamlets in the secure areas near the base, and branch out if we are successful." The chief Medical Officer removed the boots from his desk and planted both feet close to Herb's, "Klein! I think I can promise you the transfer and the other things I discussed, if you agree to tackle this Civic Action program. Forget about the F-4s. Your new squadron would be the 341st Air Commandos. These are the boys who fly C-123s and supply the Special Forces, and a lot of the small camps in the boonies. It'll give you a chance to see the countryside, get a feel for what other people are doing in the field, and zero in on the needs of the 'friendlies.' Are you with me Klein?"

"Sounds good, Colonel."

"Outstanding! Then it's settled," Lieutenant Colonel Stalley reached for Herb's shoulder, "I have confidence in you, Klein. Our medical team will serve as a model for all future Civic Action programs. I'm letting you call the shots. I attach the utmost importance to this mission, and you'll get full cooperation from everyone at the hospital."

"Thank you, Sir."

"Klein, I also understand you are taking care of Jarden's patients. The Captain and I had a nice working relationship. He apprised me of his patients, and I offered him off-the-cuff advice. I would like to continue this kind of an exchange. How do you feel about that?"

"Absolutely, Colonel. I wouldn't have it any. . ."

"Captain! I think we're going to be okay," Stalley arose, and Herb came to attention. "Klein . . . I don't want you to feel rushed. Do you have any questions?"

"No sir! I'm fully satis . . . ," said Herb, as he watched the back of Lieutenant Colonel Stalley, and heard him mutter something unclear to the sergeant in the adjacent office.

"Do you remember the stripper last week at the Doom Club? What was her name? . . . Frankie . . . Frankie. . ."

"Fe–line," said Herb, licking an envelope flap. "Frankie 'Purr, Purr' Feline."

"Number one, man, number one. I heard she gave an unbelievable show for some bigwigs the following night in downtown Da Nang. They were counting the pubic hairs. God, when she came over to our table and spread those legs, and told that guy to screw his mother . . . oh, shit!" said Mark Jarden, his right hand reached for his groin as he lay flat in the lower bunk. "Ever see anything like that before?"

"Never," Herb stated emphatically. He turned away from the desk, and faced his roommate. "I used to go to the Troc Burlesque Theater in Philly when I was a kid. A group of us waited for intermission, slipped in with the crowd, and sneaked up to the balcony. A few of the girls were okay, but I enjoyed the comedians and especially the huckster at intermission who used to sell the playing cards with dirty pictures. A friend of mine, Izzy Gold, bought a pack expecting to see the big action. . . There were girls in swim suits waving."

"Hi sucker," Mark then imitated a bathing beauty's 'show' smile.

"That's about it. We did have strippers at my medical school fraternity who went all the way, but they didn't have the body, style, or moves of Frankie. I'll never forget my senior year. Remember I told you about the nice relationship we had with the Police Department. Traffic tickets fixed, free admission to sporting events, stag films . . . the whole bit. The Police Clinic was at Osler General. . ."

"You needn't elaborate, Herb. The whole fuckin' Air Force is an extension of your Police Clinic."

"There was a guy on the Vice Squad by the name of Ron Whitsky. He arranged for a strip-teaser to entertain the Brothers of Beta Sigma Tau. She was supposed to be a real beauty queen, her name was Jackie LaRue. Out came this old hag dressed in a cowboy outfit with cap guns and a whip. It was terrible, absolutely terrible. The brothers were hissing. When it came down to removing the G-string, there were yells of 'No, please No.' She was shooting her cap pistol and pleading, 'Bang, Bang . . . Bang me," and a chorus chanted 'not on your life!' It was a real horror show."

"I guess your credibility was damaged among the brethren," laughed Mark.

"To the point where there was an impeachment proceeding involving Vice President Larry Lewis, Treasurer Sam Stein, and yours truly."

"How did it go?"

"It started out badly. Even the pledges were vocal for our ouster. There wasn't one positive thing said on our behalf. They were ready to vote with no doubt about the result, when John McFadden, the beverage chairman who I had shit on for the whole semester, requested the floor. Well, in a very flowery and eloquent manner, he proceeded to review the whole history of Beta Sigma Tau and the role of its officers. The thrust of his argument was that the most inept and inferior brothers have always held office in the past, and the three of us were eminently qualified to carry on that tradition."

"And the vote?"

"Unanimous . . . against impeachment. Reason had prevailed," said Herb as he walked to the little kitchen alcove. "Still some coffee left, want a cup?"

"No thanks, but I could use a beer. Herb, I spoke to Lincoln. It seems he was a bit pissed off about our little joke. He thinks I blame him for Lee's refusal to taste the better things in life. After all, it's not every girl that I offer my cock to."

"Mark, I have a strong suspicion she will survive without you. If you can finish your tour without the clap and with your wang intact, then you ought to get the Bronze Star."

"Can I make a confession," Mark took a quick swig of beer as Herb resumed sitting in the chair. "I dig Lee. In the real world she would be worth getting to know. There's a certain charm, an innocence . . . it's beyond the screwing bit. You know what I mean?"

"In the 'real world' we call it liking. Some brave souls may even talk about love."

"Deep, hey that's really deep. A real philosopher. . . I'll bet your Colonel Stalley was impressed with your wisdom after that pow-wow," chuckled Mark.

"Man, what an asshole! I couldn't get a word in. He's everything you said, and then some."

"I told you Herb, the only way to reach him is to concoct a plan to connect with new pussy, or pass on some info that might in some way contribute to a promotion. He wants to be a big bird so badly, his heart skips a beat everytime he hears 'Full Colonel.'"

"I had the whole thing planned. I was ready to tell him I didn't mind the flying, but I just don't fit in with the jet-jockey image. I don't drink, I don't like scarves, or understand or appreciate the lingo, and I'm not into the espirit de corps. I like the boys in the 420th fighter squadron, but I'm not the right flight surgeon for the job."

"I'm glad you didn't say anything. He's everything you're not," offered Captain Jarden.

"He knows about my dislike for regular sick call. . ."

"Don't you like VD clinic. Drink your coffee, it's getting cold," said Mark as he turned to the foot lockers. "Oh, how'd you like to make it with the one wearing the white and red sweater," he added, glancing at one of the many Playboy centerfolds that adorned the lockers and back wall next to the desk.

"The big five—clap, syph, chancroid, granuloma inguinale, lymphogranuloma venereum. Give me just a few of those cases a day, and sick call could be interesting," continued Herb.

"Look at Miss July, the one with the open purple blouse and skirt up around her navel. Now that's eating stuff," countered the short time flight surgeon.

"Stalley knows about my taking over your 'special patients' and offered his services as a consultant. He's also changed my squadron. I'm now the Flight Medical Officer for the 341st Air Commando. My sick call day has been decreased to three mornings, and even that may be eliminated. I also don't have to rotate through the Casualty Staging Hospital."

"Now the blond with . . . ," Mark Jarden stopped, abruptly sat up, and peered at Herb curiously. "And what, my dear friend, is the reason for the Colonel's generosity, other than your easy disposition and winning smile?"

"There's a new program to help Vietnamese people at the village level. I volunteered to organize the medical phase of the Civic Action initiative. . ."

"Holy shit!" screamed Mark, "Can't you see the Colonel is using you. . ."

"We're starting with the secure villages around the base," Herb said weakly.

"What does that mean? Look! There are over fifty thousand

Marines, fifteen hundred Air Police, Army types, and who knows how many ARVN to provide security for this base. Charlie can make his presence felt anytime he wants. Ask anybody in the know around here. And the villages around the base are not safe. . ."

"Come on, Mark! Not everybody in this country is VC."

"I'm not saying that! You're going to get your ass greased if you start going into those villages. It's Boonie country, and Charlie calls the shots. For Christ's sake, you're a doctor! It's not like you're a nineteen year old Marine with a M-16, and your fly open to show the folks back home who's got the meanest cock. This is a fucked up war. Don't you see what's going on back in the States? Here in the Nam?"

"I admit I was pissed off at first. Then I started to think about the possibilities. At this point, all I want to do is take a good look. If I don't like what I see, then I'll pull out. Believe me, I'm no hero."

"Hero? Hero my ass! The only hero in Nam is the guy who doesn't leave in one of those green body bags. Heros return to the States with both balls intact."

"I'm going to give it a try."

"What the fuck are you, Herb, a do-gooder? You'll give some dink a Penicillin tablet for his pneumonia, and within an hour, it'll be in some VC's stomach."

"I appreciate your concern. . ."

"Herb," Mark's hand reached for his roommate's knee, "look at her." Both men turned toward the deak, and a full color portrait of Christie. "You owe it to your wife to keep your nose clean. I'm not asking you not to do your duty. The base is bad enough. He's coming, Charlie's coming. You heard the news. The North Vietnamese have sent some crack regiments down through the DMZ. Do you think they're on a camping trip? They're waiting for the monsoons to end, and then it'll be time to kick ass. You'll be able to see the war from your window."

"We're on different wave lengths. I'm not a combatant, and I don't have strong political feelings either way at this point. I'm not looking for a rumble. I just want to find out what the hell is going on," said Herb.

An exasperated Mark, beseechingly sought his friend's eyes and cried, "Don't you understand. . . There's not a swinging dick in Washington or Saigon who knows the answer to that question."

* * *

10

. . . there was no stopping Stacy. A lively tongue darted into John's ear, and her hand reached for his belt buckle. The young woman's passion had surprised John, and he felt new strength arise from an awakening groin. Trembling fingers now sought new treasures only dreams had. . .

"Sunny!"

"Yes, Captain," he said, putting the book down.

"Major Frantz and I would like to indulge in a game of 'Gottcha.' Would you make everybody comfie?"

"Yes Sir," said Tech Sergeant William 'Sunny' Watts.

The Load Master of the C-123 aircraft released the head set button, turning off communication with the pilot. He folded the page end as a marker, and put the paperback novel underneath his seat. "Just when I was coming to the good part," he thought. "Why does it always happen when I got a hard-on?"

Sunny arose, and all of the forty Marines seated along the two sides of the plane turned in his direction. He smiled, pointed to the seat belt of a nearby passenger, and simulated a tightening of the strap.

A blond, crew-cut second lieutenant smoked a small cigar and waved to Sergeant Watts only a few feet away. "Sarge," he yelled above the roar of the two engine prop aircraft, "is Victor Charlie throwing some shit our way?"

"No problem, Lieutenant, everything's A-1," said Watts, and added a 'high sign' with his finger and thumb to reinforce the message. "We're movin' around 200 knots at about 5,000 feet. Our ETA is gonna be delayed a few minutes. Captain Pellham and Major Frantz have a little business to take care of . . . ain't nothin' to worry about."

Sunny walked the length of the plane to check that all of the seat belts were safely secured and returned to his own place to notify the pilot. "Captain Pellham, everybody's tucked in. She's all yours."

"Thank you, Sunny. Shall we proceed for a little Sunday cruise down the Mississippi? . . . over and out."

The C-123 went into a dive descending rapidly toward the river. The plane leveled off at 300 feet and flew directly over the water. Fishing boats and their occupants were clearly visible, as Captain Pellham took the aircraft into another sharp dive which cleared the sails of boats by no more than ten feet. The mouth of the river was approaching, when the pilot directed the plane into a wide bank increasing his altitude gradually until he reached the coastline; DaNang Air Base was due south.

"Five!"

"Four!"

"Five, damn it! Your vision must be shot. I told you Major, that boozing is not good for the eye sight. I think you're going blind . . . three off the red sail, and two on the other boat."

"Bullshit Pellham! Two and two, not even close," squealed Major Frantz.

"This is ridiculous," howled an indignant Captain Pellham, "let's ask the Doc. He's neutral. Doc! How many dinks did you see jump into the water?"

"On no you don't. I'm not getting involved in this one. I had a bad angle and I couldn't see anything," swore Herb.

"It looks like Doc Klein's eyesight is also failing," said the Major.

"Ahhh . . . I guess it's compromise time. Sunny!"

"Yes, Captain Pellham," returned the load master.

"How's everything back there!"

"Fine, Captain, I'm just sorry that I forgot to bring a roll of toilet paper," said a giggling Sergeant Watts.

"Sunny, what's the score?"

"Hold it, Captain," said the Sergeant reaching for a notebook in a side pocket.

After a moment of silence, the Captain asked: "What are you doing back there, Sunny, wackin' off over one of those dime novels you read? What's the score?"

"Sorry Capn', but every count I have in my notebook has a 'half' attached to it and that's the reason for the delay. The score is twenty-nine and a half gotchas for you, and thirty-one and a half gotchas for Major Frantz."

"Shit! And the inning?" asked the pilot.

"Let's see . . . you're the Pirates and the Major is the Dodgers," mumbled Sergeant Watts, "that completes seven innings. Pirates are home team."

"Thanks Sunny," said Pellham as he switched off the head set, and then said softly, "Son-of-a-bitch still can't count."

"Doc, I like the smell of your tobacco. Can I try some," asked Major Frantz, a pipe in hand.

"It's called Balkan. Expensive, but really good stuff. One of the advantages of coming to Viet Nam is that people back home are tuned in to your needs," said Herb as he handed the pouch to the Major.

"So why hasn't my wife sent me a one-way ticket to L.A. via Pan Am? You been making the rounds?" asked the Major while refilling his pipe.

"Yep," said Herb, relighting his own, "Hue, An Hoi, Dong Ha, Tam Ky, Hoi An, a few of the Special Forces camps, but this was my first trip into Khe Sanh. Wow! That was one helluva crazy approach."

Major Frantz took a few quick puffs to help maintain the pipe's flame. "I tried to warn you about our landings. Low flying through the valley has cost us two planes and some real good people in the last few weeks."

"It was still the hairiest touchdown I've ever experienced. I felt like we were dropping off a ladder. And then the incoming mortar and artillery fire. . . Charlie was just waiting to cream us. It's a good thing you taxied near that bunker. Did you see the big sign near the entrance?"

"How could I miss it Doc. It said . . . 'Khe Sahn. The Seabees built it, the Air Force enjoys it, and the stupid ass Marines die for it,'" quoted Major Frantz.

"Hey Doc," Captain Pellham blurted, "I was talking to Bud Rich the other day. I understand you're the new flight surgeon for the 45th ACS. Damn! Ol' Spooky, the 'Dragon Lady' . . . now there's a piece of machinery. Ever see one of those C-47s at work?"

"Nope!" Herb tamped the tobacco over a match cover.

"Each one of those babies has three mini-gattling guns controlled by the pilot, that let's loose about 5,000 rounds per minute from each gun with a little press of the button. What a beauty!"

"And what a deathtrap," volunteered the Major. "Spooky's old, slow, and it doesn't take much of a punch. It's not even allowed to shoot a wad at anything under 2,500 feet. It should be more like 5,000. All that fire power doesn't mean a thing when you're so vulnerable."

"Dudes like Bud Rich make up for the deficits. He is one gung-ho hell raiser. A few more like him around this place and we'd all go home early. Doesn't he live right next to you, Doc?" asked Pellham.

Herb cupped the pipe's bowl with his thumb, and tried to remove moisture from the steam by vigorous shaking before responding. "No . . . two units down. The 45th ACS occupies three quarters in the Medical Officer's barracks. Bud's roommate, Josh Trent, was the one who approached me about being the squadron's flight surgeon. Mark Jarden had been their man. Colonel Stalley's approval was no problem. I'm now the official Flight Medical Officer for the 341st and 45th Air Commando Squadrons . . . no big deal."

"You are going to be one busy fella. Aren't you involved in some medical program with Civic Action and village pacification?" asked the Major.

"Yep, and we're ready to give it a shot. There's a village about a mile from the base that I've targeted. In about a week or two, we should be organized and ready to roll. It's a bigger job that I thought."

"What do you mean?"

"You see, it's a pilot program and strictly voluntary. Technically, people can refuse my requests, but for the most part, I've received excellent cooperation at most levels. I may even ask the 341st for some help," smiled Herb.

"What do you mean?" Major Frantz removed his pipe, "Permit me to be redundant."

"I'm extending the project to include Special Forces Camps, assuming the Village program is a success. The Montagnard tribesmen have no medical care program short of a Green Beret corporal who's been cross-trained to function as an emergency medic. If you people," Herb glanced at both pilots, "can provide the taxi service, airlift our people and the supplies, then. . ."

"Great idea, Doc! Sounds fantastic. Major Frantz and I will talk to some long timers, and try to generate interest. The 'gnards are good folk. You shouldn't have a problem finding a few friends in our squadron."

"Speak for yourself, Pellham. Let me think about it, Doc," said Major Frantz.

Both men silently smoked their pipes as Captain Pellham made radio contact with the tower at DaNang Air Base.

"Sunny," said the pilot on the intercom.

"Yes Cap'n."

"We've been cleared and we'll be landing in a few minutes. Collect the barf bags and offer my apologies. 'Gottcha' was never meant to include air-sick Marines," chuckled Pellham.

"Okay Cap'n, and by the way, there's a Marine lieutenant here who would like to know your name."

"I'm sure there are others, Sunny."

"Yes Sir. Next time he gets a chance to leave Khe Sahn for a R-and-R to Da Nang and you're the jockey, he *ain't* goin'. Now you know you've made a big impression on these boys. Over and out, Cap'n, over and out."

Pellham turned to the left and saw the South China Sea. Small boats dotted the coastal beach and a large freighter steamed toward DaNang as a Huey helicopter hovered over the big ship. To his right were rice paddies and small clusters of huts, a small mountain range was truncated by low hanging clouds. The cockpit was silent, each man alone with his thoughts. The pilot broke the silence. "Doc, how would you like to land this big bird?"

"Thanks, Captain, but I think I'll pass. I want to stay in one piece for Mark Jarden's going away party, and I think the Marines in the back have had enough excitement for the day."

Major Frantz turned to Doc Klein, "I think I'd like more info on the Special Forces Medical Program and the Montagnards."

"Anytime, Major. You know where I live," smiled Herb, as he gently smacked Frantz's shoulder.

"Shit!" Captain Pellham looked at both men and snickered, "You better include me, Doc. The Major can't take a piss unless I show him how."

"How do you like it, Colonel?"

"Medium well."

"Lieutenant?"

"Well done, but not charcoaled."

"Airman? How do you like your steak?"

"Toward the rare side, Sarge."

Frank Lincoln reached for a handkerchief to wipe his brow and then waved to a thin, tall, youthful looking Negro leaning against the wall of the hospital drinking a beer. "Airman Thomas! Could you help me out? It must be 150 degrees around this grill." He turned to the men in line, and said perfunctorily, "Beans, potatoes, and onions over there; beer and soda in the back." His hand moved in the appropriate direction to guide them. Sergeant Lincoln took off his apron, handed it to Thomas, and added, "A rare, a medium well, and a well done . . . we still got a lot more left." He pointed to a box of steaks on the table with large black letters: PROPERTY UNITED STATES MARINES. The Airman nodded his approval while tying the apron strings.

Lincoln walked over to a makeshift podium. From that vantage point, he saw a stocky officer standing against the hospital bunker. The Sergeant briskly made his way through the crowd until he reached the huge man sipping a soft drink. "Captain, when would you like to start this thing?"

"How about now, Sarge. There are only a few left in the chow line, and it's hot as Hell," said David Wyatt, General Surgeon of the Casualty Staging Hospital.

Dave made his way to the podium, and frantically waved his hands. "May I have your attention . . . fellow warriors . . . Gentlemen . . . Gentlemen. You too, Mark!" The men began to clap, and Mark Jarden took his place next to the Hospital Surgeon.

"It is . . . ," hollered Dave, an arm on Mark's shoulder, "with the utmost disrespect, profound disgust, and utter revulsion that we've gathered here together to say goodbye to this outstanding patriot, soldier, and humanitarian . . . Captain Jarden introduced me to the horrors of war when I came to the Nam five months ago. It was Mark who showed me where the best bunkers were and the proper crouch position. He introduced me to the bar girls at the Hotel Touranne, some of the finer whore houses in DaNang, and China Beach for sunbathing. Doc Jarden furthered my medical education by permitting me to become a guest lecturer for our 'Preventive VD' programs. On three separate occasions, Mark allowed me to take over his emergency medical call while he participated in sex orgies and became inebriated. I might also add that I didn't sleep any of those nights, and I'm still waiting for him to pay me back in some way, other than telling me 'what a great guy I am.' Finally, I also want to thank Mark for helping me in my bridge game. Because of his efforts, I am a vastly improved cheater. Indigestion at this point forces me to relinquish my master of ceremony duties to Sergeant Frank Lincoln."

A side door of the Hospital opened, Sergeant Lincoln and 'Untouchable' proceeded to the podium. The young Vietnamese beauty was wearing the usual white Ao Dai, a radiant smile and expressive eyes could not hide her embarrassment. In her arms were two brass vases, they had been the casings of spent artillery shells skillfully restored and molded into ornaments by a Vietnamese artisan. Sergeant Lincoln spoke: "In appreciation, the housekeeping staff would like to give Captain Jarden a momento. One vase has this inscription, 'Viet Nam—Oct. '65 to Oct. '66—DaNang', and the other vase lists the medical officers who have been at the hospital over the course of the last year. I'll ask Lee to give the Captain his due, and make a few comments. Lee?"

The nervous, but elegant woman, gave Mark the gifts and paused to collect her thoughts; their eyes met, and she then proceeded in a genteel and soft voice, barely audible even to those closest to the podium. Bowing, she said, "We thank Doctor 'Arden who help Vietnamese people. It's hard to leave mother, father and loved ones . . . we thank Doctor 'Arden again. We wish him to be happy."

Lee quickly kissed him on both cheeks. Mark was startled, and remained expressionless as he watched the housekeeper return to the hospital.

"I think everyone ought to know," cried Lincoln, "that Captain Jarden took care of the housekeeping staff and other Vietnamese nationals on his own time. He was their doctor and he'll be sorely missed."

The Sergeant was not comfortable addressing officers and hurriedly left the small stand. Dave Wyatt resumed the speaker's role, "Unfortunately, our next speaker called an hour ago, and will not be able to make this fiasco. Lieutenant Colonel Daily of the 453rd Tactical Fighter Squadron conveyed this message: Mark, the Colonel excuses you for upchucking on his person at the Doom Club. I'm not going to bore you with his other less favorable comments, but Colonel Daily did offer to support any attempt by Captain Jarden to curtail his military obligation at the earliest possible date. Captain Jarden's other squadron is the 45th ACS. Representing the 'Dragon Lady' is the one and only—and if Charlie is listening, I got some bad news, this bad dude has just extended his tour of duty here at DaNang for another twelve months—will Major Rich come up here and say a few words?"

Bud Rich was tall and lean, but sturdily built, something like an outside linebacker. His light complexion, auburn crew cut, pug nose, and clean shaven baby face belied his thirty-seven years. Bud's popularity with the rank and file, and peers remained unparalleled at the air base. An aggressive pilot, he was vocal in his dislike of the enemy, and the combat restraints imposed by American military strategy. A heavy drinker, the Spooky Pilot was a daily fixture at the Doom Club.

A product of the old school, he had not attended a military academy or college, but worked his way through the ranks and Officer Candidate School by sheer guts and determination. A bar stool, loose mouth, and quick trigger-finger had stifled recent promotion ambitions.

"I want to . . . ," Major Rich raised his arms to halt the applause, "Thank you fellas. I want to wish Doc Jarden the best of luck at his next base. By the way Doc, where are you goin'?"

"Andrews. I have a C-141 MAC squadron. I'm also close enough to Washington, D.C. so that the bigwigs can consult with me on how to conduct this war," suggested Mark.

"God-al-mighty, we're in deep shit," murmured the Major, who then turned to his audience. "Let me say on behalf of the 45th Air Commando Squadron, we're going to miss the Doc. He's been a good drinkin' man, and he was always around when we needed him, regardless of the problem. I know he won't mind if I tell you all about the only time he flew a mission on Spooky. Do you remember Doc?"

Mark put both his hands over his face, nodded, and squealed, "Oh no, oh no!"

"It started out as a totally uneventful night. I even remember letting Doc Jarden play pilot for about a half hour flying around the base and out to sea. About three hours after taking off, HQ tells us about a party at the Nha Ninh Special Forces camp. We took a look, let out the flares, and would you believe, a few hundred spooks were in an open field advancing on the base. Josh Trent was sitting next to me, and couldn't believe his eyes. I got a fix, and let loose with the mini's . . . over one hundred and fifty confirmed body counts by the Green Berets the following morning, and who knows how many VC were dragged away. We took a few 50 cal hits, and lost an engine. Had to put a parachute on the Doc, but limped home without a hitch. After it was all over, I remember Josh asking the Doc for his impression. He said something like, 'Captain Trent, from here on I stick to what I do best: docterin', drinkin', and screwin'.' And damn it, he turned out to be a man of his word. Good luck Doc," Major Rich reached for Mark's hand and then jumped off the podium.

"Thanks Major," grinned the master of ceremonies. "At this point, I'm happy to report, we have only one speaker left. The other good bit of news is that I've been assured the Colonel will be brief. I know

this will be the case, because I asked our commander here at the
hospital to restrict his comments to only nice things about Captain
Jarden. . ."

Herb listened to Dave Wyatt's introduction of Lieutenant Colonel
Stalley, and decided to return to his office. He was hoping to finish
the report and recommendations relevant to 'Civic Action' . . .
Comprehensive Medical Care Initiative . . . Village 142.' Colonel
Stalley's approval would be a mere formality, Herb had consulted with
the commander, and composed the whole project as a joint effort. If
the program was successful, Harold Stalley's contribution would not
be overlooked.

Herb's military education had been orchestrated by a reluctant
Mark Jarden. He strongly disapproved of his friend's actions. Herb's
involvement with Civic Action and Air Commando Squadrons was an
unnecessary risk with a high potential for disaster. Herb knew about
the flight on Spooky, it was the only instance in Mark's tour of duty
that he flew a combat mission, and it was to be his last. A flight
surgeon was technically prohibited from flying a combat sortie, but it
was common practice to permit the good Doctor to understand the
job profile. Additional benefits were group acceptance, morale en-
hancement, and as Mark so succinctly described: "To show through
your actions, both to the pilot and other members of the crew, that
your presence in a mission of combat, or the potential of combat,
qualifies you as an outstanding, first rate asshole. After all, he has to
be there, you don't."

Mark stressed the kiss-ass routine. If you want to get anything done
in the military, imply your proposal has built-in brownie points for
future escalation in the ranks. Military life is simple for a doctor, Mark
had stressed over and over again. "Never volunteer, and when the
General comes to you with the clap, show him on his chart where you
put 'non-specific urethritis' . . . with a wink."

Herb listened, smiled, nodded approval, thanked Mark for his
interest, and then proceeded to take dangerous flights and formulated
the Civic Action Medical Program. A frustrated Mark Jarden gave up
on what he thought was a common-sense approach, and sought to
teach his friend how to get things done in the Air Force. Survival
techniques would remain a problem for Herb Klein to resolve in his
own way.

Herb sat at his desk with the Civic Action report in his hand. There
were still bases to touch, and a little more hand holding. He put away

the report in his bottom drawer, reached for the pen and wrote out the following list.

— *Call Air Police about security measures for any villager who needs to have an x-ray at the base hospital.*

— *Lab: stool cultures for parasites, malaria smears and blood samples, electrolytes. Time factor?? Capabilities?? Talk to Sgt. Cropple . . . get's things done without a hassle*

— *Tom Surrick, Podiatrist at Cam Ranh Bay. Once a month?*

— *Immunization program . . . check with Sgt. Lewis about the final protocol*

— *Since dentist refused to participate, would Mackle let a volunteer dental technician go in his place? Sgt. Lincoln knows a tech . . . let him handle if Mackle approves*

— *See Major Goode about two additional interpreters. Advance sessions needed for medical lingo . . . see Captain Ky*

— *Ask Motorpool if . . .*

"Dr. Klein! Dr. Klein!" screamed a shrill voice that was accompanied by violent knocking at his door. "There's a woman with excruciating chest and lower belly pain . . . come quickly . . . please!"

Herb darted to the door, and jerked it open: "I'm coming, Where is she? What the . . ."

". . . and her name is Frankie 'Purr Purr' Feline, everybody's favorite pussy," said the now familiar voice of Mark Jarden. With shirt out, eyes injected, hair disheveled, alcohol on his breath, he continued, "Herb, I know we said our goodbyes, but I just wanted to reassure my good buddy he can rely on me. I'll be in Philly in three days. I have Christie's ring, necklace, snapshots, slides, and your letter. You're a good boy. I don't know a fuckin' thing about Civic Action, Special Forces Camps, Air Commando trips to spas like Khe Sahn, or medical care programs for geeks in the boonnies. Mums the word, you can trust me, good buddy."

"I never had any doubts about you, Mark, you know that," smiled Herb as they both slowly walked toward the Hospital entrance.

Mark was ready to enter the jeep as Airman Treek looked straight ahead awaiting orders to take the Captain to the plane. "Hey Herb," he yelled to his friend now holding the hospital door partially ajar. "I changed my mind. I think I'll tell Christie the ring and necklace are my gifts and you have a mistress. Maybe I'll get laid!"

"Good luck! If you're successful, I can guarantee it will be the best screw *you* ever had."

Mark grinned, and jumped into the back seat: "Herb, you take care. If I can do anything. . ."

"I know, Mark. You have a safe trip home."

Captain Jarden leaned over and touched Treek's shoulder. Herb watched the vehicle head toward the airfield, the jeep stopped at the main gate, and Mark turned back to have a final look.

Herb stopped at the water cooler, and alternated drinking with letting the cold spray splash over his face, a handkerchief removed the excess water. His office door was open, and he was surprised to see a visitor.

A middle-aged civilian stood by the window. He was thin and medium height, and wore a white short sleeve shirt and khaki pants. His partially greying sideburns contrasted with his chestnut brown hair, and he peered over half-moon glasses. The stranger said, "I'm sorry I startled you. The door was unlocked, so I thought I'd wait in your office. Sergeant Lincoln told me where I could find you. I came here for Captain Jarden's party, and to have prescriptions refilled. I'm one of Mark's patients. My name is Mo Balen."

"Balen, Balen, Mo Balen . . . I know I've heard the name before," said Herb turning away and staring at the ceiling. "Of course," smiled Herb as he walked toward the window, "Mark told me about you. . ."

"I hope they were nice things."

"Very nice," replied Herb as he shook Mo Balen's hand. "You're the guy who works for the CIA."

* * *

11

"S'IL vous plait . . . Escargots et Pâté de Poisson . . . et je pense pour les entrées, Coquilles St. Jacques et Crevettes aux Herbes," said the patron without reading the menu.

The Vietnamese waiter, dressed in a formal black tuxedo, nodded. "Merci beaucoup, Monsieur Balen." Then he turned and made for the kitchen.

"That's my great uncle, parents, and yours truly," Herb responded to Mo's inquiry.

"The infamous Uncle Otto! He would have been right at home in DaNang. Vietnam is a paradise for the unconscionable fast-buck artist."

"I don't think so, Mo. During World War II, my uncle played an active role in bond drives and money raising. He was an air raid warden, a volunteer at the big Army hospital center at Valley Forge, and conservation coordinator in our area for recycling paper and metal. Otto adhered to the gasoline and food rationing when he could easily have avoided any sacrifice. The man was really very patriotic."

"Funny," said Mo Balen looking at the photograph album while adjusting glasses that had slipped almost to the tip of his nose, "Patriotic is a word never used in this little police action over here. Is it?" Without waiting for Herb's answer, Mo turned the page and pointed to another photograph.

"Those are some of my medical school fraternity brothers. Larry Lewis was the vice president of Beta Sig and he's now stationed at a State-side Army base. Sam Stein, the house treasurer, is on the Berry plan, and the military won't see him until he's through his cardiology training. Dave Garret . . . I think he's in the Public Health Service. Stu

Levin is in an Ob-Gyn residency in Boston. The fellow on the far right is Pete James. He was asked to leave Osler Medical school when he refused to shave his beard and moustache. Pete appealed his case twice and was finally reinstated. Now they allow any kind of hair growth, as long as it's neat. He'a a senior and heads an organization of medical students against America's involvement in the war."

"Christie and your father . . . Who's on the other side of your wife."

Herb bent over, "Horace and Molly Flint. They own the house in the background. My wife lives there on Kerr Street. Doesn't this picture stuff bore you?"

"Not in the least. Didn't I *ask* you to bring the album? That must be Amanda. Who are the others?"

"Karl Werner is the big fella, he was our fraternity chef. Amanda's son, Franklin Williams, is on the other side of Christie."

"It almost looks like Christie is holding Amanda up. The woman looks like a skeleton."

"She died a few weeks after that photograph was taken. Death had resolved her biggest problem. She didn't want to be anybody's burden. Christie visited her every day. Took care of the nursing and medical end, and the cooking and housekeeping when she could. Women from the Open Love Baptist Church were always willing to help, but Amanda was happiest when Christie was around. In those last few months, Franklin and I were the bit players, Christie was always in charge. Amanda would knock both of us in the usual manner, but she never had a harsh word for Christie. Franklin and I used to study together, read, and watch TV while the two of them carried on private conversations that would frequently last hours."

"Sounds like a combination of mother-daughter, and best friend. . ."

"At the funeral, Reverend Tucker gave a eulogy and referred to Christie in just that way. Did I ever tell you about that scene?"

Mo repositioned the candle closer to the table settings of fine blue china and sterling silverware. The restaurant's few windows with partially closed shades, permitted the strong midday sun to lighten only small sections of the large dining room.

"The Open Love Baptist Church is a small store-front place that seats about one hundred people. It was standing room only at Amanda's funeral. I never saw such an outpouring of emotion. . ."

Mo was moving the candle in a to and fro motion, the light flickered as Herb's face and words had the effect of a disjointed memory beginning to take shape.

" . . . the tears. . . . It wasn't just the colored church members. There was a rabbi, and some of his people wearing yarmulkas from a Synagogue called Ohel Zadek that Amanda had tried to help. I visited the place, and believe me it was a hopeless case. I've never seen such a run-down sanctuary, and it may well not exist any more. Some of the old men cried; a few of my fraternity brothers and Karl Werner were sobbing away. Christie and Franklin lost it completely. Reverend Tucker had tears streaming down his face. He waved the Bible and screamed religious epitaphs, and the members of the congregation answered back. 'I hear yeh, Jesus,' a woman behind me kept repeating. And then the kicker: the Jews all stood up and recited *Kaddish*, the Jewish prayer for the dead. I could see a few of my Catholic frat brothers genuflecting, making the sign of the cross, and I could hear 'Hail Mary full of grace, the Lord is with you.' Later, people were kissing each other and the crying continued. I remember thinking to myself, 'am I at a church or is this a love-in?' It was an eerie feeling."

"It sounds like a genuine outburst of grief. What was your reaction?" Mo withdrew his hand from the candleholder, and moved his chair slightly away from the table in order to cross his legs.

"To begin with," Herb fingered the chinaware, "I was caught off balance. I expected the same old stuff from the pulpit . . . dedicated churchworker, wonderful mama, good woman . . . standard stuff for your everyday religious funeral. A few tears and the same old sermon with a name change. It struck me as odd. Catholics kneeling, Baptists sitting, Jews standing, all praying in their own way. This poor, colored, illiterate woman achieved in death a spiritual harmony I never thought possible. It wasn't the real world. I'm more at home with good old fashioned religious hypocrisy. In everyday living, these people would have had nothing to do with each other. Death brought them together."

"Did you ever discuss your feelings about Amanda's funeral with your wife?"

"No. At the time, Christie and I were locking horns. I couldn't marry her in a Catholic church, and the synagogue wasn't a better choice. I opted for a civil ceremony, but Christie insisted on a Jewish wedding, and that's the way it finally happened."

"Did her family approve?"

"Christie's father died a few months before Amanda. He leaked his

approval of me and our marriage through some old cronies who
worked at the same coal mine. I attended the wake, and at the funeral
parlor, a few came up to me, joked around, and let me know what had
been on John Loreski's mind. They made me feel at home, but the rest
of the family never acknowledged my presence. Christie's mother is a
good woman, honest and hard working, but she is totally consumed
by her faith. I respect my mother-in-law, but Christie's brother, Paul,
is something else. He says one thing and does another. Claimed to
support our marriage, but never came to the ceremony. Always
walking fences. Politically unclear about his position on Vietnam
until about four months ago, when he finally realized his strong
religious convictions would not allow him to get involved in a
shooting war. Now he's a conscientious objector working as an
orderly in a Philadelphia hospital. The guy's a real scholar. Has a PhD
in literature and can tell you anything you want to know about Joseph
Conrad, including his shoe size. But he can't remember his sister's
telephone number."

"Herb, you said that Christie insisted on getting married in a
synagogue. I don't get it."

"You're not alone, Mo. I didn't understand it then, and I don't
today. I suspect Amanda was influential in some way."

"I would have thought that Amanda wanted a Christian wedding."

"You're too logical. The CIA has you good and brainwashed."

Mo laughed. "If the CIA taught logic, its operatives would either be
killed or unemployed. The only thing logical about the agency is its
need to exist."

The Agency was not involved totally in cloak and dagger affairs in
the Nam. Many of its operations were not covert and had nothing to
do with intelligence and gathering information. Mo claimed to be
involved with flight operations and scheduling for Air America, the
CIA's private airline. It was at the Air America terminal that Herb had
met advisors and consultants to various South Vietnamese depart-
ments, who openly admitted their Langley affiliation. Herb was aware
that Mo's duties took him throughout Indochina and the Orient. A
few days before, his friend had returned from a one day trip to Laos,
and presented him with a bow and arrow made by a Hum tribesman.

The CIA captivated Herb's curiosity, but the evasive Mo always saw
through the verbal traps, no matter how subtle. The insistence that he
was nothing more than an airline scheduler only added to the mystery.

The secretive Mr. Balen never discussed his personal life, and Herb didn't pursue the issue. The medical chart in the dispensary file room contained the basics: born in St. Louis in 1921, youngest of four children, parents alive, divorced, no children, and no previous history of major illnesses with the exception of asthma with an allergy overlay.

"Yesiree, the only logical thing about the agency is its need to exist," Mo repeated with a chuckle.

"Amanda," Herb countered, "made little distinction between Judaism and Christianity. When we told her of our plans to marry in a Jewish Reform temple, she said, 'Thank you Jesus. He'll be there with you. It's what the Lord wants.'"

Mo resumed looking at the photographs, but then glanced at the maître d' standing near the kitchen door, their eyes met and both men nodded.

"Christie had a great idea when she put this album together. It must have been a major task, but it flows nicely, from your baby pictures to the goodbye shots at the San Francisco airport for your Saigon flight. I guess you're ready to start a second album," said Mo, pointing to Herb's Spotmatic Pentax camera on the floor between their chairs.

"It's not everyday I'm invited to the best restaurant in DaNang, if not in all of Vietnam. My wife has a thing about French restaurants and candlelight. If the food is as good as you say, then I want to document the occasion. Who would believe our eating a sumptuous meal like this in a war torn country?"

"I quite agree with you, Herb, and I hope 'La Maison' won't disappoint—it never has in the past. I think our meal is ready."

Three well-groomed waiters stood next to a serving cart in full view of the two men. There were different shaped pans, small glazed earthenware jars, and a food burner rested on an asbestos mat. All had lids, preventing Herb from enjoying the visual delights of French haute cuisine. One waiter moved a pan over the bright flame in a circular motion. Another sharpened a long stainless steel carving knife, the resounding clang filled the room, as all eyes focused on the service table specialties.

"Have you ever tried snails?"

"Are you kidding? I'm an onion soup man at a French restaurant," grinned Herb.

"What about wine sauces?"

"Hey Mo! Ask me about a corn beef special or a roast beef sandwich on white bread smothered with gravy. Before I met Christie, my idea of a good restaurant was the automat at Horn and Hardart."

"I'm sorry you don't imbibe the good stuff, this place has a remarkable wine cellar. Are you sure I can't interest you in something like a. . ."

"Not interested, Mo. You ordered the meal, and all I want is an explanation of the food so I can tell Christie. When you're writing home everyday, it's nice to discuss something other than the weather."

"I understand perfectly. Garçon! Shall we proceed with the feast?"

The waiter rotated the pan over the fire, removed the lid, and inquired, "Rye, plain, onion, or pumpernickel?"

Another followed: "Captain, Nova lox or fresh herring?"

"Smoked salmon with scrambled eggs and onion," added a third waiter, "you like?"

Herb, pupils dilated and mouth open, struggled for words, "Son of a bitch . . . well, I'll be. . ."

"Kraft cream cheese, Philadelphee brand to go with your bagel, Sir."

"Captain, here are your prunes," announced the maître d'. The new arrival reached for a ladle.

"Good for whatever ails you," said Mo as he winked at his befuddled friend.

"Sir! Would you like your Maxwell House coffee now or later."

"Out with it, Mo. What gives?"

"We can handle the rest, Cam . . . Cam Ong." Mo's polite thank you was accepted by the Vietnamese, who for the first time collectively smiled, and then scurried off to resume their duties.

"A little bagel and lox on a Sunday afternoon at an exquisite French restaurant in Da Nang. It's a Vietnamese tradition . . . very common," continued Mo.

"Ah, that's my mistake," a puzzled Herb responded. "I knew this kind of meal was popular in Laos and Cambodia, but I wasn't sure about the Nam."

Mo smiled and reached for an envelope in his back pocket. Balen scanned the room and satisfied no one was observing, deftly passed it under Herb's monogrammed LM linen napkin. "Can't be too careful these days, the VC are everywhere," Mo said furtively.

Herb reached for the envelope, and saw it was stamped CIA, TOP SECRET. He removed a letter, and read aloud: 'Captain Klein . . . Enjoy, Enjoy, Enjoy . . . May God Bless you . . . Shalom Aleichem.' A card said:

**MOISHE'S DELI
28 YULAND ST.
KOWLOON, HONG KONG
TELEPHONE 3582361**

"Great guy. Moishe is one of our key operatives for the China Section. He passes secret information in bagels, so watch out for the pumpernickel . . . it changes every month . . . I think it's onion in January," said Mo, softly.

"I'm going to send a letter to your super spy, but if you, or one of your Air America boys gets over to Hong Kong, then please convey my special thanks. Who is this guy?"

"Moishe Lieberman is an Israeli who's been a fixture in Hong Kong for about ten years. We go back to the late fifties. When I told him about you during my last visit, this . . . ," Mo's fork skimmed the herring and salmon, "was his response."

"Do you like this kind of food, Mo?"

"Love it, except for the herring. We had a great deli in St. Louis, but Murray's doesn't compare with Moishe's. He's a household word at Langley."

"Now that you have successfully pulled off this caper, it's time to share the booty. Like the man said, pass the Philadelphee cream cheese . . . No one back home is going to believe this, I just know it."

"Why do you say that, Herb? I'll be your witness. Here, let me take pictures with the Pentax. The evidence is incontrovertible."

"It has to do with images, Mo. War is blood and guts stuff, not bagels and lox, cream cheese, herring."

"Don't forget prunes," Mo added with a warning finger.

". . . and prunes. There's a certain decorum, rules of the game. It almost makes me feel ashamed I'm here. This is Vietnam. I ought to be in the field helping a wounded grunt, or eating old C-rations prepared in the 1940s."

"You'll get your chance soon enough. Isn't your Civic Action medical program about to start after all of those delays?"

"Yes, but that's not the point, there's a certain war aura . . . this whole scene doesn't fit." Herb picked up a bagel and twirled it around his index finger.

"Do what you have to do," Mo's somber mood now reflected in his serious tone and slow, calculated speech. "But don't ever believe, in this toilet bowl that all of us are swimming in, eating bagels and lox makes any less sense than Ho eating Peking Duck and LBJ enjoying ribs at the ranch."

"In that case," said Herb imitating his friend's dramatic manner, "pass . . . the Nova."

* * *

12

AIRMAN Lewis made the final adjustment on the receiver's volume, and then handed the headphones to the Commander of the Civic Action Medical Program. "Captain Klein," he said smartly, "Colonel Stalley is ready to talk to you."

"Sir!" spoke an enthusiastic Herb, "the response of Village 142 has been incredible. With your permission, I would like to extend for another hour before returning to the base. We won't be able to handle everybody, but we will have made our presence felt. You can't believe the lines, Colonel."

(pause)

"No problem at all. Air policemen have surrounded the school. I can see ARVN soldiers patrolling the rice paddies. A marine helicopter periodically buzzes the area. Security is real good."

(pause)

"Space and people. We've had to improvise. Immunization is in one of the ambulances, and the podiatrist has set up shop in the other. There's a little hut in the back of the school that we're using for dental. In the school house, Dave Wyatt controls the surgical end, Freddy Black is doing the pediatrics and OB-GYN, and I'm handling the internal medicine. We underestimated. . ."

(pause)

"Affirmative. We're okay so far as shots, drugs, and surgical supplies go. We have many of the little flags and propaganda sheets that the South Vietnamese government provided, but we ran out of candy for the kids, and the pencils and pads for the adults."

(pause)

"The village chief, council elders and their families were seen first. We weeded out the emergencies. . ."

(pause)

"Sergeant McNally of photo reconnaissance, but . . ."

(pause)

"It's all unofficial, Colonel. The village chief needs an x-ray, and I thought it would be appropriate that a *Stars and Stripes* photographer be available to include you, since you are the prime architect. . ."

(pause)

"Yes sir. I appreciate your interest, and I certainly understand your need to remain at the base. Thank. . ."

(pause)

"Thank you for offering, but we don't need . . . I take that back, Colonel. If you could contact the *Stars and Stripes* newspaper, 'Da Nang Weekly,' Saigon. . ."

(pause)

"Affirmative. Thanks again, sir!"

An overjoyed Herb Klein stooped down to retrieve a red rubber ball, and threw it back to a smiling youngster dressed in a multicolored sports shirt and a cowboy hat. The schoolyard had a festive air—children playing, mothers holding their babies and chatting, old people comparing bottles and little vials of drugs. Herb returned the smile of three young women dressed in black pajamas and bamboo hats; they giggled as he passed.

"Airman Thomas," Herb smiled as he entered the school room, "would you please inform everyone that Colonel Stalley has graciously permitted us another hour."

Herb turned as he heard his name, and acknowledged Dave Wyatt's frantic waving. The portly surgeon, like most of the medical team, had removed his shirt to offset the oppressive heat. Herb maneuvered through the crowded but organized makeshift clinic to where his friend was standing. The surgeon's hand now rested on his patient's abdomen, as he reached for a towel with his free arm to help relieve the excessive perspiration.

"This man needs an internist, Herb. He got in my line because of his leg ulcers, but that's the least of his problems. He's got a big liver and spleen, fluid in the belly and lungs, can't lie flat because of labored breathing, and I can't even hear heart sounds. The poor guy consented to visit us after being persuaded we could help him, and was given assurances that we wouldn't dump him in the province hospital. It looks like he's ready to have a cardiac arrest."

Herb nodded his head in agreement, and pointed to the portion of the room that was his territory. The interpreter and a medic, aware of the serious problem and the need to act quickly, cradled the sick man in their entwined arms and carried him to Herb's examination table.

"That is one fucked-up gent," said the surgeon as he continued to move the towel over his upper torso. "A lot of that skin shit is self-made. The patches over his body are supposed to cure him and eliminate the pain and misery. I think it's some kind of Chink medicine."

"I'll handle it, Dave. No problem. And by the way, I just talked to the Colonel and he gave us an additional hour before we have to close shop. Thanks for the consult; it looks like an interesting case."

"Hey Herb, you don't have to be so accommodating. Don't worry, I'm here to stay. I know I just dumped a horror show into your lap; you don't have to act like you just got the greatest blow job in your life. Just consider me a permanent fixture in your Civic Action medical program."

Herb's grin turned to a wince. Dave Wyatt was right on target. He reached for the surgeon's towel, and jokingly rubbed it against the crotch of his sweaty fatigues before returning it to his friend. Both men laughed, and Herb added the vertical finger sign, and then quickly made his way through the line of villagers waiting their turn to see him.

He examined the dying man, now propped on the table behind a large sheet that provided privacy. Captain Ky, his Vietnamese ARVN interpreter, was already asking the standard protocol questions. The patient's illness could easily consume his efforts for the remaining hour, but at the expense of other villagers. In addition to the pressures of manpower and time, there was the dilemma of his own competence. Medical school, intern training, and Brooks Aerospace flight surgeon training had left Herb with a huge void in the understanding and appreciation of tropical diseases indigenous to Southeast Asia. An American with a similar problem was sent to a huge hospital where specialists and excellent laboratory facilities were available.

Herb was keenly aware of his own inadequacies. He had visited Province hospitals, observed and discussed the problems with both civilian and military doctors, and had begun an ambitious program of reading Hunter's *Manual of Tropical Medicine*. He was overwhelmed by the new vocabulary and a whole different way of looking at a disease. There was no one available for a consultation in the boonies, as Dave Wyatt so poignantly demonstrated, except the recent Osler graduate, and this was an affront to his own self-respect.

He reached for his stethoscope and began to examine the elderly patient. Herb held the man's hand and smiled; he tried desperately to reassure and convey a message of confidence and hope.

Captain Ky perfunctorily recited the history: ". . . is a 38 year old farmer. . ."

"God! 38?" growled Herb.

". . . 38," repeated the interpreter, "who has had. . ."

Herb listened to the symptoms, impressed once again with Ky's capacity to extrapolate information and convey the essentials in the short time allotted each patient. He had no additional questions for the interpreter, and completed his examination as Ky finished.

Herb, drawing upon his total absence of expertise in tropical diseases, stroked his chin, aware that both men were following his every move. He nodded, as if struck with a sudden divine inspiration, and turned to the farmer; his left arm encircled narrow shoulders, the right arm sought a frail hand. Herb peered into the patient's deep orbital sockets, and said smilingly as Captain Ky leaned over, intent on not missing a word. "Tell our friend that we will do some tests on his blood, urine, and stool. I am confident we can help him. He should continue taking his Chinese medicines—the plasters on both the neck and abdomen, moxa*, lotions, and the drugs I will give him to help his breathing, diarrhea, and fluid excess. He will also get two shots by the medic to give him added strength. Thank him for permitting me to help in this period of temporary distress, and ask him to return at our next session."

Herb reached for a pad and wrote the prescriptions on one sheet and the injections on another. On a separate card, he briefly indicated his physical findings, diagnosis, lab studies, and treatment. The diagnosis was simply a list of symptoms followed by the words, "Etiology Undetermined." He waited for the two men to finish their conversation, and again smiled as the farmer turned away from the interpreter to seek his physician.

"Dr. Klein," Captain Ky paused, "the patient would like you to

---

*Powdered leaves ignited and crushed into the skin to form blisters.

know that it is he and his family who are honored to be in your presence. He knows you are kind and good-hearted with the best intentions, but he does not believe he will live much longer. He wishes to you and your family, a happy life with much joy. He thanks you for all that you have done for him."

Herb said nothing. Captain Ky, noting his silence, reached over for the two sheets and repeated aloud the names of the drugs. Herb approved, and sought a pencil and pad to divert his attention from the punishing glance of the patient who had spoken with an unwarranted reverence.

"Hey Doc," squealed the Sergeant as he stood before Herb holding the prescriptions, "are you sure you want me to give this Gook a shot of sugar and B-12?"

"I'm sure," he replied, not bothering to look at the medic. Herb stared at the pad, and smiled at what he had just written. His amusement was short lived; Captain Ky was already showing the next patient into the examination area.

"Is everything okay," asked the interpreter, noting the doctor's mood change.

"Captain Ky, my good friend . . . everything is great, and you know something, we are going to have the best damn clinic in Vietnam. This is only the beginning. We're going to help those villagers, and I don't even care if they are VC. Screw the war! These are good, decent people. Look at today's response for starters," Herb said, and then he focused his attention on a new patient. "I'm Dr. Klein," he said, extending a hand in friendship.

"How curious," thought Captain Ky, as he looked at the open pad in front of him, "what does it mean?" He turned to a bemused Herb, and mumbled softly, ". . . take two aspirin and call me in the morning."

"I'm telling you not to push things. Look what you've accomplished, and it's not even a week since we've been to the village." Dave Wyatt pointed to the front page picture of the *Da Nang Weekly*. A photograph showed Herb and Wyatt watching the Colonel examining the village chieftan at a base hospital office.

"Stalley promised me two, and possibly three Civic sessions a week. It's important early in the game to maintain the people's confidence. They must get the message that we're not going to abandon them."

"Herb, no way the Colonel's going to abandon this village stuff.

Not as long as the big boys in Saigon are hot for the idea. I figure this Civic Action Medical Program is worth four, maybe five brownie points. What do you think, Mo?"

"Too high. A five is when Walter Cronkite has some nice things to say about you on prime time. In the *Da Nang Weekly* this story has no value. The *New York Times,* or even *Stars and Stripes,* that's the big score."

"Yeah, but I got good vibes about Civic Action," countered an excited Dave. "Do you know that a few lifers have volunteered since the word got out. I gotta believe this thing has real promotional potential."

"I don't give two shits about motivation. I just want to get the job done. These people need us desperately," Herb said.

"I've been trying to sell Untouchable the same message, but Lee doesn't want my help," chuckled Dave.

The door to Dave Wyatt's office opened abruptly. . . "Captain! We got a grunt with a gun shot wound in the belly and his bandages are bloody." Dave bolted through the open door and the medic followed.

"I guess I better leave."

"That's not necessary, Mo. If Dave needs help, he'll let me know. It's probably just some bleeding from the suture site. So tell me, what's happening in your life?"

"Not a thing. I try to make sure Air America planes are on time . . . coming and going. My worst moments are when I have to bump somebody. You should hear the language."

"Isn't the cargo a little different," snickered Herb.

"Don't believe the spy stories. My hands are in clear view," Mo rested his arms on the table. "What you see is all above board. That's the nice thing about Nam, company matters are out in the open."

"Okay, when something interesting happens, let me know about it."

"It's a deal. You have an insatiable appetite about Vietnam. It's not worth the effort, Herb. There's no master plan locked in a safe about how to win this war, or even how to fight it. This thing is a day-to-day affair. You know . . . walk a little to the east and then to the north . . . before you know it, you're back to square one."

"You sound like Mark Jarden. Was he one of your protégés?"

"Mark was a team player. He never had his fly open in public, remember that. I don't think Mark ever asked me a question about the CIA. He just didn't give a shit. He used to say about the Nam. . ."

"A hero is a guy who doesn't leave in a green body bag and returns to the states with both balls intact."

"That's right," sighed his friend, "there are no other rules."

"And I'll tell you the same thing I told Mark. I'm no hero. I'm here so I'm going to attend to sick people, because it's the right thing to do. I'll tell you something else, Mo. I've seen a lot of this country—Dong Hoi at the DMZ, Highlands, and right through to Saigon. I have talked to mucho guys, and I've heard a million theories. Right now, the issue of who's right is dead so far as I'm concerned. I'm going to help as many people as I possibly can."

"Herb, I like you. I truly and sincerely like you. Honestly, you're great, but. . ."

"But?"

"But . . ." Mo repeated, and then added, "Do you know I have a dozen bagels and lox sitting back in my apartment and damn it, I forgot to bring them."

"I thought you were preparing me for a variation of Uncle Otto's favorite line," grinned Herb. "He used to say, 'you can think and talk idealism, as long as you don't practice it.'"

"I've done too much preaching. What the hell! You think you've got some good ideas, let's see what happens. How's Christie?"

"She's fine, Mo! No bullshit, what the hell do you really do?"

Mo deliberated a moment, then looked at the young flight surgeon with amusement. He shook his head, and shifted in the chair. "I schedule airplanes. Now no bullshit, do you want me to go back to my place and get those bagels?"

"Boy-oh-boy," said an incredulous Herb. "Is there anybody in this country who knows how to be serious."

The road from Da Nang Air Base to Village 142 was paved for a mile as it paralleled the perimeter of the base. An eight foot metal fence interspersed every twenty yards with huge utility poles and their flood lights stood on one side, the rice paddies on the other.

Beyond the first fence was an area of barren ground that varied from ten to twenty yards—a heavily mined 'no man's territory.' A second metal wire fence of the same dimensions with manned watchtowers every seventy-five to one hundred yards was the last barrier before reaching the confines of the base.

Herb could see the hospital was no more than one hundred yards from the second fence as the jeep slowly traveled the single-lane macadem road. A grunt in a nearby watchtower trained his binoculars on the convoy as it neared the end of "Interstate 69," the nickname for this narrow road that led nowhere. No one Herb asked had the slightest notion of why it had ever been built.

A few yards from the last watchtower, just before the turnoff, an air policeman with an M-16 strapped to his back walked slowly along the edge of the mine field with his German shepherd. The guard dog's life was made easy—his only two friends in the world were the trainer and the base veterinarian. Other mortals were his enemies; a simple command by the sentry-trainer made it so.

Captain Joe Hurlock, like the guard dogs, was also Herb Klein's friend; the base veterinarian sat quietly in the jeep behind his buddy recalling their first encounter. . . *"Would you believe! I'm in this shithole six months, and it's the first time. If Jenny finds out, I'm a goner, Doc! You've got to help me."*

The jeep followed an ambulance as it left Interstate 69, and the convoy proceeded in a northwesterly direction away from the base. Potholes were filled with water, and dust from the vehicle ahead made visibility difficult, as the dirt road cut through the rice paddies.

The convoy halted as it was about to enter a wooded area. The schoolyard and clinic were only a mile away. Herb heard the familiar hum of the helicopter. He could see a helmeted gunner direct the 50 caliber machine gun below, as the chopper, barely above tree level surveyed the area leading to Village 142.

After a short delay, the order was given to resume, and the convoy made its way through the most treacherous stretch of the journey. The dense mass of trees on both sides of the small road made excellent cover for an ambush. It was impossible to prevent an isolated skirmish with the few VC who were interested in kicking a little Yankee ass.

"I don't know if it's the penicillin you gave me, or whether it's going through these woods like one of those pigeons in a shooting gallery, but I gotta take a shit. Not to mention the sweating and belly pains," said Joe Hurlock in the jeep's back seat, as he rested his hand on Herb's shoulder. "You know, Jennie's father was in the Army in World War II, and the only advice he ever gave me was not to volunteer for anything. The idiot is one hundred percent right. You've made my father-in-law look smart, and that's hard to do. All of you are nuts!"

"Calm down, Joe. We're almost there. I've made this trip many times, and we've never had a problem."

"Many times . . . many times, eh? You're talking to Joe Hurlock, Herb. I know I've got a heavy dose of clap, but I'm still thinking okay. This is no countryside road leading to picnic grounds where we can split open a sixpack, sing songs by the campfire, and reminisce with the boys. There may be mines on this road, or VC in the trees who don't like me. You know, you're a sick boy. I can't believe that I volunteered to come out here in the boonies to help some Geek's buffalo."

"Joe, you did the right thing," said Herb, not bothering to add how Sergeant Lincoln conveniently entered his office to talk about certain deficiencies in the Village Medical Program at the precise moment Captain Hurlock was dressing behind a screen. "You'll have some nice war stories to tell your friends and kids. You'll thank me, Joe. Look ahead. We're almost there."

A Marine patrol had secured the road. He saw mine sweepers, and realized there were only a hundred yards left to the school. A sergeant directed traffic, and waved the convoy on at a faster speed.

There was unusual activity in the yard. Near the dental hut, three Marines smoked and rested in the shade. An Air Policeman was motioning to his colleagues. ARVN soldiers actively patrolled the rice paddies surrounding the school on three sides. All of the vehicles were now parked. More grunts walked down the two trails leading out of the village into the compound.

Three officers, two Americans and a Vietnamese, stood by the entrance to the school. Herb was joined by Dave Wyatt, Freddy Black, and Sergeant Lincoln. Hurlock remained in the jeep and muttered, "Look at this show! You're nuts, Herb. Jennie won't believe this."

"What gives?" Dave asked in a subdued tone. "Where the hell are the Geeks?"

Herb shook his head in despair, and remained riveted as the three officers at the school entrance approached him. His attention was diverted toward two helicopters, and the clatter of machine gun fire.

"Are you the head honcho?" screamed the Marine Captain.

"Yep! I'm Captain Klein, the medical man in charge."

"Oh, you're a doc then. Hey, don't pay any attention to that crap. The choppers need some gunnery practice, so we called a little strike. I'm Winger, this here is Lieutenant Buck with MAC-V, and Captain Tuh is with ARVN."

"Look's like everybody's here but our patients." Herb said.

"And that's the way it's gonna be, Doc," said Captain Winger lighting a cigarette. "Last night, about twenty-one hundred, there was a fire fight about two miles from here. Charlie was probing for something. There was activity throughout the night to the south and a little east. Now we know what the Spooks were up to."

"It was all a diversion Doc," said the young crew cut Lieutenant Buck. "Charlie did a real fine job, first rate. They got into the village and wiped out the chief, his wife and kids. They also greased a few other officials whom they didn't like, and made it known that they don't care for your medical program."

"You mean nobody wants to come here? After the response we had? I can't believe it!"

"Doc, they're afraid. We were there the whole morning," the Lieutenant glanced at the Vietnamese captain, "trying to persuade some key people to show up, but it was no go. Charlie's got the upper hand right now. Maybe with a new chief. . ."

"A new chief? That could take weeks," said a frustrated Herb.

"Doc, listen, this is one of the better villages. An average chief around here lasts about six months. He gets it from both sides, and has to be a good man to survive."

"These people want us. We're not interested in politics. For Christ's sake, we just want to take care of their diseases. . ."

"Herb," Dave Wyatt interrupted, "the Lieutenant is doing his job. This is not the end. We'll be back in no time flat. It'll be standing room only."

Captain Ky approached the group accompanied by an elderly Vietnamese villager who needed a walking stick to get around. His sunken cheek bones and emaciated appearance suggested a sick man with many serious problems. "This man would like your help," said the interpreter.

"Shoot," squealed a curious Dave Wyatt.

In front of the assembled officers, all of whom were impressed with the bravery of the one soul who dared to defy the Viet Cong, Captain Ky translated: "Morning before I eat . . . afternoon when I take my walk . . . during my sleep . . . my children tell me all the time . . . I feel good, and have no other complaints . . . but all the time I . . . I. . ."

"What's the problem, Captain Ky," asked Dave noting the interpreter's hesitation and embarrassment.

"This man . . . he pass. . ." The translator turned around, so that his back faced the officers, and reached for the seat of his pants.

"Are you trying to tell me that this man's only problem is he farts all the time?"

"Yes, Captain Wyatt."

"It looks like Charlie is sending us all another message," said Lieutenant Buck, breaking into a wide smile.

* * *

13

"THE membrane still looks red. I have to ground you for a few more days. It's certainly better than last week. I think you should be ready to fly by the weekend." Herb returned the otoscope next to the x-ray box, and placed his stethoscope on the desk near Christie's photograph.

"But Doc, I'm feeling fine. Let me make a trial run today, and if I have any problem, I'll be back in a jiffy. We're really hard pressed at HQ. A few of the boys are putting in double time without me."

"I'd like to help you, Brad. I feel terrible when I have to ground anybody. But middle ear infections and flying don't mix. You are not able to Valsalva. If you can't clear your ears, you can't go upstairs, it's that simple. I also have you on antibiotics and antihistamines, and that in itself is a contraindication to flying. Stick it out for a few more days."

"Okay, but never let it be said that Bradley Frantz is an unreasonable man."

"How do you handle it, Brad? Here you are with a legitimate medical excuse . . . if you kept on complaining about your ear, I could find good reasons to keep you grounded for weeks. But I know damn well you would be flying into Ky Sanh, a DMZ strip, or a Special Forces camp this afternoon if I gave the word."

"Some of it is military conditioning, the rest is personal pride. If you screw up, your buddies and a helluva lot of other people are going to suffer. Walt Pellham and Sonny Watts are like my brothers. You look around, and say to yourself, 'Hey, I'm one of the lucky ones!' Last week I saw a young F-4 jockey freeze on the line. He was stuttering, totally incoherent. I've seen others like him. I know damn well I would've reacted the same way, if I was flying up to Haiphong and had to face those SAMs and all that anti-aircraft shit."

"I don't believe it. I've seen your act. It's a tough one to follow."

"I have three teenagers and a wife waiting for me, and I intend to spend by retirement days with my family. Right now I have a job to do. You know, Doc, sometimes it's just not possible to explain why you act in a certain way. You don't plan things, they just happen. And when you analyze how you reacted in a situation, you're more surprised than anyone. Major Frantz rose to leave. At the door, he turned to his doctor friend for one final request. "Could I stop back tomorrow and have the ear checked. I have a gut feeling everything's going to be okay."

"Be happy to take a look," said Herb, not the least bit surprised at his patient's persistence.

Alone, Herb peered through the window in the direction of the air field; a C-130 was approaching the runway for a landing. The sonic boom of an F-4 jet could be heard in the distance. Last night a B-52 had made an emergency landing and was now being repaired. Herb changed his mind about visiting the giant bomber and inspecting it before it returned to its home base in Guam. There would be other opportunities.

His mood was much improved since the unmitigated disaster at Village 142. Colonel Stalley no longer took a let's-see-what-happens attitude, and had given Herb approval to explore available options. The medical team, with the exception of Joe Hurlock, was still intact. Nobody else had offered his resignation despite the killings. He even had an ace up his sleeve for the veterinarian and the other 'shakies'— if they didn't want to make the trip to the boonies overland, then door-to-door chopper service would be arranged.

He glanced at the In basket; mail from Ben and Christie awaited his scrutiny. Letter writing was a task for Herb, as was his constant battle with a guilty conscience. His wife wrote everyday, and some days twice. He claimed in his letters to be writing every other day, but his habit was to write a few letters in advance of their actual postmark. The format included comments about the weather, amusing anecdotes, and half-hearted replies to her questions. Unopened mail in hand, Herb sought the privacy of his quarters.

The hallway was empty, though he could hear voices from the pharmacy area bordering the main foyer. He left the hospital by a side entrance near the medical barracks. A bright, late morning sun greeted him, it was only a short walk to the comfort of his air-conditioned room. He welcomed the letter writing with unnatural enthusiasm.

As Herb turned the street corner and passed a few trailers shared by the officers of the 45th Air Commando Squardron, the hell-raising Spooky outfit, a familiar figure greeted him at the steps of a room only two doors away from his own.

"Hey Doc, how you doin'," asked the beaming, red-haired Lieutenant.

"Great," Herb said, returning the smile. "How are you feeling?" Herb recalled seeing the young navigator at sick call, but could not remember his problem or name.

"Hey Doc," he repeated, "you really cured me of the runs."

"I'm glad you're better."

"Doc," the Lieutenant approached him with a stagger. "One favor deserves another. Wanna get laid? I got sloppy fourth's and you can have left-over fifth's," he whispered. The alcoholic stench of the Lieutenant's breath was so strong that Herb took a backward step.

"What's going on?"

"Shhh!" The Lieutenant's finger went to the doctor's lips. "We got ourselves a helluva gang bang goin'. Major Rich, Major Bickter, Captain Trent, and your's truly are partyin'. I think ol' Bud's in the saddle right now. And we got ourself some real prime meat. I mean A-number one prime. You know that little housemaid, the one they call 'Untouchable'! Well, she ain't no more."

Herb hurdled the steps and reached for the knob in one motion. The door offered no resistance, and he found himself standing in the quarters of Bud Rich and Josh Trent.

The size and layout of the room was similar to Herb's. Bunk beds were against one wall with an adjoining desk. The lockers, however, were catty-corner, and a small table and chair present in the space where Herb's locker would have been. The tiny kitchen and bathroom location were identical. Another chair was in the middle of the room and faced the bed; it was occupied by Josh Trent, a whiskey bottle in his right hand. Herb could see his left arm above the elbow moving in a rhythmic motion. The only sounds were that of the air conditioner's hum, and the metal springs recoiling from the weight of Lee and Bud Rich on the lower bunk bed.

"What are you a fuckin' Peepin' Tom!" said a nude man standing at the bathroom entrance. A middle-aged six footer with short black hair and a full moustache, the stranger added, "Who the fuck are you, Captain?"

"Doc Klein . . . fellas, Doc Klein's here and wants a piece of the action. You have to wait your turn, Doc. It's worth it. Yahoo," yelled Josh Trent as he turned around to face Herb, his hand firmly wrapped around the shaft of his erect penis. "Captain Klein, meet Major Cal Bickter. Cal's from Nha Trang. He's taking Bruce Evans' spot."

Cal Bickter stood at the door, and berated the carrot-topped navigator: "Shape up! This ain't no fuckin' open house, Lieutenant!"

Herb heard a snappy, 'Yes Sir,' as the door slammed shut.

"This is some piece, Doc . . . nice and tight," mumbled a breathless Bud Rich. He thrust his pelvis against a motionless Lee; her head propped on a pillow, vacant and expressionless eyes focused on the upper bunk-bed springs. Bud's massive arms pushed under Lee's knees; her one foot rested against the wall; the other in space, almost touched the desk.

"Tight my ass," chuckled Cal. "Bud drew a third, Josh and me made it easy for the sucker. She was damn tight when I had her. Shit! There's room for the whole 45th Commando Squadron right now. Make yourself at home, Doc. Take your clothes off . . . have some whiskey," said Bickter, pointing to the bottles on the table. "I think the Lieutenant forfeited his squirt. You all agree with me!"

"Sure," seconded Josh, who had resumed masturbating.

"Fuckin' A . . . Doc is an okay dude," panted Bud. "Boom, Boom, you fuckin' cunt. Boom Boom . . . Boom Boom," roared Major Rich imploring Lee to move her motionless body.

"Fellas, you ought to stop this. It's . . . not right," said Herb, his hands shaking and heart pounding.

"What!" A disbelieving Bickter squared his shoulders, "Say that again."

"I said this is not right. This gang bang is a rape job, pure and simple. You know it and I know it. Get off her, Bud," Herb moved quickly to the bedside and put his hands on the Major's broad shoulders.

"Get this fuckin' Jew boy off me," screamed Rich.

Strong hands encircled Herb's chest and then he was slammed into the locker. Josh pinned one arm, the other hand yanked on Herb's hair immobilizing his head. Cal reached for the other arm; Bickter's free hand held a blue handled scuba knife, it settled on the tender spot on Herb's neck.

"One fuckin' move, and I'll slice you . . . you Kike son-of-a-bitch. Just give me the word, Bud," said Cal.

"That's too good for the cock sucker. Bring him over here. Put him on his knees and let him watch me fuck this lousy whore."

"Rape! You cunt lappin' Kike. This ain't no fuckin' rape, it's a party, and you're the only one here without an invitation," Cal growled.

Herb was thrown to the floor, his head held inches away from Lee and Bud Rich's genitalia.

"I know all about you, Klein. You're a fuckin' Geek lover. You help those Viet Cong villagers, but you don't give a shit about any of us. Whose side are you on?" yelled the sweaty, fast moving Major Rich.

"Charlie must give him free ass," Josh said while fondling himself.

"I got a great idea." Cal tightened his grip on the flight surgeon, "Why don't both you guys come in the Doc's mouth and his lover's at the same time. Josh'll handle the whore, and you. . ."

"There's no sheeny in the world good enough to swallow my cum. Let him watch. Boom Boom . . . Boom Boom," reiterated the hard working Bud, his strokes now long and penetrating. "Make sure his eyes are open . . . Boom Boom . . . I'm comin' . . . Ohhh . . . Oh, Yea!"

Major Rich jumped out of the bed quickly, and grazed Herb's head with his knee. The semen gushed out of the vagina. Herb's face was thrust between Lee's legs.

"Lunch time for the Doctor," announced Cal.

"Pussy a-la-mode is now being served," added Josh.

"Give Charlene a milk shake. Get it? . . . Charlene? . . . Charlie? . . . Charlene is a VC whore," laughed Major Rich. "While Josh gets the mouth, why don't you take her ass, Cal!"

"Can't handle it, Bud. I'm lucky to pop off once with all this booze," replied Major Bickter.

They sat Herb next to Lee in the bed. She continued to stare into space, oblivious to all around her. Arms remained limp at her side. Bud moved her hand under Josh's testicles, and at the same time Josh tried unsuccessfully to open her mouth while his penis strayed over her lips. Trent continued to masturbate, and then let loose with his orgasm yelling, "Charlene! You fuckin' Vietnamese whore!"

"Look at them . . . look at them. Fuckin' mannequins, that's what they are," Major Rich ridiculed the couple's lifelessness. "Now I'm gonna tell you both something, and I want you to listen very carefully. The three of us are getting dressed, and we're goin' over to Cal's place for a few rounds. When I get back, I want this place clean, and I mean spotless. . . You gotta stop helping the Dinks, Klein! I had a feelin' you were a real fuck-up when I heard about your ideas. You can't hold Mark Jarden's jock strap. I want you to know that the whole squadron will back me up on whatever I say about you, or what happened here today. You see, this whore promised to take on a few of the boys and now we're goin' to keep our end of the bargain, even though she wasn't as good as advertised. I'm giving her twenty dollars American money, not the Vietnamese shit we use for toilet paper. A gift from the four of us, though she doesn't deserve it. Do you understand Doc, do you?" asked Bud, reaching for Herb's shirt collar.

"Yes," Herb answered in a barely audible voice.

The men dressed into their flying fatigues, and as Cal Bickter opened the front door, Herb Klein heard the red-headed Lieutenant ask, "My turn, Major?"

"You're first, next time around, Lieutenant. Didn't we tell you no visitors allowed," growled Cal.

"Yes, but the Doc was . . . ," said the Lieutenant as the door was shut with a deliberate and forceful bang.

Herb arose and stared at the Vietnamese girl, so admired for her beauty and countenance. She remained unmoved, with the same expression and demeanor present when he first entered the room. He checked her quickly, careful not to frighten her more with any sudden moves. Her skin was cold and clammy; her pulse was regular, but weak. She's going to break down and go into shock, he thought. She won't hold up. "Listen to me, Lee. Please listen!" He reached for her small hand, gently held it in his own, and then rubbed the palm in a gentle circular motion. "I know a Marine doctor who was a ladies' doctor before he came to Vietnam. He will give you medicine so you needn't worry about a baby. He'll take good care of you, and make sure everything is the way it ought to be. Do you follow me? Please nod your head if you do."

Lee said nothing, did not move a muscle. "Oh God," he whispered. This poor little girl can't hold out much longer, he thought. With all that she's been through, it's not possible. She's going to crack. What can I do?

The sobbing started; a stream of tears were soon joined by un-abashed moaning, tremors shook the whole upper body. The doctor's trembling hand rested on her bosom. He sank into her lap and she gently stroked his hair.

Her first words, said softly and with uncommon tenderness, "Don't cry."

Herb had lost control.

* * *

14

THE first snowball missed its mark; the second grazed a shoulder; but the third smacked her nose. She sought cover behind a park bench, but not before being pelted on the leg and back. The snow was soft, and the thrower's aim, though accurate, was not hurled with forceful conviction.

As she huddled behind the bench, the young woman quickly reviewed her options. She had good protection from a frontal attack, but the flanks were unguarded. There was an adequate amount of snow to stockpile armaments but there was also a major problem, she was already feeling the affects of a bitter cold winter day, and had forgotten to take the warm leather gloves from the kitchen table. Valor will have to give way to prudence, she thought while waving a small white handkerchief. "No fair," she shouted to her adversary. My hands are freezing, you caught me by surprise. I think I'll call you 'Mister Sneaky.'"

"You didn't expect to walk in Independence Square, the very spot where the American fighting spirit was born, without a snowball fight. I think I'll call you 'Miss Sore Loser.'"

"Come on, 'Mister Sneaky', admit you're wrong!"

"No way! But if you tell me what this wooden cubicle is, I promise to take you to a nice, warm restaurant."

"It's called a watchbox. In Colonial days, a guard would stand in here and look for fires. Let's ee . . . eat," she shuddered.

Southwark Tavern was located on Georges Place, a small cobblestone alleyway between Pine and Queen Streets. It was a neighborhood bar and hangout, away from the tourist traps surrounding the historical attractions of Old Philadelphia. There were no overhanging signs, nor did the owner advertise, with the exception of the one-eighth page in the local high school yearbook. He lived or died, by the oldest communication technology known to man: word of mouth.

The interior had a long oak bar with twenty stools, none with back supports. A half-dozen tables, each capable of seating four people, encircled a massive fieldstone fireplace, eight feet wide, five feet high, and four feet deep. A huge iron-throat camper evacuated the smoke. Giant andirons with ball tops of ebony finish were on both sides of a five foot grate. A four-fold black brass spark screen stood on firebrick in front of the huge cast iron grate.

The menu was limited to one side of a single sheet, and included both lunch and dinner specialties. For people in the know, and the owner-chef wished it to be few, there was one item of exceptional merit.

"Two chili con carnes," she whispered to the bartender, coats in hand. "Coffee, Mister Sneaky?" An affirmative nod prompted her to add, " . . . and two coffees, Ted."

The bartender, holding the telephone, puckered his lips and smiled to acknowledge her request.

"Twelve inches, maybe more. It looks like a real blizzard out there," said the only patron at the bar, an elderly man, with a ruddy appearance suggesting he was no stranger to Southwark Tavern.

"I believe it. Thanks for the update, Jeb," said the young woman as she led her escort to a table directly in front of the fireplace.

The raging fire provided the only source of light other than two small bulbs overhanging the bar. She lit her cigarette, and then the white candle on the checkered red and white tablecloth.

"I'm pooped. Where do you get your energy?" Arms extended, he rubbed his palms, then turned away from the fireplace and rested warm hands on the table. "Betsy Ross House, Ben Franklin's pad, Carpenter's Hall, Independence Hall, the Liberty Bell, and . . . the oldest street in America, Alfred's Alley!"

"Elfreth's Alley," she grinned, and removed a beret. Long auburn hair, loose and wet, clung to the back of her heavy woolen, blue, turtleneck sweater.

"The grand tour. What's your fee?"

"Later. I hope you enjoyed it. Perhaps it's a little different from your previous visits to the City of Brotherly Love," she said, with a smile.

"Historical shrines and the like were not turn-ons. My energies were devoted to 'sisterly love'."

"So the grapevine reports, but I don't put much stock in rumors. What I really want to know 'Mister Sneaky'," she took a deep puff on her cigarette, "is about that trip you took to Chile and Easter Island."

"Santiago's okay. Some good restaurants and nice churches. The Commies are very big. There's a great deal of the Yankee-Go-Home sentiment. Easter Island is something else. I had heard about the mammoth stone heads around the island that face the sea, but it was the people that were fascinating. They're a mixture of Polynesian and probably Peruvian, living on the most remote island in the world. Money has no meaning, so I brought old clothes to trade for woodwork, statues, and handicrafts. There is a priest who spreads the gospel and conducts Mass, but the people are a primitive sort who still keep up the old ways. A woman will approach you and let you know that she's interested in love making, and it's all done so naturally."

"Why did you make the trip in the first place?"

"Easter Island is supposed to be an Air Force weather station. The truth is we are monitoring DeGaulle's nuclear bomb blasts. I went down to resupply the medical stocks and advise the medic."

"You mean to tell me we are spying on France, one of our allies? It's been downhill since Dallas," she sighed.

"Hi, stranger." The bartender held two steaming bowls of chili and placed them next to the diners. "Where have you been? Horace was here a few days ago, and said you were okay but I must see for myself."

"Please excuse me, Ted. I'm not busy, just thoughtless."

"Christie, Christie . . . " mumbled the thin, elderly, silver haired man as he admonished her with a warning finger, "You cause an old man grief." He hugged and kissed her on both cheeks, "The doctor is okay?"

"Herb is fine. Ted, I'd like you to meet a friend from Washington. This is Captain Mark Jarden who's stationed at Andrew's Air Force Base. Mark's a doctor who served with Herb at Da Nang."

Graciously, Ted said: "Consider this your home. God bless you! Do you drink wine?"

"Yes, thank you, but. . ."

"Leave the rest to me," said Ted, who embraced Mark and scurried off to the bar.

"Did you see the look on that guy's face, Christie? I though he was going to kiss me."

"Herb took care of Ted, Jeb and a lot of the Tavern clientele . . . curbside consultations, free drugs were standard fare during his internship. This is a blue collar, working-class neighborhood. Most of the people around here are very pro-war."

"Don't they know how you feel?"

"Passions are thick in Southwark, so I don't advertise my viewpoint. I'm not interested in confrontation. Ted thinks I share his opinions, just like he believes Herb and you are on his side, because you were there. People assume. If it makes them happy, I don't want to be the one to burst their bubble."

"I know what you mean," Mark paused to sample the chili. "For me, the war is over. I don't want to deal with it. I just don't give a damn. And while we're on the subject, Peter James has been trying to get me to enlist in his Medical Students and Doctors Against the War crusade. How do I say no nicely?"

"Let me handle it."

"Christie will do a good job, no matter what the problem," said a voice behind her. Ted put two small glasses next to an open wine bottle, and placed hot coffee mugs next to the chili bowls. "Is it warm enough? Let me put on another log. Take your shoes off, and put your feet on these little stools by the fire . . . like you and Herb used to do, Christie. If you need anything, holler," smiled the bartender as he left.

"Herb would have loved travelling to Easter Island and Chile," said Christie, not the least bit surprised by Ted's hospitality. "He joined the Air Force to satisfy his wanderlust, and because of an interest in things he knew nothing about, like flight and related medical problems. We never discussed Vietnam."

"Don't ever try to figure out a computer," said Mark, who had gulped down his first glass of wine, and started to pour a second. "I heard a rumor. Are you doing volunteer work at the Naval Hospital?"

"Yes."

"Not busy enough? Long night shifts at Osler, Herb's father, your own family, countless hours at Amanda's church and a run-down synagogue. . . I know quite a bit about what's happening in your life. I think you ought to slow down, and I know damn well Herb would be pissed off if he ever found out."

Christie sipped her wine, and sampled the chili. The light of the candle flickered as Ted added another log to the raging fire. She continued to eat and waited for the old man to leave. "You've been talking to Peter James. It sounds a lot worse than it really is. I enjoy pediatric nursing. The pay is lousy, but I can pay the bills without touching Herb's salary. And Herb's father? He's a joy. Ben's proud that his son is doing his share, instead of burning American flags . . . Amanda Williams was someone very important to Herb and me. Continuing her work is something we owe her, sort of a tribute to her memory; more importantly, its the right thing to do. My mother and I have never been closer. She has accepted our marriage and the situation. She even writes Herb. I mean it. She just sent him a necklace with a Jewish star . . . that I'm sure he doesn't wear. Herb has been going through a religious denial period ever since his mother died. My brother Paul works at a Philadelphia hospital as a conscientious objector based on religious grounds. If I know Paul, the only praying he does is to thank the Lord his testicles are not in range of a Viet Cong bullet. My brother is like a lot of people, I guess—he has a knack of finding the happy safe road on a dangerous journey. Paul drifts in whatever direction the wind blows while the rest of us fight the current. The Marines at the Naval Hospital . . ." Christie reached for the wine glass, and turned to the window, there was an accumulation of snow on the sill blocking a street view. Her eyes then turned to the blazing fire. All that could be heard was the harsh blowing of the winter wind, the crackling of fresh firewood and an occasional ember sizzling as it was caught in the firescreen. "They're so young. What do you say to someone who can't walk or use his arms? How do you deal with hopeless dreams that can never be restored? Mostly, I just listen. When it gets real tough, I have to imagine I'm talking to Herb. The propositions are no problem. It's a good sign when a guy wants to go to bed with you. It means he's on the road to recovery. I like to think I can say no, and still make a fella feel like he's a great lover who'll get his chance tomorrow. And then there's the tough, handsome Marine who puts the make on you, and you know the mind is willing, but the body can't do the job. Believe me, it's tough to deal with these young men." She turned away from the flames, crossed her arms under firm breasts to seek added warmth, and scowled, ". . . it's even tougher when I think how unnecessary it all is. For what? A total sham; an affront to every ounce of decency I possess. But don't get me wrong, if a quad believes his sacrifice was in the name of Freedom and Democracy, I just put on my best smile and agree. The customer is always right."

"Christie, you don't need it. Walk away. They'll survive. Those guys have their own families and friends. The VA hospitals aren't the best, but they're more than adequate. They will be taken care of by the government for the rest of their lives, and in time most of them will recover. Nobody's going to forget them. It's never happened before in this country and it never will."

"Mark," her hand reached for his, "I'm really doing fine. For some reason, I picked you as a sounding board for some of my frustrations. If things get out of whack, I'll shape up."

"I understand. I want you to feel free to discuss anything with me. It's important not to keep your emotions pent up. You've got to have an outlet."

"I know you are someone I can trust. . ."

"Christie, I think the world of you and Herb. You know that."

"Mark," she leaned forward, "there is something else I'd like to discuss with you. Please tell me what's happening with my husband."

It had been a wonderful day, despite the whipping wind, numbing cold, and heavy snow. So many new and interesting places to visit and enjoy. It was all so cozy, but suddenly for the first time, Mark Jarden felt horribly uncomfortable. Could it be, he wondered, is it possible this beautiful, intelligent 21 year old charming, sweet thing has my balls in a vice, and is now squeezing. Well, fuck me!

"I don't know much. Doesn't he write you every day? Is Herb okay?" he asked.

"Yes, so far as I know. He writes often, but his letters are part of the problem. Have you ever read one of those masterpieces?"

"I can't recall Herb ever sharing any of his letter writing with me."

"He starts out with the weather report, and that usually takes up a half page—though during the monsoon season, when wind velocity and rainfall are big items, it takes a full page. You didn't know I married a frustrated meterologist. He usually concludes his letter with intimate insights into the horrors of Viet Nam, like . . . 'I ordered a steak medium, and Sergeant So-and-So-burnt it to a crisp.' He never answers my questions about the war and complains constantly about the mail service. This is his excuse for not responding to anything he considers sensitive."

"The mail service really is terrible."

"It must be one way, Mark. I get mine every five days after they're postmarked. I know my husband, and there is no way he's going to stay put at Da Nang and look after a bunch of healthy fliers and watch over their gonorrhea. I know you're in contact with Herb and that big surgeon. . ."

"Dave Wyatt," he said softly while refilling his wine glass.

"Yes, and there are others. There is something going on with Herb, I can feel it. I'm a big girl. I need to know the truth."

"Herb's great and. . ."

"Please, Mark. I beg you."

Their previous conversations about Herb and Vietnam had always been light and cheery. Mark would tell Christie amusing stories about Da Nang; it was all fun and games. But it had become obvious she was biding her time, taking notes and waiting for the right moment. Now her face told the story: no more bullshit. He turned to the fireplace for respite. Christie's silence offered no support, the next move was squarely on his shoulders.

"It's hard for me," he said painfully, "to tell you these things. I need to know that neither Herb nor anyone else will know we've had this chat. People have said things in confidence."

"I understand."

"Herb is a bright guy. I'm not just talking about medicine. He has street smarts, good intentions, and he's sincere in his convictions, but damn it," he said angrily, "it's the military and there's a war on."

Christie nodded her head in agreement.

"Herb's always asking questions, probing, digging below the surface. If he would only stay put on the base and do his job. It's only a year. But it seems as though your husband is on a crusade."

"You're right," she said in an encouraging tone.

"It all started with the Village Pacification Program," Mark was now eager to share his secrets. "Colonel Stalley knew that only Herb could pull it off. All the other doctors would have laughed in his face, and he knew it. Mind you, a voluntary Medical Program that goes into Boony country loaded with VC to take care of some Geeks that couldn't care less if we all got our asses greased—I wouldn't have gone, and I told Herb that before I left. But somehow, he got a team together and they were so successful, they pissed off Charlie. The VC slaughtered the village chief and his family, along with some other bigwigs. When Herb renewed the program, the VC responded by killing some more people. He looked around for other villages, but by this time everybody had gotten the message, and his medical team was in shambles. Maybe he could have filled a jeep with crazies like himself, but the idea of making house calls on the needy was kaput. The sick folks would have to go to the province hospitals which they hated, and I can understand their reservations, I've been to one of those places . . . Do you remember the last big rocket attack on the Da Nang air base?"

"Yes," answered Christie softly.

"A helluva lot of guys were hurt, some badly. A doctor sees somebody after one of those attacks, and signs a certificate stating the man is injured in action and entitled to a Purple Heart. It's a judgment call, and not an easy decision to make. A medal always looks good at promotion time, and it makes for a good war story back home. I guess Herb was overworked, but he refused to sign for a few officers—A fella jumping out of bed and stubbing his toe, that kind of thing. He was heard to say by a few people, Frank Lincoln was one of them, that one Major's hand injury was the equivalent trauma of jerking off twice in one day. A few officers complained to Stalley. If he'd only learn to keep his mouth shut and play the game."

Ted stood over the table with another bottle of wine, "I notice you're a little low. Can I get you more chili?"

"No thanks, but everything is just great. Christie may disappoint, but you'll be seeing a lot more of me around this place," Mark said with a grin.

"It looks like we're the only people here, now that Jeb left. If you want to close early, we'll gladly leave."

"Relax, don't rush. The lights are off outside and the door is already locked. Stay here as long as you want," said Ted.

"Why don't you give me the check now and we can settle, so I don't have to bother you again," said Mark reaching for his wallet.

"Doctor," said the owner of the Southwark Tavern, "you are a friend of Herb and Christie and a Vietnam Veteran. I am honored. There is no check. Please! This is your home. Add as much wood to the fire as you want. I'm going upstairs to watch the news."

"Now you know why I don't come here," smiled Christie, as they listened to the old man slowly ascend the old, creaky stairwell.

"I feel terrible. I'll leave a big tip."

"Not necessary, Mark. Ted would be insulted if you left a penny . . . You were speaking about my maverick husband."

"Christie, it's not my intention to cause you anguish about Herb. I . . . ," he stopped to open the second wine bottle.

"You're doing super, Mark. This is vintage Herb. I'm still waiting to be surprised." He thought she looked as beautiful at that moment as any woman possibly could.

"I guess you didn't know he spent a few weeks at one of those Geek hospitals. Yes Ma'am! Another brainchild of you-know-who. Herb requested—and of course Stalley approved—a pilot program at a civilian provincial hospital near Hoi An, about fifty miles south of Da Nang. A real hole with about two hundred beds staffed by two Vietnamese doctors who spent a few hours in the morning making rounds. Nurses and aids actually ran the place. Dave Wyatt worked one afternoon a week at the hospital and said it was the pits. Remind me to show you the photographs I got from him."

"What's it look like?"

"Big wards. Maybe fifty to a room. Dumpy cots and bamboo mats on the floor. A kitchen in a little hut that served only rice. A small lab where a technician did everything by hand, and in one corner was an old French fluoroscope that must have been the hit of Paris in the roaring Twenties. Whole families slept together at a bedside. Can you imagine Herb walking into a set-up like that?"

Christie smiled, but remained silent.

"He had a ball with the tuberculosis ward. A nurse determined the schedule, and the doctors saw the patients on a nearby porch. You got a small card with the patient's name and drugs, and that was the extent of their whole record. The Geeks must have thought Herb was nuts when he walked into the TB ward and insisted on bedside examinations. But here's the biggest joke. Herb shipped an x-ray unit to Hoi An and got chests films, skin tests, and found out that many of the patients didn't have TB. He also insisted every patient be seen once a day and have charts with notes. Then he made up a twenty-four hour schedule for emergency calls. Of course, Herb was the only doc available at night. No way the Vietnamese doctors would sleep at the hospital with just a few grunts around to maintain security. The Geek docs were very accommodating and agreed to everything. And why not? It all made good sense. But you see, they understood the American need to change and get things done quickly. They knew Herb was only going to be there for a year, and that would be the end of the war for him. Not for them. Dave told Herb to go slow, and more importantly, work through channels. Your husband did neither, a week after Herb was called back to Da Nang, Dave went to Hoi An for his surgical clinic, and guess what?"

"Everything had reverted to the old way."

"That's right. It's like our friend was never there. You are one smart cookie, Mrs. Klein."

"Why was Herb called back to the base?"

"Some other matter. He doesn't know when to look the other way. There was a small ward for Viet Cong prisoners. They were chained to their beds, and ARVN soldiers patrolled the building. One day, a chopper landed in the hospital compound, and some ARVN bigwigs went to the VC ward and started roughing up some of the patients. Herb interfered and had to be restrained. ARVN took a few of them for a ride, and Herb claimed he saw two VC thrown out of the helicopter at high altitude. Captain Klein made a big stink with the higher-ups and there was an investigation. They couldn't find a single soul to corroborate his story . . . like a refill?" He picked up her wine glass while holding the bottle.

"No! . . . No, thank you, Mark. Who is Mo Balen?"

"Nice guy . . . works for the CIA. Has something to do with Air America, the airline the CIA operates in Southeast Asia. Mo was one of my patients, and Herb inherited him when he took over my 'specials.' He has an allergy problem."

"Is that all you know about him?"

"Yes. Well, no—come to think of it, there was one other thing," Mark stroked his forehead. "I visited a flight surgeon friend at Nha Trang, and there was an outdoor barbecue . . . I met a fellow who said he was with the CIA and a consultant to the police. I casually asked whether he knew Mo, and he had the strangest look on his face."

"What did he say?"

"Not a damn thing. He just walked away. Why do you ask?"

"No particular reason. Herb mentioned him in his letters and likes him very much. They eat bagels and lox together." Christie laughed.

"Do you hear that wind? Look at the frost on the window. I have to take you home," declared Mark, surveying the empty tavern.

"I think I will take a refill. It's a woman's perogative to change her mind," she said jokingly. "I want to thank you for your candor, Mark. I know how difficult it's been. Is there anything else you think I ought to know?"

"That's the major stuff," he said, as he polished off another glass of Ted's favorite wine.

"I can cope with the realities. It's the not-knowing that plays silly tricks on the imagination. Your honesty, Mark, that's all I really have. You're the only person I can rely on to tell me the truth."

"There is something else you may want to know about. Herb got into a little fight. He's okay, but there's a little cut on his face. Men playing a kids' game. Tempers flew! No big thing."

Christie nodded a knowing smile, sipped wine, and patiently waited for Mark to continue.

"Boys will be boys. Herb got into an altercation with a guy named Bud Rich. Herb's friends pitched in, and Bud had his friends. Someone pulled a knife, another dude pulled his . . . people were cut. It all happened at the Doom Club, in the Officer's mess. Dave Wyatt told me he felt like a seamstress after suturing half the night. Nobody got killed, and there were no major injuries. Herb has a little momento; simple as that. Okay, Mrs. Klein, let's go home."

"Why did Herb and the other gentlemen fight?"

Mark tried to stand, but his legs gave way and he fell back into the chair. "It had something to do with a Vietnamese girl. Her name is Lee, but everybody called her 'Untouchable.' I tried myself, and believe me, the name was right on target. Boy was I surprised when I heard she took on a few pilots from the 45th Air Commandos. They slipped her a few bucks, but I understand she was available to the whole base. Playing it real coy. You know, the virgin scene? I knew I should've tried a little harder."

"But how was Herb involved?"

"Herb claimed she wasn't a slut. He said she was the victim of a gang bang, and that she was raped by Major Rich and his friends. Can you imagine? They are some of the toughest damn people we have over there, and Herb yells 'Foul.' A week before this happened, Captain Evans' plane was shot down. That made three out of five crews destroyed from the 'Old Spooky' squadron in less than a month. A 60% mortality figure! Lots of pressure on Bud, Josh Trent, and others . . . Did they need that aggravation?"

"It's not like Herb to make wild accusations, unless he has proof," mumbled Christie, more for her own ears than Mark's.

"Yep, old Herb screwed up this time. He should have kept quiet. There were a half dozen witnesses that called him a liar to his face at the Doom Club, and then all hell broke loose. It was all hushed up, no newspapers or TV. Some of the boys were sent on R and R to Bangkok, Tokyo, Singapore, Kuala Lampur . . . a few were transferred to other bases," said Mark shaking his head from side to side. "Excuse me, I feel a little woozy."

"Please answer one more question, Mark. Why did Herb say it was rape?"

"He was jealous. Herb was shacking up with Lee, and we all thought she was untouchable. She is one piece of ass. I can't blame him for not wanting to share her with anybody else." Mark felt dizzy, and reached for the second empty wine bottle, but the hand fell short. He slumped on the table with arms outstretched and mumbled, "Any more questions?"

"No," she said softly.

"How did I do? How was I Christie?" he asked while raising his tottering head, his eyes rolling in and out of focus.

She stared at the blazing fire, her silhouette aglow. His eyelids were about to close, when he heard her say, "You were fine, just fine . . . Thank you, Mark."

* * *

15

Both men warmly shook hands, and tried to isolate themselves from the noise and confusion of a busy medical ward.

"You look good, Wally. How do you feel?"

"A-number one. Have a seat, Chris, and pull the screen over. It's the only privacy we are going to get. Good to see you ol' Buddy. How are things over at MAG-11?"

"Fabulosa. There are mucho Marine pilots interested in your ass, shithead. I'll bet you didn't know you were so popular. Gee, you look terrific. I can't get over it."

"I guess it wasn't my turn. I'm just happy to be alive."

"I've heard so many different stories, Wally. I was in Okinawa when I heard about it. What the hell happened?"

"Oh brother! It's even hard for me to put the pieces together. Would you prop me up, Chris? Yeah, just put those two pillows behind my back. Now if you'll give me one of those non-filter jobs.

"The last couple of times we had been in North Vietnam in the Panhandle near Dong Hoi, there had been heavy cloud cover. I was glad to hear at the briefing that the weather was real good. Our first objective was a huge ferry complex. The bridges in the immediate area were already knocked out, so we knew they had a lot at stake and the place would be heavily fortified. The NVN usually keep the MIG's in the Hanoi-Haiphong area, but we had some Air Force F-4 Phantoms around for cover as a precautionary move. Our concern was with the SAM's and the anti-aircraft fire. We picked up a lot of heat at the Huu Hung ferry side. I got into a bad angle, made a sharp dive and let loose my jollies. I have to make a wide bank while climbing. Fortunately, I was pointed toward the Gulf of Tonkin. I remember hearing over the phones, 'Jackpot! Look at those secondary explosions.' And then came a thud. I'd bought it. I tried to level off. I knew if I could reach the shore line and parachute into the water, chances would be better, that I wouldn't have an all-expense-paid vacation to the Hanoi Hilton. I think I was about five thousand feet and around 300 knots, when I pressed the ejection trigger. I'm damn sure I broke every rule in the manual. . . My left arm was not placed properly on the ejection seat arm rest, and my elbow slammed into the edge of the cockpit when the seat catapulted. My feet were on the rudders, not the foot rests. The calf muscles were bruised, but luckily I didn't break my legs. I wasn't sitting straight and felt a sharp pain in my back. No compression fractures of the vertebrae but the Doc says some muscles were torn. I don't know how many G's I pulled, but I had no trouble with windblast or tumbling once in a slipstream, and the separation of the ejection seat and the opening of the parachute went without a hitch. I could feel the pain; man, it was sheer agony. I could see the water clearly, and with my good hand, I reached for the bailout zipper bag, and the fastener released. The life preserver and the raft inflated. I tried to gauge my position, but damn, it's tough to judge water impact. I was waiting for my feet to hit the water before starting my canopy release, and I remember feeling for the safety clips just before impact, but the pain destroyed my concentration. The next thing I remember was being entangled in the shroud lines of the parachute. My left arm and legs were totally useless. Friendlies were in the area. I remember looking up and seeing two F-4 Phantoms. I guessed the shoreline was over a mile away, but it turned out to be less than half a mile. A Navy helicopter was on the scene first, but it disappeared quickly. I found out later it had developed mechanical problems, and just made it back to a carrier. A Jolly Green Giant chopper followed a few minutes later, and it hovered right over me. I could see the hoist being lowered down but then it got stuck. I was trying to point to my bad arm with my good hand. No way I could have made that hoist even if it hadn't malfunctioned. By this time, I was cold and numb, two choppers had tried and failed, and I thought it was all over. Then I heard a noise, turned around, and saw a HU-16 Albatross Rescue Seaplane. I watched that baby land right near me, and all of a sudden . . . bang, boom, bang! Would you believe! The NVN were watching the whole show, and when the Jolly Green and the Albatross were on the scene, they opened fire with their shore guns. I could see the muzzle flashes, and bullets were hitting the water all around me. The last thing I recall was seeing a guy in a frog suit pushing a raft in my direction, and then I blacked out.

"Chris, I'm sliding. Would you please prop me up? This bed is so damn hard," said Wally angrily. "The rest of what I know," he continued after finding a comfortable position, "is what I've been told by medics and friends."

"Is it true your heart stopped, and that," Chris hesitated, ". . . that you were dead?"

"Yep! That's right. The water was rough, and the pararescueman had a devil of a time getting me back to the plane. Two other guys had to jump into the drink to help him out. By the time I was hauled into the Albatross, I had stopped breathing and had no heart beat. There was also a question of whether the plane could become airborne. It had taken enemy fire, and I'm sure it would have been curtains were it not for air strikes by the F-4s. They destroyed the shore guns after their positions were revealed. The seaplane was a sitting duck. Can you imagine how those dudes must have felt when they found out they were breaking their balls for a dead man?"

"How in Hell were you revived?"

"A million to one shot, a medic told me later. Try this on for size. Fractures of my elbow and arm, leg and back muscle tears, bullet wounds in both thighs, overexposure to the cold water, in a coma and shocky . . . a real basket case, but somehow they got me going again on the Albatross. I ended up in a special hospital that deals with my kind of problem—a shock unit—a few miles outside of Da Nang. I was in a coma for seven days and snapped out of it, and the only damage that may be permanent is to my elbow."

"You were lucky to have a paramedic who could handle that shit while you were on the seaplane. Unbelievable!"

"That's part of the miracle. The medic was the frogman and he got into deep trouble—leg cramps, vomiting, and a bullet wound in the shoulder. Remember, I told you two other guys jumped into the water to help out! One of them was a flight mechanic and the other was a fuckin' doctor. The Doc put me together."

"What the hell was a doc doing in a seaplane in North Vietnam? Must be whacko. I never heard of that."

"Beats me. But, hey, I'm not about to question his sanity. I never got a chance to talk to him, but they tell me he called the hospital a few times to find out how I was doing."

"You don't even know his name?"

"Not a thing," grinned Wally. There was a medic who remembered one detail when I was brought into the shock unit for the first time. He said the doctor had a big scar on his cheek. And that's it!"

"I shouldn't be surprised at this crap," Chris shook his head in bewilderment. "Do you remember flight training school in Pensacola, the night of the big poker game, and I had a full boat with aces up? Biggest fuckin' pot of the night, and you had four tens. You always win when the stakes are high."

"Yep! I guess it was in the cards for me to make it," laughed Wally.

"Time for a celebration. Are you allowed?" asked Chris removing a flask from his flight jacket.

"You bet," said Wally eagerly.

"I'm returning to the Nam tomorrow." Chris paused, and then he carefully poured the whiskey into two paper cups. "What's happening with you?"

"I'll be leaving Yokohama in a few days, and taking one of those nice Polar C-141 med-evac planes. A stopover at Elmendorf, Alaska, and then direct to Andrews where there's a nearby hospital, that's going to totally rehabilitate my elbow. I'll be back with you assholes real soon."

"No way they're going to ground you, Wally. No way! A toast to our buddies at MAG-11, the best damn pilots in the world. And to you old pal, the luckiest Marine pilot of them all."

"And to the dudes that got me out of the drink. Especially the Doc," added Wally.

"Okay," agreed Chris. "Here's to the whole lot of them. May your beer runneth over, as you watch a sweet sunset in the warmth of a new day, especially you, Doc Scarface!"

* * *

16

ALONE in his office, he reached for the Oom-Paul, its shank was rounded, the stem deeply curved, and the chamber enlarged. The style and shape of the pipe had been popularized by Sherlock Holmes. "Maybe some of the magic will rub off," thought Herb as he filled the bowl with his favorite Balkan tobacco.

He sat speculating about Mo Balen's visit to the Hospital earlier that day. The CIA operative was about to leave after a routine allergy checkup when he said in a casual, but calculated voice, "Still interested in learning about my company's business?"

Past discussions about job profile were always treated lightheartedly. Mo never admitted he was anything more than an employee involved solely in flight scheduling for Air America Airline; it was Herb who manufactured wild stories of intrigue and adventure to explain his friend's mission. "Was this meeting to be a practical joke? Why had he chosen tonight for his coming out party? And why were they to meet at the morgue? Why the morgue?" Herb wondered as he silently puffed on his pipe.

The idea of returning to the morgue did not sit well with Herb. He hadn't been there in weeks, and was hoping his presence there would never be required again. A doctor shouldn't feel squeamish around the dead, he knew, but that's precisely what had happened.

Captain Bruce Evans had been the last straw. His death, along with the other members of the crew, represented the third C-47 Spooky destroyed by enemy fire in a month. There were no survivors.

Herb's task as the squadron flight surgeon of the 45th Air Commandos was to identify the corpses, look for contributing medical circumstances, oversee the preparations of the remians, and tie in any of the loose ends. The first plane shot down offered no great challenge. The bodies of the crewmen, recovered within hours of the crash, were intact, and though the faces were not recognizable in a few cases, dogtags, jewelry, wallets, insignias, and other paraphernalia made the mandatory identification a routine matter. Herb had just become the squadron's Flight Surgeon, and knew none of the men socially, or even from sickcall visits.

Two weeks later it was a totally different scene. The plane had been destroyed near a Special Forces camp under siege, and rescue operations had been delayed three days because of the bad weather and the dangers of unfriendly turf. Herb was there when the body bags were opened. The men were burnt beyond recognition, and there was not one body totally intact; dismembered limbs, torsos with no heads, exposed viscera, heads with half trunks, missing body organs, black charred skin and muscle. Insects and bugs, saporific organisms of every conceivable kind crawled over their host in search of a good meal. And that smell—never would he forget that mixture of jungle rot, burned flesh, and decomposed human tissue.

Identification was difficult, but the remaining tissue revealed scars, tatoos, and birthmarks. Fingerprints, footprints, and dental records helped match a name to the remains. But even science has its limitations, and mixing body parts was sometimes inevitable.

Herb knew three members of the crew, though none were identifiable by conventional means. The flight mechanic had a skin rash that defied diagnosis and treatment. He was on the list the dermatologist from Cam Rahn Bay would see on his monthly visit. The navigator was a friendly type, and a fixture at the Doom Club poker games; a "Hi Doc" and a smiling acknowledgement by Herb, had been the extent of their contact. The copilot was stocky and muscular, a recent graduate of the Air Force Academy and a newlywed of a few short weeks before coming to Vietnam. He occasionally jogged in the early morning with Herb and a few other brave souls. The flight surgeon remembered him as the only runner who wore combat boots instead of sneakers.

The day after the Viet Cong had destroyed the second Spooky plane, Herb decided to fly the scheduled night mission. It was tense on the line that evening, a no-nonsense approach with none of the usual kidding among crew members. The Doc tried to break the ice, but he could never get past the small talk. His presence hadn't created the desired effect. Each man was absorbed in his own thoughts—

perhaps, like him, wondering if they were next. Herb needed conversation, if only for his own sanity. He had a sense of fear and foreboding that tonight would be his last. He conjured up all kinds of critical situations: What if the North Vietnamese had moved some big guns down from the DMZ and were just waiting for an easy mark like one of these old C-47s? What if the pilot was pissed off enough to take a few extra chances to pay Charlie back for the squadron's losses? What if . . . ? The actual flight turned out to be uneventful. The plane flew around the base and then out to sea, but never more than a few minutes from the mainland. He tried to break the monotony with additional small talk, but his efforts were in vain. Herb was convinced that his symbolic presence did nothing to allay anxiety and boost morale.

He was surprised when Captain Evans, the pilot and commander of the Spooky crew, visited his quarters to thank him personally for making the flight. Herb's presence was recognized and appreciated by the crew. Herb was not only gratified but felt he had gained a friend.

Bruce Evans was a quiet fellow who didn't like to ask questions, but never hedged on answers. You always knew where you stood with him, the archetypical straight shooter. He hated the VC as much as anyone, but he had great respect for their resiliency, courage and determination. As a professional soldier, war was his business, and Vietnam was the testing ground. Though only in his early thirties, he had prepared his family for any eventuality; the two small children had college funds, and there were letters they could read later from their father about his attitudes toward life in case the worst happened. Herb was convinced that Captain Evans was not a fatalist, just a very intense man who came to grips with the issues. "To do your duty," he often said, "is to accept a greater risk, that death may be a required prerequisite . . . it's just that simple."

Or was it simple? It certainly wasn't for Herb the day the body bags arrived at Da Nang morgue and his friend was among them. It wasn't an easy task. The bodies were dismembered for the most part, but not in the same league as the previous carnage. The airman who loaded the devastating mini-gattling guns was originally thought to be the flight mechanic. The headless, badly burned torso revealed laundry marks under a metal belt buckle, the gunner's initials and a few digits of his serial number were the first clue that the original identification impression was incorrect. The flight mechanic was never accounted for; his final resting place a mystery. Bruce Evans and the copilot were the only crew members totally intact, though burned in many places. The others were badly charred and distended with gas.

Herb watched as his friend was washed with a hose. His body cavities were immersed in formaldehyde, as were the viscera. The organs that had been removed were then returned to their natural setting, wrapped in muslin. The whole body was then swaddled in a similar fashion and gently put into the casket. A folded Captain's uniform from Bruce's wardrobe was placed on top of the glass lid of an inner liner, and the casket was closed.

Herb tapped the Oom-Paul pipe against the ashtray to remove loose ashes. The memories of the morgue and Bruce Evans rekindled another painful experience. He opened the bottom drawer, and found the partially written letter to Bruce's wife. It was the standard "good man, didn't die in vain" letter. He crumbled the paper in his fist and discarded it in the wastebasket.

He needed help desperately. Herb looked at her photograph on the desk, reached for the buttons of his fly, unloosened the belt buckle, and pushed the pants and shorts to thigh level. His eyes closed, a fanciful imagination was at play.

"Hi Christie!" he mumbled.

"I have the distinct impression you are happy to see me," her glance settled on Herb's groin.

"Oh, baby! If you knew how much I miss you. I love you so much," he said as they embraced.

She wore small pearl earrings and a matching necklace with no makeup. Her soft, light blue cashmere sweater and braless breasts hugged his chest. He reached for the hem of her dark blue skirt with one hand, and massaged the upper thigh where her nylons ended and the garter belt began. Black high heels raised her just enough for their eyes to meet. They kissed with darting tongues, as he held her buttocks with both hands, his fingers stretched and grasped for flesh. She wore no panties as his unencumbered hand abruptly changed direction, and sought the wetness between her legs that first invited one finger and then two.

"Christie, Chr . . . isttie," he stuttered. "Remember the fall day in Fairmount Park by Pegasus when we held each other tightly and rolled in the leaves? There hasn't been a day since then that I haven't wanted you."

She pushed him away, gently fingered the head and then stroked the shaft of his erect penis. "I know, Herb. I feel exactly the same, my love," she said tenderly. She kissed him on the ear, then the neck, and then the eyes, then gingerly removed his trousers and shoes.

"Oh, Christie, I . . . "

'Shhh!' She put a finger to his lips, bent over and grasped Herb's penis; Christie pushed the smooth head over her soft, moist lips, then her tongue caressed, and her mouth enveloped him as his body began to shake and quiver. Stopping suddenly, she declared, "Oh, no you don't! I want you in me." She directed him to the examination table. She lifted her dress above the hips and stretched out on the table with knees bent slightly and the legs spread, her pink flesh fully exposed, she pleadingly rotated restless hips.

He asked, shyly: "Don't . . . you want to take your clothes off?"

"C'mon, Herb. I know what you like."

He mounted her, and said laughingly, "Never let it be said that I refused my wife's wishes."

"It's time to put your money where your mouth is." Her hand grasped his throbbing, pulsating penis, and slid it gently into her, warmth against warmth. Her high heels dug into his legs as she held him tightly. He pushed the soft cashmere sweater toward her neck, and sought her beautiful, shapely breasts with his mouth. Anxious hands reached for her lovely, nylon covered thighs.

"I love it! I love it when I can feel all of you. Oh, Herb. Do it baby . . . Baby, do it!"

At first, they each went their separate ways. But then the movements were in harmony. They hugged and kissed.

"Oh, Herb. It's time . . . Deeper, deeper . . . Fuck me hard . . . give us a son . . . I love you."

"Christie, I love you. Oh, oh. Ohhhh."

Herb's eyes opened. He reached for the tissues, glanced at Christie's portrait, and looked at his watch. Musn't keep Mo waiting.

It was time to go to the morgue.

* * *

17

"MY Seiko says you're right on the button," Mo signaled with a turn of his wrist.

The admissions clerk sat behind a desk reading a paperback. He appeared surprised as the two men entered the morgue, but quickly regained his composure. "Mr. Balen, I thought you were through for the day. Doc Klein! I haven't seen you in weeks. How you doin'?" said the Sergeant, warmly.

"Fine, Sarge, I guess you thought I was a fixture around here. My squadrons have had good luck lately," smiled Herb. "How's it going?"

"Good days and bad. We've been busy the last week. Everybody's been puttin' in overtime. What can I do for you fellas?"

"I'd like to take Doc back to the Specials room. Can I sign in?"

"No problem, Mr. Balen. I'll take care of it," waved the clerk. "Hey Doc, what happened to your face? Jesus!"

"I picked up some flying glass after the last rocket attack on the base. Makes me look mean."

"That scar seems to affect your mouth. Can you eat okay?"

"I'm fine. Tested it last week and there's been no change . . . I can still get down on it!"

"Well I'll be," sighed the clerk. "Another muff diver. Glad to have you aboard, Doc."

"I'm a card carrying member. Local 486," winked Herb, and then he scurried through the door in pursuit of his friend. He headed for a light coming from an open door at the end of the hallway. "I thought there were only offices back here," Herb said as he stood in the doorway.

Mo Balen was sitting in a chair holding a pack of cigarettes, a brown portfolio lay on his lap. He peered over half-moon glasses that rested on the tip of the nose, waved his arm and said casually, "It's all yours, Herb."

The room had a single light attached to a central wire that Mo must have bumped accidentally. The bulb rotated and flickered. Herb followed the light as it played over each of the five tables in the room. On each table lay a green body bag partially opened. He reached for the wire to keep the light steady, and then inspected each corpse. He was forced to unzip all the bags even further to get a complete view, all the while keeping very cool and calm—very clinical. It was this professionalism that forced him to review the bodies a second time, even when there was no additional information to be gained and his gurgling stomach was yearning for a respite.

"Hmmm. Very nice. I wonder if I could have a few snapshots to send home and have framed for the family den."

"I'll see what I can do. Any thoughts about the goodness of man?" The portfolio was open, and Mo pointed to the sheets on his lap. "Makes for a nice bedtime story."

"They are all dressed the same, but I'm not familiar with the style," Herb said softly. "They're not Vietnamese. My guess is Chinese.

"You are off to a good start. The wearing apparel is typical for your everyday Chinese Communist political commissar."

"Okay Mo, enough of the bullshit, this is no top secret operation if a dumb-ass flight surgeon like me is involved. What happened?"

"You're right," snickered Mo, "but at one stage, it was big stuff. You see, this is a Langley operation. I don't know the architect, but my guess is that one of those nice Harvard boys with a major in Greek sculpture thought the whole thing out at a coffee break. The corpses on the tables are Chinese from Taiwan, employees of the CIA. You know who they were impersonating—the mission and the particulars I can't go into. They were dropped at a sensitive spot, and their delivery was based on a variant of 'student body left' . . . the football play where everybody blocks left, but it's a decoy and the runner goes right. In this case, there was an air strike and a Mick team. . ."

"What's a Mick team?"

"It's a fighting unit of Vietnamese and assorted mercenaries headed by Special Forces types. They are used primarily after the shit hits the fan, or in a situation like I'm describing. These boys are very good, and in this case," Mo glanced at the corpses, "the Mick team was choppered into Charlie's turf and went left—including air strikes—but our Taiwan friends and their Montagnard guides went right. . . That is, right smack into a trap. But who's counting? What I *can* tell you is that we lost two choppers, twenty-eight from the Mick team, three damn good 'gnard trackers, and five Chinese."

"But why were these people tortured?"

"It's hard to say, Herb. A signal to the American Imperialists? 'This is what you can expect if you stay in our country,' or a message to the CIA about what they can do with their great ideas. Maybe they're paying back some old debts to some overzealous players on our team. The Vietnamese have a special hatred for the Chinese. They occupied this country for a thousand years and they weren't very nice. On the other hand, this could be a few boys acting independently. You know, Saturday night at the local pub and a few of the fellas letting off a little steam."

"C'mon, Mo. No normal man could do this to another human being. Whoever is responsible belongs to another species. Look at this man!" Herb walked to the far end of the room. "They've removed his cock and put it into his mouth! I guess those two bulges on both sides are his testicles. He's been disemboweled. . . This next fellow has had his penis crushed. What's that shiny stuff?"

"A small glass tube inserted into his dick, and then someone used a rifle butt to finish the job. Nothing original here, Herb. The French used this little diddy in Algeria and Indochina in the 50s and 60s."

"Good God, he's been scalped . . . and has multiple stab wounds in the chest. Number three has had his nails removed, eyes gouged, was castrated, and it looks like the rectum has been cut with a blunt instrument."

"A knife. It was left in its original position, but I guess somebody now has a souvenir."

"Look at this woman! Total evisceration of her genitalia, the ears and nose sliced off. She must have the fella's penis in her mouth," cried Herb pointing to the remaining corpse. "He has excrement over his body. Animals kill for food, or self preservation, or fear . . . but this!"

"A German philosopher," replied Mo, "once said, 'Man is more cruel than the tiger, and has less pity than the hyena.' His own people tested the idea a few years ago. Not only did they prove the theory correct, but the Nazis provided a new standard to shoot for. This just goes to show, nobody has a lock on the marketplace."

A cloudless, moonlit sky greeted the two men as they started their walk back to the hospital along the dirt road parallel to the airfield. At first neither man spoke. Then Herb said, "What's it all mean, Mo? How could any man, other than a deranged, sadistic mental case, do something like that?"

"There's no mystery. There may be a guy or two, who when he cuts flesh, comes in his pants, but I'm more impressed with the so-called normal chap without the big hang-ups. I would guess the men who carved up the Chinese were nice, young farmers who would have more problems killing a pig. It's all a matter of conditioning."

"You can teach someone to torture and then defile a corpse?"

"It's simple, Herb. You break him into little pieces, hold onto his mind, and then you let the guy reassemble."

"You're talking about mind control. . ."

"Brainwashing, thought manipulation . . . Same thing."

"All countries do that sort of thing, including ours. Why shouldn't the other side?"

"Couldn't agree more. They just do a better job. The American way is to bombard a guy with ideas, give him access to information, encourage independent choice, even if it's not in harmony with the boys in charge. All you can really do is hope for the best, that he'll buy your viewpoint if it's a quality selling job. The VC and the North Vietnamese come at you from a different direction. Information is screened and intentionally one sided; the other view is distorted to enhance your own argument. They use dialogue, but in a totally different context. Have you heard of Khiem Thao?"

"Who's he?"

"Khiem Thao is not a person," spoke Mo after a short-lived smile. "It's a special session of the Commies used for indoctrination, a kind of self-catharsis. You cleanse your soul, and you are given another chance but with preconditions. For example, a soldier might admit he raped a girl or stole rice from a farmer. He is then severely criticized by his peers, but in the end the deed is forgiven and his sins absolved. But there's a price to be paid. You must not act and think like an individual—the party knows what's in your best interests. If you buy it, then they have you by the balls. It's simply a case of peeling away the layers."

"So Khiem Thao is designed to make you a dedicated party man. I still can't see the connection with the slaughter and mutilations."

"No, but it's a natural consequence. When you peel away the layers and get to the very core, at what keeps him going and makes him the dedicated believer willing to make any sacrifice, its simple, unadulterated hatred. Its the air he needs to breath his revolution. Spiritual, political, and philosophical considerations—they're just incidentals. You're not born to hate, it's something you learn, and Charlie has some excellent teachers. What happened when that ARVN Colonel visited your VC ward at the Hoi An provincial hospital?"

"They shot one patient, physically abused others, threw two of them out of a helicopter . . ."

"And I suspect they would have done a lot more if you hadn't spoiled their fun. But what was the reaction of the VC who remained when you made your medical rounds?"

"They were hostile, but it didn't bother me. I don't need any thank-you."

"That's not the point. It didn't matter that you were a doctor trying to cure a sickness, or that your intervention prevented a shot in the head or another chopper ride. You're an American, and they hated you. Given the opportunity, they may well have treated you the same way they treated our Taiwain friends. What you saw tonight in the Specials room is not an isolated incident. I've seen it many, many times."

"Some of the VC patients were young boys, no more than 14."

"Let me tell you something. . . " The noise of a jet's sonic boom made Mo suddenly stop walking. The silence that followed was punctuated by the distant clatter of machine gun fire. They were no more than fifty yards away from the entrance to the base compound. "Look at every country in the world, and you'll find that most violent crime is caused by one segment of the population: young males from about 14 to 25. No other group is as mean, as vicious, more aggressive, or hates like them. In peacetime they are a real pain in the ass, but no politician or military man would ever undervalue their importance in a war. Not only are they highly maleable, but teaching them to hate appeals to their sense of manhood. At this time of their lives, the basic needs most of them possess are to eat, fight, and fuck. The rest is negotiable."

Herb stroked the contour of his facial scar as both men resumed walking. "So what you're telling me is that Kheim Thao can make a monster out of a choir boy?"

"It can and it does. And with enough consistency to make a very effective weapon."

Herb reached for the Oom-Paul, and put it into his mouth without filling the bowl with tobacco. He held the stem tightly; his speech was slurred and barely comprehensible because of the pipe. "Mo, I know I've been buggin' you about your work, and I have this insatiable curiosity about the war. But I'm not sure whether I'm getting the message about tonight, and I'm still in the dark about you."

"All of these nasty things that have been happening . . . Bud Rich and the rest. I wanted you to see what the other side is like."

"Not necessary, Mo. Remember the Village Pacification Program? I saw first hand what the VC did to those officials and their families who cooperated with us."

"I just wanted you to appreciate that VC horror shows are more plentiful and a lot worse than our side."

"There's something else, Mo. You gotta spell it out for me."

"Okay. I'll give it to you straight." They had entered the compound, and Herb clumsily returned the airpoliceman's salute. The street was deserted. They passed Photo Reconnaissance and the Judge Advocate's office before Mo continued. "I wanted you to feel utter revulsion, to be overwhelmed with terror. This is what man is really like, and what Vietnam is all about. You got to see and feel the horror. We are caught in it. It's contagious; it's cyclic. As long as you stay in this country, there's no escape. Those who survive will be the guys who keep their noses clean and do their homework. The one's that have something to prove and the humanitarians will get fucked, they always do. Herb, I'm concerned. You have to change course. You're an honest-to-goodness do-gooder. There's no place for you in this shithole."

"Okay, I'll change. I'll become the prototype for your kind of man," said Herb glibly as he pointed to the base's theater marquis. The evening's movie was *Dracula, Prince of Darkness* with Christopher Lee and Barbara Shelly. "Would you like me to become a blood sucker? Somebody who gets a kick out of hurting other people and controlling their minds. Dracula must have been the inspiration for Khiem Thao."

"Oh no you don't. I'm not letting you off the hook so easily. Not only do I want you to think about what I said, but I want you to promise me you'll stay put at the base. Screw the Village Medical Programs, province hospitals, and those rescue missions up north! A doctor is not supposed to be on those seaplanes. You're actually violating military regulations. If you have to visit the flight line, then come over to Air America and we'll shoot the crap. . . I know the Colonel wants you to go on R and R. What's wrong with a week in Hawaii with that piece of ass you have for a wife?"

"Sounds good. I'll write Christie and see what her schedule is like."

"Then it's a deal!"

"You're not the first guy to suggest a vacation. The question I have to ask myself is whether the American war effort will collapse in my absence."

"Herb, I promise you, at the first sign of deterioration, you will be notified and I will provide the wings. Compliments of the CIA."

The two men passed the airmen's eating hall, and were approaching the Doom Club. Herb had to return to the Hospital where he was the medical officer on call that evening. Mo enjoyed a nightcap, and would occasionally get involved in one of the late night poker sessions that was a daily event at the Officers' mess. The doctor removed the empty pipe from his mouth and returned it to a trouser's pocket. The mood had changed, perhaps Mo's guard was down.

"Now that your plan to penetrate the VC with Chinese spies has failed. . ."

"It's not my bag. I'm only responsible for moving the bodies out of here. Once the cargo is on the plane. . . "

"Okay Mo, I give up. I promise not to push you on the job profile," said Herb. "It's none of my business anyway. Thanks for letting me have a look-see, and for your concern about my welfare. You made your point."

"Good. I'm not comfortable about preaching, but in your case, I thought I had to give it a try. I have no more advice to give," Mo's arm moved to Herb's shoulder. "Stay put and do your job. Keep out of the way of all the mean mother-fuckers—on both sides—who are out to make a name for themselves. And get your ass over to Hawaii. One week with Christie and you'll be a new man. I'll underwrite it."

"Sounds good, real good."

Herb watched Mo enter the Doom Club, and then began to walk along a dirt road close to the huge fence with its watchtowers encircling the base. He heard a rumbling noise and looked skyward; it was 'Old Spooky.' Herb watched as the moonlight swallowed up the old two engine cargo plane, with more fire power and destruction in its belly than any machinegun conceived by man. There was a frightful *clap-clap-clap*, and he observed the tracer bullets of thousands of rounds showering on the poor souls below. There was a quiet interval, laughter came from a nearby watchtower, followed by the shrill voices of Marine grunts.

"Fuck 'em, Spook. Fuck 'em."

"Hey Charlie, you sons-of-bitches. We got you by the balls, motherfuckers."

"Kiss my ass, Mister Charles! Don't fuck with the boss!"

There was more laughter and then silence. Spooky had disappeared, the youthful sounds of teenagers at play no longer filled the air. Herb glanced back at the Doom Club, and whispered, "Khiem Thao . . . Khiem Thao."

* * *

18

"**C**APTAIN Klein!"

"Speaking," replied Herb softly, as he cradled the telephone under his chin and completed a memorandum.

"This is Colonel Reed. How ya doin'!"

"Fine sir, and yourself?"

"Real good. Did I catch you at a bad time? I know you docs are always busy."

"No Colonel. Sick call is over, and Captain Black is taking care of the emergencies. I guess you're calling about my report."

"I'd like to review a few things if that's okay with you!"

"Shoot."

Herb opened the bottom drawer and put the duplicate copy atop the desk, its front page was torn in half, but the title remained.

AF FORM 14 A-AIRCRAFT ACCIDENT INVESTIGATION BOARD
MEDICAL REPORT-MAJOR WILLIAM STRICKLAND
MEDICAL INVESTIGATING OFFICER-HERBERT KLEIN, CAPTAIN MC USAF FMO

"He's drug free, right Doc?"

"Yes, sir. He wasn't taking any medication for an illness, no downers or uppers, and there wasn't any alcohol found in his blood."

"What's this lactic acid level and all the other blood work about?"

"If the lactate was high, Major Strickland may have suffered from lack of oxygen, but his wasn't. The other blood chemistries and gases were also normal. This doesn't exclude a transient black-out spell, due to hypoxia, because the samples were taken forty-five minutes after he ejected and the plane crashed. But based on the available information, there is no evidence for physiologic abnormalities and the Major is clean from a medical view."

"Okay Doc, then there's nothing about his physical or mental state that might have impaired his judgment."

"That's correct, Colonel. Any of the other board members suspect pilot error?"

"No, Doc. The aircraft maintenance officer feels there was a mechanical problem with the fuselage, but we're still in the preliminary stage. What do you suggest we do with Major Strickland at this point?"

"Colonel, I think he's ready to fly, but a more prudent approach might be to send him on R-and-R to someplace like Hawaii. The Major hasn't been out of Vietnam for five months, and a week with his wife might just tie all the loose ends together."

"Good idea. Why don't we do that. Thanks Doc, I know how valuable your time is."

"No problem, Colonel. Anytime."

The good Doctor always recommended R-and-R to a superior officer inquiring about an underling's disposition, it was the only panacea he knew. But like the proverbial medicine that treats symptoms rather than cause, R and R was purely a temporary cure.

For some, R-and-R was rest and relaxation. For most, it was a time and a place to forget. Armed with a pocketful of money and an attitude that there may not be another tomorrow to spend it, the American serviceman was hurtled by Pan American Airlines into a strange and exotic foreign country. What awaited him was a familiar sight, that cut across alien cultures—quick change artists, pimps, whores, live-in companions, junkies, drug pushers, omniscient taxidrivers, human parasites and leeches at every bar and streetcorner. They all offered a piece of heaven in return for a piece of their wallets. A few kept on walking, but many didn't.

The unattached had a choice: Hong Kong, Seoul, Tapai, Bangkok, Penang, Kuala Lampur, Singapore, or Manila. The picture postcard of Southeast Asia was 'GI Joe' dressed in light khaki pants, a multicolored short sleeve sport shirt, penny loafers, sunglasses and toting an Olympus pen camera. Hand in hand, he strolled with his miniskirted Oriental girlfriend.

Hawaii was different, a place reserved for couples, marrieds or singles with attachments. American-style restaurants and hotels, luaus, the Kodak picture show, International Bazaar, Catamaran cruises, car rentals and a tour of Oahu, a walk through a pineapple field, and that all-out search for the isolated beach where two people in love sought to insulate themselves from a world that had been less than fair.

The Pan-Am planes returned to Vietnam with silent and tired men; with R-and-R completed, the "short-timer" became a revered and honored position in the vernacular of the military.

Herb Klein was not a short-timer with more than six months left of his one year commitment, but he too, faced a familiar countdown. He picked up the two page letter on his desk and reread the last paragraphs:

> *. . . with that kind of heat and humidity, but it must be better than the rain and the monsoons.*
>
> *The best news for last. My reservations have been confirmed by both United Airlines and the Hotel Kuilana in Honolulu. I will be in Hawaii two days before your arrival. I've given myself extra leeway, in the event of any unforeseen difficulties. The mere thought of missing one possible moment in your arms is enough to ruin my day.*
>
> *With Everlasting Love,*
> *Christie*

> *P.S.: I forgot to mention that Sol Pincus is Ben's new pinochle partner. His old partner, Abe Cohen, finally retired to Miami Beach. After playing one night with Sol, Pop said he was sorry Abe hadn't left ten years ago, when he began complaining about the weather.*

He folded the letter and put it into his shirt pocket. He was suddenly aware that someone was standing at the door.

"Herb?" Freddy Black was holding the door open and prepared to knock a second time. "I need an expert on skin rashes."

"There must be another Herb around here. The only think I know about skin disease, is that a dermatologist comes to the hospital once a month from Cam Rahn Bay."

"Then have a voluntary look," said Fred while grabbing Herb's arm and guiding him into the emergency room.

Both men stood at the side of the examination table and examined the skin lesions. The patient, a Sergeant, was nude above the waist, and his pants were open at belt level.

"The damn thing is diffuse. It's present on the area around the ear, neck, upper chest, back," said Fred as he began to pull down the pants and underwear. "The groin is loaded. Pustules, comedones . . . are those cysts?"

Herb shrugged his shoulders, "Looks like pimples to me."

"Pimples? The Sarge is thirty, and never had an adolescent skin problem. I never saw a case of acne like this!"

"That's what it looks like to me, Fred."

"Pimples!" The Sergeant thought a moment and then turned to the doctors. "There is something I didn't tell you, Captain Black. I'm married, and I don't fool around like a lotta other guys, but I get the urge and everything. . .and, eh. . ."

"Yes, Sarge, we all have the urge. What are you trying to say?"

Hold it, Fred. I think I know what the Sarge is getting at. Are you talking about masturbation?" Herb spoke as he continued to study the curious lesions.

"Yea, Doc. I've been pulling on it a helluva lot these last couple of weeks, and some of the guys say you can get pimples."

"If jerking off caused pimples," Herb's gaze met the Sergeant's, "then clear skin would be a medical curiosity. Fred, I would try a sulfur ointment, and let's see what the dermatologist has to say."

"Then I can still fly?"

"Sure, Sarge," said Herb. "No reason to ground you. Who are you with?"

"Ranch Hands. I'm a load master."

"Doesn't your outfit defoliate trees and destroy crops?" Fred asked.

"Yes, Sir! The Ranch Hand's motto is 'Only We Can Prevent Forests,' and you better believe it. You oughta see us in action, Doc. Six C-123s can destroy a half mile by ten miles of one of those hardwood forests in no time flat. By the time we're through, the only thing that's going to grow is bamboo. Charlie can use them for blow guns," laughed the Sergeant. "I can tell you one thing for sure. No way those sons-of-bitches are gonna hide or eat anything from the ground after we're finished sprayin'."

"Has your skin ever been exposed to the herbicides?"

"Yes sir, Captain Black. I got sprayed accidentally, and I've touched the stuff. It's a gooey brownish-orange liquid, thick like oil. This agent is the most common one, and we use it against mangrove and hardwood forests. There's another white herbicide we use against certain trees and jungle, and a blue type for crops. But it's that brown stuff that gets the biggest play."

"What do you think, Herb? Could there be a connection . . . The acne and the herbicides?"

"Captain Klein?" Frank Lincoln stood at the door awaiting recognition, "Excuse me, sir, but your next appointment is a few minutes early. Should I have him wait?"

"That's okay, Sarge. You can put him in my office. I'm finished." Herb's darting eyes once again focussed on the Sergeant's skin lesion, as he once more confirmed the extent and characteristics of the puzzling disease. "Fred, I just don't know," he said with a shrug of the shoulders.

Herb left the emergency room, walked to the bathroom at the end of the hall, and angrily shut the door with a loud bang. He relieved himself, drank water with cupped hands and rubbed his tired eyes with wet fingers; looking into the mirror, his index digit slowly traversed the scar from above the orbit to his mandible. Herb reached for his wallet and his mother-in-law's gift; the necklace in place and fully exposed, the Jewish Star of David glistened as it rested on a shirt button.

"Mind if I smoke?" A lit cigarette dangled from the side of his lips; he wore flying-fatigues and combat boots, but had not removed the standard Air Force sunglasses used by pilots. "Go right ahead," said Herb sitting in the desk chair a few feet away from his visitor.

"I'm here to apologize to you and Lee, not to be forgiven. What I did is inexcusable . . . "

"That's not necessary. I really don't want to hear your confession. Why don't you see the Chaplain?"

Captain Josh Trent took a few deep puffs, recirculated the smoke through his nose, and then squashed the cigarette into an ashtray. Ignoring Herb's remark, he spoke in a crackling voice, his head bowed toward the floor. "I remember every second. I might've seemed drunk out of my mind, but nothing could be further from the truth. After the VC destroyed Bruce Evans and his crew, everybody was on edge. The tension was indescribable. The night mission before the rape had been a laugher. Charlie slept, and the only bangs from Spooky that evening were the Navigator's farts. Bud Rich is usually talkative, but he was quiet as hell. When we debriefed at HQ, Cal Richter was waiting for us. I knew he was Bruce's replacement, we had chugged a few beers at the Doom Club, and he seemed like an OK guy. Cal had flown B-52's for SAC, and volunteered when he saw a chance to get his feet wet in the Nam. Bud suggested a pick-me-up, and we all went back to the trailer. After a few shots, Bud started to talk about a surprise party. Cal said something like 'you mean a sweet little pussy like. . .' Bud never let him finish, and that was the first inkling I had of the morning's activities. I'm sure our navigator, Lieutenant Foley, was in the dark. He kept on asking questions."

"I hope you're not trying to condone your actions and Foley's because you weren't involved in the planning. Shit! I know you fellas were under tremendous pressure, but you went off the deep end."

"Doc, you're wrong about Foley. By the time Lee knocked at the door to clean the room, we were plastered. I heard Bud whisper to Foley that Lee had consented to a gang bang, and that he should be lookout. They pushed Dan out, and friendly Cal asked Lee to remove some trash in the kitchen. It got ugly real quick, and Lee sensed trouble right away—you could see it in her eyes, the fear. They grabbed her and she resisted up to the point of threats made to mammasan and pappysan . . . the family bit made her into a passive lamb. Bud kept on saying we were putting our lives on the line for her country, and she laughed at the Americans behind our backs. 'You owe us,' he kept yelling, 'you owe us.' Sure, I knew it was a bunch of shit! It was rape, but I wanted Lee, and I stood by and didn't raise a finger. At that moment, Lee became more important to me than anything in my life . . . my wife, kids, parents, Country, self respect . . . and yes, even you Doc." Captain Trent raised his head, and Herb realized he was hiding embarrassed tears behind those sunglasses.

Then Trent continued. "I let them rough you up, and even helped in the trailer. My mind drew a blank and my prick took over. I listened as they spread those filthy lies about you shacking up with Lee, and your trying to protect your own ass by accusing us of rape. I watched Bud Rich pick a fight, pull a knife, and cut you with no provocation on your part. I agreed with the CO and Colonel Stalley to keep my mouth shut for the morale of the base, and the bad publicity that the anti-war press. . ."

"When did you talk to the CO and Colonel Stalley?" interrupted Herb.

"Two days after the big rumble at the Doom Club. That same night I was told to button up, and they would handle the whole matter. The three of us were sent on R-and-R, and I understand you went away to a Vietnamese hospital. When I got back, it was as if nothing had happened."

"Would you repeat this to the authorities and testify in a military courtroom?"

"You bet. That was the whole idea when I went to the CO in the first place. I can't live with this thing on my conscience. I ought to be strung up by my balls in a cell."

"It's not going to happen, Trent. I've already talked to the Judge Advocate's office, there is no case without Lee's cooperation, and she refuses to press charges. Your testimony wouldn't change a thing. All of you are free men in the eyes of the military and the law."

"Great! So I guess my punishment was a week of R and R in Bangkok," sneered Captain Trent. "Maybe I can get another week in Hong Kong if I rape the ARVN commander's wife."

"Listen," Herb spoke in a comforting voice, moved in spite of himself by Trent's contrition. "Spooky is a ball-buster. I don't know how you guys fly that death trap night after night. You messed up, but nobody's going to touch you. A guy with a conscience who wants to pay back debts can be a big item around here."

"Since we're on the subject of Spooky, Doc, let me dispel another myth. Bud Rich and yours truly are not gung-ho heroes in the sky. On more than a few occasions, we let loose with our little mini-gattling guns at high altitudes to protect our ass. I know for a fact that Bruce Evans never shot his wad over 3,000 feet. That would be a first for Bud Rich's crew."

"Would you like to hook up with another crew?"

"I've thought about that, but HQ frowns on transfers. Let's say I consider it part of my punishment to be his co-pilot. He's aware of how I feel about him, and I want both majors to know that if they don't behave themselves, I'm ready to blow the whistle."

"Let me think about a few things, and I'll get back to you," said Herb as he stood up.

"God, I'm sorry Doc. What else can I say or do?" sighed the pilot. Herb said nothing and concentrated on having no expression whatever on his face. He walked out of the room and Trent followed him into the hallway. Dave Wyatt and Freddy Black standing together nearby, quickly turned away, and made themselves busy with a medical chart. Frank Lincoln stood at the foyer entrance conversing with Airman Brent, a huge muscular medic who was the hospital enforcer and appropriately known as 'Moose.'

"You and I are even. I'm here, if you need me. Good luck, Captain," said Herb in a loud voice meant for the others to hear.

Why was he letting Trent off the hook? The answer eluded him. Herb's problem all along was trying to find a punishment to fit the crime. The solution turned out to be a pat on the back, and a warning not to break into the cookie jar. Was that justice? Was this the whole revenge package he had conceived those many sleepless hours?

Then again, what was he to do? Lee had closed the door to other remedies. Not only had she refused to testify, but had left Da Nang and disappeared. She believed, along with most of her countrymen, that raising your hand and crying foul had become a national pastime that would elicit only laughter. The Judge Advocate's office had made its position known, and finally Herb was made aware of the base leadership's position.

Colonel Stalley, the hospital commander, had always implied that he believed Herb's account of the 'Lee Incident' even though no one had corroborated his version. Trent's confession had never been mentioned. Herb also understood why after many refusals to initiate a Civilian Aid Program at the Provincial Hospital level, the Colonel had finally consented to his recommendations. It was all part of the cover-up. How naive he was to believe that improved health care for Geeks should take precedence over base morale and bad press.

But there had been something glaringly missing from Trent's confession. He wished the Captain had apologized for the anti-Semitic remarks. Hadn't the 'Spooky' pilot seen his Star of David? Perhaps a gentle reminder at their next meeting would be in order.

"Airman Brent," said Dave Wyatt in a strong voice, "would you please return this chart to the record room?"

Herb's actions had been clear; Moose's services would not be required after all.

* * *

19

CHRISTIE Klein climbed the narrow, winding spiral staircase, opened an old creaking door, and walked to her favorite seat in the last row of Osler General Hospital's original surgical amphitheater. No longer of any practical value, this medical curiosity was in need of repair and the painter's brush. For a hundred years it had been a primary source of instruction to eager medical students, both as a lecture hall and a surgical arena in the era prior to the advent of sterile technique. It had been rumored, though never substantiated, that Sir William Osler's earliest lectures at this very Hall, were the basis for his *The Principles and Practice of Medicine;* a leading textbook of its time and the standard by which future medical writers would be judged.

The circular old amphitheater was capped with a dome. A huge round window at the apex was the room's only source of sunlight. Above the two adjoining, massive oak doors that were the main entrance to the Hall was an oil painting Christie admired. Its setting was the hospital lawn; medical students, attending doctors, and nurses watched as Sir William Osler examined an elderly woman in distress. There were twelve figures in the painting and ten of the spectators wore expressions of gloom and despair. Only on Sir William's face was there a suggestion of a smile.

Christie turned away from the painting and peered through the skylight. It was another cold, cloudy day, devoid of sunlight with the promise of snow. She removed her nurse's cap, and silently cursed the nursing supervisor for making this monstrosity mandatory wearing apparel. She eagerly opened her brown bag and took out a peanut butter and jelly sandwich, half-pint of milk, an apple, and six of Herb's letters.

It felt good to be alone, an opportunity to enjoy silence and a few minutes to daydream—a walk along the river, a park bench, a beach with thunderous waves, a picnic in the countryside, a roll in the golden leaves of autumn, a snowball fight, a newborn flower, a bed to hold and to be held in, Herb and Christie, Christie and Herb.

The old amphitheater had become her refuge. She could no longer eat in the cafeteria without nurses, hospital workers, technicians, medical students, House staff, fraternity brothers stopping by her table and asking about Herb. There was always that serious look of concern; many would ask for his address to write, and a few did; all offered their regards and an offer to "help." Her life had become a series of on-going encounters with well-intentioned good samaritans.

Molly and Horace Flint insisted she eat her meals at their table. Ben was just as vehement about Christie spending Friday evenings in his company at the Wyal Street row house. Thursday evening was the mandatory telephone call to Neschaunk; Momma returned the call on the weekend when the rates were lower. Even Paul was seeing her regularly, though she suspected his own problems had created a need for sibling togetherness. Her brother was a conscientious objector, exempt from military duty but unhappy as a hospital orderly.

Herb insisted that his wife attend social events, and had solicited the assistance of Peter James and Mark Jarden. Peter was a recent escort at a Beta Sigma Tau fraternity party. (Swenson House was no longer the site of swinging blasts and rowdy brothers blowing off steam.) The changes were pronounced. Beards and moustaches were common, and brothers wore blue jeans and work shirts; gone and forgotten were the ties and jackets, and clean-shaven faces that were standard in the Fall of '64. The conversations had political overtones, that invariably included the war. This group of brothers, particularly the underclassmen, did not have the care-free style of Herb's contemporaries; group singing, guitars, and laughter had been replaced by pot, Dylan, and political activism. Beta Sig's collective sense of humor was clearly in rapid decline.

And no wonder—the fraternity had become a focal point for a small but growing anti-war movement at Osler General Hospital with Peter James as leader of the revolt. The transition wasn't complete, but the die had been cast. Peter had called a few days earlier to tell Christie, that a bare majority of the brotherhood had approved his proposal to invite a Quaker peace activist as a guest lecturer, to advise interested students on ways to avoid the draft. There was another vote at the same meeting just narrowly defeated (Peter was not the sponsor, nor a supporter), a resolution to dissolve the Keller Report and Sisters of Mercy Proclamation. Beta Sigma Tau was losing its reputation as the Osler Hospital playground. The fraternity had set its course. No longer would it provide strip shows, smokers, and beer parties that got out of hand. Women and booze were being replaced by events in Southeast Asia. It was a time to get serious or freak-out.

Christie wholeheartedly endorsed the transformation, but rejected Peter's request for a more active role in the anti-war movement. In the hospital, she sometimes wore a peace button, and her opinions were available when asked, but this was the extent of her involvement. And there was another bothersome consideration: what was Herb's view of the war?

Her mind reasoned that it was an irrelevant question. She had always been an independent thinker, a rebel in the eyes of her family and friends, yet loyalty and devotion to Herb had become more important than the movement. Herb was aware of his wife's anti-war stand, but he never gave the slightest hint of his own position. The subject had become taboo, and Christie's subtle inquiries about the war were simply never answered. Herb's letters continued unchanged; they dealt with minutia and never with substantive matters. He was covering up for her sake, but he resented the protective, child-like tone of his mail. Her own letters had taken a similar turn, man and wife tried to reinforce each other's fantasy that they lived in a trouble-free world. It was this uncertainty—not of Herb's position, but of his failure to state it—that created a dilemma for Christie. Why? It all seemed so clear. Was she missing something? Christie decided to temper her enthusiasm until she could raise the issue with Herb. She wasn't after his approval, so much as a compelling reason why she shouldn't walk the streets with a placard protesting the horrors of Vietnam. Despite her strong convictions, she would await their conversation.

The other pipeline to Da Nang was Mark Jarden. He vacillated, his information was uneven and unreliable—more questions were raised than answered. She was not surprised when told of her husband's rebellious spirit, his constant probing and seeking to understand, tackling tough problems with tougher solutions. Herb was never the kind to walk away from a wrong, when he felt it was in his power to right it. Uncertainty of the physical and mental cost of those decisions continued to disturb Christie. The Vietnam War would take its toll, but had her husband been touched in a way that would alter and possibly destroy what they had worked so hard to build? She had no way of knowing, and Mark's revelations only added to the confusion.

The evening of the great blizzard spent in Ted's Southwark Tavern had been typical. Christie had broken through Mark's resistance, and a week later he was telling her another story; there had been a rape by Air Force officers, no romance took place between her husband and Lee, but it was true that Herb sustained a knife injury to his face (he wasn't sure about the size). His previous information had been based on rumors, but now he was sure of the facts; this was the truth, but there were other truths.

Herb was a hero, and was to receive two medals. He had been awarded the Silver Star for bravery in a sea-rescue operation in the Gulf of Tonkin that saved a marine pilot's life, and a Commendation Decoration from the South Vietnamese government for his work in Village Pacification and the Province hospital at Hoi An. Her husband no longer was thought of as a carefree, reckless doctor trying to set the world on fire and rectify all its evils. He now had the respect and the admiration of the flyboys, as well as his peers. A few of his friends had intervened, and Herb was content to spend his time on base. The message had finally registered: Don't look for trouble, and trouble won't look for you. Mark had also mentioned the possibility of her meeting Herb in Hawaii, so she was not totally unprepared when that came to pass. Hawaii gave her strength, it was to be one of the great times of her life.

The anguish and frustration of that evening at Southwark Tavern had been overcome, but not without a battle. After Mark had fallen asleep, she borrowed blankets from Ted (refusing his pleas to sleep in the guest room), and added another massive log to the hearth. Sitting in front of the blazing fire, listening to the howling wind and crackling embers, she tried to assimilate all that was happening to her husband. She feared for his safety and their love. Her meeting with Mark had been designed to get at the truth, and now her mind sought to make it a big lie. Christie refused to believe that Herb could love another woman. What they had before Vietnam, remained unchanged until she could hold her husband, seek his eyes, listen to his voice—then she would know. It was a conclusion not reached easily.

She did not sleep that night. Fantasies of a different Herb—wild, noncaring, lustful, crazed by war—had to be played out. Visions of a disturbed and callous husband returning home—understanding, time, infinite patience, and her presence would be necessary to reawaken his dormant love. Her imagination played nasty games in front of dancing flames of the fire until she was spent. Cigarettes and hot coffee could not stifle the dirty tricks. The mind continued to unravel the worst possible scenarios: their love was in jeopardy, a separation was imminent, a divorce inevitable.

The tears and hurt were replaced by the realization that only seeing Herb could make a difference. The inventions of a fanciful imagination was one challenge, Mark's second-hand information another: Christie knew she had the strength and determination to meet both, and anything else that might develop. As the morning light seeped into the Tavern, a tired but relaxed Christie was at peace with herself. Nothing had changed.

Mark Jarden's new pronouncements were received with a sense of amusement and detachment. The real world was the Island of Oahu. She was to meet him at the Fort Zama Army processing center, and not at the Honolulu Airport as she had originally envisioned. Her imagination reeled at the prospect of that first encounter. How different from the evening at Ted's place when the thought of happiness seemed as chilly as the wind, the whirling snow drifts, and the shivering cold of that colossal winter storm.

Hawaii was warmth, a dreamland, a place to build castles, a Garden of Eden. Herb was the magician who would make it all possible. He would turn her dark reverie into sunlit reality, and bring joy back into her life. Christie Klein returned the half-eaten sandwich to the brown bag, the milk and apple were left untouched. It was important that her lithe body retain not one extra ounce. Herb would know and gently kid her; she mustn't give him the opportunity.

She gazed across the circular benches of the old amphitheater and focused on the podium. Sir William Osler had lectured from that platform, she could see it all in her mind's eye: the house staff listening attentively, trying to understand the great man's every word.

Her husband had never mentioned this surgical area. "Together," Christie mumbled to herself, as she started to daydream, "we will share in its delights."

She thought she heard him whisper softly: "I need you."

"It's crazy, but I feel the same way," she answered.

"Stand-up, and let me hold you tightly," said Herb in a firm, gentle voice.

He held her in his arms. Sunlight poured down from the massive window at the top of the amphitheater dome. Christie's hands massaged his back, and then danced over his curly hair. Her lips kissed a barely perceptable scar on the cheek. His soft-spoken, tender manner enhanced her excitement.

"I love you. I love you, Christie."

"I must have you Herb. I must."

She gently pushed him away and pulled down his slacks and underwear. Mouths and hands fervently explored the targets of their passion. She positioned him on the bench, and then sat on his lap. Christie's legs entwined Herb's back, they were one.

Slowly and methodically, with care and precision, they moved in harmony to the rhythm of life. They smiled and their eyes met, expressions of joy in each other's happiness. Their breathing became rapid; body movements were coordinated over a longer range of motion.

"Herb! Fill me up. Oh, my love, fill me up."

As the warmth of Herb became part of Christie, their lips and bodies merged in a sweet caress. It was not over. They continued to hold each other, exchange endearments and share the rapture. She delighted at his compassion and tenderness. They hugged each other over and over, and then . . . a final kiss.

There was silence in the amphitheater, except for Christie's sobs. She reached for a tissue in her uniform, and wiped away the tears. She cried, not so much out of despair or self pity, but for the happiness that awaited her in Hawaii.

Christie's gaze again surveyed the lecture hall, it halted at the painting of Sir William administering to the sick patient. "I want so much to believe that Osler can aid that poor, suffering woman. Maybe . . . " she thought, and then added aloud, "No! He did help her!"

She smiled and glanced at the wall clock. It was time to return to the Pediatric ward, and care for her sick children.

* * *

20

"C'MON, Freddy! Out with it. How many times?"

"Shit, Dave! There are some personal things in a man's life. What's *your* hack-off rate?"

"Funny you should ask. Since my surgical residency days, I've learned to suture with my left hand. In response to my distinguished colleague, the eminent Dr. Black's question," Dave Wyatt waved his shot glass, "I'm a southpaw on Tuesday, a rightie on Thursday, and I combine my skills on weekends."

Brad Frantz and Mo Balen chuckled as Sergeant Frank Lincoln entered the medical conference room of the base hospital. Herb grinned from one side of his mouth as he puffed on a favorite pipe—it was a straight grain briar, squat bulldog design with a diamond-shape shank, cutty stem, and wedge bit; a gift from Christie.

"Now here's a guy who'll give me some honest answers," continued Dave. "Sarge, you are the only guy other than Freddy who's been to Hawaii. How many times did you get laid and who holds the Da Nang record?"

"The lab tech, Sergeant Cropple, claims he shot his wad twenty-two times in under six days. As for me, I did a lotta boozin' in Honolulu. I wanna be straight with you Cap'n," moaned Lincoln, "Me and the little woman only went at it four times."

"Sarge, you're kidding!" lamented a disbelieving Major Frantz.

"I'm not jokin', Major. I only remember the first day, and I'm sure of the number. My ol' lady won't tell me the final score. But I know one thing! She walked around bowlegged for a month."

"Hey Doc! Do you think you can become the new champ?" Brad spoke after the laughter subsided.

Herb nodded affirmatively: "I'll give it my best shot. If I can screw as well as you fellas can bullshit my chances are good."

The surprise party for Herb was Brad Frantz's idea. A few of his closest friends celebrated the Philly doc's recent good fortunes; Hawaii, kudos, and the 'Lee Affair' had been put to rest with Herb smelling like a rose. The good Doc had finally come around.

He was no longer flying dangerous missions to fire bases and hot spots like Khe Sahn to help improve morale within the squadron, or to determine the medical needs of grunts and Geeks. The sea rescue of the Marine pilot had been his last trip north. A new directive from Colonel Stalley prevented flight surgeons from flying sea-rescue missions unless authorized by him. Spooky and all other planes flying combat missions were off-limits to medical personnel.

There were no more planned medical trips to the boonies; Victor Charlie didn't like the idea of Herb making friends on his turf. And when he turned to the Hoi An Provincial Hospital, the South Vietnamese government candy-coated a similar message: Thank you for your offer, Doctor Klein, but we prefer to handle our own problems in our own way.

And no longer were Herb's accusations against Bud Rich and his cohorts a divisive nightmare for the base hierarchy; an issue that had created two armed camps, undercut base morale, and was potentially devasting to a war effort in desperate need of a good press.

Herb had become a model flight surgeon: sick call in the morning, 'special clinic' in his spare time, Hospital rounds at the Casualty Staging Unit, participation in medically related aviation problems, emergency duty every fourth night. Doc Klein had finally shaped up. His days as a boat rocker were over; he would simply do his job and in a little more than six months, return home. Vietnam would be a memory, and someone else's problems. If there were lingering doubts, Hawaii and Christie were sure to dispel them.

"You've hurt our feelings, Herb," said Dave in a small voice barely above a whisper. "Twenty-two squirts by Sergeant Cropple is a prestigious accomplishment. You're going to need help my friend. Mo!"

"To set the right mood and compensate for your many inadequacies, we chipped in and got a few things to help lighten Christie's load. Living with a mess like you has to be awfully stressful." Balen continued to speak as he picked up a box beside his chair, and opened it on the table. "From My-Hanh's shop, the best damn tailor in Da Nang: a pair of red pajamas, matching robe, and ao dai, and undergarmets. All hand made, and the measurements are Christie's. Don't ask me how Mark Jarden got the numbers."

"Silk, pure silk!" an astonished Herb felt the material.

"Pewter from Malaysia," Mo handed the flight surgeon a huge mug with the inscription, *TOGETHER, WE RIDE PEGASUS.*

"How in the world did you know . . ."

"And last, but not least," Mo interrupted Herb, and opened a jewel box. "Tokoyo. Mikimoto's. A string of pearls. There are other screwballs not here, who contributed, when the word got out that your wife was taking you away from Da Nang for a week."

"If you don't go, we have to give them their money back," added Major Frantz."

"You fellas are nuts. I don't believe it. I'm speechless."

"Don't be, Herb. Enjoy Hawaii, and while we're at it, congratulations on your medals," smiled Freddy Black reaching for a glass to propose a toast.

"I should have told you," Herb shook his pipe to remove the moisture from the stem. "I've refused the awards."

"What?" cried Dave Wyatt, angrily. "You earned the fuckin' medals. Take 'em. What's with you?"

"Look Dave, Maybe it goes back to the rocket attacks on the base, and some of those fellas on their knees begging for purple hearts, as if a splinter in your ass is no differint from a shot-up Marine with a bullet in his head. I just have a sour taste in my mouth over the whole business. Every grunt who totes an M-16, or jockey that flies a combat mission puts his life on the line every day. They are entitled to a Silver Star a helluva lot more than I am. The South Vietnamese Commendation Citation is just a way of putting a lid on the Hoi An Hospital incident when those VC were tortured and killed. I'm not knocking kudos for guys who do more than their share, but I'm not one of the deserving."

"Maybe we ought to give the medals to Bud Rich for his outstanding service above and beyond the call of duty," suggested Brad, sarcastically.

"Since you mentioned it, Brad, I want you to know that I've been thinking a lot about the 'Lee incident' since Josh Trent visited me, and am seriously considering reopening the case with the Judge Advocate's office. Maybe Trent's confession will make a difference even in the absence of Lee's testimony."

"Herb," Dave Wyatt squared his shoulders and frowned, "this party is not turning out the way we planned. We thought we were celebrating a new beginning, not a rehash of the old crap. Now, are you going to Hawaii, or do we send this stuff," he pointed to Christie's gifts, "back to Philly with your name on it?"

"Sure I'm going to Hawaii," laughed Herb. "But first, I have to go away for a week, and then I'll return to Da Nang to prepare for Christie and the world's screwing record. Don't worry gentlemen, I intend to give Cropple a run for his money."

Mo looked troubled. "Where the hell are you going?"

"Good news! I finally got Colonel Stalley to approve a medical assistance program for Montagnard tribesmen. I got a guarantee of no interference from either our people or the Vietnamese. I just go there, set up shop, and the Colonel will provide the supplies." There was a brief, thick silence. "Look, these people have never seen a doctor. I think the pilot program will work. . ."

"Excuse me Cap'n," said a puzzled Frank Lincoln. "The Montagnards are in the mountains with the Green Berets. That's injun' country. Are you gonna be in a Special Forces camp for a week?"

"That's right, Sarge. This garden spot is called Bia Vuc, and it's in the Central Highlands. The gnards are aborigines, a real primitive type, but I understand they're good people." Herb turned away from his friends and looked through the window. "I see this as a real opportunity. Nobody telling me what to do, just me and the 'gnards. Fellas, I really feel good about this one."

The party guests, immobile and speechless, stared at their honored friend. His pipe, held tightly at the angle of the mouth, rested almost perpendicular to the linear, reddish cheek scar. The sunlight illuminated his side profile, smoke from the bowl made concentric circles over the conference table. Herb Klein's words pierced the air, sharp and crisp like a cutting edge. "This may be what I've been looking for," he muttered. "It's a fresh start, a new vision. Bia Vuc has great possibilities."

* * *

21

THE reader eagerly turned the page, moved a hand into his front pocket, and gently stroked his erection. "Wow!" he thought, "Banging the gardener, and her husband's sleeping in the next room!"

"Sunny!"

An attentive Sergeant Watts forcefully pressed the speaker button of his head set: "Yes sir!"

"We're going to be landing in a few minutes. Why don't you make sure our guests are comfie!" chuckled the pilot, Captain Walt Pellham.

"Son-of-a-bitch does it everytime," cursed the loadmaster as he tossed the paperback into a bin.

The two water buffalo remained passive. Their head movements were slight, legs and chests were held tightly by overriding belts attached to the sides and floor of the aircraft. The animals had not been affected by either the engine noise or the bad turbulence earlier in the flight. Sunny retightened the straps and then made his way toward the cockpit while checking to see if the containers of food, ammunition, and medical supplies were properly anchored.

"A-OK," radioed Sunny.

He secured his seat belt, and studied the clip board. The cargo weight data was reviewed, and the loadmaster rechecked the addition. The passenger list had one name: Capt. Herbert Klein, FMO. "Holy shit! What a layover. ETA 0800 and Departure 1200!" mumbled the Sergeant.

Sunny never liked flying into a Special Forces camp, a four hour stopover made him jittery. The short dirt runways were always a hazard, and you knew that Charlie was watching your every move. On more than a few occasions, the plane would land, quickly unload, taxi, and go home. The engines were never shut off, and Sunny's boots never touched the ground.

These camps, located in desolate, remote mountainous areas, were virtually impossible to secure. Two Special Forces camps, Tu Lin and Ga Ku, had already been leveled and were no longer on the flight itinerary. Why the others weren't overrun by the VC was a mystery to Sunny. He believed the Green Berets were off their rockers; only loonies could live with savages right smack in the middle of Charlieville. He had no such death wish. Once in Bia Vuc, the loadmaster would find the nearest bunker and return to his novel.

The C-123 came to a halt and the two engines suddenly shut off. The huge, rear panel was opened and sunlight bathed the plane's interior. Sunny felt the cool mountain air as he looked into the faces of the Montagnard porters. They were mostly older men with a few young boys scattered here and there; all were thin, small, brown skinned, and had dark, stringy hair. They wore loin cloths, some had turbans, and all were barefoot. The sight of the two water buffalo gave rise to frantic gesticulation and animated conversation among the tribesmen

Montagnard soldiers in fatigues, combat boots, and ranger hats encircled the plane; they faced the river and mountains surrounding the camp, their M-16 rifles in a ready position. A tall, wiry, muscularly built American soldier stood with arms akimbo, a blond burr haircut was partially hidden by a beret. He barked out orders in the porter's native tongue to empty the cargo into an Army truck.

A double row of barbed wire fences spaced a few yards apart encircled the area. Skull and cross bone signs warned of mines. The gate and entranceway to the compound had another sign which caught the Sergeant's attention:

THE PROS
CO "C" 6 SPECIAL FORCES (AIRBORNE)
R" SPECIAL FORCES (RVN)
BIA VUC

"Jesus, Mary, and Joseph," thought Sunny, "now I gotta find the sign that says BUNKER."

"What do you think, Doc?"
"It's great. You didn't exaggerate."

They stood on a hilltop overlooking the valley and Bia Vuc. Herb absorbed the beautiful sea of green that danced before his eyes, the low hanging clouds and the truncated mountain tops, and a river winding its way through the wilderness.

It was because of the commanding view and strategic position, that Mount Servin had become an important observation post to the defense posture of Bia Vuc. The summit was well fortified with interlacing tunnels and bunkers. In the middle were dug out holes covered by straw roofs.

The families of the men who guarded the outpost lived in those straw covered pits. Herb peered through an opening and saw a young woman, her hair held together by a white cloth. She wore only a black wraparound skirt from the waist to her ankles. Four necklaces covered the upper chest and an infant suckled a sagging breast.

Herb counted twelve Montagnard soldiers, all armed with M-16s and grenades. A few wore standard military fatigues, but most were dressed in traditional tribal attire. Two machine guns remained unattended as the flight surgeon strolled around the periphery of the bunkers. When he met a 'gnard, his smile was always returned.

"Over here Doc," said the lean, jaw-boned soldier. His blond hair glistened in the mid-afternoon sun as he sat on a small grass patch, its location provided a superb view of Bia Vuc and its environs. "This is the designated picnic area," continued Captain John Bixler, the top ranking Special Forces Officer and Herb's personal guide. "Today's menu . . . Chateaubriand Steak or Prime Roast Beef?"

Herb adroitly caught the C-rations box in midair. Its label read: Hot Dogs And Beans—U.S. Army, Packaged 1951. "Only sixteen years old. The food in Hawaii may be a big letdown after this feast."

It had been a hectic day. Captain Bixler had supervised the removal of the C-123s cargo. The discovery of long overdue supplies prompted an immediate visit to the village school; a small room with twenty smiling children of various ages, and a distressed Vietnamese teacher who looked like he would willingly trade his chalk for a rifle. One side of the room had a large map of South Vietnam, propaganda photographs and drawings depicting VC atrocities and the exploits of the Saigon government. It was the back wall that amused Herb: anatomy charts of the eye, gastrointestinal tract, heart, and brain with detailed explanations in the French language. A huge red and yellow Vietnamese flag dwarfed a small blackboard behind the teacher's desk.

On the return trip to the military compound, the jeep narrowly missed one of the water buffalo in from Da Nang. It was in the camp, prior to the start of a requested tour of the village by Major Frantz, that Captain Bixler was apprised of a VC probe: Sergeant Pralley and his Montagnard scouts on patrol, had located unfriendlies on a nearby slope.

Lieutenant Alan Stone stood by the 105mm Howitzer, and Sergeant Tom Flaherty assumed his position behind a 50 caliber machine gun. They were the other two members of the Special Forces team stationed within the confines of Bia Vuc. Bixler contacted Pralley by phone; coordinates and fixes were obtained, and instructions relayed. One of the Montagnard soldiers assisting in the artillery loading motioned to the three Air Force officers to cover their ears. After a few minutes of Howitzer and machine gun fire, the Captain signaled cease fire. He reported a few kills; the other VC had scrambled. Pralley and his troopers would mop up.

Captain Bixler described to his Air Force visitors how the VC constantly probed the camp's defenses and its state of readiness. To combat this threat, patrols of Montagnard soldiers headed by a Green Beret, scoured the countryside around the vicinity of Bia Vuc in pursuit of the enemy. Telephone and electronic devices planted in strategic areas allowed them to communicate with the commanding officer who planned and coordinated countermeasures.

In addition to the four Berets in or around Bia Vuc (the present rotation kept Bixler, Lieutenant Stone, and Sergeant Flaherty in the camp and Sergeant Pralley patrolling the perimeter) two other members of the Special Forces team were on a two week overnight with an unspecified number of Montagnard soldiers. The Captain was vague about the team's mission. They gathered information, harrassed, and interdicted the flow of supplies in the enemy's backyard.

A stationary C-123 and the VC presence called for an earlier departure than planned. Sergeant Watt's absence was the only delay, but two 'gnard youngsters playing tag recalled seeing a stranger peeking out of a bunker near the main gate.

Herb had taken photographs throughout the morning with his Pentax camera (another memory to share with Christie and the children), and gave the roll of film to Brad to develop. In one week Major Frantz would return, unless Herb needed emergency medical supplies or requested an earlier Da Nang arrival.

It was at the landing strip, watching the big bird winging its way back to Da Nang, that Captain Bixler turned to Herb and suggested the long treck to the Mount Servin observation post overlooking Bia Vuc.

"Peaches!" Herb offered the can to Bixler, but the Captain nodded his disapproval.

"I can't stand canned fruit. Well, Doc, what do you think of our little corner of the universe?"

"It's a little different than I thought when I first saw it at ground level. There are clusters of houses that only partially surround the compound."

"That's right. They are actually four separate villages—A, B, C, D— in a semi-circle around the core. You can see how the runway is parallel and between the river and the compound. The dirt roads interconnect like the spokes of a wheel."

Herb peered through the binoculars. "What's that plot of ground between the two villages on the far right?"

"Burial grounds. You'll get a chance to see it close up, soon," Bixler pointed. "We'll be visiting a house on that nearby slope."

"Why are there two fenced-in areas toward the river side?"

"They divide two separate mine fields, the French's and ours. The French mines date back to the days of your C-rations. We don't even know if they'll detonate. Our mine field is more extensive, and is only a year and half old."

"What are those three round dug out areas between the metal framed buildings? They appear camouflaged." Herb went to high power, and then handed the glasses to their owner.

"Mortar pits." Captain Bixler took out a cigarette, and then threw the pack like a grenade to a gnard sentry in combat fatigues. "He's fourteen and a veteran. Real mean. His sister was raped, and father killed by the VC. He'd like to be out in the field killing Charlie, but we rotate. Everyone is treated the same around here."

The young soldier raised his M-16 above the head (the other hand held the Lucky Strikes) and yelled, "America, number one . . . America, number one."

"That's for you, Doc. He knows you're the new boy in town. That's probably the extent of his English."

Herb approached the Montagnard trooper, and offered the peaches and other untouched cans from the C-ration boxes. He put an arm around the youngster's shoulder, and whispered into his ear. Herb's comments created an immediate reaction. The excited soldier barked an order and other tribesmen appeared. Women with small children emerged from their straw covered adobes and joined in the banter, they too waved and smiled with obvious pleasure. Many of the men shook hands with the American newcomer, before he returned to an amused Captain Bixler.

"What the hell was that all about, Doc?"

Herb once again waved his hand at the tribemen, and then turned to the Captain. "I said 'Bia Vuc and Montagnards, number one.'"

Herb waited for the giggles and the laughter to subside before continuing. "I understand the topography, but what about the people and history of Bia Vuc! Where do you and your boys fit in? And by the way, Captain, forget the bullshit you fed my two pilot friends about security. I'm not a Congressman in search of good answers, or a reporter trying to meet a deadline and looking for a scoop. Charlie and the NVA can walk into Bia Vuc and kick your ass. The only thing you can do is spread your cheeks."

Bixler took a deep drag on his cigarette, his sweaty skin glistened under the hot afternoon sun. "You're alright Doc, and I don't use those words loosely. Let me first start with your last point. Yeah, the bad guys can take over this place, but they're gonna pay a helluva price. My guess is it would probably take a regiment to do the job, and it better be a good one. I'm talking two thousand men versus my Special Forces team, and three hundred 'gnards. And Doc, don't let their size, good nature, and primitive ways throw you. These fellas are damn tough. When they buy what you're selling, they fight to the death with no questions asked. Do you know about Spooky?"

"I'm familiar with her act," nodded Herb.

"Aside from air support, the Army has special fast reaction units, and there are Mick teams to help out when the shit hits the fan. Intelligence stays on top of things, and makes sure there are no big surprises. So far, Charlie has been content on stealing rice and bypassing Bia Vuc for bigger and better prizes. Sure, there are a few 'gnards here who are VC sympathizers, but this camp is better than most."

"Why are you any different than Tu Lin and Ga Ku? They're in ashes right now."

"Special Forces learned a lot from those two fuck-ups. For openers, there was a big contingent of ARVN at both camps. There were also a lot of VC plants. Neither one of those places would have folded without inside help. There were VC regulars in the compound when the general alarm was called, and let me tell you, Charlie still paid a heavy price. We have a few ARVN advisers in Bia Vuc and they get along fine with the gnards, but they are the exception. Fact is, the tribesmen don't give two shits about the Vietnamese. Saigon, Hanoi, Charlie—all the same."

"Who do they like, Cap'n, ugly Americans?"

"Gnards are like anybody else. They want to be left alone and follow their own way. Because they are different, the Vietnamese are on their asses. They are actually a lot of separate, well defined tribes that differ from the lowland Vietnamese in language, value systems, religious beliefs. They are all mountain dwellers—that's what the French word Montagnard means: people of the mountain. What they do best is cultivate rice and a few other crops. They are mainly wood gatherers, simple folk. If somebody has a problem, he goes to the Shaman and gets an answer. The 'gnards are animists, believers in the spirits of animals, nature, and their ancestors. Let me tell you about two water buffalo that were your traveling companions in the C-123."

"You almost ran over one of them with the jeep," recalled Herb.

"Yep, but they escaped a closer call about a week ago. A farmer's kid got hurt by one of those buffalo. It's unclear why it happened. The kid could have provoked the animal, nobody knows. We choppered the youngster to a province hospital, and I understand he's doing quite well. But the farmer believed the buffalo were cursed, and to appease the evil spirits, they would have to be killed. Now understand something, a water buffalo to these people is equivalent to your life savings. I talked to the Shaman and we found a solution: put the water buffalo on the big bird and fly the animals to the heavens where the evil spirits can be washed away. We kept the animals at Da Nang for a few days. You saw the results this morning."

"So that's what the commotion was all about when we landed. And they bought it?"

"You better believe it. Those buffalo are cleansed," said Captain Bixler, sternly.

"How would the Vietnamese have handled the same problem," Herb asked.

"If they were controlling the purse strings, then the buffalo would not have died. Rice is more important than evil spirits."

"And the French?"

"The French had a hands off policy; the buffalo would have been a 'gnard problem. They were well liked by the people. Bia Vuc was their brainchild in the early fifties."

"How so?" As Herb spoke, he turned and watched the Montagnards disperse. An elderly lady remained and resumed giggling when their eyes briefly met.

"When the old women take a liking to you, then you know you've got it made. Their words are golden. The Montagnards revere senior citizens," grinned the Special Forces Commander. "You asked about the French. They never paid much attention to the 'gnards. They were interested in the coastal areas and the big cities when they first came here as a Colonial power. France never could develop industry or exploit any of the Nam's resources. All of Indochina was a big failure economically. The Montagnards were left alone and treated as a non-entity because they didn't figure into the dollar and cents scheme of things. Of course, this is just what the tribesmen wanted. After World War II, Nationalism became the big cry in Southeast Asia, and the French made the mistake of staying and getting involved in a 'liberation war.' The military plan was to defend the big cities, and to develop outposts in the countryside where the enemy had its strength. Guess where they looked when they wanted a friend? It was easy. The Vietnamese were still up to their old tricks while fighting the French. They stole rice from the natives, raped their women, and continued to ridicule their savage ways. No arm twisting was necessary. Montagnard enclaves were formed all over the highlands. They understood that the French offered them protection in return for their military assistance. Bia Vuc is still pretty much the same as it was when they left it in '54. The only real additions are Village A, the mine fields, and an expanded compound. It's amazing how this place survived. Throughout the late fifties and early sixties, it was a playground for both ARVN and the VC. Bia Vuc changed hands so many times, it was like the swinging doors of a tavern on pay day. Both sides treated the 'gnards badly. Saigon made an about face in '63. It was decided that a permanent presence in Bia Vuc was desirable; rehabilitation and indoctrination of the infidels was necessary. Special Forces got their feet in the door, and the Montagnard camps became a joint project. Except for Bia Vuc—this is my baby. Want to take a walk?" Bixler jumped up, and was on his way before Herb ever got his feet off the ground.

He caught up with the Captain at a little knoll not far from the picnic grounds. Herb observed a wooden marker inserted on a mound, and now understood the significance of the observation post's name.

"Dave Servin was my predecessor," said the present commander proudly.

"Two 'gnards on the outpost that night were VC. Charlie was here before they knew what was happening. This place was a slaughter-house. Dave could've asked for air support, but he knew women and children were up here. He led a team that regained the hill, but he was greased. There's something else I'd like you to see."

Herb followed Bixler across the summit to an area that had a massive bunker, an oddly placed wall of sandbags blocked a view of the surrounding countryside. They skirted the curious bunker, and traversed a small ridge that led to an abutment. It was here that they rested. Bixler remained silent, as the stunned doctor tried to unravel the mystery of what he saw, but couldn't comprehend.

"I don't want to give you the idea that the Vietnamese and the French are the only fuck-ups around this place," the Green Beret officer said finally.

Herb detected a change in tone and mood. The Captain was agitated; teeth gnashed, arm and stomach muscles were taut as his left hand formed a fist.

"What you're staring at Doc has the 'Good Housekeeping' stamp of approval. Thank Uncle Sam for this shit."

Herb shrugged his shoulders: "What happened here?"

"Two monstrosities! Take a good look at the one along the slopes and into the valley in front of us. What you see is a wasteland. Remember Village A? I told you it was a recent addition to Bia Vuc. Now you know why. The people in that village lived in this valley. They produced crops on these slopes, near the ravine and river. All along the mountain ridge they grew rice in terraced fields. This was productive land at one time, it fed a lot of people. Our master planners in Saigon and Washington refused to believe that Montagnards could grow rice on stepped terrain, and decided all that food belonged to the Viet Cong. Of course that's bullshit! The whole concept is mind boggling! Nobody bothered to ask me what I thought. The Vietnam-ese knew better but they can't stand the Montagnards, so they agreed to destroy the crops and deprive the enemy of its' food supply. The trees had to be removed because of the potential for hiding places. Beats me where the hell Charlie's cover is, and our boys have been humpin' this valley with a fine tooth comb. Real Indian country is right up the gutter, north and west!" The Captain made a wide, sweeping motion, and then continued into his pocket for a pack of cigarettes.

"Is that Laos and the Ho Chi Minh trail?" Herb made a similar gesture.

"Yes Sir! There are trail terminals both south and north of here. There's an interdiction team at one of them right now."

"Is that what you were referring to this morning when you mentioned the two absent members of the Special Forces sent on special assignment?"

"You don't miss a trick, Doc. I won't go into the logistics. Let's just say Laos is okay for NVA and Charlie, but it's off limits to our people," said the Captain with a snicker.

"Cap'n! I still would like to know what happened in this valley. I've never seen anything like it."

"Doc, Have you ever heard of the Ranch Hands?"

Herb nodded. It all gelled. He recalled the sergeant with the crazy skin condition who equated jerking off with his disease. The loadmaster was laughing, " . . . the only thing that's gonna grow is bamboo. Charlie can use them for blow guns. No way those sons-of-bitches gonna hide or eat anything from the ground after we're finished spraying.' And their motto! What was their motto, 'Only We Can Prevent Forests'?

"I wasn't in the valley the first day. I understand the people were elated when it happened. Their land and their bodies had been sprayed by the American 'big birds' with a potent magic medicine." Bixler lit a cigarette and inhaled deeply. "It was a great omen. The Montagnards believed that their American friends were moved by good spirits. I got on the phones and tried to find out what was happening. An Operations Officer told me the valley would be sprayed for three days with defoliants. They had already hit the terraces, and were ready to tackle the forest piecemeal. I pleaded with mucho people, but nobody was able to authorize a stop order. I even called Bien Hoa and spoke to a big honcho in Special Forces. He was powerless, but offered to try channels. I knew it would be no go. The second day I stood on this cliff and watched. They came out of the northeast, eight C-123s in formation, swept down one in back of the other, and flew a couple of hundred feet above the tree line. Each plane targeted an area and there was very little overlap. All I could do was look up at the sky, and scream 'mother fuckers.' The next day I stayed in my room and worked over a bottle of Seagrams. Look at it now. A wasteland, tree stumps, branches on the ground, without leaves or greenery, no more rice, a denuded forest. Herbicides do a very thorough job—believe it. Doc."

"I guess the Montagnards soon understood that the spraying was not a blessing."

"You better believe it. Evil spirits had invaded their land. They had misinterpreted the signs; a curse had swept through the valley. All hell broke loose. They slaughtered livestock, even water buffalo that hadn't been sprayed. They burned their own homes. We tried to get the Shamans to intervene, but in fact, they turned out to be the ring leaders. No Montagnard will ever farm that land even if it should become fertile again. And he wouldn't touch that wood. He would rather freeze than use it for firewood. This valley is cursed!"

"Do they blame the Americans?"

"Shit no, sports fan! The Americans carried out the will of the evil spirits. It's something the Montagnards did, and they have to find a way of ridding themselves of this curse. Less than half of the people in this valley relocated in Village A, and we promised to provide them all with food and housing. The others left with the clothes on their back and who knows where the hell they are?"

Herb's muffled sigh was barely audible. He reached for the binoculars and pondered the other part of the puzzle. Beyond the Ranch Hand's wasteland, into the belly of this macabre valley and mountain range, lay Captain Bixler's 'gutter zone' as it snaked its way into Laos and the Ho Chi Minh trail. Thousands of pits and concave depressions dotted the landscape. The pocked forest and hilly terrain stretched for miles, no demarcation line on the horizon left the imagination to grapple on an end point. Herb focused the glasses on high power and examined the closest excavations. The huge holes were devoid of vegetation, but between the massive pits were areas of grass and foliage, small pockets of trees were interspersed, but many stumps and pale, barkless branches covered the earth. It was eerie. Signs of wildlife were absent, no animal walked the ground nor were there birds winging over the honeycombed landscape.

"Looks like the moon with all those craters," said Bixler, casually discarding one cigarette and lighting another.

It all fell into place, a single word had solved the mystery. Herb wrapped the strap around the casing, and placed the binoculars on the ground next to the Captain's 'Luckies'. Addressing Bixler, he mumbled: "Craters . . . craters . . . bomb craters."

"Let me tell you somethin'. You're looking at a supply route off the Ho Chi Minh trail in a free fire zone, and Doc, you never want to be in a free fire zone eating pussy with a bunch of B-52s overhead at 30,000 feet ready to unload their jollies. It just ain't good for your appetite."

"You sold me," smiled Herb. "I'll stick to steak and potatoes. Did the B-52 raid accomplish anything?"

"You bet your ass! You met Flaherty. We were here on Mount Servin about 0300 when our friends from Guam came to visit us, and the Sergeant took some of the best night photographs you'd ever want to see. I told command that we only get a trickle through this valley, most of the action is further west. My boys were pissed off that there was so little activity, and hopin' for more business. If there was a heavy movement of people and supplies through the valley that we couldn't handle, I'd be the first one to ask for a B-52 raid. The timing was lousy. We were just recuperating from the Ranch Hands' visit."

"What a sight!" Herb's gaze surveyed the valley. "How many bombs hit this place? God, those craters are big!"

"I thought you'd never ask, Doc," replied Bixler removing a wrinkled paper from his wallet. "Alan Stone is an engineer. The Lieutenant loves to play around with numbers. Interested?"

"Sure."

"A B-52 raid—and by the way Doc, you don't see these fuckers and you don't hear them; the bomb just hits the ground and there's an explosion, and that's their calling card—a B-52 raid usually involves seven or eight planes, though they may have used more on the three missions in this valley and up into the gutter. Each bomb weighs 500 pounds, and a full bombload is 110 of these babies. There were probably around 900 bombs dropped on each raid, and there were three of them so Stone estimates there are 2,500 ro 3,000 craters. The first raid saturated an area of a little more than a half mile wide and about three miles long . . . about 1,000 acres. Remember, there were three attacks!"

"I hear you, Captain."

"Now this is where our engineering friend comes in handy. Stone claims that the average crater size is 30 feet in diameter, 15 feet deep, displaces 131 cubic yards of earth, and—get ready for this one, Doc— each crater-producing bomb disperses fragments over 1.25 acres."

The numbers were dazzling, but the view morose. The valley was a skeleton forest with man's signature. "I think I've had enough," said Herb.

They left by the same route they had come. When Herb passed the huge bunker wall that obstructed the cursed valley, he murmured aloud, "One less question to ask." Captain David Servin's memorial illicited another glance, but the Commander of Bia Vuc's Special Forces kept on walking.

The two men were ready to descend the slope, when Herb spotted the same young Montagnard soldier in combat fatigues, who had been the recipient of the unused C-rations. He was smoking a Lucky Strike, and talking to a young girl. She wore a wraparound black skirt almost to the ankles, and a white blouse. The top four buttons were opened and three necklaces rested on her small firm, exposed breasts. Bracelets adorned both her ankles and wrists. Her hair was loose and free flowing as it swayed in the warm mountain air.

He kept on walking, not wanting to disturb the young lovers with so much as a 'Hi.' It was their moment, and he would not be an intruder. Herb had taken a few steps on the narrow path leading to Bia Vuc, when he heard voices. He turned and saw the trooper waving. The couple stood arm-in-arm, and together in a loud and synchronous voice, they happily proclaimed, "America and Montagnards, Number One! America and Montagnards, Number One!"

* * *

22

THE Americans called him Frenchy. He was in his early thirties, but his appearance was distinctive even for a Montagnard. He dressed in camouflage battle fatigues, an artist's blue beret covered his crew cut. The hairstyle and beret set him apart, it made a statement about his Francophile loyalties.

The defeat of French colonialism, and their departure from Bia Vuc in 1954 was a watershed. The American presence had not restored past glories. The Special Forces were honorable men, indefatigable workers, skilled warriors, excellent diplomats, purveyors of wisdom, respectful of Montagnard culture and tradition—but where were the parties and the good times?

Frenchy fondly recalled the French occupation of Bia Vuc: memorable feasts, evenings of wine and laughter, and the painted ladies.

They came from the big coastal cities on the supply planes to the garrison at Bia Vuc. Women of many nationalities, but mostly French and Vietnamese. The ladies were friendly, always smiling, used strange pigments to color their faces, made peculiar noises, and moved their bodies in funny ways.

The Montagnard teenager soon discovered the meaning of the rituals, but their favors had a price. What could he give in return? The painted ladies wanted Francs, but he had none to give. He correctly concluded his greatest asset was to offer a formidable array of services, the price would always be negotiable. Frenchy became a pimp, tourist guide, chef, errand boy, lookout, servant, hairdresser—all requests were considered, and rarely was one refused. And so they opened their legs, but the joys of the flesh were not his only rewards. There was the excitement of learning about a world that went beyond the Central Highlands, and even the great coastal cities of Vietnam; exotic lands, and people with unusual customs and mysterious ways who worshipped different spirits. To break the barrier of ignorance, he needed to understand another language. The whore house at Bia Vuc had become a university, the harlots his faculty.

The French departed Bia Vuc; their star student and most fervent admirer followed on their heels. He was armed with an address book of soldiers scattered throughout France, and an idea of getting work on a freighter that would find its way to Marseilles. Saigon would prove to be his downfall. Vietnamese officials ridiculed attempts to leave the country. His Montagnard heritage was a severe handicap in the streets of the big city; the Mountain People were the lepers of Vietnamese society. He returned to his colony, the trip was long and arduous. He had come to Saigon, 'Paris of the Orient', by plane; he would return by foot. Beautiful dreams had given way to painful blisters.

Another war replaced French adventurism—Vietnamese against Vietnamese—and the Montagnards were once again caught in the middle. Bia Vuc's survival hinged on its ability to placate both sides, a difficult balancing act, and the master juggler was Frenchy. His knowledge and linguistic abilities made him a bridge between the Montagnard world, and whoever else wanted a favor. He had the confidence of the Council of village elders, and skillfully manipulated the conflicting interests. In the intervening difficult years between the French and American presence, Bia Vuc successfully walked the tight-rope and retained its identity. The emergence of the Special Forces in the early sixties helped sway the great majority of Montagnards to any uneasy alliance with Saigon. Bia Vuc, with Frenchy at the helm, understood the wind direction. Neutrality no longer a viable option, the safest bet appeared to be Uncle Sam.

Frenchy didn't recall her name, she was half oriental and half caucasian. Afternoons were quiet at the brothel, and patrons appreciated. The reward for helping the Eurasian with more customers was a small, tattered black book that fit into his hand. She claimed that in the world of commerce, this little prize was indispensible, it had helped her, and would be a passport for a secure future. And Frenchy would soon agree, studying the French-English dictionary made good common sense.

"Bon Matin . . . Good Breakfast, Docteur Klein?" asked the 'man of the mountain' with the blue beret and crew cut.

Herb answered with a nod and a thumbs-up. It was the day before, on the road from Mount Servin to Village A, that Captain Bixler first discussed the virtues of Herb's translator. Frenchy was a good linguist (though he often interchanged French and English), bright, resourceful, dependable, and had an excellent record for getting things done. An exalted view of the French had earned him his nickname. "He talks and acts like one of us, but he thinks like a 'gnard," said Bixler prior to their visit with the Council of Elders. "Give Frenchy a problem, turn your head, and let the little fucker do it his way, you won't go wrong." On this second day at Bia Vuc, Herb was beginning to understand.

"Number one idea, Docteur Klein . . . real fine . . . beaucoup Montagnards like you very much," said Frenchy, referring to Herb's plan for making morning house calls to the villages, and then encouraging visits to the new clinic at the compound for ambulatory patients in the afternoon.

"We'll see," he replied cautiously.

"No problem, Monsieur," smiled the diminuitive interpreter, "you a winner!"

"Hey, get a load of this stuff," said Sergeant Flaherty, the other member of the medical team, as they walked along the small dirt path leading from the compound to Village B.

Two Montagnard girls scurried past the men as they approached a small bamboo fence, only a few yards away from the first house they intended to visit. Well endowed, their fully exposed globular breasts bounced with the aid of a fresh mountain breeze. No glances or words were exchanged, but the giggling of two teenagers was appreciated as the medical team entered the yard.

Frenchy turned to the two Americans, raised his right hand high in a patriotic gesture, and shouted, "Viva la pussy!"

"You didn't know this guy's a big cunt man," chuckled Flaherty. "Frenchy, tell the Doc about the whore house when the French ran the show."

"Oo la la! Good time in Bia Vuc. Nice women with painted faces, big asses," Frenchy spread his arms in front of an amused Herb.

"You love a wide ass, don't you, good buddy," said the Sergeant, his arm rested on the shoulder of the Montagnard.

"Number one. You bring wide ass woman to Bia Vuc. Frenchy do the rest."

"You have beautiful women here," Herb said, containing a laugh. "Why look elsewhere?"

"It is a lesson I learn from the world beyond the mountain, Docteur Klein: pussy and power, man never have enough."

Frenchy fascinated Herb. Yesterday, at their first encounter in Village A and the strategy session at the compound that followed, the Montagnard was silent except for his translation duties. A few of Herb's questions were directed squarely to his translator. His concern was to make Frenchy comfortable and involved in the decision-making process of the Bia Vuc health care program. The response was a nod of the head or a single word answer.

The afternoon chat with the Council of Elders was nothing more than a courtesy call to strengthen rapprochement. The doctor's mission had been discussed and approved by the village hierarchy before his arrival. Herb reinforced the notion of cooperation; health care decisions would be made jointly, and implementation of any proposal would require council approval. He had no intention of degrading Montagnard ritual and healing practices. He was determined that Western medicine complement their own. A long range plan would be formulated soon for their scrutiny, assuming the next few days proved successful. The reception was cool, but polite. Herb recognized these men had lived with a string of broken promises. Results, not words would dictate their actions.

At the dinner table, Herb explained the game plan to his eating partners—Bixler, Stone, Flaherty, and the reticent Frenchy. He wanted to visit the villages in the morning to make house calls, and introduce himself to the natives. The idea was to diminish anxiety, instill confidence, and allay fears of a whole new approach about looking at their bodies. He would show the people his equipment and let them leaf through some medical books with photographs, a technique found useful in the village and Province Hospital programs.

Out-patient hours would be at mid-day. A small, rarely used supply building was to serve as a clinic and a four bed dispensary. All of the Special Forces men were cross-trained in a variety of specialties, but Sergeant Flaherty was the designated medic. Herb expected to work closely with the sergeant, and in the future would try to set up a direct communication line with the Da Nang Hospital for immediate consultation and coordinating emergency air lifts. Herb also planned to visit Bia Vuc once a week for sick calls, and if possible, bring specialists.

The three Green Berets were ecstatic. For three months they had tried unsuccessfully through regular Army channels to get a part-time physician for Bia Vuc. Lieutenant Stone mentioned the problem to a pilot in the 341st Air Commando Squadron who had delivered supplies to the camp and was ready to return to Da Nang; Bia Vuc had its doctor a few weeks later, and now a workable long range plan to boot. The crew-cut listener in the blue beret remained noncommital. He continued eating, only half-attentive to the discussion. His only response to Herb's proposals was a shrug of the shoulders.

A relieved and overjoyed Captain Bixler recalled how a Special Forces physician had once come to Bia Vuc with different suggestions. The doctor was interested in doing malaria research. He wanted to take blood samples and put needles in the spleen for tissue specimens. In return, he would see a few of the sickest patients, and advise the medic on how to handle other problems. "I couldn't believe the jerk," Bixler said bitterly. "I told the sucker that Bia Vuc ain't no Auschwitz and to get his fuckin-ass out of here! You should have seen the size of the needles."

Bixler stopped talking. He suspected Herb was Jewish and immediately apologized; no religious slur was intended. Frenchy said nothing, but was clearly more interested. He set down his fork and followed the give-and-take carefully, wondering why the words were suddenly being weighed. Herb quickly defused the issue and made it clear that the Captain's remarks did not bother him. With the aptitude of a skilled diplomat, he moved the discussion away from concentration camps to the mundane world of professional football. An in depth analysis of Green Bay's victory over Kansas City, the first Super Bowl game, ended the evening meal.

Herb returned to his room in the center of the military compound. Originally, his quarters had been a French built pill box, which then served as a storage place for explosives because of its sturdy concrete construction. The slits in the walls were covered, machine gun terrets had long ago been removed, a small opening designed for ventilation and observation overlooking the main courtyard was situated right above the bed. The top of a huge trunk containing emergency medical supplies held a photograph of Christie, a dozen pipes thrown together in a single pile, a humidor filled with Balkan tobacco, and six medical books lying in a single stack within easy reaching distance of the bed. A foot locker and a chair in one corner of the room were the only other furnishings.

He was preparing to smoke, having selected the woodstock, a sickle-shaped pipe with a long shank and a small stem. The briar was a combined flame and straight grain, the surface smooth and the finish shellac. An examination of the bowl's undersurface showed a burnt out area that could spell doom for the pipe's future. The pipe was a gift from Ben the week Herb started medical school, he associated the woodstock with Morty Zucker's first year anatomy class.

Morty Zucker! Herb frowned when he thought about him and his fellow Osler Professors. They had stuffed innumerable bits of irrelevant scientific facts up his ass, but what about Malaria, nutritional diseases, Dengue Fever, a host of intestinal and skin afflictions? He knew more about genetics and embryology than tropical medicine, felt more comfortable with RNA than the life of an Anopholes mosquito and the Malarian Cycle, was at ease with mitochondria, but uneasy with the diagnosis of early malnutrition. The thought was scary. In a few hours, he would march off to the village and engage in the only battle he ever wanted to fight. How could he help some of these sick people? And if he didn't understand their problems, he would do no harm and at least leave them with the hope of a better tomorrow. For the first time in his brief medical career, Herb would enter the fray alone. No doctor was available to lean on, and he felt woefully unprepared.

His fingers rubbed the surface of the smooth, darkly stained burn-out on the pipe's surface, the bowl was then filled with tobacco. He turned to what had become a familiar companion: Hunter's *Manual of Tropical Medicine*.

Herb's reading was interrupted by a knock at the door. "Pardon Moi, Monsieur," said the man with the blue beret. "May I speak with you?"

"Sure," said Herb with a wide grin. He directed Frenchy to a chair near the bed.

"Captain Bixler was not himself at dinner. I think he wants to please la Docteur," smiled Frenchy, now seated.

"How so?" asked Herb.

"The other docteur . . . with the big needles . . . made the Captain angry. Why?"

Herb smiled. "It has to do with my, er, gods, and something that happened years ago."

"Is it . . ." Frenchy strained to pronounce the word as he had heard it. ". . . Uschweetz?"

"Yes. Auschwitz."

Bixler's slip of the tongue had opened the flood gates; an unlikely topic for starters, but a first step. The translator's enthusiasm and cooperation were essential to a successful medical program at Bia Vuc. Herb welcomed the opportunity to improve his image with Frenchy after his icey reception, but was not looking forward to discussing a distasteful subject he had already artfully dodged at the dinner table. A plan was formulated—a few tidbits to satisfy the Montagnard's curiosity, and then a rapid shift to Bia Vuc and more important matters. But Frenchy was determined.

"So you come from a different tribe than the painted ladies." He was recalling the Catholic rituals practiced by some of the prostitutes.

"Yes," Herb said cautiously. "The tribe I belong to has different ways."

"Different from Captain Bixler's?"

Herb paused a moment, took a puff, then said, "Yes. Different."

"Ah!" An excited Frenchy smacked his knees and shook his head; his broad toothy smile betrayed a sense of discovery. "Tell me more."

"We're a very old tribe, and we have suffered a great deal."

Herb sat on the edge of the bed and slowly puffed on his pipe. Frenchy was a few feet away on an old metal chair. His body was arched forward, a hand rested on each leg while his searching eyes never wandered from Herb. Together, they burnt the midnight oil. The interrogator was unrelenting, unwilling to retreat from half answers or from ground already covered. . . . Who are the Jews? What do they believe? Why don't people like them? What is a ghetto? What do you mean by 'Final Solution'? How can a water shower make gas? Aren't ovens for warmth and making food? But why the children? And the women who lived were given x-rays to prevent Jew babies? Six million! How many Bia Vucs is that? What about decent burial grounds? Don't the Jews have friends? You are 'chosen'! Chosen? Chosen for what?

It wasn't as if Herb didn't try; he drew upon every meager bit of information he could remember, much of it from childhood. But nearly every explanation only added to the confusion. Frenchy had read a few books, the barracks and whore house at Bia Vuc had provided him with exposure to the Western world. Special Forces maintained the continuity; nevertheless, he still possessed a

Montagnard mentality, a mind and a way of life that more closely resembled the Stone Age.

And Herb's personal convictions became another source of controversy. He hadn't experienced anything like this since the late night fraternity sessions in college. How could he be proud to be a Jew and not accept the Jewish religion? Did the men at "Uschweetz" accept the distinction? Or was the problem an identity crisis? It's okay to accept the Jewish faith, but don't be labeled a Jew! Frenchy would ask a question, Herb's response required clarification and more questions were raised.

There were other moments when the Montagnard retreated, and Herb was left to ramble; a walk with Sophie in the rose garden at Horticultural Hall, Ben's pinochle game, Uncle Otto's antics at the World's Fair, Grandpop Jacob and a red wagon loaded with jugs of spring water, a colored housekeeper . . . Christie.

It was 0450 when they stood at the door. In a few hours the two men would be together again, with the sick and needy of Bia Vuc ready to greet them. Frenchy departed, there were no goodbyes or handshakes. At the mortar pit, he turned to find the Doctor at his side. In the moonlight Herb handed him a shiny necklace. "This is for you. It is called a Star of David, a Jewish star. It's the symbol of my tribe . . . of my people." The man of the mountain nodded appreciation, but said nothing.

"I'm a tit man myself," smiled Sergeant Tom Flaherty, "A wide ass doesn't do anything for me. Frenchy! Have a look and see if our first patient is ready."

"Real fine. Real fine," said the translator, lightheartedly.

Herb felt relieved. Frenchy's cheerfulness was quite a contrast from yesterday's stark performance. His new friend had a flair for the unexpected; a frisky, free-wheeling, bullshitting Montagnard who could hold his own in the big leagues was a pleasant surprise. Herb leaned against the porch of a typical 'gnard abode built on wooden stilts about two feet off the ground. Herb bent over and counted twenty poles, four rows of three and two rows of four. The house was constructed with wooden slats interlaced with bamboo. The slanted, two side roof was layered with straw. There were no window openings, a side entrance and an open front between the porch and interior provided ventilation. Twenty feet long by seven feet wide, the house had a small porch and an enclosed living area compartmentalized into an eating and sleeping section.

"A-OK. Please come in and see your first Montagnard patient," said Frenchy with a wink.

"Where did you learn that?" asked Herb as he passed through the door, the Sergeant at his heels.

"Women at Bia Vuc whore house do all the time," mocked the Francophile. He grinned, blinked, alternated both legs in rapid succession, rotated his hips in a bump and grind motion, and concluded the act with wild thrusts of his pelvis. An old woman sitting by a boiling pot chuckled, a young girl holding a cloth on the sick man's brow giggled, even the patient smiled despite his difficulty in breathing. Frenchy's comic pantomime antics had struck a harmonious chord.

They encircled the sick man, he remained motionless and stared at the ceiling. Sergeant Flaherty gave a quick history and his reasons for administering water pills and antibiotics; swelling in the feet, and poor breathing. Frenchy directed Herb's questions about his patient to the young woman, a thorough physical examination followed. After a half hour of listening and poking, the Doc needed a break to sort out the pieces. The outside yard and mountain breezes was a welcome respite.

In the vernacular of Osler General Hospital, this case was a 'blue balls special'; a certainty for Medical Grand Rounds with a high potential for creative bullshitting. Herb could visualize a respected Professor standing at the podium in a huge auditorium in front of the entire House staff. He would be citing cases from the medical literature, referring to patients with similar problems, concluding with an exhaustive differential diagnosis and a spirited finale synonymous with 'I don't know'; words never spoken, but implied by the length and certainty of the discussor's convictions.

He pressed against the bamboo siding and rehashed the salient factors of a troublesome case history, present illness, past problems, review of systems, physical examination, diagnosis. A logical approach to his patient's illness was systematically reviewed, distilled, and coordinated into a meaningful therapeutic program.

Herb then stood by his patient's side. He was propped against the wall staring at the floor rather than above. Herb squatted and reached for the old man's hand. The knowledge and wisdom of modern Western medicine, previously unknown in this primitive village, was about to be unleashed.

"I assume he won't go to a hospital," said Herb, peremptorily.

"He no leave Bia Vuc," confirmed Frenchy.

"Gentlemen," Herb pontificated, "I don't know what's going on. I feel a little better about what he doesn't have. I don't see any reason for his medications, so let's stop the pills. I think he'll feel better if he sits up like he's doing now. No lying down."

Frenchy never hesitated, his translation was delivered in a monotone with no hint of emotion. The sickly old man spoke for the first time with the Montagnard interpreter. Frenchy's retorts were terse, head and hand motions animated. As he spoke, the old man looked at Herb; deep-seated eyes sparkled, head nodded affirming words not understood, a toothless mouth broke into a warm smile and an even warmer thank-you.

"Old man want you to know," said the man with the blue beret, "that he like you, and you a good healer. He no like pills. In only a short time since you come, he feel much better. I tell him his ancestors send you to Bia Vuc on big bird. He know all about the water buffalo returning yesterday on the big bird. Make much sense. You make old man very, very happy. He ready to die now."

"You don't mind, Doc."

"No problem, Sarge. Frenchy and I are going to make some courtesy calls, we'll see you in the clinic at 1400. Thanks for your help."

"You fellas ought to catch a few Z's. I'm beat. I don't know how you guys do it," said Flaherty. Medical chest in hand, the Sergeant returned to the military compound.

It had been a tiring morning. A few patients had been diagnostic dilemmas, but all were manageable. Frenchy was there to bail him out. Montagnard ritual and Western medicine collided with no noticeable casualties. Frenchy permitted no vacillation, a master at extemporization, the finished product always produced hope for the patient. Herb had the good sense to keep quiet even when the truth was abandoned, no one seemed to be hurt, and he had nothing better to offer.

The Montagnard's response exceeded his expectations. Children followed him everywhere, they tugged at his fatigues for recognition, and squealed for joy when he acknowledged their presence. Cordial villagers went out of their way to make him feel at home and they succeeded; Herb was overjoyed. After such a cool reception by the Council of Elders, he anticipated a confidence gap and a difficult uphill battle to close it, his early triumphs were a pleasant surprise.

"Frenchy, ol' buddy," said an exuberant Herb, proudly. "I want to thank you for your help. No way this program is going to make it without you. I see a brighter future for the Montagnards."

"Docteur Klein, let me show you the Montagnard future."

The two men walked to the sacred burial grounds, and observed the grave sites from a partitioning fence. The village elders and other important members of the tribe were interred in replicas of the typical Montagnard home—worldly possessions (vases, knives, pottery, eating bowls) lay scattered, and within the small, narrow, stilted miniature houses only slightly larger than their deceased occupants.

"Montagnard stay with family and ancestors long time in other world . . . very happy place if good spirits like Montagnard. You are much too serious. If your medicine fail, you must not be so unhappy. No big thing. No one like my people. You care. That is enough, Monsieur."

"But caring is not enough for me. You can keep your burial grounds and tradition, and borrow from my world . . ."

"Docteur Klein! You, Captain Bixler, Special Forces someday leave Bia Vuc like the French. Only Montagnard can save Montagnard. My people like Jew people. No one like us unless we help them," said Frenchy as he reached for the Star of David hanging loosely around his neck, and obscured by a green undershirt. "I tell you what I borrow from your world, Monsieur. If Montagnard survive, he must kiss ass. No other way."

Bia Vuc is in good hands," replied Herb, who then jokingly asked, "Since when did you decide to become Jewish?"

"I walk around village all night after our talk in your room. I think much about what you say, and come to burial grounds for help. It was here that it all made good sense. Ancestors send Docteur Klein to drive away evil spirits. People of Bia Vuc must listen, respect your wisdom, and honor your wishes. I tell everyone this morning, and show them the star necklace from the heavens for proof."

"So that's why everybody in the village was falling over me! They think I'm some sort of a messenger boy."

Frenchy grinned: "You be a Montagnard messenger, and I be a Jew. Okay?"

"Outstanding! In my book, anybody crazy enough to call himself a Jew, *is* one. Sholom Aleichem, partner," said Herb, affectionately.

* * *

23

THE distant, crackling sound of rifles preceded bursts of machine gun fire. Herb knew the small arms fire wasn't near the compound, but peered through his quarters' only window anyway. Northwest of the compound, at the river bend, flares lit up the sky. Two Montagnard sentries in the courtyard stood by the Howitzer and exchanged a joke. Their wholesome laughter brought a contagious smile to Herb's face. His mood was festive, there was much to celebrate; a few 'gnards having target practice to break up the evening's monotony only added to the party atmosphere. There had been no VC probes since the first day. Short bursts of small arms fire at night was routine, and signaled restless soldiers rather than enemy troop movement.

Herb released the mosquito netting and prepared for bed. Three days remained at Bia Vuc, two at Da Nang, and then there was a little unfinished business waiting in Hawaii. Only a short time left, and still no gift for Christie. She would be thrilled with the presents from friends—but what about his own? He put his hand under boxer shorts already wet from perspiration around the waistband; first the shaft was massaged with long, synchronous strokes; the soft, smooth head followed. In jest, he thought: maybe this will be enough.

He loved her with an intense passion. In an atmosphere where the prevailing maxim was 'If it moves, shoot it or fuck it,' Herb Klein remained untouched, he traveled a straight and narrow course. Not that he cared or passed judgment on others, but a side order of sex did nothing for the appetite; his own release was a fanciful mind and quick hands. Christie had captivated his imagination. He stretched out in the darkness and remembered the beautiful moments she had woven. Quick hands moved to the mark.

'Christie, my love! And wow, what a lover you are! Oh, baby! . . . Talk to me honey! Who taught who? What moves? Turn it on . . . Roll 'em!'

'I hear ya big fella . . . Homework time! I need you now or no pancakes in the morning . . . I want all of that big thick cock . . . C'mon Herb! Work hard . . . deeper! . . . deeper . . . Did you forget your vitamin pill this morning? I can only feel you up to my chest . . . Be good to your little girl, Herb. Ride me high and hard lover . . . Fill me up Herb. Hold me tight, real tight . . . tighter. Let's make it together . . . together . . . together . . .'

"Doc! . . . Doc! . . . Doc!"

Herb opened his eyes, and heard a knock on the door. "Coming!" he yelled with a wide grin.

"Sorry Doc," cried an apologetic Flaherty, the door was slightly ajar, with only Herb's head in view. "I know you can use all of the z's you can get, with all the patients you've been seein', but we got a little problem and the Cap'n wants you to take a look. VC prisoner with bullet wounds. I thought I could handle the fuckin' thing, but the gook's still bleedin'."

"Be right with you, Sarge."

"No hurry. Charlie's not gushin'; just a few red cells. Sorry Doc."

Flaherty was right. Herb could use the sleep, the last three days had been exhausting, but in a somewhat pleasant way. The reception of the villagers had been nothing short of spectacular. The clinic hours were extended into the evening until every patient was evaluated. A codified chart system was developed, documentation and verification were the key to good records and a viable long range health care program. An immunization schedule was established, and Montagnard women taught to administer the injections. All patients were given revisit appointments, continuity was essential. Even Frenchy was impressed with his thoroughness and attention to the smallest detail, a personal approach that made each person feel special, an attitude that Bia Vuc would not be short-changed.

The two men had become inseparable. All of their waking hours were spent together sharing each other's thoughts. A strong attachment had developed that transcended the normal boundaries of friendship. Perhaps the man of the mountain had summed it up: "Docteur Klein," he said holding the Jewish star of the necklace (a little gesture Frenchy made to assure Herb of his sincerity), ". . . the Montagnards no longer alone . . . you are one of us."

Herb put on his Bermuda shorts, slipped into sandals, and reached for a pipe and pouch—time to make a housecall.

A large closet with a single light bulb and no windows adjacent to the dining area, served as an interrogation room. Captain Bixler sat in the lone chair with legs crossed and a cigarette dangling from his lips, a pencil and writing pad resting on his lap. Stone, Flaherty, and Frenchy stood erect and used the wall for support. All of the men scrutinized the Viet Cong prisoner seated on the floor.

"Doc's here. The Sarge tells me you were occupied with a lovely from Village D," kibbitzed Stone.

"No sweat, Lieutenant. A piece of ass is easy to get around here, when you consider the competition," countered Herb.

"Let us know when you're finished with our friend, Doc," Bixler was all business. "Coffee anyone?" the Captain's glance suggested that Stone and Frenchy were thirsty.

"I could use Frenchy for translating," yelled Herb, the three men were already in the dining room.

"Not this gook. He speaks damn good English," chipped in the Sergeant, medical chest in hand. "Better than Frenchy."

Charlie was barefoot and wore tattered black pajama pants, a blood stained shirt and a clean blindfold lay on the floor next to an extended leg. He was a young man, early to mid-twenties; enlarged, flattened nostrils almost covered the length of his mouth; straight, unparted black hair reached the nape of the neck.

Herb observed that he was in no acute distress. The compression bandages were removed and revealed gunshot wounds in the upper arm and shoulder. The rest was routine: local anesthetic, good exposure, probing, tying bleeders, debriding dead tissue, irrigating and cleaning the wound, examining for major vessel and nerve damage, suturing and closing. Fortunately for the patient, his wounds fell just barely within Herb's limited surgical skills.

"You are a lucky fellow," commented the medical officer, "your problems are soft tissue. You will have some pain and tenderness for a while, but I don't anticipate a permanent problem with your arm or shoulder. It was a dirty wound and there are some signs of infection, so I'm starting you on antibiotics."

"Doc," said Flaherty, the Sergeant had been uncharacteristically quiet and pensive. "Why don't you see the Cap'n. I'll clean up."

"Doctor," it was a strange voice, clear and gentle. "Thank you for helping me."

Herb returned the prisoner's smile, and then proceeded into the eating area, his presence created a definite change in mood and had apparently severed the conversation of the somber faced men sitting at the dining table.

"Everything okay, Doc?" asked the Captain with a noticeably forced grin.

"Yes Sir. The patient's fine."

"Have a seat, Doc. How do you like your coffee?"

"A little cream and sugar will do."

"I hope you don't mind the powder, can't stand the stuff myself. Doc! You gotta be wondering what the hell's happening, so let me level with you." The Special Forces Commander handed Herb his cup, Stone doodled on scratch paper, Frenchy remained silent and sullen. "Maybe you can make some sense out of this whole thing, I sure as hell can't. Charlie-boy . . . ," Bixler removed the pencil from behind his ear, and pointed it in the direction of the interrogation room, "is an officer in a hot-shot Viet Cong regiment. He wasn't captured, but walked right into one of our patrols. Claimed to be a defector, and said that he was shot by one of his VC comrades during the escape. Charlie-boy knew all about Bia Vuc, it was his destination, and he wanted to see the American Commander right away—American, not ARVN. Telling ARVN your secrets, according to our new shot-up friend, is like whispering into Ho's ear. I'll buy that, it's the rest of the story that I have trouble with. The defector has no papers or documents, says he had a packet of goodies that was lost when the shooting got hot and heavy. Charlie-boy wants us to believe that Bia Vuc, a few other Special Forces camps, some villages and towns—he's not sure of the exact number—have been ticketed for destruction in a single coordinated strike, and I mean total . . . every man, woman, child, water buffalo, outhouse . . ."

"C'mon Captain," scoffed Herb, "Bia Vuc, according to your own appraisal, would be a major undertaking and result in unacceptable losses, let alone a synchronized attack involving a whole group of places. Do they have that kind of manpower?"

"Doc, I told you from the start this fuckin' thing is way out. Charlie-boy says it's a kamakazi mission. They come in, set up shop, wait to get their asses kicked, and nobody retreats. They intend to use some of the best people they have, at a time when they're definitely hurting. We have big operations going on in the Highlands and DMZ, not to mention numerous search and destroy missions in this region. We've never been in a better position. The other side is on the run."

"So," a bemused Herb playfully fingered his unlit pipe, "an enemy getting its ass kicked is going to commit its crack troops on a suicide mission that they believe is doomed to fail. It makes no . . ."

"Sense," Lieutenant Stone finished the thought. "I couldn't agree with you more, Doc. It all sounds like a fairy tale to me."

"I'm not finished, Doc. Let me tickle your balls with this one," Bixler arched backward, the two front legs of his chair were lifted off the floor. "Our friend says this signals a change in the direction of the war. The Commies can't win militarily, so their efforts are geared towards mobilizing world and more specifically American public opinion. They believe we're more vulnerable at home than on the battlefield, so they'll exploit our divisiveness . . . whoever wins in the streets of American cities, will win the war in Vietnam. Doc, it's nuts. This whole situation is out of my league. A Green Beret is just a plain, ordinary grunt with a bigger hard-on, that's why I'm getting on the phones and asking the smart boys to handle this one. I like my pussy straight, if things get a little kinky, I look for help."

"Fuckin' A," seconded Stone.

"When's D-Day?" kidded Herb.

"D-Day! It already was according to Charlie-boy! We were supposed to get hit on the Tet holiday, but for reasons that he doesn't understand, it was called off at the last minute. So there's another jump-off date: tomorrow night."

"The Tet New Year of 1967 . . . Tomorrow night." Herb mumbled loudly. "Is there any activity outside the camp?"

"Within a few miles of Bia Vuc, Charlie can't fart without our knowing about it. I've checked with our patrols and intelligence, there's nobody out there, nothing, let alone a couple thousand men ready to hit us in a suicide attack. As a precautionary move, I'm putting us on a full alert until we can sort it all out. Frenchy will explain to you what this means." Bixler arose and started toward the exit door, "Frenchy! I want the Council of Elders contacted now, but we needn't bring in anybody unless the situation changes. Stone!

Interrogate the defector again and see what you can come up with. I'll be on the phones."

"Captain. Is it okay if I tag along to the interrogation room to listen?"

"Sure Doc! Ask questions; give him truth serum . . . anything!" said the Special Forces Commander as he rose and left.

"Docteur Klein," Herb heard his new brother's voice. Frenchy had reverted to the quiet, reflective mood of their first day's encounter. "Full alert means Spooky airplane nearby and ready to help. Patrols more active, and we send more men out to scout. Elders and their families, some other key people we are sure of, come into compound from village. To all others, our camp off limits. They fight in other places."

"What do you mean, 'off limits'?"

"Montagnard come into compound who not belong here is shot, even women and children. Everyone know, elders approve, only way. Some Montagnard are VC, can't take a chance. Every camp overrun by VC have inside help. Soldiers fight better with families nearby."

"Is there anything else?"

"We give out more guns, grenades, ammunition . . . you want, Docteur?"

"Nope," Herb held his hand up.

Frenchy hastily departed for an emergency meeting with the council. Lieutenant Stone refilled his coffee cup, topped off Herb's, and picked up Bixler's pencil and pad. Both men entered the small, windowless room; Flaherty sat quietly on a chair. Charlie-boy was asleep, but continued to lie on the floor with his back against the wall.

"Wake him up, Sarge," said Stoney. "Cap'n called a full alert. Why don't you meander down to supply and check out the hardware."

"Hey Doc," Flaherty's hand rested on Herb's shoulder, "This alert stuff is like a fire drill. We have them all the time. Keeps you on your toes; doesn't mean a thing."

"My pants aren't stained yet Sarge, thanks anyway." Herb turned to the awakened defector, "You are welcome to have my coffee." He drank a little, and placed the cup by the VC's side.

"Doctor, you need not drink out of cup. I trust you. I have nothing to hide," smiled Charlie-boy. "I like coffee very much. Have not had in a long time."

"Do you smoke?" Herb was now methodically puffing on his pipe.

The VC asked for cigarettes. Herb scurried back to the dining hall, an unopened carton lay on a shelf above the range.

"You are Captain Chac Duo Trang of the 3rd Viet Cong regiment," the Lieutenant's voice was clear as Herb approached the room with a pack of Bixler's 'Lucky Strikes.'

"Please call me Chac," said Charlie-boy.

"Okay, Chac. Why don't we start?" Stone paused and looked at the pad, "Saigon, 1963. Now, you say you attended an antigovernment rally. Buddhists Monks were set on fire? . . ."

* * *

24

"Do you know what I fear most when I visit your pad?" The bearded youth took a hefty gulp of beer, and then placed the mug on the table in front of the huge picture window overlooking the river. "That your landlord is home. I love to visit Southwark . . . the old homes, cobblestone streets, views of the river. But when I make my turn on Kerr Street, it's time to say a prayer. 'Dear Lord! Somehow, someway . . . you, who are all knowing and all powerful, find a way not to shake hands with old man Flint'."

"Horace can be a little over-zealous."

"'A little' did you say? I feel like my hand has been through a wringer, and it gets worse as he gets older. What's he, seventy? I'll bet you he could go to the docks and still do a good day's work."

She smiled and nodded. "Yes, he is very strong."

"So, Mrs. Klein! How does it feel to be on vacation?"

"It hasn't sunk in yet. I have been so busy trying to prepare for this Hawaii trip. I hate shopping. What a day!"

Christie took a deep breath, removed high heel shoes, and lifted tired legs onto the chair snuggly under her buttocks. The sound of sleek nylons rubbing together brought a smile to Peter James' face.

"Wow! Herb's going to have a ball," he said looking at her well shaped calves, a tight fitting blue skirt rested slightly above the knees.

"How's Beta Sig? Osler?" parried Christie.

"Fraternity! The Fuhrer still rules with an iron hand, and you have to count your testicles after a visit to the kitchen. Emma Mae complains bitterly that she is overworked and underpaid—that is when you can find her, which isn't very often. The Brothers are shaping up—Vietnamese genocide and napalm are slowly replacing the new entries on the Keller Report and Sisters of Mercy Proclamation as the hot topic of 1967. Osler Medical College? Same crap. Christie, Are you feeling okay? You look troubled."

"It's been a tiring day, Peter. I guess it shows. Your being here eases the tension. I'm glad you called," she said, smiling.

Herb was a poor liar, his little white lies often accompanied by a twitching of the left upper lip, shifty eyes and a change in the tempo of his pipe smoking. His wife knew all the signs and when caught, Herb could only shake his head, baffled by her clairvoyant powers.

Christie, on the other hand, was an expert liar with flawless technique. Tonight's opening fib was a hackneyed but proven winner: praise you guest, and label him a good samaritan. The truth was, Peter James was a despised and unwelcomed visitor.

Peter was a complex problem, his presence required deft maneuvering and fancy footwork. Tactful avoidance was the primary goal, but this morning's telephone call had a plea of urgency and there was no chance for a rain check. Her uneasiness was complicated by Herb's trust and explicit request that his good friend be an escort and confidante to combat her loneliness. If she alienated him, her fear was that Herb would somehow get a distorted message adding to his burdens, a violation of each other's sacred unwritten code—protect thy mate. She felt it was best to avoid confrontation and oppose his advances in a way that would not strain their relationship.

He was smooth and clever; Pete's repertoire included innuendoes, sex jokes, double entendres, many variations of a 'live for today' theme, pats on the shoulder, hand squeezing, massaging the back, lingering 'hello and goodbye' hugs and kisses on the cheek. There never was a hint of encouragement on her part, and subtle pleas to back off fell on deaf ears.

Christie was used to come-ons. At the Naval Hospital, a young Marine's passes were regarded as a therapeutic success, and a surefire sign of recovery. Working at Osler General Hospital went as expected. Herb's fraternity brothers and friends were amicable and respectful, a hands off policy rigorously adhered to, though understandably painful to some. The rest of the House Staff outside of Herb's world made advances; she understood and good naturedly destroyed a shared notion by doctors on the make. She was neither depressed nor horny; a year's celibacy was no big deal—and, yes, she knew what she was missing.

Mark Jarden and Peter James fit into another category. They were

Herb's trusted Lieutenants and designated chaperones. Mark was a well-intentioned harmless soul, who, like her brother Paul, preferred the middle road. Anything suggesting commitment or intimacy was enough to send him scurrying to the nearest bar. Mark was at a stage in his life where musical beds had become the game of choice, and, bullshitting the time-honored and revered technique used to achieve his aims. Nobody knew this better than the nursing staff at Osler where Mark was fast becoming a living legend. An operating room RN friend gave Christie a copy of a circulating petition making the rounds.

Re: Dr Mark Jarden, Captain USAF (stationed at Andrews AFB, Washington, D.C., but frequent visitor to Philly and Osler General Hospital on weekends)

I (the undersigned) will become Mark's lover for the night if he fulfills *one* of the following:

(1) Does not feign an old war injury (e.g. back pain, headaches, blackout spells, impotence, stress syndrome)

(2) Refrains from war stories about the 'horrors of Vietnam'

(3) Tells the truth more than 50% of the time (judgment call)

(4) Admits the only reason he's dating you is that he wants to get laid.

Rumor had it there were many signatures, but no takers. Mark always offered to accompany Christie out for dinner or an evening of entertainment, but was happily relieved when she refused (the fiasco at Ted's tavern had been their last social event, and his actions still haunted him). The Vietnam veteran had fulfilled his obligation to his buddy Herb, and was now free to utilize all his time, skill, energy, and cunning in pursuit of a loftier goal, where persistence and resource-fulness would pay handsome dividends; little did the poor slob know, it was his for the asking.

Peter had become more daring. He persuaded Christie to attend a Saturday night party at Beta Sigma Tau ('Herb would be happy'). It was a pleasant evening; the usual small talk, a chance to unwind, a change of routine, and the opportunity to renew friendships with old acquaintances. She had an enjoyable time until the living room at old Swenson House became a dance floor, soft romantic music filled the air, and candle light added to the ambience.

John McFadden, an old friend presently a Medical resident at Osler, was an excellent dancer; a master of the whirl and the dip. Christie had fun as his partner, but was in no position to refuse her chaperone's request during a quiet interlude.

The melody began, they stood near the wall of the darkened dance floor swaying lightly to the music. He held her tightly, standard protocol for the setting, but with a fully erected penis rubbing against the Vee of her tight skirt. Christie whispered, 'Peter . . . Please!' but to no avail; his breathing became shallow, pelvic movements more rhythmic. Fearful of creating a scene, she tightened her gluteus muscles and rotated her hips ever so slightly; Peter's body became rigid in concert with a barely, perceptable moan.

On the return trip back to Kerr Street, he discussed the difficult times following his suspension from Osler Medical School. Her husband was a true friend, he had provided housing and a job as Karl's assistant chef, sound advice, and direction for an uncertain future. Herb Klein was responsible for his rejuvenation, and he would be forever grateful. The dance floor incident was never mentioned.

"You know Christie, we ought to get together more often. It's been a few weeks. I feel like I'm letting Herb down . . . not doing my share. I haven't seen you since the party at Beta Sig."

"I don't want to be a burden, Peter. I know how busy you are with school and the Peace movement."

"You could never be a burden." His eyes darted back to her nyloned, exposed legs. The shrill sound of foghorns made him turn in the direction of the river. "I guess you're wondering why I had to see you."

"The thought crossed my mind. You're welcome here anytime, but why tonight?" she asked, the charade in full swing.

Peter reached into his jacket pocket and handed her a small box: "He's a tough guy to choose a gift for, so I went with old reliable. I like the shape myself—a Dunhill straight grain, Saddlebit Dublin style. I know how much Herb loves the saddle. How about you Christie?"

There he goes again, she thought. How I'd like to shove this pipe up his ass. "Oh, Peter! You really shouldn't have," she said graciously. "Herb will love it. Thank you. Let me show Molly and Horace."

"There is something else I want to talk about, if you can just contain your enthusiasm about the pipe for a few minutes."

Christie had found her opening. She would have preferred to throw the pipe in the Delaware river than show it to the Flints. Her main objective was to plant a message in Peter's mind: that ox of a longshoreman, who almost made you into a cripple is downstairs and available for instant consultation.

"I don't want to sound like a broken record," said a somber Peter, "but we really could use your support. The rally is only one day. You'll still have plenty of time to prepare for Hawaii."

"We've been down this road before Peter. You *know* how I feel. I just want to talk to Herb and get his feelings about this. He's been there for over six months and I still don't know where he stands."

"Suppose he's pro-war! Is that going to change your mind?"

She paused. "I'd listen . . . to his reasons, then make up my own mind."

"Christie!" he cried angrily, "There is nothing Herb or anyone else could say that would justify our involvement in a civil war that's none of our business. It's immoral. It's just plain wrong to kill thousands of innocent people because of an idiotic pretense of resisting Communist aggression! You mark my words, this thing is going to escalate into World War III and a nuclear nightmare. The pigs have got to be stopped now."

"You don't have to convince me, Peter. I still want to hear Herb's views. For the next few days, I'm not going to read a newspaper, or listen to the radio, or turn on the TV. I desperately need to take a vacation from this thing. Maybe it's best that I don't discuss Vietnam when I get to Hawaii. Right now, I just want to spend all my time preparing for Herb."

"Can't be done, Christie. You're talking about stopping the clock. No way! The anti-war rally will help Herb get home early. It will be the biggest peace march this country has ever seen, and you have a chance to be part of it."

"I can't do it, Peter."

"It's not just you, Christie. Herb is only one of a handful serving in Vietnam from Osler's house staff. Be a part of this rally and you symbolize Herb's rejection of the war. Everybody at Osler will make the association. For Herb's sake, join us."

"What if Herb is a Hawk, and for his own reasons, doesn't want you or any of his other friends to know. Do you still want me at the rally?"

"I don't believe it. He couldn't be. . ."

"Peter . . . ," she put the pipe on the table next to the beer mug, "my husband has always admired your strength of character. It took a special person to stand up against the Osler dress code."

"So? What are you driving at?"

"He's always said you were a man of high moral courage, but . . ." Christie turned to the river.

"But what? Stop talking in circles."

"Peter, Herb doesn't want to hurt you. He realizes how strongly you feel about the war."

Christie's implication that Herb was Pro-War had no basis of fact, nor was the suggestion deliberate. She was bothered by Peter's insistence that she play a more active role in the Peace movement, and by the overblown symbolism he attached to her presence. So far as she knew, Herb remained uncommitted. Neither side could claim him; no one was entitled to speak for him so long as he remained silent. She wanted to inflict a little pain on Peter (Lord knows, he had it coming) and Vietnam was his Achilles heel.

Peter turned from Christie, looked about the room, and then looked intently back at her. "Everybody's allowed to make a mistake, including your husband."

"I'm glad you feel that way. I'm sure Herb will feel relieved. Your friendship means so much to us." She looked at the saddleshaped briar on the table and joked, "I think I'll present your gift as 'peace pipe'. A reminder that men of good will can differ, and still be friends."

A voice bellowed from downstairs: "Christina! Christina!"

"That's Horrace. He's a little hard of hearing and yells all the time," smiled Christie. "I'll be there in a sec," she shouted down.

She opened the kitchen door, Horace stood on the first floor landing at the bottom of the staircase. A trip to the pharmacy was necessary to renew Molly's ulcer medication, and then another stop at Sam Green's grocery store. Did she need anything? Christie returned to the dining room to find Peter standing with a folded sheet of paper in his hand.

"The chartered bus leaves for New York at 8 A.M. from 10th and Oak. We meet first in Central Park. Our estimate is about 200,000— assuming the weather's good and there aren't any great screwups. There's a march through the streets to the plaza, and then the rally. With luck, we could be back in Philly by 9. . . . I'd still like you to come."

"And I still want that vacation," she said in a gentle, but firm voice. "Give this to Herb with my regards," he said with a touch of bitterness. He handed her a folded sheet and hastily departed without even a goodbye.

She waited until she heard the front door downstairs close before opening the flyer.

> **UNITED NATIONS PLAZA PEACE RALLY**
> — A Protest against American Genocide in Vietnam
> — A 'Hell no, we won't go' Draft Card cookout
> — Prominent Speakers
> **INNOCENT CHILDREN WILL NO LONGER BE MURDERED. WE ARE MORALLY OUTRAGED! ARE YOU?**

She crumbled the circular in her hand and wondered aloud, "Herb, my love, are we not in the eye of a hurricane?" Christie removed the beer mug from the table; as she did, she noticed the straight grain, Saddlebit Dublin 'peace pipe' was no longer there.

* * *

25

"YOU were confronted with evidence . . . photographs of you watching the burning bonzes, struggling with a Buddhist monk, and a signed confession by a shopkeeper who said you forced your way into her store, and that she overheard some nasty comments from you and a monk about the government. You never suspected that it was a hoax?"

"No. I believed everything, because it was true. My friends presented these documents in a way that made me look like a VC collaborator, and it was consistent with the way the Saigon government would slant evidence, assuming that I would be one of the lucky ones and have a trial. Many others were not so fortunate. At the time, I had no idea that the VC were following my every move at the rally, and that they had taken the photographs and forced a confession from the shopkeeper. My friends claimed the file was in their possession because of a security leak, it was common knowledge that VC sympathizers were at every government level."

"But you said that you were aware that the friends who were trying to help you were critical of the Saigon regime, and yet you still didn't suspect a VC inspired plot!"

"Lieutenant Stone! Many of the students and faculty at the University who were anti-government were not Communists. They wanted a meaningful constitution, land reforms, free elections, a government free of corruption and in harmony with the needs and wishes of the Vietnamese people. As events have shown, their cause was a just one."

"A trusted friend of your family and your university advisor, a certain Professor . . ."

"Ling. Professor Ling of the history department."

"Professor Ling arranged for a hiding place. It was during this time that you decided to become a member of the National Liberation Front. No one coerced you in any way!"

"Correct. I was no longer a student sipping coffee at an outdoor cafe on the Rue d'Catinat admiring the magnificent trees lining the boulevard, and debating other students on the value of Buddhist monks becoming human torches. I was a wanted man. A fair trial was impossible. I believed then and still do, that the Saigon government is corrupt and unfit to rule. I would like to emphasize that in 1963, the National Liberation Front had many dissidents who were not Viet Cong, only anti-government. In the beginning, I fitted into that mold."

Stone paused a moment, then continued, his voice still loud and strident. "Okay Chac, let's jump to '64. You were stationed in a base camp in Svay Rieng province, in Cambodia, about forty miles from Saigon. You graduated your indoctrination course with honors and your job was in Information and Intelligence. You read American newspapers and stolen documents as a translator. Then one day a political commissar hot-shot told you that you'd passed all the tests and were entitled to know the truth."

"Yes."

"You estimate it had been about nine months since you left Saigon."

"Six."

"Six months. In that period of time, you considered yourself not just anti-government, but a committed and hardcore Viet Cong."

"Correct."

"Hot-shot informed you that it was all a set-up. The whole incident—getting you to the Buddhist rally, photographs, confession, warrant for your arrest, hiding place, escape—all of it orchestrated by the VC. You had been targeted, along with others at the University, as a good catch with above average potential, at a time when the VC were in desperate need of skilled people with your kind of brain power. The master planner was none other than your loyal family friend and trusted advisor, Professor Ling. None of this bothered you?"

"Correct."

"What do you think would've happened when you were hiding in Saigon, if you had chosen not to join the National Liberation Front?" asked Herb.

"Professor Ling would have ordered my execution."

"Does that bother you?"

"Not in the least, Doctor. Professor Ling was a dedicated Communist. My recruitment and possible elimination tested his loyalty. The party teaches that the individual's role is to serve the needs of the people, all other actions are secondary. The state. . ."

"Let's get to the nitty gritty," Stone interrupted impatiently. "When did you leave Information and Intelligence? How long were you in Operations Planning? I want dates and places."

"I was in Intelligence until '65. It was a gradual phaseout starting in mid to late '64, and was related to increasing participation of the North Vietnamese. From '63 to '65 the National Liberation Front relied on their own people for gathering and interpreting information. As Hanoi's presence grew, our role in these areas diminished. I was transferred and spent most of '65 involved with planning and operations in Svay Rieng and O Rang provinces."

"In Cambodia. Neutral Cambodia."

"Cambodia, but hardly neutral, Lieutenant. 'Neutral Cambodia' is a seed developed in Hanoi, planted first in Phnom Penh, which now grows only in the minds of American newspapermen and peace activists. Cambodia has always been a sanctuary for the VC and North Vietnamese. Within its boundaries are large caches of military supplies and rice. Base camps in 'Neutral Cambodia' provide communications, housing, rest, hospital facilities, medical care—even entertainment. The war would soon end if Cambodia had an even-handed policy. The Communists interpret 'neutral' as a place where they alone can roam free."

"Operations, Chac, operations! Let's hear about . . . ," Stone scanned Bixler's notes. "Payback."

"Operation Payback. The VC taxed and collected rice from the farmers. There was hoarding and uneven food distribution among our own military cadres. I devised a plan which set up food depots and made sure quotas were met and maintained."

"Riverboat."

"Latter part of of '65 and '66. I helped coordinate the movement of supplies from the port of Sihanoukville to base camps along the Cambodian border in Svay Rieng and O Rang provinces. The ships were from Russia, China, Eastern Europe, and some third world countries."

"March of '66. You came back to Vietnam. More than two years had passed, since you left your homeland."

"Correct."

"You returned to Tay Ninh province as a Special Field Commander. 'Teach' was your job?"

"Operation Teach. A plan designed to assure that the villages were run efficiently and in the interests of the people."

"People, meaning Viet Cong?"

"Yes, Viet Cong. My teams dealt with the village leadership. Those who did not cooperate were punished, many executed, a few reindoctrinated and returned to assume their proper role. Many of those killed were school teachers . . . Operation Teach."

"Summer of '66, Chac. You were then in the Central Highlands attached to a regular Army unit in full scale combat maneuvers. 'Scissors.'"

"The Central Highland provinces of Darlac, Pleiku, and Kontum were major targets. Once strength was established, an attempt was to be made to cut Vietnam into two parts. Weakness in coastal provinces made the plan unworkable."

"Where was the trial run?"

"Trial run?"

"The probing action. The test to see if the plan could be operational."

"Binh Dinh province. Only best NVA troops used. ARVN no problem, but assault by First Air Cavalry showed American forces to be too mobile and strong."

"NVA regiments involved?"

"Eighteenth, Twen . . ."

"You were attached to the Third VC regiment. What was your role during the probe?"

"Attacked Poleiking in Kontum province, cut off Highwa . . ."

"Highway 14 . . . Let's go right to Tet '67, and the events leading up to a change in strategy and this 'suicide mission'. Could you be a little more specific this time around. I'd like more details. Who were the officers that told you these things? Where? When?"

"I never said that someone told me about a strategy change, or that the attacks scheduled for Tet were suicidal. I gave you my impressions. You must first understand the language of the revolution and then you can make certain inferences. I told you what I thought, but I did have in my possession certain documents that would have proven a planned, coordinated attack of many places on Tet. And then there was a new timetable. I have no idea why the Tet attacks were cancelled, or why tomorrow is the new target date."

"Okay. The language of the revolution and its . . . inferences."

"Operation Scissors was a major disappointment. A military victory on a large scale had been our objective. A few years ago, we fought government forces with their own American weapons. Guerrilla tactics had been successful. We were armed with modern Russian weaponry, and organized into fighting units of the conventional type alongside regular NVA. There was a feeling that a major victory was imminent. Scissors was to be the American Dien Bien Phu. The American imperialists and their Saigon puppets were to be replaced by a Peoples Government. The First Air Cavalry's performance, and the defeat of crack NVA forces in Binh Dinh province proved what a few of us had felt all along: the Americans were not the French, nor could we expect them to weaken. More men and supplies arrive at our shores every day. New tactics were needed after our comrades fought so courageously against the better armed and numerically superior 'American Dogs' . . . May I have have a cigarette?"

"Sure," said Herb. He lit a Lucky and then put it into the defector's mouth.

"Thank you, Doctor. The first hint of a strategy change came from the Political Commissars, who began lecturing our troops with increased intensity. Their message: The People's War had many friends in America who supported our struggle, but others remained silent, not convinced of our sincerity. Renewed dedication was necessary. The Revolution would soon require great sacrifices that were to test our resolve. The Commissars also intensified the sessions dealing with self-criticism. . ."

"Khiem Thao," nodded Herb.

"Yes. How did you know that, Doctor?"

"Hi guys," Captain Bixler stood at the doorway. "Anything cookin'?"

"Big zero. No go, Cap'n. Our friend Chac hasn't budged."

"Okay Stone, why don't you put this thing to sleep." Bixler squatted next to the Viet Cong defector, and gently put a hand on his good shoulder. "I want you to understand Chac that I kept my end of the bargain. I just talked to Command, and told them you didn't want anything to do with ARVN or their security branch. I supported that view and they share your concern about leaks. But something like this requires their presence. An ARVN security officer, along with some other top level people will be here at day break. Policy is policy. Sorry."

"I understand, Captain. Thank you for your help."

Bixler left, and Stone reviewed his notes again. Before resuming, he asked Herb for an explanation of Khiem Thao. The interrogation continued. "If I understand you correctly, the behavior and the language of the Political Commissars is the tip-off that something of major importance is about to happen."

"Yes. Soon after these sessions, came new orders. Our regiment was to prepare for an all out attack on Tet. The enemies of the revolution were to be dealt with severely. Privately, the officers were told to expect heavy losses, and that retreat, even in the face of overwhelming resistance, would not be tolerated."

"And the porters?"

"Many, many, Lieutenant—more than I have ever seen."

"I don't get it," Herb looked puzzled.

"When the VC are ready to kick ass, they always get helpers. Peasants who move supplies, remove the injured and dead bodies. Porters on a large scale means trouble. Everything was in place, and then suddenly the operation is called off, and you don't know why?"

"Correct."

"It was quiet for a while, and then you got a new set of orders: the Tet thing all over again, and your regiment has been ordered to destroy Bia Vuc tomorrow night. You estimate that your old buddies were about thirty kilometers southwest of here when you made your escape."

"Correct again, Lieutenant."

"That's it for me. I have no further questions. Chac, I want you to listen very closely. A Montagnard guard will be watching you. He'll be sitting on the floor and looking right into your eyeballs. He won't budge, even to take a piss or a shit. He'll sit in the stuff the whole night. We've told him you're not like the rest of the VC, and you're important to us, but you never know with these boys. You can talk to him and he'll listen, but if you're out of line, he'll carve you into little pieces with his knife—a gun's too quick. An then after he's finished with you, he'll go back to the village and fuck his girlfriend, and then they'll have a party. Do you follow me, Chac?" He nodded, and then Stone turned to Herb. "Are you coming, Doc?"

"I'd like to resume the discussion, if it's okay with Chac."

"I would be honored to talk with the Doctor."

"Goodnight gentlemen," said Stone, not bothering to close the door.

"Are you sure you want to continue? Tomorrow morning is going to be tough. You can bet the intelligence officers will be very thorough. Every detail of your story will be examined closely. Your mind and body should be well rested."

"I have nothing to hide, Doctor. I speak the truth."

"How does your shoulder and arm feel?"

"Much better," said the defector, but his thoughts were elsewhere.

Chac focused not on the Doctor, but on the open door. Herb turned and he too saw the youthful Montagnard guard sitting on the floor. He immediately recognized the face. The Doc said, smilingly: "Montagnards and America . . . Number 1."

The teenager said nothing and remained motionless; his vision focused on one thing and one thing only. His senses and piercing eyes had reduced the cosmos to a single Viet Cong prisoner.

* * *

26

THE three-man intelligence team arrived in Bia Vuc by helicopter at daybreak, all were armed with the ubiquitous weapon of their trade, the attache case. A tired Green Beret commander working on only a few hours sleep was present to greet and debrief the investigators. An exhaustive interview of Chac followed. It had not dampened enthusiasm or satisfied their appetite, another source of information was available to the inquisitors.

It was no secret that the interrogation room was bugged. The Montagnards knew of this electronic marvel, a source of fascination and amusement, especially when their own voices were reproduced. As a member of the Viet Cong's intelligence community, Chac was indifferent to a taped session, though he assumed as much; the idea never crossed Herb's mind. And in the excitement, no one had bothered to apprise the doctor of standard Special Forces procedure.

Sunlight bathed the military compound's dining room and Operations center. A weary Captain Bixler was flanked by a U.S. Army Major and his ARVN counterpart; an American civilian adviser and consultant to the Vietnamese Major, chose to stand by the window and observe Bia Vuc going about its business.

The tape recorder faithfully regurgitated events of the previous evening to an attentive audience, Chac's conversations with Captain Bixler, Lieutenant Stone, and Doctor Klein were analyzed and collated with the intelligence team's own interview. Selected parts of Bixler and Stone's segments were repeatedly reviewed. All of the officers summarily dismissed Herb's taped session as irrelevant to the important military considerations of Chac's revelations. Only the civilian consultant was interested in reviewing the doctor's portion.

When the officers were finished, he quietly strolled to the tape recorder, and found what he was looking for.

PLAY

Chac: ". . . the peasant belongs to the land and village, family and ancestors. He knows nothing of Communism or Democracy, cares neither for Hanoi or Saigon. The VC say, 'We are the earth-worms who enrich your soil.' Saigon counters, 'We are the elephants, strongest of the strong, and we rule the earth.' And the peasant asks, 'Who among you will help me make the land more fertile?' . . ."

STOP—FAST FORWARD—STOP—PLAY

Chac: ". . . the peasant who becomes a VC soldier. . . He is a Buddhist who worships at the family shrine and the pagoda, and believes strongly in family honor and ancestor worship. Yet, he has primitive beliefs similar to the Montagnard guard at the door, who would very much like to help me see my own ancestors this evening. Also, there is the reverence for the Emperor, and the traditional view that the Imperial House of Hue represented with its emphasis on Confucianism and Taoism. You must understand the mixture."

STOP—FAST FORWARD—STOP—PLAY

Klein: ". . . help me to understand the problem."

Chac: "My father used to tell me a story from the Analects. He would say, if you were a ruler and were forced to give up one of the three, which would it be: sufficient food, sufficient armament, or sufficient confidence of the people?"

Klein: "Armaments!"

Chac: "Of the remaining two, which would you abandon?"

Klein: "I don't see the sense . . ."

Chac: "Confucius would say to abandon the food. There have been deaths immemorial from hunger, but no state can exist without the confidence of the peop . . ."

STOP—FAST FORWARD—STOP—PLAY

Chac: ". . . haps. You may be right, but the kidnapping and murders of the school teachers in their view was okay, because it served the interests of the people. You imply, Doctor, rules of conduct and a code of morality that is common to all. Not so! The political Commissar dictates to the VC what is immoral. The Vietnamese character has had no experience with Democracy. Historically, the correct answers to the peoples' questions were supplied by the

Mandarins and the Emperor. They want to be told, and not given a choice . . . "

STOP—FAST FORWARD—STOP—PLAY

Chac: ". . . There is no distinction in the eyes of the political Commissar. If you are not a friend of the 'People's Revolution' then you are its enemy. There is no middle ground. You either give your total devotion or none at all. Your mind is theirs, or it is contaminated, and needs cleansing and reeducation. Khiem Thao is but one technique . . . "

STOP—FAST FORWARD—STOP—PLAY

Chac: ". . . When I first joined the NLF there were many voices. Under Hanoi, we spoke as one. Saigon was no better. I find virtue in neither camp; my own survival was more important. . . . Men defect because they are either hungry, poorly armed, or believe their chances are better on the other side . . . conscience and values are secondary considerations. I was caught in rough waters like so many others in this war . . . my only option was to swim. You try to line up on the side of humanity and rightiousness. I was raised in that tradition by my parents, but in the end you understand it's not all that easy . . . there are obstacles everywhere . . ."

STOP—FAST FORWARD—STOP—PLAY

Chac: ". . . good person, respect and honor your fellow man. Jen is humanity . . . Jen! The other is the Chinese word Shu . . . Do not do to others, what you do not want them to do to you . . . Shu! Shu and Jen . . . both sides preach, but unlike my father, neither side acts in a way that confirms their words . . ."

STOP—FAST FORWARD—STOP—PLAY

Klein: ". . . Americans in your country?"

Chac: "Your intentions are honorable. Your leaders are correct in assuming that Hanoi fuels the revolution in the South, but who started the fire! . . . And surely Saigon's actions keep it ablaze. Hanoi is gambling on America's will to persevere. . . Nothing is more disturbing to a Democracy than something that is not clear cut and well defined, but few issues are . . . Freedom to protest and dissent is a great strength, but in the hands of your enemy, it may well turn out to be a greater weakness. Your resolve will always be challenged, because your system invites controversy. A totalitarian government knows that it is right, a Democracy can only think it . . . no one knows this better than your enemies."

STOP—FAST FORWARD—STOP—PLAY

Chac: ". . .it is everywhere in Vietnam. Evil is a cycle of terror that is broken by a single man's actions. . .I return to my father's ideal. I walk the path he has chartered, his wisdom will guide me. . .Jen and Shu . . . Shu and Jen! Nothing else matters. You must watch the direction of the wind, and you'll see how the grass bends . . . you can see it's effects, hear and feel it. Move in the proper direction! . . . Ah, the sweetness! . . . But you must always remember that in the eyes of many, your actions will never be like the grass . . . the wind blows, and you bend against it."
STOP

The Civilian Advisor had heard enough, pensive and uncommunicative, he returned to his place at the window overlooking the compound. The consultant to the Vietnamese major thought, "He's too sure of himself. There's no hesitation; it's all too pat. What the hell am I missing?"

The three military men sitting at the table resumed weighing the evidence. The American Major removed the tape recording and slipped it into his attache case. "Captain Bixler, would you update us on what's happening in Indian country?" he asked tonelessly.

"We doubled our patrols last night and we've checked some of our critical electronic sensors on key trails. A big goose egg. There's nobody out there. We've gotten negative reports in from long range reconnaissance teams in Laos and on the border. I think it's safe to say that a large scale attack in regimental strength tonight is not in the making."

"That pretty much sums up the whole situation from the Delta to the DMZ. There's nothing happening that would substantiate the defector's claim of an all out attack on multiple localities," agreed the intelligence officer. He then turned to his ARVN colleague. "What do you know about our new friend, Major Thu?"

"I'm afraid our file adds nothing of importance to Chac Duo Trang's own story. He was a brilliant student, and excelled in linguistics. We know that he was framed and part of an elaborate plan to acquire certain skills needed by the VC in 1963. His record is clear of anti-government activity, and there is no mention of any participation in Buddhist protest rallies. In December of 1964, Professor Ling was identified as a collaborator involved in a scheme to recruit University students for the VC. A leak in our Saigon bureau prevented his arrest, and he disappeared. Chac's father died in 1962. The mother and sister interviewed after his disappearance were of no help, nor were friends at the University. Initial thinking was that he had been kidnapped or killed by VC because his record had been spotless. After three and a half years, there was not a single new entry in his folder. Chac's file was reactivated last night, and the case is already in the hands of high level agents. I am confident this sketchy report will be enlarged by this evening, if not . . ."

"Well, what do you know!" cried Captain Bixler. Dressed in fatigues, Herb had entered the dining room. "I thought you'd be sleeping a lot longer. We're ready to have some chow and discuss Charlie-boy. Why don't you join us. Remember I told you last night about an Intelligence Team? Doc Klein meet Major Markle . . . Major Thu, and his consultant . . ."

"Hi, Herb," interrupted the ARVN Intelligence Advisor. He reached for a brown paper bag on the window sill, and tossed it to the Doctor. "Would you believe that I forgot your favorite kind of bagel, so I got a few of each."

"Pumpernickel. It's pumpernickel. When are you ever going to learn, Mo?" said Herb, disgustedly.

* * *

27

"A bunch of spoiled college brats. Most of 'em haven't worked an honest day in their lives. Burnin' draft cards, American flags . . . Walkin' around with VC flags and shoutin' cuss words about our President. Fine fix this country would be in if we had to rely on those whippersnappers to fight our battles. Thank God, we got people like your Herb, and my George," said Horace Flint, working himself up to a spitting rage.

"Come on now, Horace, relax and drink your tea. This rally in New York isn't worth getting upset about. Remember what Herb said about your blood pressure and excitement," warned Christie.

She was concerned and with good reason. The old man's face was flushed, eyes teary, and his upper lip twitched. Trembling hands picked up a tea cup only to have its contents spill on the kitchen table. Christie cleaned the spill and placed a chair next to Horace; one hand rested on his broad shoulder, the other sought the thick and calloused palms that had toiled in the dockyards for so many years; she nestled her head against his wide chest. The stillness was punctuated by the longshoreman's sobs.

It was over twenty years ago that George Flint had been killed at the Battle of the Bulge. After a long period of quiet, another war in Southeast Asia reintroduced the same basic problems. Vietnam, Horace reasoned, was just an extension of an on-going process: the preservation of freedom and democracy, and the maintenance of our way of life were still the overriding issues for him.

In World War I, Bismark and the Germans took it on the nose. Horace wanted to be a Doughboy, but an inguinal hernia kept him out of the Army. The hernia was repaired and then Hitler came along, but by then he was too old; George would take his place. The Commies were stopped in Korea, and now they were up to the same old tricks in Vietnam, only the tactics had changed. First Indochina, then Thailand, Burma, Malaysia, Singapore; soon, we'll be fighting in California. Horace asked: "Hasn't anybody heard of the 'Domino Theory?'"

It all seemed so unreal. Tony Marrelo, a steel worker friend, had a son in the Nam. A retired longshoreman, Bill Louten, had a grandson who lost a leg in combat. Willie Carter's boy Durell, used to help his father with the janatorial work in the union hall. He was a Marine fighting in Vietnam. The blue collar folks were sending their sons off to the war while the grubby, rich kids with the long hair went to college, got their military exemptions so they could parade in the streets, and protest against the war by mutilating American flags and screaming obscenities at the President. "Hadn't anybody heard of fairness and dignity for the working man?" he yelled suddenly.

The old man believed in his President. Sure he was a Democrat—what true union man wasn't—but it would have been the same if a Republican was in the White House. The Congress, with the exception of a few mavericks, had supported their leader's position, as did the public opinion polls. In times of crisis, the American people have always rallied around their President. In the past, when things got tough, everybody did their share. Duty and commitment was the price people paid for their freedom, and some, like George Flint, had to make the ultimate sacrifice. An anguished patriot cried, "Hadn't anybody heard of dying for the American way of life?"

Christie understood Horace's frustrations, the depth of his agony, but she had no remedy. The gigantic peace rally at the UN was a beginning, not a climax. Anti-war demonstrations would intensify as American involvement in Southeast Asia increased; further polarization was inevitable. The universities had become the leaders of dissent; the local blue collar bars that dotted Southwark, the government's symbol of support. In the evenings, the retired longshoreman would walk into Ted's Southwark Tavern and undergo his almost daily catharsis. Old friends from the same school (Hard Knock U), and a few belts would erase the pain, if only for a few short hours.

"Horace," Christie pleaded, "could you do Herb a favor?"

The response was immediate, the hand tremor stopped, so did the tears. In a clear voice that did not crackle, he replied: "Don't ask the question, just tell me what you want me to do."

"You know how much Herb likes Southwark, and talks about someday opening a practice here. . ."

"Yes, yes!" he answered excitedly, his hand running through Christie's long, auburn hair.

"It's not definite, but I'd say there's a fifty-fifty chance he won't do a residency. He might want to open an office as a GP. Would you scout the area, and let me know . . ."

"Christina, you mean Herb's going to practice medicine in Southwark, and wants me to find him an office?"

"Yes. Herb still has over a year to go in the Air Force, but he thinks it's a good time to start looking. Nothing's definite, but. . ."

"Christina, you can rely on me. Tomorrow morning I start. No, tonight. Ted and our friends at the tavern will be overjoyed, and they will help. This is great news. Wait till Molly hears!"

"Herb just wants to explore the possibilities . . ."

"I see a problem," he said standing. His huge arms raised Christie from the chair, her penny-loafers dangled and were in danger of falling to the floor. "It's the waiting room," mumbled Horace while returning her to the kitchen linoleum. "I can see it as clearly as your smiling face, Christina. A street covered with old bricks, and a pre-civil war clapboard house converted into a doctor's office. There's a shingle next to the gate, and it reads 'Herbert Klein, M.D.' The waiting room is packed with old geysers like myself, and also young'ns with kids. There are toys for the children, papers and magazines for reading, a little music or even a TV. . . People are a little scared, but they know they're in good hands. Herb greets 'em with that big smile and a handshake. A little small talk about sports or a joke about sex to make 'em feel good. I've seen the way your husband operates, and then it's 'How can I help you?' or 'What's our problem?' Folks around Southwark don't have much money, but they're hard workin' and honest. He'll make a decent livin'."

"Herb loves Southwark. I don't think he cares about the money."

"He should, Christina. You gotta pay the rent. Nobody around here wants a free ticket. They'll pay with dollars or workin' odd jobs, that's the Southwark way. Herb talks like he knows the score, but he's too much of a dreamer."

"What's the problem with the waiting room?"

"No way you're ever goin' to find a waitin' room big enough to hold all the people! No sirree," answered Horace as he made for the door.

"Horace. About the rally. . . . It's going to be in the papers and on TV. . ."

"Don't you fret, Christina. I'll be fine. If it's a fight those peaceniks want, then old Horace'll give it to them," he said with one hand on the railing, and then added, "By the way, are you going to be Herb's nurse in the office, or start that family Herb always talked about."

"A toddler requires a full time mother," she said calmly.

"I guess a couple of sons and a daughter would be a big job," laughed Horace, as he descended the stairs.

Christie closed the kitchen door, she thought: So, Herb Klein, you never mentioned anything about the size or gender of our family. Whatever I wanted was okay. Apparently you told Horace what you really want. Why not say what you feel? Why be so secretive? And you, Christie Klein, you ought to be ashamed of yourself. What an absurd lie; Herb never asked anyone to look for an office in Southwark. It sure made the old man happy. What a bearhug! My chest still hurts. I think he cracked a rib.

Christie's smile faded as she entered the bedroom, and surveyed the disaster. The dreaded moment had arrived: it was time to pack for her Hawaii trip.

On the bureau rested a legal pad, she checked her lists and started the task. Was there anything missing?

Large Blue American Tourister Suitcase (me)

> 1 peignoir set, 2 lacy nitegowns, 1 garter belt, 1 girdle, 3 pair stockings, 5 bras, 5 panties, 1 half slip, 3 pair shorts with coordinated tops, 1 pair of white slacks, 2 extra mix and match blouses for either slacks or shorts, 1 yellow and white knit suit, 1 peach and white dress, 1 lavender and white dress, 1 pink moo-moo (matching sheer head scarves for dresses), 1 white handbag, 1 pair flat sandals in white, 1 pair white dress heels, 1 pair sandal heels, 1 pair penny loafers, two-piece bathing suit, white coverup, 1 white sweater

Round Overnight Blue American Tourister (hand carry on plane)

> jewelry—3 pair earrings, gold chain, white beads, shampoo, conditioner, suntan lotion, solarcaine, first aid cream, tampax, bandaids, safety pins, electric razor, make-up, aspirin, nose drops, plastic bags and ties, address book, stamps, writing paper, envelopes

Leave Out to Take (morning of flight)

white A-line skirt, R-W-B blouse, half slip, stockings, garter belt, bra, straw sandals, summer coat, carry straw bag, airline tickets, $350 cash, check book, wallet, I.D. info on Fort Zama, time and place to meet Herb, Hotel Kuilana reservations, sightseeing info on Honolulu, wrist watch, book to read on plane, tissues, Orthonovum packet

Smaller Blue American Tourister Suitcase (Herb)

2 knit shirts, 2 Bermuda shorts, 3 sets of underwear, 2 polo shirts, 3 pair socks, 1 pair Converse sneakers, 1 bathing suit, gifts

Herb's Gifts

Ben—Foremost Salami, hamantasch, letter

Mama—Polish cookies, letter

Paul—Book . . . 'Tales of the Sea and Adventure,' Joseph Conrad

Molly and Horace—Whitman Chocolates, Fralinger's Salt Water Taffy

Ted—Subscription to Phila. Inquirer for the next five months, and a promise for the best 'Welcome Home Party' that Southwark has ever seen

Southwark Tavern cronies—'God Bless America' plaque

Karl—Apple Strudel

Beta Sigma Tau Brothers—Dunhill pipe, minutes from the meetings, updated lists of the Keller Report and the Sisters of Mercy Proclamation

ER Staff—Comoy pipe

Peds Nurses ICU—Butane lighter, 3 huge boxes of safety matches

Peds Nurses Floor—Bracelet inscribed 'Christie and Herb' with the date of our marriage

Cafeteria Workers—Set of coffee mugs (2) with our names inscribed

Mark Jarden—Book . . . 'A Guide to Sexual Abstinence'

John McFadden and Dave Garrett—'Stained' back issues of Playboy

Me—Pipe accessories . . . reamer; companion; cleaners; sweetener fluid; 3 large cans of Balkan; Superbowl 1 Book . . . Green Bay vs. Chiefs; Books . . . 'Short Stories' and 'The Castle,' Franz Kafka; 3-way Dorich Stethoscope; Photo album additions—Ben and Wyal St. . . . Mama, Paul, and I at a recent family reunion at Neschaunk . . . 'Memory Lane'—Memorial Hall, Swenson House, Open Love Baptist Church, Congregation Ohel Zadek Synagogue

After reviewing the lists, Christie couldn't think of a single addition. She wondered whether she'd exceed the 44 pound limit, but decided to pay the penalty fee rather than leave anything behind. The cost of their Hawaiian rendezvous was already more than a thousand dollars; a few pennies more or less wouldn't make a difference.

The trip to Honolulu was to be her first flight on an airplane. At 22, Christie's world had been Neschaunk, Philly, summer trips to the New Jersey beaches, a weekend in Boston, and three one-day visits to New York. Travel and adventure had always been the product of a vivid imagination, the reality was always disappointing. Herb was excitement enough. He had that indefinable—and irresistable—sense of discovery, the kind that drives everybody crazy.

Her environment had been a sheltered one, no arguing that, but not detatched from the rapid changes America was undergoing. Vietnam may have been most important, but there were others. Many of the institutions cherished by the older generations were crumbling. A disillusioned youth took no prisoners. The leaders whom Horace Flint believed in were now the symbols of their discontent. Cynicism, distrust, rejection, questioning authority, rebellion, challenging the status quo were no longer the perogatives of a troubled youth; it was now a matter of policy. Christina Klein had become a non-conformist; but she did not endorse change just for the sake of change.

At Osler General Hospital, nurses refused to remove bed pans, change soiled linens, brew coffee for doctors. They considered these unprofessional and undignified—not part of the job profile. While the controversy raged, patients suffered. Despite peer pressure, no child in Christie's care would lie on wet sheets. When a nursing supervisor suggested she was overzealous in her duties, Christie offered to resign.

At a coffee break, a married nurse friend asked Christie if she was interested in "doing the town." Sex was okay, provided it didn't lead to emotional attachment. Inhibitions were destroyed, and fantasies took on a new meaning. Marriage was stronger because of the freedom and understanding a couple mutually shared. "What do you think Herb's doing? The double-standard is a relic of the past. Believe me!" said her friend with conviction. "It's a fantastic feeling when you can see the ceiling, legs wrapped tight, urging on your partner . . . *your* orgasm is what counts, not his. Love isn't even a passing thought. This is a new age. Get into the groove. Swinging is in; get with it, girl. Herb wouldn't disapprove."

Christie's response: "I'm into romance, and Herb's approval changes nothing."

"Do you want a little 'herb?'" joked a pediatric resident standing by the chart rack.

"Herb! Herb?" asked a bewildered Christie.

"Kif, herb . . . hashish. It's all the same," he whispered reaching into a white medical jacket and palming a brownish-green oblong, flat cake a half inch thick. "A friend of mine returned from Morocco with these goodies. I also have some fine grass back at my pad. I'm not into hard drugs, and I never will be. Cannabis is the end of the line for me. Herb would be the first to tell you the medical literature doesn't show that grass is any worse than cigarettes or booze. Ask him in your next letter. Smoking grass puts you in touch, it's relaxing, no worries, you want to laugh not cry. Whatever you see, touch, or hear has a special meaning. It's a real high. You got to try it once." Christie felt a sense of well-being, a firm belief in her own self worth, she was in control, a firm 'no' was her only response, nothing else was necessary.

Good samaritans continued to be found everywhere, even the unit secretary of the pediatric ward offered advice and a helping hand. "There is so much of ourselves that needs to be explored. I never realized the range of possibilities, the untapped potential that needs to be set free. I truly feel fulfilled. I have a challenging job, sculpture classes in the evening, my own Studio flat on Spruce Street. I'm my own person now. Tom and the kids have their lives, and I have mine. The awareness sessions don't offer you a cure, but it helps you see the signs and symptoms. I can even identify problems that I never thought about before . . . thanks to the other women in my group. Why don't you come to our next meeting," suggested the Secretary.

"I'm definitely interested. Sounds like a great idea," said an enthusiastic Christie, "but let me clear it first with Herb."

Christie was a non-combatant, and a nonbeliever. She avoided rap sessions, meaningful dialogue, playful repartee; discussions dealing with self help, self improvement, self analysis, identity analysis, conscience lifting, conscience awareness, crisis intervention, and the new self exploration techniques developed to create and sustain self esteem at the expense of self gratification. America was at war with itself, and the Vietnam rubberstamp made it verifiable.

She tried to understand. The issues of the times were clear cut; the answers less so. She saw the need to question and analyze her own beliefs—but who to share them with? Her prize pupil and respected mentor was eleven thousand miles away. But Hawaii beckoned; only a few days remained before they could make sense out of all the confusion.

There was something else that bothered Christie as she picked up the legal pad. She couldn't think of anything to add to the lists, but pondered a question.

Horace had mentioned Herb's wanting a family. The military and Vietnam prompted Herb to delay the start of their family. She reluctantly acquiesced, and even agreed to take a contraceptive pill prior to the Hawaiian trip.

"Who knows? Maybe we'll be lucky," she thought while crossing out "Orthonovum packet" from the list. Her hands began to massage the lower abdomen in a circular motion: "Could you imagine the look on his face six months from now when he arrives at the Philly airport after a year in Vietnam, and sees me in a maternity dress!"

At heart, Christie was a rebel.

* * *

28

AT the dining table a plan of action was formulated. An observation plane was due to arrive at Bia Vuc, and would be used to retrace the escape route with the Viet Cong defector as an on-board director. In the event of an unlikely successful search, fighter plane support already on alert at Pleiku Air Force Base could be called in for an immediate strike. Charlie-boy was then to be flown to an unspecified camp area for more intense questioning.

Chac's motives, honesty, and the content of his information was in dispute among team members, but no one felt Bia Vuc in serious danger of a major confrontation. A full alert removed, Captain Bixler decided to continue increased patrols, and maintain an on-call ready vigilance with Spooky. There was another precautionary move which surprised Herb; a crack 'Mick team' would be put on ready alert. In nearby Moon valley, an area had been prepared for an emergency helicopter assault, and close by was a parachute drop zone. It was assumed that the Bia Vuc air strip would be cut off in a large scale enemy attack.

Frenchy joined the Intelligence team during breakfast, and was informed of the changes. Bia Vuc would conduct its village affairs in a normal fashion, and this included the sick-call schedule Herb had organized. The feisty Montagnard suggested that sick-call be cancelled, and that Herb should return to Da Nang with the other team members. Holding his Jewish necklace, he argued: "Docteur Klein work too hard, and there is strain of possible VC attack. He needs more rest for Hawaii trip so he can make wife happy." The idea that Herb's sexual performance was in jeopardy drew laughter, and offers of assistance from the other diners.

Frenchy departed for another meeting with the Council Elders; Mo declined to accompany the two Majors and Bixler to a nearby bunker where Chac had been transferred. The dining table remained cluttered, two bagels were left from the dozen Mo had brought. Sitting opposite each other and alone for the first time, both grinned as they simultaneously reached for the remaining bagels.

"How about a switch? I'll take your 'onion' and you can have my 'plain'," suggested Herb.

Mo, having already ravenously devoured an 'egg' and 'garlic' stood his ground: "Thanks, but I'm happy with the present arrangement."

"The food is still fresh. I don't know how you do it Mo! Don't forget to thank Moishe Lieberman again next time you get to Hong Kong."

"It's his pleasure, Herb. He keeps on telling me, 'anything for a *lantsman*'."

"What's your pleasure, Mo?" asked Herb while smearing a generous portion of the cream cheese spread on his bagel. "Putting a glass rod in Chac's penis and then smashing it with a hammer!"

"Maybe. Pass the cream cheese, please."

"How about cutting off his balls, sticking a ten inch blade up his ass, and making him whistle Dixie?" Herb sipped his coffee, then added a teaspoon of sugar.

"Don't be unreasonable, Herb," answered Mo after a first bite. "I'd never ask a man to whistle a tune he didn't know."

"What would you do to Chac if you didn't think he was telling the truth, or was withholding information?"

"Because he's your friend, I might use an old but proven technique. Some of Major Thu's stable of ladies could jerk him off until he breaks. Do you think he'd make double figures before giving in? . . . When did you figure it out Herb?"

"I suspected this was your line of work the night we visited the morgue to view our Chinese friends from Taiwan, but this morning cinched it. What is your official title?"

"I'm a consultant to the security branch of ARVN. My specialty is behavior modification, or if you prefer, information extraction, or try this on for size—communication analysis."

"I felt all along you weren't just a scheduling officer in Air America. Your job isn't a covert operation. Why the secrecy?"

"Let's just say I don't like to advertise. It's an old habit. Even some company chaps don't like what I do," the CIA agent put down his bagel and peered over half-moon glasses, "You've heard the story many times, Doc. I'm misunderstood. Nobody loves me."

"Help me to understand, Mo. What will happen to Chac?"

"Let me dispense with one misconception. Occasionally you have to break somebody up. It happens, but it's not part of our usual 9 to 5 day. Defectors like Chac are rarely a problem, though his story is far out. A suicidal attack of regimental strength, and mass executions, as a plan of action to mobilize public opinion is a hard pill to swallow, especially when it comes from a low level Viet Cong officer. His information about Cambodia confirms other reports, though our people will want to pursue this thing about Sihanoukville as a port of entry for supplies. He'll get special attention . . ."

"Torture?"

"Always possible, but unlikely. The captured and committed VC with something to hide is the guy who gives me a bad reputation. A little candy or threats will get the job done more often than you would imagine, but occasionally you need muscle."

"How much muscle?"

"Enough to win the ball game. The rules are made by my supervisors, though I'm at a level where I can usually freelance."

"How often," Herb traced the outline of his facial scar, "do you encounter someone you can't break?"

"Personally, I've never met the man. In fact, the stronger his belief, the greater the vulnerability. Let's take Herb Klein, for instance. I know how much you love your wife, and if that was your great strength, then I would attack it. There are no great secrets in this line of work. Failures occur when there is not enough time, or when the interrogator is unskilled."

"What's the satisfaction? I've always considered you a reasonable man. I can't believe you're a sadist with no conscience. You must draw a line like everybody else. Where's yours? . . . What gives you the right?" said Herb angrily. His hands pounded the table; plates rattled and a fork fell to the floor. Herb moved closer until they were eye ball to eye ball. Mo calmly leaned back in the chair, and wiped his mouth with a napkin, a slight smile on his lips.

"I got to hand it to you, Doc. You come to the Nam and help people . . . peasants, VC, Montagnards, air jockeys, grunts, even Mo Balen. There you are on the sidelines watching the boys mix it up. Nobody even asks you to pick a side. Herb Klein stands for goodness, decency, honesty, and a fair deal. . ."

"Cut the bullshit, Mo!"

"I've said it before, you're a legitimate do-gooder. But what about the rest of us, Herb? The pilots who drop the bombs and the napalm, the grunts with the M-16s, and little ol' me. Once you become a soldier, your hands get dirty. The rules tell you how it is, not how it ought to be. How many of those nice boys in the green body bags lined up in the morgue ready to be shipped home to Momma got zapped in a fair fight? Show me a guy that plays fair—I'm talking about either side—and I'll show you a fuckin' loser. Fairness my ass! I'd work for my country for three square, and a roof over my head. There aren't many people in the CIA who look at it as nothing more than a way to make a buck. I will do anything to save the life of an American serviceman . . . Remember the two VC thrown out of a helicopter at Hoi An hospital? It was a set-up, Herb. They had no information to give, but another one of your VC patients did. He spilled his guts out and American lives were saved. I had a part in that operation, and I'm proud of it."

"And what about saving Vietnamese lives?"

"If they support us, then they're entitled to equal treatment. The ones who don't! Fuck 'em. Sure, good people are going to get hurt and you feel like shit when it happens. The other side plays the same way, only a hell of a lot harder. We're just well-fed kittens, and they're hungry tigers . . . Think of what Chac said. I know it's crazy, but what if they went through with those attacks? Tens of thousands of innocent people would have been killed, and for what? They'll lose the battle, but gain a few extra percentage points on next month's Gallop Poll. And believe me, most of the Vietnamese civilians don't give two shits who wins this war, they just want to survive. Don't talk to me about conscience. I sleep very well, thank you!"

"You make it sound like Vietnam is one big cage, and all of us are trapped animals. Somebody throws in a little meat, and there's a big free for all."

"That's exactly what this place is, because our government is indecisive, and sends out mixed signals. Anytime a man questions why he has to die, then he's in the cage."

"Okay Mo, why don't you spell out what the message ought to be."

"Why are we here? And what's it going to take to get the job done and go back to the states? We're here because the North Vietnamese and their Commie brethren never gave the South Vietnamese a chance to set up shop and see what they could do. The only boys capable of handling the bullies on the block are the Americans. If we succeed, maybe the ballot box will replace the gun as a legitimate method of acquiring political power. If we fail, then our enemies will remember and they'll play the same game on other street corners."

"Fine, just fine. Now, tell me how we're going to end the war."

"Ask a man to die for an idea, then you've got to have a game plan that he can believe in, understand, and work to achieve. A grunt gets in a fire fight and celebrates a big victory. A few months later there's another fire fight, and he's taking a shit in the same rice paddy wonderin' what the hell's going on. Search and destroy, enclave theory, containment . . . it's all bullshit. Our planners have a preoccupation with numbers: body counts, villages pacified, captured supplies. The only number that really counts to the grunt doing the dirty work is how many days he has left before his tour of duty is over. We need a blueprint for success. Fortunately, I think we've turned the corner," his tone reflected an awakened confidence. "I can see the light at the end of the tunnel."

"Shit, Mo, I must have blinders on."

"I've got news for you," the CIA agent edged closer to his listener anxious to share a revelation. "We are going to win the war. This whole thing will be over by Tet of '68 if, and it's a big if but a realistic one, if my sources are correct . . . We're going after them in Cambodia and Laos. No more sanctuaries. The show is over, the enemy isn't going to cover itself with a neutrality umbrella. No more sparring; we start playing for keeps."

An amused Herb squared his shoulders: "And what do you intend to do with Peking and Moscow, not to mention a growing anti-war movement back home? Do you think they will applaud this new plan for victory?"

"The response is part of the equation. The big powers will scream, but back down from anything more than verbal support and supplying a few more guns. The Peace movement is easy. A great majority of Americans will support us when they're convinced we're fighting to win and not draw. The public will support an action that may lose a few more lives initially, but will get the job done and avoid a protracted war."

"You know what I like about true believers, Mo," Herb spoke in a casual voice. "Issues are always clear cut. It's all so simple, an either/or situation, nobody knows what the color gray looks like. Everything's been stripped and the basics exposed, dissecting an idea is never a surprise. Press a button and the argument is over; confusion is never the enemy, clarity is like music to them. When the war is over, I wonder whether anyone will ever understand the agony of looking for an answer, probing for an insight, and maybe, just maybe, still coming up a little short."

"Still the dreamer. The American psyche will only tolerate a winner. Nobody will give two shits about your agony or confusion if they know you played on a losing team. And that, my good Doctor, is the only difference between a hero and a prick."

The noise of an aircraft broke the silence. Mo walked to the window and watched the observation plane make a routine landing. The aircraft stopped near the helicopter, Chac would soon be airborne.

The arrival of the big bird generated excitement, little children scurried to the airfield from village play areas, older men made the trek but at a slower pace that betrayed their years. Young Montagnard troopers assumed a combat-ready position; airplanes on the ground were easy targets for enemy fire.

"How do you like Bia Vuc?" Mo had returned to his chair.

"The natives are kind and decent. When I get back from Hawaii, I intend to implement a comprehensive medical program that will act as a model for other Montagnard villages throughout the Highlands. It's about time we pay attention to their needs. The 'gnards have been neglected and abused for centuries. I think Uncle Sam can turn it around."

"Good old Uncle Sam! The world's biggest troublemaker and leader of the Imperialist camp until you have a problem, then Sammy's a misunderstood blood relative with a chance to redeem himself. When are you going to open your eyes? First it was Village Pacification in the boonies, and that failed. Then you got your ass whipped at Hoi An hospital. You ended up with a thank-you medal from the Vietnamese, and a pat on the back from Colonel Stalley, and not a damn thing was changed. Bia Vuc is next. Primitive Montagnard tribesmen who fart and believe they're blowing away evil spirits, and you're their savior. This project is doomed just like the others. You take a piss in the ocean and think you're making a tidal wave. Uncle Sam is not going to pick up the tab. He's too thin now, and everybody wants a piece of him—there's not enough to go around. Bia Vuc is good copy, a nice place to take a congressman who wants to see the real Vietnam; propaganda bonus points, promotion and a medal for the guy who invented the idea. The plan called for a sucker to volunteer and play doctor, and you're their man. The publicity boys will milk it for all it's worth, and then the Montagnard Health Care file will be stashed away in a big cabinet. Ask Frenchy, he seems like a smart fella, what he thinks about the future of American medicine in Bia Vuc? Whoever wins the war, will continue to shit on these people. Governments don't like non-conformists. They always take it personally." Mo rose, briefcase in hand, and approached his friend. "I've often thought about you and your situation, Herb. The marchers back home look at you and your captain's uniform and see a childkiller; anybody in the military helping the American cause is committing genocide in their eyes. Your peers think you're a two karat jerko for volunteering your ass in what they correctly see as no-win situations. Bud Rich, and a whole lot of his kind, regard you as somebody more interested in helping the other side, than the people you're supposed to help. The Colonel exploits your altruism; suckers like you, after all, are a rarity. And of course, there are the VC and the NVA . . . so who cares about you? A few guys back at the base, that Montagnard Frenchy . . . and me." His arm reached for Herb's shoulder and he squeezed tightly. "A few of us have tried to reach you but failed. Our only hope is Christie, maybe she can fuck some sense into you. I'll see you back at Da Nang, m' man . . . By the way! All of Christie's gifts are wrapped. Thank Sergeant Lincoln."

Herb stood at the window and watched Mo walk toward the airfield. At the compound gate, Frenchy greeted him, and initiated a lively discussion. Both men turned in the direction of the Dining Room, and he could see the Montagnard holding the Star of David necklace. Herb smiled at his friend's antics, and returned to the table to clean up the mess. The bagels were all gone and only a small chunk of the cream cheese remained. Herb made a mental note: Frenchy likes onion.

* * *

29

Accompanied by a Stanley lunch pail and a one pint thermos of hot tea, John Loreski entered the Neschaunk underground coal mine at the tender age of twelve. As a trapper boy, he stood by a door and pushed it open, so coal cars would pass from one chamber to another. The youngster was determined to do a good job; the Loreskis needed the money, and the promise of a higher paying position in the mine was possible, if he proved equal to the task.

The door was heavy, but John was a strong and determined lad; smoke, dust, and gas were other occupational hazards. But his biggest obstacle, along with other co-workers, was to overcome the darkness that was their working world. Fear, lonliness, and boredom had to be dealt with in a responsible manner if the trapper boy was to succeed. The emotional strain of working in oppressive conditions was devastating for most, but John would survive the ordeal.

Christie's father would credit his success in part, to a little mental exercise he invented: choose an object or an idea—something nice and uplifting—create a setting, and then develop a happy story. The duration of the images were seconds to minutes, depending on the activity of the coal cars. A fanciful imagination, ingenuity, and a sense of beauty were all one needed to be good at it.

In the pitch black darkness of the earth, John created his fantasies at a frantic pace. His first love was exploring mountains: high cliffs, fast moving streams, gentle brooks, roaring cataracts, an extinct volcano crater filled by a lake, a grotto shaded by immense trees.

For many years his little mind game remained nameless. Little Christina was well schooled in the basics, and also an avid player. One day she sat on her father's lap, pulled on his bright red suspenders, and said playfully, "Let's do 'Pretty Things'!" A game that had been a favorite pastime now had a name and a new twist. Either one could initiate the action; taking turns, they yelled out whatever came to mind, closed their eyes, and when each fantasy was over and ready to be shared, they simply whispered softly, "Pretty Things."

So many wonderful memories, thought Christie as she recalled her Dad. She rested on the living room couch, her preparations for Hawaii were complete. The packing chores had already been painfully executed, all that remained were telephone calls to Momma and Ben.

It was time to unwind; she needed warmth and sunshine to soothe the senses and rekindle the spirit, expunge the uncertainties and think about the possibilities. Christie closed her eyes, and reflected on the little game that bonded father and daughter.

Pineapple Herb is wearing dark blue bathing trunks, Christie a two-piece aquamarine bikini. They sit on an isolated beach on the North shore of Oahu. There are no other people, a majestic crashing surf roars its endless melody. A ripened pineapple sits on a multicolored beach towel, and Herb's knife is making little headway. "I hope you're a better surgeon than you are a fruit cutter," Christie jokes, who then proceeds to cut the pineapple into small pieces. The juices flow, succulent fruit is still in their mouths as their lips meet. The aftertaste lingers. "Sweet Herb," she whispers.

Catamaran The boat travels along the Waikiki coastline in the direction of stately Diamond Head. A strong wind carries them swiftly through the rough waters. Near the shore, through the water spray, two native Hawaiians can be seen surfing on their koa-wood surfboards. One of the boat's two hulls is out of the water, the other skims through the waves. Herb and Christie feel the water, wind, and each other's warmth; they are propelled into another direction. "Faster, faster!" she says as they sail into the sunset. Laughter hastens the adventure.

Pali Lookout In the Koolau Mountains, Herb and Christie share a kaleidoscope of color, and the panorama of Oahu. A rainbow is the focal point of their portrait; sloping, verdant hillsides gracefully merge into sugar cane and pineapple fields, creamy sand and emerald green waters clash on desolate beaches. Herb is mesmerized by the beauty, quietly and methodically he puffs on his pipe. Christie turns away from their landscape, one arm encircles his waist, and the other dances through curly hair. Her head rests on his chest, the aroma of Balkan tobacco penetrates and delights; silence rings loundly. The moment is framed and captured.

The game over, Christie felt refreshed as she strolled to the kitchen. On the table was an address book, and a letter containing another list of restaurants and native Hawaiian dishes recommended by a nurse friend who had lived in Honolulu for two years. Christie's arrival would precede her husband's by a few days, she'd have ample opportunity to explore the dining-out possibilities.

Herb enjoyed basic American fare, Jewish cooking, and a few Polish dishes, he had always been reluctant to experiment until Christie insisted on a change. Now that his culinary tastes had enlarged, he tended to concentrate more on the price than the quality of the food. In a restaurant he deemed unreasonable, she could count on her husband picking the lowest priced entree, and complaining about the poor selection of appetizers and desserts before selecting none. At the same time, he would insist she eat a complete meal, regardless of the cost. In Hawaii, there would be no compromise, and they would eat well. Her plan called for a light breakfast and a gourmet experience involving different restaurants each afternoon and evening. She intended to ask for a single menu and order for both. Herb would scold her for treating him like a child, protest his having no voice in decision making, lecture on the necessity of being frugal; the rest of the evening would feature glowing compliments of the restaurant and her choices. Life with this guy, reasoned Christie, as she prepared to peruse her friend's suggestions, may be predictable, but never boring.

. . . with my tastes in mind, Christie, here are my selections for Honolulu restaurants:

Tony's Fish House: near Waikiki Palace Hotel—terrific opakapaka (like red snapper) and the mahimahi is great. Best place for Maine lobster, or Maryland crab. . .$10 for two (prices don't include drinks)

Ala Moana: near the shopping center of the same name—great native dishes—try poi, chicken luau, lomiloni salmon, and limu-kohu . . . $15 for two

Imperial Inn: near the International Market Place entrance (next to Manny Ho's Drugstore)—traditional Chinese fare, very good and unbelievably low prices . . . $3 a piece gets a banquet, doggie bag for leftovers, and a pleasant headache that you can live with

Kamakura: Kapiolani Blvd., across the street from Hotel Kapiolani—knockout Japanese cuisine—sauteed beef, a winner from the teppan grill, but shabu-shabu is spectacular (similar to Swiss fondue) . . . $8 a couple

Kalini: in the Hotel Kalini—mainly Hawaiian dishes—Roast Duckling Waialae (with bananas, litchi, and peaches) is mind boggling . . . a deuce sets you back about $15 to $20

Walter's: same street as Tony's, but on the other side—stark, but exceptional island seafood (a 'locals' hangout)—try ono (wahoo), hapauu (grouper), and Opelu (mackerel) . . . $5 for two, tops-do *not* order cole slaw

Pierre's: in Hotel Iolani, at beachfront level—best French food in town—great ambience (overlooks ocean, fresh flowers on table, candlelight)—House pate is a treat, and so are the escargots—everything breathtaking, including the check . . . in excess of $30 (knowing Herb, you better blindfold him for this one)

Luau: the food is uniformly poor, but the shows are fabulous and seeing one is a must—the Hotel Royal may be your best bet, but don't forget the Alka Seltzer

I know you've been bombarded with sightseeing suggestions, and I've none to offer. My guess is that with the exception of meals and sunbathing, your hotel room will have all the attractions you need.

Give Herb my love, and tell him the medical ward is not the same without his ashes on the charts. Since he left, no one carries extra matches. Have a great time, Christie!

ALOHA
Sharon

Christie carried the address book and Sharon's letter into the bedroom, and slipped it into the small overnighter. Compulsively, she reached for the legal pad and rechecked the lists. All accounted for, she paused before returning to the kitchen. Herb's small blue tourister suitcase was slightly ajar, and the three white cans of tobacco were in view. It was okay for others to buy Balkan as a gift, but her husband always insisted their budget could not accommodate this luxury.

"Oh Baby . . . please Honey!" she said aloud to herself, foreseeing another little squirmish. "Don't give me a hard time over the Balkan tobacco. You deserve the best, my Love . . . the very best."

* * *

30

THE day had been hectic. Soon after Chac, Mo and the Intelligence Team departed, Frenchy accompanied Herb on his routine village sick call. The Montagnard was talkative, moody, and irritable, understandable in light of Chac's revelations, and the possibility of Bia Vuc's destruction. Herb tried unsuccessfully to ally his friend's fears by restating Captain Bixler's optimistic military assessment.

On their way to Village A, they stopped at the cemetery, always a focal point for contemplation: renewed questioning about Herb's religion and family had a calming effect on the little man with the blue beret.

A late start and a few more house calls than usual set the tone for the day. A heavy patient load in the afternoon made lunch an impossibility, and a medical emergency put the schedule in total disarray.

A six year old girl was brought to the infirmary in a comatose state, she had two seizures in Herb's presence. The child had been active and alert until that afternoon, when she suddenly became ill. Herb's diagnosis after an extensive evaluation: A very sick youngster, etiology undetermined. A short visit with Hunter's *Tropical Medicine* and a twenty-minute chat with Dr. Black at Da Nang changed nothing: Freddy simply agreed with the plan of action which included good hydration, anti-convulsive medications, and antibiotics for possible pneumonia. The youngster would be airlifted to a hospital the next morning.

It was while Herb was at her bedside attending to the needs of the convulsing girl that the Shaman approached him and offered—through his translator, Frenchy—some ideas for a remedy. Herb wasn't insulted, but thought Frenchy overreacted. He yelled at the 'witch doctor' for interfering, criticized the suggestions, and angrily threw his blue beret to the floor to emphasize his displeasure.

The rest of the afternoon was a juggling act. Herb was determined to see every patient with a complaint, despite the interruptions necessary to assure the seizuring youngster's well-being. When the last patient left the clinic, he breathed a sigh of relief, nobody had departed prematurely despite a long wait. He believed the intimacy and confidence he had established with the natives remained intact. A good image and a high profile was necessary if his medical plan was to succeed at Bia Vuc.

It was almost nightfall when Herb and Frenchy joined the three man Special Forces team. Their paths had not crossed during the day, and the evening update remained unchanged. No large scale enemy movements were observed, not even small unit probes appeared imminent based on field reports.

Dinner was a pleasant surprise: fruit cocktail, mashed potatoes, baked beans, juicy steak, doughnuts, coffee, and Seagrams 7. It wasn't necessary for Captain Bixler to confirm Herb's suspicion but he did: Mo Balen had provided the goodies. The meal was familiar to Herb, and he guessed Sergeant Lincoln was the middle man. The missing part of the puzzle was how many bottles of whiskey passed into Marine hands to complete the transaction.

The post meal conversation took a familiar direction; a rehash of Superbowl I, condemnation of the American Football League, and of Kansas City in particular. This was for the benefit of Lieutenant Stone, a diehard Chief's fan. The Lieutenant's recent fallout with his girlfriend was then mercilessly exploited by his Green Beret colleagues. Stone answered with a diversionary ploy: "Did you hear the news? *What's My Line* is going off the air. Would you believe! 17 years. Only the Ed Sullivan Show has a longer run."

It worked. Sergeant Flaherty suggested the Lieutenant be the guest with an unknown profession, but it had to be something he had actually done in the past. Stone agreed, and eagerly wrote his trade in block letters on a blank paper.

"Are you in a service oriented industry?" Herb's first question set the mood.

"Yes Sir!" said the Lieutenant snappily.

"Is your fee fixed?" asked Flaherty.

"Negotiable," was the terse reply.

The panel far exceeded the routine twenty question limit, but with no success. The frustration level was high when Bixler, who had been the most persistent interrogator conceded defeat. A humble Lieutenant Stone acknowledged victory, and quietly revealed his secret by turning over the paper. It read: Professional Muff Diver.

Shouts of "fraud, cheater, and liar" followed, but it was Flaherty who provided the telling blow: "He calls himself a professional and that is false advertising. I knew his girlfriend . . . traveled the same territory . . . and compared to me, she called him an amateur!"

"Sarge, you shouldn't be so hard on Stone, even the best lady's man has a bad day. I remember at Fort Bragg, there was this Civie chick who worked in the accounting office . . . Jo Anne Lasher, Lister, Lisher . . . I can't remember. A real piece of ass, Triple A prime, solid eating stuff . . . Stone, you'd gladly do this job for free. I took her out to a nice restaurant and a movie, and was a perfect gentleman. I think it was our fourth date, when I grabbed for titty. I figured there was so much there, maybe she wouldn't notice it! You know what that cunt did? She called me an animal. Do you believe that chick? Why don't we have a true confession session, and let each man tell about a girl he had the hots for, but never made it with. Doc, you're the lead-off batter."

"I can't comment, Captain Bixler," said Herb apologetically. "I never faced the problem, but I can sympathize with you. Failure can be a terrible blow to a man's ego."

"Never happened. In Bia Vuc, women ask Frenchy to maky love all the time. I try my best to help out pussy, but sometimes I'm very busy, and must say no."

"Cap'n, I know how you feel. It happened to me once," commiserated the Lieutenant. "Her name was Rosalyn, a real knockout. I was in sixth grade . . ."

"Fuck you, Stone . . . Flaherty!" barked Bixler in a stentorian voice.

"I picked up this girl at a local gin mill. I think her name was Judy. A fine woman . . . real fine. I had a load on that night, but I'm pretty sure I didn't get into her pants . . ."

"Holy shit! I'll be a son-of-a-bitch," Captain Bixler said disbelievingly. "You mean to tell me that I'm the only guy here who ever failed with a lady?"

"Sounds that way Cap'n," said a straight-faced Lieutenant Stone, as the other men soberly nodded their heads in approval.

Herb started it, and then the others followed. A salvo of paper plates, napkins, and towels caught the Captain by surprise. The chair tumbled backwards as Bixler tried to avoid the missles, the sight of his lean, muscular frame sprawled over the chair and floor prolonged the laughter.

Captain Bixler stood up with a wide grin and a flushed face as Herb left the dining hall to visit the infirmary. Waving hands and a chorus singing 'Good Night, Doc' ushered him into the pristine mountain air. Herb took a circuitous route along the perimeter of the compound, the stroll was restive and therapeutic, an opportunity to recover from the feverish pace of the last twenty-four hours.

An elderly Montagnard guard dressed in a loin cloth and armed with a rifle, emerged from the darkness to open the clinic door. The nurse did not even turn her head as Herb approached the bedside, so entranced was she with the welfare of the convulsing child. Herb looked at the vital signs chart, then a nod of the old woman reassured him that no problem had arisen in his absence. The patient remained asleep as he examined her. Breathing was not labored and the skin had a noticeable sheen. Perhaps it was the lack of good light, but he could not see the eye and skin hemorrhages, nor could he feel a spleen or hear the rales in her chest. He had a warm feeling, but he realized a sick child tested his objectivity. The need to separate the disease from the flesh was distasteful, but necessary.

Once more, after a deep, mind-clearing breath, he re-examined the patient. The rales in her chest, hemmorhages in the skin and eye, palpable spleen, skin pallor . . . it was all there. Nothing had changed since the last examination before dinner; her condition remained precarious and her life in jeopardy.

The reality dealt with, Herb held her closely. He rubbed his face against the straight black hair, massaged dark skin with an open hand, rocked the beautiful little girl in a gentle to and fro motion before returning her to the bed. She had not stirred, only her chest and protuberant belly swayed to the cadence of life. Herb was moved. He sought her forehead first, then the bridge of the nose and the chin, and concluded with the cheeks. Percolated with tenderness, love, and hope, delivered lightly and with moist lips, a kiss had become the instrument of his despair.

The old Montagnard nurse watched without a hint of emotion. She nodded when Herb returned the vital signs chart, and again, when he explained by a series of gestures where he could be found in the event of an emergency. When Herb was ready to leave for his quarters, the elderly woman reached for his hand, and placed it between the sick child's and her own. The nurse then uttered strange words in an eerie, melodic chant. He guessed it was a primitive healing prayer, but would ask Frenchy in the morning about the ritual's significance. As Herb approached the door, it suddenly opened; the old Montagnard guard, his keen sense of hearing still razor sharp, awaited his departure.

The elderly sentry was not the only one aware of Herb's movements. In the infirmary, behind a makeshift screen that overlooked the sick girl's bed, lurked a man who had witnessed all that had transpired between doctor, nurse, and patient. He quietly stepped from behind the screen and total darkness, a single light from the bedside cast his long shadow. The little girl and the old woman became the sole objects of his penetrating gaze.

Herb sat alone on the cot in the concrete fortified bunker that served as his quarters. He meticulously reviewed the child's condition and the most likely complications he might encounter during the night.

Know the odds, play the favorites, but think of the longshots when the stakes are high, an astute Osler physician whom he had admired and respected once summed up. The subject of that lecture was disease and probability, but the implications were far-reaching. A sick little girl and an inexperienced nurse in a critical care situation was a lethal combination to uninterrupted sleep. Herb understood the odds as he prepared for bed. The courtyard's soft light filtered through the only wall opening, and rested on the chair where his clothes and stethoscope had been placed. In the event of an emergency, he would dress in partial darkness, and not use the room's strong electric bulb. The short, brisk walk in the fresh mountain air to the girl's bedside would enliven the senses.

At Osler General Hospital or Da Nang, it was a loud ringing telephone that would alert him to a problem. In Bia Vuc, he could expect frantic knocking at the door, or ear-splitting screams of help through the room's one window. As fatigue set in and heavy eyelids began to droop, Herb expected no more than a short nap. He fully anticipated a return to the infirmary where his medical judgment would again be tested.

On previous evenings, the main deterrant to a good night's rest had been a shared joke by Montagnard sentries near his quarters. An awakened Herb would merely chuckle before resuming his slumber.

But tonight it was not laughter, nor banging at the door, or an urgent plea for help that startled him from a deep sleep. Instead, it was a *ping*, followed by repetitive *pings*—the unmistakeable sound of gunfire.

Herb jumped to his feet, and peered throught the window. A clear view of the lit courtyard indicated that visitors had arrived. Bia Vuc was under siege. The People's Army had successfully penetrated the military compound without a warning shot being fired. Charlie was right outside his quarters and setting up shop. Crackling rifles and flashing muzzles, popping machine gun fire, exploding grenades and deafening thumps. The clamor of men scrambling: virulent shouts and curdling screams.

A raging battle in full swing, Herb's mind kept company with the barrage: How could it have happened? . . . The Intelligence reports! . . . Chac called it! . . . How did Charlie escape the patrols and the land mines? . . . Spooky! Where's Spooky? . . . The troopers on Mount Servin and the village guard, maybe they're preparing for a counter-attack! . . . A Mick team assault . . .

Suddenly, the back of a Viet Cong cadre appeared directly in front of Herb's vision, only a few feet away. He muttered, "Is that . . . ? It can't be!" The black pajama clad soldier turned around and looked directly into the bunker's window. He stood still a moment and then dashed to a nearby mortar pit.

Herb was trembling and sweating. He turned away from the window and the carnage outside, and staggered to the medical chest that served as his bureau. He realized how the enemy had infiltrated the compound, how Bia Vuc's defenses had collapsed so decisively—he had seen it in the face of a single VC soldier.

Herb sought a pipe. The blazing fires surrounding the bunker set his room aglow; it made the selection process easier. He looked at all of them, each had a separate personality and a host of memories. His choice—a briar with a saddle bit bulldog shape, diamond shank, and saddle stem—had been her first gift. Sweaty hands shook as he reached for the pouch of Balkan tobacco. Teeth chattered as he held the pipe stem tightly in his mouth. Heart pounding, he struck a match, then a second; success came on the fifth try.

He felt better sitting on a chair, and puffing on the pipe. Her photograph was on his lap, the sounds of death and destruction remained unchecked, if he chose to listen. But Herb had another idea . . .

Herb saw himself dressed in shorts, polo shirt, sweat socks, and sneakers while running in a drizzle in Philadelphia's Fairmount Park. There's Grandpop Jacob putting the jugs of spring water into a red wagon. He's racing past a fenced-off bush, and waves to Uncle Otto selling religious articles. Sophie smiles as he sprints through the rose gardens at Horticultural Hall. It's a downpour as Herb approaches his house on Wyal Street, and Ben nods approval. Into 'Old Philly' and Bainbridge Street where Amanda sits by her apartment window and urges him on. Doctors, nurses, and hospital employees cheer as he passes Osler General. His fraternity brothers make a pathway outside of Swenson House—"You can do it. Only a little bit longer," shouts a Brother. The rain falls in cascades, Herb is splashing in giant puddles approaching Southwark. As he nears Kerr Street, the deluge intensifies, a tumultuous cloudburst makes it impossible to see. Herb goes faster and faster into its eye—he is caught in a torrent. It is the monster monsoon of Vietnam . . . Swiftly! Run quickly! Faster! Go Herb! . . . He emerges into the sunlight. The rain has ceased. The sky is blue and cloudless. Warm sunshine bathes his wet body. He has reached Kerr Street, and stands in front of the Flint house. She waits for him at the doorstep . . .

Herb removed the pipe and raised her photograph, he kissed the lips, and fingers danced over a long sensuous neck, rosy cheeks, and silky auburn hair. She had given him so much joy.

There were loud voices on the other side of the bunker door. The knob was turning; clockwise, counterclockwise, clockwise again, and one final counterclockwise rotation.

"Momma! Papa!" spoke the devoted son. "I have tried to be a good and decent person to all whom I've touched . . . the rest was nonsense."

There was shoving and pushing against the door; a short quiet interval, and then more thumping.

"Shema Yisroel, Adonoi Eloheinu, Adonoi Echad . . . Hear, O Israel, the Lord Our God, the Lord Is One." An embarrassed Herb shook his head in disbelief, surprised by his own words. He added in a resigned smile, "Born a Jew, I'll die one. A few misunderstandings along the way, but . . ."

An argument had ensued, men were shouting at each other. A gun clamored. The lock gave way. The door swung open.

"The universe is collapsing, it's getting smaller and smaller," Herb sighed. And with the knowledge of a man who had known happiness, Herb Klein whispered for a shrinking world to hear, "I love you, Christie."

* * *

She stood in the darkness of the huge bay window admiring the river. Her senses were alive. It was a clear evening in old Philly town. The glow of the river boats, flashing white streaks on the nearby Benjamin Franklin bridge, glittery old bricks on Kerr Street: Southwark had a special feel.

Her field of vision encompassed even more than the lights, colors, and shadows of a great city on the edge of sleep. Tomorrow morning, she would board the plane at International Airport, and start the long, arduous journey to Hawaii. But tonight, even more pleasure awaited her. With eyes closed, She mused.

Sunset An oceanfront balcony at the Princess Kuilani Hotel high above Waikiki beach. Near sliding doors, a small table with a glass top has two tumblers partially filled with coconut milk, and a large bowl filled with oranges, peaches, bananas, litchis, pineapple, and papaya.

They stand at the balcony railing holding hands. She wears a pink mumu. A lei embellishes her bronzed neck. The purple orchid in her hair is pushed gently by the ocean breeze. He is also well tanned. His rainbow colored Aloha shirt falls loosely over white slacks. A lei adorns his neck. The pipe he smokes is her favorite, as is the alluring aroma of Balkan.

On the horizon, sitting atop the ocean, is the glowing sun. Its deep, dark, fiery red radiance sets the sky ablaze. Gold and silver clouds look down on sparkling waters. A Pacific sunset in all its splendor weaves its magic, and they watch the spectacle.

"It's ours, Herb, it's ours."

"And it always will be, Christie."

* * *

PART III

31

EXPOSURE

"Do you like Gypsy music?" asked the young man wearing a Grateful Dead T-shirt.

"It's different, Henryk," answered the bearded man with a grin, not wanting to offend. "An unusual combination . . . two guitars, cello, concertina, and a dancer with castanets. Yet, there is a pleasant harmony."

The gypsy musicians were out of tune, but the harshness was diminished by their energy and enthusiasm. Smiling faces, fast moving hands, full-mouthed cries, and whistles spurred the dancer into a frenzy. Her swirling movements and uplifted skirt were more in keeping with tempo than melody. No one in the crowd standing on the river bank appeared bothered by the cacophony. The dervish dancer set the mood, young and old clapped hands and swayed to the music.

"Are you sure you don't mind, Professor? I see a raft coming."

"I will be fine," said the lean, middle-aged man.

"Good. You're in for a treat. A boat ride on the Dunajec River, the Pienny mountains—one of the most beautiful sights in all of Poland."

"Then you must mean the world," corrected the Professor.

"Of course," smiled Henryk. "The car will be parked near the big bus."

He watched the young man walk to a nearby kiosk, and then turned to the river and the surrounding countryside. A huge castle with stately turrets sat atop a mountain on the opposite bank partially immersed in clouds, surrounded by a huge brick wall and circular archways leading into a courtyard. The bearded man marvelled at the Renaissance design and its idyllic setting.

The raft arrived at the small dock. Its flat surface permitted three abreast, and a seating capacity of fifteen. The boatman, dressed in native folk costume—blue baggy pants, red vest, white ruffled shirt, and a black hat with tassels—stood astern with a large black pole ready to maneuver the craft.

The boat filled quickly. The Professor was seated in the middle of the front row; a priest in a clerical frock occupied one side; on the other flank sat a baldheaded older man dressed in peasant garb—plaid shirt, tapered pants, and knee-high boots smeared with mud and debris. Three youths, loud and boisterous, sat in the next row.

The raft had just started its journey when the friendly priest commented on the weather, and asked about the bearded man's hometown. The Professor was depressed and in no mood for small talk, though fluent in Polish, he diplomatically replied: "Polonia Amerykanska . . . Polish American. I understand very little Polish. Do you speak English?"

"Ah, Amerykanska! English . . . no," sighed the priest.

The boat pilot started his dialogue in a monotone, indistinguishable from a recording, as the raft accelerated in mid-stream. No explanation was necessary for the American, he was already captivated by the mountain slopes of massive trees and the sweep of the river with its crystal clear water; cataracts above high precipices were already in sight as the raft made its first bend and one great vista replaced another.

The Professor responded to a pat on the shoulder. One of the cantankerous youths thrust a canteen in his face; the smell of alcohol helped explain their behavior. He refused the offer, but with a placating smile. The priest sought his attention and pointed to the shore, huge boulders were smothered with water from a massive waterfall cascading into the river. But the biggest surprise for the bearded man was not a delight of nature.

"The Sears building in Chicago is like the Palace of Culture in Warsaw. Is it not, Professor?" asked the old peasant with the massive muddy boots. "Don't turn around. Continue to follow the good Father's hand. He is one of us, and the three young drunks behind you are friends. Do not look at me, except if the sightseeing dictates. The packet you seek is now at your feet. I'll tell you when to pick it up."

"Is it all there?" asked the American, his composure regained.

"Yes, Professor. Photographs, microtape recordings, sworn affidavits from the prisons and detention centers . . . delivered as promised.

When you return to Chicago you will be notified of a change in Swiss banks and an appropriate telex number."

The river was widening, streams and brooks were frequent, the raft passed one tributary and approached another. The American could hear the sound of the pilot's pole splashing through the water.

"I had just about given up hope. I expected an earlier contact. Why the delay?"

"The Ministry of Internal Affairs has big ears. The only time you have been out of sight is on your trip from Warsaw to Crakow. You've been followed since the moment you checked in at the Hotel Cravinia. The Ministry's people are everywhere. Henryk, your guide from the Orbis travel bureau, is on the MSW's payroll."

"Well I'll be!" said the Professor. "Smokes pot, loves acid rock, dresses like a beatnik, and works for the Polish KGB."

"You've been a busy man. We tried to make contact in Crakow in the Old Market Square when you listened to the bugler, and then at Wavvel Hill at the Zygmunt Bell. In the salt mine at Wieliczka, you had a soda at the refreshment stand before the Grand Chapel visitation," recited the old peasant. "We are very cautious, my friend."

"What if Henry had decided to take the raft trip?"

"There was a back-up plan, but we felt reasonably assured of success. Do you recall seeing a young woman in the parking lot? She wore black boots, a short skirt, and was very robust."

"No."

"Your Orbis guide did, and I suspect that after Yola's finished, Henryk will be a tired young man . . . and poorer as well. We are coming to another bend in the river, and there will be a monastery on a mountain cliff. When everyone turns toward the boatman to get a good look, reach for the packet."

The transfer succeeded without a hitch. After the raft had turned, a long straight section followed where the river narrowed. The three rowdies were singing and laughing, and the priest berated them. An unperturbed raftsman continued to drone on about the wonders of the Dunajec.

"What do you think will happen when we go public?" inquired the Professor.

"A little noise and no action. The United Nations, International Labor, Amnesty International—what's their record in Eastern Europe, or in the Soviet spheres of influence anywhere? Our revelations keep issues alive, and bring in a few dollars. We still make good print in the Free World's newspapers and magazines." The old man turned to the shoreline, his voice quivered. "Self-determination is still the major problem. We raised the question at Gdansk, and the Russians provided the Polish people with the answer: sixty Soviet divisions pointed their guns in our direction and told us to be quiet. Most of the world governments called our dash for freedom an 'internal affair' for the Polish people to resolve, knowing full well that Poles will never be allowed to chart their own destiny under the present Moscow formula. Now, my friend, how many mountains do you think we will move in the West with that packet in your possession?"

"Then what was gained by it all," said the Professor gloomily, "except to show the Free World's disunity, and its weakness to act in the face of adversity and a clear cut issue?"

"Our struggle is the best example to date, of what the Kremlin and their puppets fear most, an open election and the choice of alternative ideas. It is the one experiment the Party and the Revolution will never make and that is the irony, for it is the only test to prove their credibility. I was at Oliwa, near Gdansk, for the First Congress. The atmosphere was electric—the delegates debated issues, cheered and laughed. We were in awe of our own power. The power of a new voice with a world wide audience. All of us were so proud; the honor, the pride of Poles, who believed they now had a share in the decision-making power of the state. We thought of ourselves as patriots. They branded us counter-revolutionaries to be ridiculed, jailed, and tortured. Enemies of the state who needed rehabilitation. The world can pretend no longer. There is no place for the people's voice in the Soviet bloc."

The river was at its narrowest, a small segment of fast, white water was no challenge to the skilled boatman as he churned through the rapids. The nearby shoreline continued to be desolate with no signs of life. The castle and the monastery was the only evidence of a wilderness instrusion. The passengers squealed each time an occasional spray threatened to get them. The raft slowed as the water became more calm. The noise and excitement aboard the craft subsided as well. The hum of the pilot's pole remained the only constant. The unruly drunks were again sternly rebuked by the priest.

"How do you like Chicago?"

"Very much," answered the Professor. "Right now, my girlfriend and I are rehabing a house. The amount of time and work involved is tremendous, not to mention the expenses, even though it's shared."

"How does your 'arrangement' work out? In Poland, marriage is still an honored institution."

"Monica is a career woman. She's an advertising executive, travels a fair amount, and loves her work. Like me, an independent type, but smart enough to understand that she can't have it all in our situation."

"Maybe if you ask her hand in marriage . . ."

"I did, twice," interrupted the Professor, "and have been refused both times. It was difficult to understand. I was always a believer in the biological instincts of motherhood, and the idea that love conquers all. Monica has forced me to revise my thinking, and she is right, marriage and a family at this time would be disastrous."

"Have you eaten at the Kasztelanda and Orbit restaurants on Milwaukee Street? They were my favorites," sighed the peasant.

"Sure, many times! I love the Czarnina and the Golabki at Kas', and the Orbit's Kielbasa and Szpinak z Czosnkiem. A little Chrussieka for dessert . . . Then you've been to Chicago!"

"I lived in the States for a while, including Chicago for a few months. I made enough money to buy a Czeck automobile—a Skoda—and then returned to my family. I still get 'care packages' from a brother in Connecticut," grinned the old man.

"Now if we can mobilize the conscience of the Free World, package it and then ship it off to the Kremlin, maybe we can salvage something out of this mess."

"My friend," The peasant took note of the Professor's sarcasm and replied, "The Polish contribution to truth has been made, no matter how the West chooses to respond. Our working class has proven that Marx's dictatorship of the proletariat is not possible under Soviet direction. The inspiration of our struggle comes from the shipyards, the factories, the mines. The state is opposed to the very forces it claims to represent."

The raft continued to flow in calm waters. As the river widened, man's presence became noticable—an occasional cabin, waving children, two men chopping wood. The boatman's pole continued at the same cadence, but his lecture on the Dunajec was over. A repeat performance would be forthcoming as the craft approached the final river bend. The landing dock was already in sight.

The men in the front row were quiet, they had been partners in a mission about to conclude and it was unlikely that their paths would ever cross again. Neither tried to renew the conversation, but the silence was broken by gypsy music and clapping hands.

At dockside, disembarking from the raft went smoothly. The Professor could see the back of the priest, and the three rowdies, as they ascended the short hill to the parking lot. He would have to take the same path to meet Henryk, who should be tired if Yola was nearly as talented as the old man had hinted. He assumed that the elderly peasant was behind him, or perhaps he had strolled in the direction of the kiosk, along the bank of the river.

As the bearded American slowly made his way to the car, he reflected on the mystery surrounding his recent encounter. Who was the old man, and what was his position in the movement? As a courier, his contacts had always been brief, and today had been the first instance of any verbal communication. There had been no direct contact. He was still unaware of the old man's facial features; he had caught only a side profile out of the corner of his eye.

The Professor had reached the parking lot, and saw Henryk standing by the car. He was forced to walk through a group of sightseers boarding a bus in order to reach his Orbis tourguide. It happened quickly and the shock was shortlived. Another memory to be cherished, one that would surely never go away. The bearded man was jostled as he passed through the crowd. A quick backward glance revealed familiar garb with muddy knee high boots. The peasant had said in a tiny voice, but with immense pride and power, "*Solidarność.*"

The airport at Crakow was not busy. From his chair, the departing Professor had a good view of both the airfield and the entrance to the terminal. At his side sat the cheerful and outgoing Henryk. Never at a loss for words, the tourguide expounded endlessly on any issue that he believed stimulated his client's interest. The young man was a marked contrast to the reserved and formal style of Poles the American had known. In a country where history and tradition was still a revered way of life (kissing a woman's hand was still in vogue and considered an act of gallantry), the effusive and back-slapping antics of Henryk were more in keeping with a used car salesman, Chicago-style.

The Professor really didn't need the old man's warning of Henryk's affiliation with the Ministry of Internal Affairs. Except for Solidarity contacts, he assumed all Poles were somehow associated with the MSW. As a noted scholar who had access to Poland even in a crisis, it was important to maintain a position as an impartial academician

uninvolved in internal political affairs. Criticism of any Polish institution could jeopardize his position.

"What do you think of the Zomos?" asked Henryk. One hand
scratched his Ozzy Osbourne–Blizzard of Oz T-shirt, the other
playfully patted the Professor's shoulder.

"I don't think about the Zomos," grinned the bearded American.
"But I guess someone has to maintain peace and order in difficult
times. Anarchy won't solve Poland's problems." In a place far removed
from the present location, where free speech was possible, he'd have
answered the question by echoing a Warsaw University student's
appraisal: "Zomos! SS! One eats perogi, the other weinershnitzel."

Satisfied with the response, Henryk became a one man talkathon.
He rambled on about the wonders of America, and how he intended
to visit the bearded man's homeland. The Professor, irritated by the
young man's chattering, reached for a pen and card. He recognized
the ploy and diplomatically offered the tourguide an invitation to
Chicago. Henryk's discourse on American history and life-style was
replaced by a humble inquisitiveness about the "real America," one
that in the near future he would investigate under the guidance of his
newly acquired friend for life.

At customs, Henryk continued to reaffirm their friendship. The
Professor needn't worry; he would sustain the harmony and they
would soon be reunited in Chicago. Both men appeared equally
puzzled when the custom's officer told the American to go to a nearby
room for routine questioning.

The policeman who greeted them at the door was well-mannered
and congenial. The Professor considered his manner cause for concern; he would have felt more at ease had the officer been formal and
business-like. The Solidarity packet was concealed in a briefcase that
held his research for a forthcoming book. The possibility of detection
no longer seemed remote, but he remained composed and relaxed.
Henryk was neither. He angrily shouted at the policeman, and
expressed his displeasure at the very implication of impropriety.

"How dare you detain the Professor! He is an honored guest of the
Socialist Republic of Poland, and a world authority on our literature.
His book on Joseph Conrad is read at our universities. . ."

"Henryk," interjected the Professor, "let the man do his job."

"Thank you," said the officer graciously. He then turned to Henryk.
"Would you please have a seat . . . Mr. Ozzy Osbourne!"

"I warn you, even the Party First Secretary knows of the Professor's work. You will be hearing from him," mumbled Henryk.

"Excuse me, Professor." The policeman, middle-aged with slick black hair parted in the middle and dark eyes to match, casually glanced at the American's passport. "You are Paul Loreski, born 1942, in Neschaunk, Pennsylvania."

"Yes sir."

"I have a cousin in Pittsburgh, Pennsylvania. Is Neschaunk close by?"

"About the same distance that separates Warsaw from Crakow."

"Were your parents born in Poland?"

"My father was born in Nowy Sacz, my mother in Neschaunk, but her parents come from Nowy Targ."

"What does your father do in Neschaunk?"

"He died, but he was a coal miner."

"Ah," smiled the officer, "I am from Walbrzych. My father also passed away, and he was a Silesian coal miner. I go home, and still see his black trade uniform with gold trim . . . a proud man. I'm sure your father was the same way."

"Yes."

"Professor, I noticed the Ministry of Education and Culture approved your visa application."

"Yes."

The officer rose, and handed over the passport with a little bow and a firm handshake. "Professor Loreski. I am sorry for the delay. I have orders and I must obey. I hope your stay in Poland has been enjoyable. I am quite anxious to read your book on Joseph Conrad, and the one you are now writing. Have a safe journey home, and we look forward to your return."

As they stood at the gate awaiting the call to board the LOT airplane, Henryk continued his berating of the policeman: "Somehow, someway . . . he will be punished, Professor. Your honor will be my sword."

Paul wasn't about to argue. A man of principle is rare in a world governed by the laws of economics. It was useless to dissuade a fraternal ally from revenge—the cement was in place and needed time to harden. Even after shaking hands and passing through the boarding gate, he could hear a final shout: "It's my sword, Professor! My sword! The government will issue you a formal apology. I'll tell you the details in Chicago over a cup of tea . . ."

As he ascended the steps leading to the aircraft, Paul could only shake his head in disbelief. The prospects of lunch with Henryk at Chicago's Orbit restaurant was a revolting thought. But sharing a cup of tea with the likes of the old man with the muddy boots, now that was another story.

* * *

32

THE HERMITAGE HOTEL OF PHILADELPHIA

Philadelphia Hypnotist Society 9 A.M.–5 P.M.	Gold Room—Floor 2
Hot Toddy Lingerie Shareholders Meeting 8:30 A.M.	Pink Room—Floor 1
Lighthouse Business Association Luncheon 1 P.M.	Green Room—Lobby
Holiday Travel Agents Ongoing 8 A.M. Coffee and Danish	Grey Room—Floor 2
Testimonial—Rabbi Max Mazer Dinner 6 P.M.	Blue Room—Floor 1
Charity Ball—St. Vincent's Hospital 7 P.M.	Main Ballroom

"It's the Blue Room, Rachel," shouted the man in the pin-striped suit. "C'mon, will ya! We're late as it is."

"Don't use that late routine on me, Harry. I asked you to help out with the kids . . ."

"Rachel, please! They expect 500 people for the Rabbi's dinner. I hate grand entrances. You know what I mean. The Duke and Duchess of Society Hill . . . and all eyes are on Rachel and Harry Weinberg as we walk to our table. By the way, what is the table number?"

"15," she said, approaching the escalator.

"Who are we sitting with?"

"Levins, Goldmans, Marlene and her boyfriend."

"Oh shit! Not Marlene. I can't take another trip to the King of Prussia Shopping Mall, and the 'divine fashions' at Bloomingdales.

You should have told me we were with Marlene. I could have prepared myself: a joint, a couple of shots . . . "

"Harry, you're a real putz. When are you going to grow up?" she said as they stood on the first floor landing. "What room did you say?"

"The Blue Room, Rachel, the Blue Room."

"My friends," smiled the honored guest, his words quieting the standing ovation of an appreciative audience. Rabbi Max Mazer waited for the noise of shuffling feet, moving chairs and chatter to subside. He adjusted his horn-rim glasses snuggly against the bridge of his nose and casually brushed a finger against a silver moustache that matched the color of his bushy eyebrows and thick head of hair. With hands holding the wide lapels of a blue suit too large for his small, frail frame, he stood at the podium and scanned his notes cursorily before responding to the silence.

"Thank you. Thank you very much for your kindness and patience. Listening to an old rabbi reflect and reminisce is not my idea of a 'swinging time' . . . (*laughter*) . . . But who knows, maybe we can reach out, touch each other, and make this evening more than a social event for a rabbi, who has served your synagogue for 42 years. Probably a lot longer than many of you would have preferred . . . (*laughter*) . . . I look around this vast room and get a warm feeling. Our future is secure. We have never been stronger. Until our building program and expansion plans are completed, we are in the extraordinary position of having a waiting list for those who seek membership in our congregation. Your Board of Directors has dedicated members, who understand the economic realities of fickle times, and have planned accordingly. The Hebrew school has a committed faculty with the highest standards. I can assure you our first priority remains your children's Jewish education. We will continue to maintain a quality program, but we are not complacent and will always seek to improve our curriculum.

"You have in my replacement, Rabbi Joseph Margolis, a young man with the enthusiasm and know-how to continue our fine tradition, and to help us climb even higher mountains . . . (*applause*) . . . Rabbi Margolis is a different breed than in my day. He's a tennis player, a karate expert, a foreign film enthusiast, and he appreciates rock music. He understands our youth, and is tolerant and compassionate towards old cronies like Max Mazer . . . (*laughter*) . . . Rabbi Margolis, to you and your lovely wife Joan, welcome to our family . . . (*applause*) . . .

I would be remiss in my duty as an observer and chronicler of our synagogue's history, if I left you with the impression that I always felt secure about our future. In fact, there was a time not too long ago, when the candle of hope was flickering and despair ruled. In fact, our synagogue was on the brink of extinction. We were in desperate financial straights, a real basketcase. . . . (*titter*) . . . Yet, we survived, and in time, prospered. How did it happen?" The Rabbi sipped ice water, and returned the notes on the podium to a jacket pocket. He had abandoned his prepared speech, and his probing eyes slowly scanned the audience.

"Let me answer my question by first asking another question. Has anyone heard of Lezeritch? . . . No! No hands or signs of recognition! Lezeritch is the name of a village in Poland, and was my birthplace. Your synagogue—Congregation Ohel Zadek—is an extension of Lezeritch. Let me explain. I want to go back in time—many, many years ago to B.C. You know what B.C. means? I see a few people nodding. No, I don't mean the Christian calender B.C.—I'm referring to another age that a fair number in this room can personally identify with. B.C.—Before Computers . . . (*laughter*) . . . In the mid-1930s I lived in Lezeritch with my father, mother, two sisters and a brother. There were a thousand or so Jewish people in our village, but just a few rednecks like me . . . (*laughter*) . . . One day, all the rebels asked a question of the Rabbinical Council. My father, Mendel, was a Rebbe and a prestigious member. We wanted their opinion about this man Adolph Hitler. Did we have anything to worry about? You see, there were rumors floating around our village, and a few of us had traveled beyond the Pale, and saw things that were disturbing.

"The Council weighed the evidence and debated the issue for a week. There were heated discussions. One Rebbe pointed to a passage in the Midrash, another cited the Kabbola, but the Rabbis couldn't agree on what to say. So, Rebbe Pinkas from the nearby town of Litz, an acknowledged Talmudic scholar, was asked to mediate. Another week of study and debate followed, and then Rebbe Rhizak was elected to announce the decision. There was no danger, and assuming that the 'alarmists' were even partially correct, the people of Lezeritch, so long as they continued to follow God's message as written in the Torah, had nothing to fear. Rebbe Rhizak looked directly at the rebels who had instigated the debate, concluding his speech with a warning to those who created an atmosphere of fear and panic. 'God,' shouted the

Rebbe, 'knows what he's doing.' I, and a few others, left the village because we believed the Reichs Fuèhrer also knew what he was doing.

"About ten years after the war ended, I revisited Poland with the idea of returning to my birthplace to rekindle beautiful memories. I had known for quite a while that all my family had become a part of the Final Solution. We all know the numbers—6 million total, 3 million Polish Jews . . . and 5 Mazers from Lezeritch. I had a rented a car and bought several maps, but I could not find my village. After many hours of searching, I traveled to the city of Litz and found the one remaining synagogue. An elderly man sat alone praying. I introduced myself and explained the problem. 'Lezeritch? You want Lezeritch?' the old man's hand were shaking as he held on tightly to his tallis. 'Lezeritch! You go up the main highway about 40 miles to Katowice and then a few miles south to Osweicum. Walk under a sign that says *Arbeit Macht Frei*, and you will pass a few blockhouses before you reach the ovens. Lezeritch is the third from the left. That's most of it. The rest can be found in Majdanek, Chelmno, and Treblinka.' The message was clear. Lezeritch, like many other Polish towns and villages does not exist today. It is on no map. It is nothing more than a memory to the few who were not there when the Gestapo and Schutzstaffel arrived.

"You see my friends, there is a misconception. Let me share it with you. A belief exists that 'survival' is a semitic word. 'Survival' is not of Jewish origin, the etymology can be traced to the old English, French and Latin. The Hebrew association with the roots of this word has been mistaken because our people have had so much practice . . . so much . . . so very, very much." Rabbi Mazer paused for more water, and then wiped his brow with a handkerchief.

"So, you want to know what Congregation Ohel Zadek was like in the late '50s and early '60s? Okay, I'll tell you . . . We were a Lezeritch about to happen. The neighborhood was then a black ghetto. The congregation consisted of a few business men, elderly people too poor to move, and a few men from the suburbs who visited us during Yizkor service on Yom Kippur. The synagogue had some problems— the bathroom sinks didn't work; the toilets didn't flush; plaster was falling from the ceilings and walls; broken windows; the benches needed to be repaired; the balcony was condemned and could not be used—enough said about the minor things. Each day was an adventure, but I was determined that Congregation Ohel Zadek would survive and not suffer the same fate as Lezeritch. I desperately needed help. It arrived right before the High Holidays in 1962. I was reading in my office, when our shamus, Morris Sipkoff, of blessed memory, informed me that a middle-aged black lady insisted on seeing the Rabbi. I said yes, no big deal! She was a strong, robust-looking woman who was well-mannered and very religious. Almost every sentence she spoke alluded to Jesus or the scriptures and her language was difficult for me to understand. In all candor, my first impression was that she was a meshuggeneh, and I admit that for a moment I thought about calling the police to take the poor woman to the Osler General Psychiatric ward. But the more I listened, the more I appreciated this extraordinary human being. Her name was Amanda Williams and this was her story. She was a housekeeper of a fraternity house at Osler Medical School. There was a student who Amanda loved like a son. He was a Jew who had lost faith; he had separated himself from God and religion with the premature death of his mother. The young man, perhaps not fully understanding the depths of Amanda's religious convictions, had made sport of his theologic views. The housekeeper sought me for counsel and advice to restore the young man's faith in God and Judaism . . . that was her story! I argued, and I thought rather convincingly at the time, that her best course of action was to do nothing. Let him work out his own problems, and let him know my office door is always open if he wants to talk turkey . . . *(laughter)* . . . She approved of my plan, and graciously thanked me for my time and thoughtful suggestions. I learned later that the housekeeper dragged the medical student out of bed and made him attend High Holiday services a few days after our conversation.

"Amanda Williams! What a remarkable woman. To this day, my friends, I still don't know what motivated her. Was it retribution for the fallen medical student she loved, a calling from Jesus, a little of both, or something I don't know about? But this poor, simple black woman decided to make Ohel Zadek her own personal reclamation project. She had seen the condition of our synagogue, said nothing, but the next day returned with several of her friends to restore our edifice to its former glory. In typical Amanda style, I was never consulted about whether I needed or wanted help. She belonged to a congregation in a South Street storefront called the Open Love Baptist Church. Their pastor was Reverend John Tucker, a lovely man who passed away in 1970, and the church closed soon after his death.

The members of this church provided the care and maintenance that sustained us in times of crisis. No task was too great—plumbing, painting, carpentry, electrical work. Okay, so they were handymen and not union, but they did a magnificent job and they wouldn't accept money, not a penny. Strong, young black men from the Open Love Baptist Church provided an escort service for any member of our congregation who requested help. Amanda actively solicited money and members for our synagogue from sources that ranged from her medical contacts among Physicians, to business men in the community. She was the synagogue's housekeeper—cleaned my study, washed the floors . . . you name it and she did it. Never was there a request on my part, nor was money exchanged. Even when she was dying from cancer, Amanda Williams continued to work for Ohel Zadek. She died in 1965. I am still saddened by her loss." The Rabbi looked up to the ceiling at the floodlights encapsulating the speaker's podium, and then removed perspiration from his brow with a handkerchief.

"Amanda's untimely death strengthened our resolve, but the many problems our synagogue faced wouldn't go away. Her legacy was an innate goodness and an enduring faith to persevere and conquer, even in the face of seemingly overwhelming obstacles. She left us something else, and that something was a Catholic girl of Polish descent who was raised in a small coal mining town in Pennsylvania. Again, the connection is the 'Godless' medical student. Eventually, this young woman, who by the way was a nurse, married the future doctor. I will not give you their names—you will understand why in a few minutes—but simply refer to the young couple as the Doctor and the Nurse.

"I met the nurse quite by accident, at Amanda's bedside in Osler General Hospital. She was a beautiful young woman—long brown hair and sparkling eyes to match, high set cheek bones and a radiant smile . . . magnificent features. And after our first discussion, I just knew that in goodness of heart, I had met Amanda's twin. The two women and I met a few times, and quite frankly our talks always took the same direction. How could we revive and maintain the Doctor's Jewish sense of identity? The pattern repeated itself. The Nurse, like Amanda, became active in the revitalization of our synagogue on a voluntary basis. The young woman was a tireless worker, and I'm not just referring to physical tasks. She also solicited money and new members, and I will be the first to admit, that more than a few men donated not because of religious or altruistic reasons, but were persuaded by her beauty and charm. The Nurse and I developed a relationship based on friendship and mutual respect. I tried to wear two hats—friend and rabbi—a difficult position to be in at times. I had to refuse her request that I officiate at her wedding because she had not converted; and conversion was out of the question because the Doctor would not permit it. They eventually were married by a Reform rabbi in a temple at her insistence, and I suspect Amanda had a hand in it as well, even though she died before the actual ceremony.

"I guess I became the Nurse's confidante after Amanda's death. I don't think I ever met a woman so completely involved and devoted to a man. Perhaps it was the romance and the exuberance of youth, but her husband was everything that really mattered to her. An old-fashioned idea by today's standards, but a refreshing memory for an old rabbi who has been a witness to so much marital discord. I believe, though I have no way of knowing, that the Doctor reciprocated in a similar way. I don't want to leave you with the idea that the Nurse was not an independent woman with her own mind— she was strongwilled and a battler. I also think her presence at the synagogue was tolerated, though not encouraged by her husband. The truth is I didn't know the doctor; my information about him was always second hand. We never even met, though I saw him once, at Amanda's funeral. He was sitting in the first row with his wife-to-be in front of the pulpit and Reverend Tucker. He had dark curly hair, a gentle face . . . it's funny what you remember. The Doctor was a pallbearer, and as he rose, a pipe fell out of his pocket. I thought to myself: this is not the doctor I want to see to help me break my two pack a day habit . . . *(laughter)* . . . We did have another encounter two years later, but I'm getting a little ahead in my story.

"I would like all of you to try to remember what our great country was like in the Fall of 1966. Drugs and LSD was 'in'—religion was 'out'. Earlier that year, *Time* magazine published an article, 'Is God Dead?' trying to document the trend. Black marches in the South and riots in the northern cities . . . the Beatles performed their last concert in San Francisco . . . Philadelphia's urban renewal program still looked good on paper . . . *(laughter)* . . . Congregation Ohel Zadek remained on a respirator . . . *(laughter)* . . . the Doctor went to Vietnam.

"The war was heating up, and he willingly served his country and helped people. That was his job—he was a doctor! The nurse would have to do the best she could for one year, and then when her husband returned, they could put some order into their lives and plan for the future. I will tell you the Nurse was vehemently anti-war. I have no idea what her husband thought about Vietnam, and I don't believe she did either. But she was about to find out. After six months of an agonizing separation the young couple planned on meeting in Honolulu for his R and R—Rest and Relaxation.

"I don't want to go into the particulars, but there were ambiguities about what was happening to the Doctor, and his letters . . . Oy! What can I say? How should I describe them? The letters were obvious attempts to lighten her burden, but actually had the opposite effect. In the name of love, honesty is sometimes stretched, and occasionally abandoned.

"So! . . . With some trepidation and great expectations, the nurse started her journey to Hawaii. She took a taxi to the airport an hour or so earlier than was necessary, and was resting comfortably in the lounge when a friend appeared. He was also a doctor who served in Vietnam, and had come from Washington to see her. The information he had was not from official channels, but was authentic—from sources that had contacted him directly from Vietnam. The news was that the nurse's husband had been killed by the Viet Cong.

"She lived in Southwark near the river, and I visited her that same day. The house was filled with mourners. People were standing around outside in the street. She was alone in the bedroom when I entered. She was sitting on the edge of the bed, a beautiful flower in her hair, a photograph of her dead husband in her hands.

"I remember that funeral very well. It was a sunny spring day in 1967. I remember after the Honor Guard shot their guns and played taps, an American flag was given to the nurse, who then handed it to her father-in-law. The old man kissed her again and again—I can still see them walking to the car, her arm around his shoulder. She was a tower of strength.

"I called her a week or so later, but I didn't see her for about two months. I was in my study, when to my surprise, a knock at the door, and there was our 22 year old widow. She was a little thinner, and smiling. Why was she happy? She was happy, she told me, because my check had arrived. She told me a story that her husband, in the few months prior to his death, had been studying Torah . . . and had reaffirmed his belief in Judaism. He wanted to help his people in a concrete way, so he decided to make me the beneficiary of his government life insurance policy. Any serviceman killed in Vietnam had $10,000 given to anyone he designated, and so, my . . . my check had arrived! I was to use the money for Ohel Zadek in any way I desired. The Nurse claimed to have a letter in the Doctor's own handwriting which verified her story, but 'unfortunately' she couldn't find it. And I couldn't help but notice the check was not from the government, but from her own personal bank account.

"My first reaction was anger. I was insulted. I wanted to shout at her: 'What kind of cockamamie story are you telling me? This is Max Mazer you're talking to, from Lezeritch—the third oven from the left! I didn't believe Rebbe Rhitzak, Rebbe Pinkas . . . my own father, Rebbe Mendel Mazer . . . I'm no fool! Why do you deceive me? It is *you* who wants to give the money to Ohel Zadek!' But I said none of these things. I reached for my cigarettes and said nothing. That way I didn't have to worry about misunderstandings, semantics, implications . . . silence is silence. I chose to accept the money and her story, because my friends, she wished me to. It was important to the Nurse that her husband die a good Jew. This gift to Ohel Zadek was a form of redemption—a *kapporoh* we will call it. The slate was clean, the IOU paid off. She wanted me to believe this story, but I must say that I do not fully understand her tactics or objective. There was another stipulation to the gift. She asked that I keep the donor a secret, and I continue to honor her request. Whether it was the Doctor or the Nurse—let's just say it was both—it does not happen very often that someone's charity fulfills Maimonides' highest degree of *Tzedakah*.

"Congregation Ohel Zadek is now self-supporting and we are in a position to help other Jews, and to this day, those who benefit are not aware of who made it possible. Now you understand the secrecy and my reluctance to tell you the names of the Nurse and the deceased Doctor. Buoyed by this anonymous gift, our synagogue held on until the renaissance of Center City and Society Hill, until the fiscal health of Ohel Zadek could once again be assured.

"A few months after our meeting I received a telephone call. The Nurse told me her father-in-law had passed away and she was leaving Philadelphia. A letter would follow when she was settled, but since her departure, no mail from her has crossed my desk. I have no idea where she is, or what has happened in her life. Congregation Ohel Zadek, this is your legacy! A Baptist black woman, a Catholic nurse, a Jewish doctor killed in the Vietnam war, Lezeritch . . . and a foolish rabbi who continues to smoke two packs of cigarettes a day . . . (*laughter*) . . . It's all yours, my friends. Ohel Zadek is all yours! Thank you! . . . (*applause*) . . . *Zei gezunt* . . . good health, continued happiness . . . And don't forget your heritage!"

* * *

33

"WE'RE still looking at Malbork Prison Camp. The man in front is Jerzy Witzcak. He works as a welder in the Gdansk shipyard. That's a makeshift sling around the arm. His face looks like it's been through a meat grinder."

"Oh, my God!" cried the svelte blond, a pink negligee touched the floor after she deftly swung her legs onto the sofa's soft pillows.

"This next slide shows Walter Gulzuski, a crane operator at the Gdansk shipyards. He was an important speaker at the First Congress. Considered a radical by even Solidarity standards . . . advocated free elections, withdrawal of Soviet troops, non-interference of Moscow in the internal affairs of Poland, and pushed for independence along the lines of the Yugoslavian model. If you'r wondering, that's a nose below the black and blue eyes. There's also a note here that says his left knee cap was shattered."

"Paul, this is dynamite! I can't wait until *Main Event* hits the newsstands."

"Jozef Zychetta, an electrician. The two men behind the barbed wire haven't been identified. Jozef's a union delegate and a moderate . . . I need a break, Monica. Is the coffee ready?" The bearded Professor turned off the slide projector, closed a small, black loose-leaf book and placed it in the pocket of his white, terrycloth robe.

"Les stopped in earlier today," said Monica from the kitchen. "Damn it, we're out of Sweet-and-Low!"

"I'll take it black . . . and?"

"Les loves our ideas about the bookshelves, but . . ."

"How much, Monica?"

"Five hundred more than we planned. You need a solid wood. The heavy books would buckle the pine . . ."

"I thought the guy was supposed to be our friend!"

"Paul! Les is barely meeting expenses. What's the matter? You've been shaky the last few days, and I know it's not just the costs of rehabing this townhouse."

The Professor stroked his beard, and then spoke morosely: "The underground has new couriers. They want me to serve as a spokesman and secret fund raiser. No longer do I preach tolerance and a 'let's see' attitude about the present Polish regime. At the Pulaski Club's next meeting, I will speak of my disillusionment with the government and my allegiance to Solidarity. It's my coming out party. It also means that I'll never see Poland again."

"How can you be sure? The present political climate will change. Isn't that what Solidarity is all about?"

"Solidarity is doomed. They don't have a chance. Their own leaders know it. They made a fast power move, and the Kremlin called their bluff."

"What's the problem, Paul? Why did you get involved in this thing anyway?"

The Professor walked to the fireplace mantle and looked at an old photograph. It was a family portrait taken in front of St. Stanislaus, the Polish church in Neschaunk. Paul stood next to a proud Mama Loreski, his six year old sister was nestled in their father's lap, the warmth of a mid-afternoon sun merged with the laughter of four happy faces. "Good question! Why did I join Solidarity? Why jeopardize a nice soft faculty position with tenure in a major university? Play by the rules and I'm set for life. If I'd been caught, it would've meant a show trial as a CIA spy and a long internment in a Polish prison. I often thought of that possibility, perhaps subconsciously wished for it."

"You always maintained that Solidarity was a question of principle. You never mentioned the martyr bit," she said while placing both cups of coffee on a table close to the slide projector before sitting down.

"Maybe it's time I told you about my past," he turned away from the mantle and met her stare.

"If it has to do with your sister, and it's painful, please don't . . ."

"I want to, Monica. It's long overdue. You know that I was a conscientious objector during the Vietnam War and served two years in a Philadelphia hospital as an orderly. But what I didn't tell you was that morality and religious convictions never entered into my decision. I was looking for a way out, without breaking the law. I had no intention of putting my life on the line in Southeast Asia."

"Come on, Paul. There were lots of fellas who connived their way out of military service. Vietnam was an unconscionable war; any maneuver to avoid the draft was justified."

"Maybe from your vantage point, but not mine. You see, Monica, I was never a member of your team. I believed the Vietnam War was a justified military response to aggression by Hanoi. I may have quarreled with our government's tactics along the way, but never with the original assumption."

"How can you stand there and blurt out this unadulterated trash. Our presence in Vietnam was a cowardly, immoral act! A civil war fought under the guise of a worldwide Communist conspiracy that was a fantasy . . ."

"For Christ's sake, Monica," he shouted angrily. "I didn't raise the issue of Vietnam to debate you. I just wanted you to understand my state of mind."

"I'm sorry, Paul. Please go on."

"One person back then—in the good old Sixties—saw through me. I'll never forget that particular night. It was a few months after Christie's husband was killed in Vietnam. I visited her with the idea of trying to ignite her non-existent social life. A good friend of mine from Harvard was doing graduate work at the University of Pennsylvania, and I wanted to be a matchmaker. It was your standard pitch: stop living in the past, don't feel sorry for yourself, now is the time to get out in the world and build a new life . . . I also told her that it was a damn shame her husband was wasted in a senseless and shameful war. Christie understood my hypocrisy and hangups better than anyone. She lashed out at me. I never saw her so enraged."

"The shock and grief of her husband's death. You were the target of her frustration and anger," said a consoling Monica in response to his quivering voice.

"Not so! I was the archetypical fence-straddler. Nobody played 'cover your ass' better than Paul Loreski."

"I don't believe it!"

"Believe it, Monica. I left my sister's apartment feeling sorry for myself, wandered through the cobblestone alleys of Southwark and ended up at Ted's Tavern getting drunk with a bunch of longshoremen. A few of the people at the bar knew that I was the Doctor's brother-in-law, and they treated me with a reverence I still can't get over. I was a fervent supporter of the war at Ted's, the following afternoon in the Hospital cafeteria I just as vehemently took a strong *anti*-war position. You see, Monica, I never rocked the boat. I wanted us to win in Indochina, but not enough to put my ass on the line. Our system makes it so easy to cop out, and at the same time be a super patriot. I saw my role in the war as an observer and commentator, not as a warrior. Shit no! I was a scholar, a seeker of truth. My superior intellect made me more important in a democracy's scheme of things. I operated in the realm of ideas, while others dealt with realities."

"Okay, so all men are not created equal."

"But what about those guys that were maimed and killed?"

"Paul, I feel terrible about the loss of life and suffering, but I can't endorse the principles those men died for. Their sacrifice made no sense! Indochina wasn't like World War II, or even Korea. Any man who served in Vietnam had other choices. Look, I was deeply involved in the Peace movement. I went into the streets and to the universities, and counseled young men on how to avoid the draft. The method, legit or otherwise, was a secondary consideration. You have a short memory. Lying and deception was standard procedure no matter what team you played on. The goal was to stop the killing on both sides; saving lives is what our message was all about." She added bitterly, "Anyone who listened to those jerks in Washington, got what they bargained for."

"Do you know, Monica, I didn't have a single friend who served in Vietnam. All of my college buddies found a way out. Most were apathetic, a few believed they had the right answers, but arguments about who was right in Vietnam always took a back seat to finding ways to save your ass. My brother-in-law was the only one I knew . . . 'who got what he bargained for'."

"I didn't mean to imply the men killed in Vietnam were fools; they were victims. The policy-makers were the assholes. Paul, I'm not happy with this conversation. Tell me, do I give Les the go ahead with the bookshelves?"

"Fuck the bookshelves and Les . . . You know I talked with him a few days before he left for Vietnam," he said with a smirk. "I tried to convince him not to go. I pulled out every anti-war line there was. I too, was heavy into the Peace and Love theme. After all, any dumb ass knows that ethics and morality takes precedence over the demands of the state! I told him he was making a big mistake, he was playing on the losing side—everybody knew that in Vietnam, it was the good guys who wore black. . .

"Please don't do this to yourself."

"Can't you see? It's important to get this out in the open. My brother-in-law told me that he was happy that I'd worked it all out, but Vietnam wasn't all that clear to him. Going there would help him sort out the pieces. And as long as there was a question in his mind, he would go along with the big boys in Washington. They hadn't betrayed him in the past, and he felt compelled to do his share. He wanted me to understand that he too was a man of conscience."

"Brother!"

"Listen, I'm not saying he was right. All I'm saying is that nothing made an impression on me. I didn't give two shits about anything or anyone in those days, except number one. It took many years for me to come to grips with the problem. Now I understand. Those who went to Vietnam, at least they did their duty. But I didn't do mine." Paul joined Monica on the couch, his hands skimmed long blond hair and rested on her shoulders. "Leaving Philly after my mother's death was an excuse for running away from bad memories. Chicago was a fresh start; only trouble was Vietnam wouldn't disappear. When the crisis in Poland came along, it was a chance to regain a little self-respect. I needed a cause, not a victory."

Paul reached under the table for his briefcase. He fumbled with the combination and the lock popped open; its contents were prominently displayed.

"I thought you said it was a lost cause, not worth wasting your time or effort," she jested.

"I've reconsidered," he said, while pinning a metal badge with the bold red-face 'SOLIDARITY' insignia against a white backgroud, onto the lapel of his robe.

"Paul," she said softly, "I'd like to be at the Pulaski Club dinner when you give your speech."

"I thought you were going out of town this weekend. You don't want to risk your job. . ."

"I'm proud of what you're doing," her hands held his as she glanced at the Loreski family portrait. "If they could only be here to see the magazine exposé and hear your speech! How do you think they'd react?"

Paul leaned back and thought for a moment. Strange that in all this time he had never considered what his parents or his sister would think about his actions. "I guess," he said finally, "my mother would approve, but be concerned with the risks. Dad would probably wear the Solidarity button twenty-four hours a day."

"And your sister?"

"Tough call. The Christina I remember from the Sixties would probably kiss me, call me a shmuck, and smile in a way that would make me wonder what the hell she really thought. She had a way of keeping me off balance, except when I pissed her off. Then she'd open up with both barrels."

"What about the Christina of the eighties?"

"Monica, my love," he sought her lips, "God only knows."

* * *

34

"LARGE pizza with pepperoni, and a small plain to take out. How long?"

"About 15 minutes," replied the middle-aged Oriental behind the counter. He quickly relayed the order to a worker preparing the pies, pointed to the cash register, and casually removed his apron. A young woman dressed in designer jeans and a tight-fitting polo shirt with a 'Charlie's Saigon Pizza' emblem gestured with a lateral movement of her arm, as her other hand reached for an unfinished glass of soda. "Kimi! Will you also check the telephone order? Sounds like a kid. May be a phony."

"Sure thing, Charlie. Don't you worry, I make everything okay. Kimi a winner—Kimi number one," she said with a wink.

Her undulating hips brought a sheepish grin to the proprietor's face as he entered the living quarters adjoining the pizza parlor. The apartment was small, but ample for his needs; it consisted of a small kitchen and bathroom, and an all purpose living and sleeping area. The escalation of rentals and condos in Westminster, as well as the rest of Orange county, had resolved the issue of relocating. Despite his lucrative business and his desire for a beach-front property along the rugged California coastline, Charlie was content with the present situation; other matters were higher priorities.

As a Council member of the Freedom Alliance, his actions were closely scrutinized by the many factions and diverse elements within the group's loosely formed coalition. The economic, political and ethnic differences within the ranks were profound, but their objective kept them together: an Indochina free of Communist domination. Financial assistance, and dedication to the Alliance's principles was critical to a leader's image at this early stage in the movement's development.

Sitting at a small desk and shuffling papers into distinct piles, Charlie paused to scan a memorandum he would introduce at that evening's Executive Committee meeting. The question of CIA assistance would surely be controversial; the Laotian tribesmen and Vietnamese would probably be receptive, but the Cambodian Khmer representatives would remember broken promises and agency duplicity. His own position had been circulated privately among a few key members: CIA help was essential to a successful guerrilla effort. Charlie had weighed the risks; he believed the propitious moment had arrived for a Council decision on this vital issue.

Something else caught his eye: a slim ladies watch rested on the base of the desk light. Kimi was so forgetful! Soon she would be looking for the lost Seiko, and he would once again come to her rescue. The poor girl was lazy, disorganized, incapable of cooking a decent meal, and a lousy housekeeper. She had no intellectual curiosity, and did nothing to improve the quality of her mind; political discourse fell on deaf ears. Rock music, gossip magazines, and sex were her only turn-ons. He tolerated the young woman who shared his bed, despite her many shortcomings. Charlie was a patient man. He believed that some day his benevolence and compassion would be rewarded.

Kimi was one of the Boat People. Charlie didn't know the whole story. Bits of the puzzle had been supplied by friends and a few details revealed by his mistress in weak moments of self-pity. Her father was a successful Vietnamese entrepreneur who had been reeducated in an internment camp soon after the war's end in 1975, and then managed a state run textile mill until his Chinese heritage became a liability. The cost of moving a wife, two sons, and Kimi exhausted his life savings; boat passage was obtained through government channels and the time honored custom of greasing the right palms.

The san-pan vessel leaving Ho Chi Minh City in early 1979 had 36 undesirables aboard, only six would survive the ordeal and Kimi was one of them. The rest of her family would not be as lucky. Two brothers were killed defending the boat from pirates off the coast of Thailand. The distressed vessel limped to an abandoned island and an ingenious captain made the appropriate repairs. Supplies had dwindled, and Kimi's father succumbed to poor nutrition and sun stroke imposed on an already weakened heart. Turned away by two countries, the captain navigated the boat into a Malaysian harbor until a naval blockade stopped his passage. The captain's order to abandon a crippled ship was a last ditch attempt to salvage lives, but only the strong managed to swim to land. Kimi's mother perished in the strong current. How the teenage girl, barely alive and completely alone, arrived in California six months later remained a mystery.

Kimi did not share Charlie's dream of returning to the Motherland or removing the bonds of slavery. She thought the Vietnamese people were fed up with war and would not support another revolution. The major problem was internal. A government unable to provide the basic needs of its citizens would crumble under its own weight. Vietnam for her was a repository of bad memories, the fun and good times resided in Orange County, California, U.S.—at Charlie's Saigon Pizza Parlor.

There were some feeble attempts to correct and edify, but Charlie was forced to admit that Kimi was a real challenge. Her world was a set of earphones with a clip-on Walkman. In the late evening, she would lie on the couch and tune into her planet's Top Twenty. Charlie's appraisal of political realities in Southeast Asia, and the ideas of the Freedom Alliance to unseat the Hanoi gangsters were goodnaturedly ignored. The boat girl would tease: "You too serious, Charlie. Why you not love me?"

He would sternly admonish the young woman; someday he would erase her ignorance. But hadn't reason eluded him in his youth? Today he was on target, and soon Kimi and her generation would be persuaded by his wisdom.

Charlie reclined in his chair, and again reflected on the CIA proposal. Assuming he could get the Committee to agree on Agency involvement, there was still the nagging question of who to seek out and how best to sell his case. He had known one man in the CIA, but it had been many years since their last encounter. On a sheet of paper, the pizza man wrote the large block letters 'M' and 'O.' "What" he wondered aloud, "ever happened to Mo?"

Charlie grappled for the keys in darkness, he guessed it was around 1 a.m. The pizza parlor closed at midnight, another half hour was needed for cleaning and putting the books in order. Kimi usually had a snack ready for him when he returned from an Alliance meeting. The outdoor light next to the back alley door was always on until he entered the apartment. "Maybe the bulb needs replacing," he thought, as the fourth try brought success and the latch gave way.

The table light was the room's only illumination. He took off his shoes and tiptoed to the couch where she was propped against a pillow. The music blared from the headphones until he turned off the Walkman. An open copy of *People* magazine lie on the floor. He had a sudden urge to awaken Kimi to share his happiness, but did nothing more than cover her with a light blanket.

He sat in the lazy-boy recliner and chuckled. His anxiety had been uncalled for. The Council had unanimously accepted the "CIA Initiative." A few of the men suggested names of possible contacts, but they were all in the same predicament. Many years had passed since their last agency connection. Reluctantly, Charlie agreed to start with an intermediary, but middle-men jeopardized secrecy and favors would have to be returned.

High ranking officials in the debunked Saigon government lived in the area, and many still had friends in high places in Washington. The Freedom Alliance tried to separate itself from South Vietnamese military and political leaders, all of whom had tainted reputations in the eyes of the American public. The Alliance was a grass roots operation, its members were patriots who had not shared in the material gains of corrupt governments. They were front-line combatants who fought for principle, not money or power. In this situation, an exception would have to be made.

General Thieu was the logical first choice. He had been the military Commandant at Dalat, the Vietnamese equivalent of West Point. A quiet, intense man with a low profile, Thieu retained many contacts in the States and abroad. He would mention Mo Balen's name to the General, perhaps a meeting with his old friend could be arranged. Charlie lit a cigarette, took a few drags, and thought about a possible reunion.

"Remember me? Chac Duo Trang, the VC Captain who defected. Bia Vuc Special Forces camp in '67? You bought my story and saved me from torture at the hands of ARVN interrogators. Nobody but you believed me about the suicide attacks . . . until they occurred during the Tet offensive of '68. You were responsible for my reindoctrination and got me a job with ARVN counterintelligence. I didn't let you down, Mo. I busted ass with the best of them. There wasn't a VC I couldn't break. You would have been proud. I came to the States in '75. Hitched a ride with one of the last eggbeaters to make it. I could see the NVA moving into Saigon. I'm living in a small town outside of LA. Would you believe it? I own a pizza parlor. Working real hard, but making plenty of bucks. Nobody knows me as Chac; everybody calls me Charlie. Never married, but I'm living with a piece of ass by the name of Kimi. She's one of the boat people. All the chick wants to do is fuck. I do what I can, but I'm a busy man. Much of my time is spent with an outfit called the Freedom Alliance. That's why I'm here, Mo. We need the Company's help. We have a lot of friends all over Indochina, and they're waiting for us. You supply the goodies and the info, we'll take care of the rest. My team has heavy hitters, and they all have hard-ons. We need some quiet action. I'll be waiting for your call. It's been too long, Mo."

Charlie inhaled the cigarette smoke, held his breath, and exhaled through the nose. He was somber and no longer interested in playing mind games designed to placate a bruised ego. Hard work and sound arguments would help assure CIA collusion, but he must also prepare for failure. Nothing should be taken for granted, the Freedom Alliance would succeed if it had the guts to withstand adversity. And yet, the prospects of not succeeding made him jittery. His earlier enthusiasm yielded to despair, it was the realization of another prolonged struggle. Mood swings came with the territory—a great leader must learn to deal with the uncertainties.

Charlie squashed his cigarette in an ashtray, and listened intently to the harsh sound of tobacco against glass. He moved to the couch, let his pants drop to the floor, and gently moved his erection over Kimi's cheek and lips.

The startled girl awoke, and smiled instantly as her eyes met their challenge. She saw a troubled lover, and understood the temporary answer to his problems resided in the warmth and wetness of her mouth. As usual, she was equal to the task, and with a fervor and tenacity that overcame his best attempts to prolong the excitement, a shaking Charlie erupted.

Supporting his weight by extending an arm against a pillow, he leaned forward for a kiss and an embrace. Her thin arms encircled his neck, but before their lips could meet, he emitted a prolonged moan. In extreme pain, he disentangled himself from a concerned Kimi.

"You have to be more careful about your shoulder, Charlie," she said. "The doctor say no weight bearing or lifting."

Charlie now sat on the couch with eyes closed, mouth agape, and the arm immobilized at his side. Kimi quickly shuffled to a nearby table, removed a heating pad and a bottle of pain pills. The therapy administerd, her hands gently massaged his chest and back. She waited for the shoulder pain to abate.

Kimi felt genuine affection for her lover. Tonight, Charlie had taken the initiative, and she was pleased whenever this occurred. His pleasure was her delight. But as she gazed into his grief-stricken face, pity and sorrow overwhelmed her, feelings of inadequacy only compounded the problem.

The shoulder pain would not totally go away, it defied Western medical wisdom; unconventional methods—holism, hypnosis, yoga, acupuncture—were no better. A bullet wound was not the only war injury. A mind was on fire.

Vietnam had become an obsession, an ongoing dialogue with a few meaningless intermissions, and no end in sight: Charlie was engulfed by the flames. It would be his undoing, there was no doubt in her mind. The question of methodology remained. Would his fate be determined in a mental institution, or could he find his way back to the seat of his illness, and play out the final act of a fantasy? He and the other members of the Freedom Alliance were the laughing stock of Orange County, among the very people they attempted to solicit for their cause. Each week a different scheme to overthrow the Communists was discussed, but soon discarded.

The ridicule and abuse directed by the Vietnamese community toward her lover only strengthened her resolve. She had refused better employment and worked fifteen-hour shifts daily to keep the business afloat. Charlie had long ago stopped participating in the affairs of the pizza shop. He made only token appearances, and invariably spent his time trying to persuade customers to enlist in the "Movement." "An invasion is imminent . . . A workable plan is on the drawing board . . . A few dedicated men are all we need. Will you be one of us?" asked the pizza man. She tried to protect him from the taunts, and the antics of young men who jokingly feigned interest in the Freedom Alliance. The vigil was constant, each day her patience was tested and her devotion challenged. He was unable to perform the simplest of tasks without her assistance. She would often hold him in her arms, and say: "I take good care of you. Don't worry . . . Charlie a winner—Charlie number one."

Lately, his behavior was becoming more irrational. In a trance-like state, Chac would mumble incessantly in a mixture of Vietnamese and English that was not intelligible to Kimi. Occasionally, a few words or a phrase was succintly shouted, punctuating the confusion sputtering from his lips. Like now, watching the sweat pour from his forehead, she distinctly hears her lover say: "Ah, the sweetness! But you must always remember, Doctor, that in the eyes of many, your actions will never be like the grass. The wind blows, and you bend against it. . ."

* * *

35

THE grass bends in one direction, a pause follows and there is stillness; the grass moves again, but takes a different course. The sun begins to assert itself, the mixture of warmth and a soft breeze makes the skin tingle. Small animals search for food, only the sounds of a trained ear can detect their presence. The chirping of birds signals the beginning of a new day.

A man sits on the ground in quiet meditation absorbing all that is available. He looks at the heavens and then the meadow, closes his eyes and listens, a deep breath and the pristine mountain air is consumed. It is comforting, a joy to the senses, crisp and sharp. "The beauty of early morning, I share it with my ancestors," toasts the nature-lover with a quick skyward motion of his arm.

The years have been kind to Frenchy. His bronze skin is smooth and unmarred. A short crewcut without a hint of gray adds to his youthful, sturdily built stature. Black combat boots, khaki fatigue pants, a worn green polo shirt and a blue beret continue to be the uniform of the day. The only obvious change is a bulging at the midriff, a source of embarrassment. He massages the abdomen while standing on a small patch of grass separating the dirt road and the cemetery fence.

He glances one more time in the direction of the family plots, and then scans the entire breadth of the valley. Bia Vuc is intact, and a vibrant community life flourishes. The mine fields surrounding the main compound have been destroyed, and the concertina wire removed. Quonset huts and other buildings built by the French and Americans have been converted into silos, supply depots, a small theater, town hall, recreation center, and an enlarged dispensary. Montagnard culture and tradition has survived another ordeal and is enjoying a temporary respite, vestiges of Western influence remain but are merely cosmetic. Life for the mountain people continues as it has for a millenium. Civilized man, equipped with computer technology and the tools of an industrial revolution, have come and gone; his legacy remains in the abandoned concrete bunkers and rusty pieces of metal scattered throughout the valley, the object of children's play and curiosity. The Montagnard way has triumphed. Bia Vuc is at peace with itself, and with the world around it.

Almost a decade has passed since a North Vietnamese regiment entered Bia Vuc and liberated the mountain people from the American imperialists and their Saigon puppets. There had been many anxious moments and a long period of uncertainty, but the village council with Frenchy at the vanguard, overcame the obstacles. Bia Vuc is considered a model village, an example of how Socialism can succeed when previous political ideologies have failed. On the surface, the land is now state owned, productivity and consumption shared, and private farming abolished. Silos filled with rice, and a model communal farm are shown to a swelling parade of bureaucrats from Ho Chi Mihn City to Hanoi. Children are taught Socialist theory, but outside the schoolroom and away from huge portraits of Marx, Lenin, and Ho, a more persuasive Montagnard way is preached and reinforced in the day to day activities of the village.

The Council members choose trusted young men to become 'volunteers' in the new Vietnamese Liberation Army. Others are recruited for work and study in the Soviet Union; a few of the young women provide entertainment for services rendered to influential commissars. Bribes continue to be paid to the right people, rice quotas are always surpassed and directed to the proper places. Bia Vuc is even showplaced to Soviet officials as an example of what Socialism can do with primitive mountain tribes like the Montagnards. And where else can they be wined, dined, and entertained by a crew-cut francophile, who actually converses in Russian?

Frenchy was prepared, just as he had been with the French and the Americans. The Paris Peace Conference was welcomed with cautious optimism, but despair followed when the accords were sealed in 1973. The military exit of the Americans except for advisors, and the continued presence of the North Vietnamese in the South, made the outcome of the war inevitable; only the Communist's exact battle plan remained unclear. Frenchy believed the Central Highlands were indefensible and that Saigon would retreat to the Coastal areas where success was possible. He felt the Americans would not tolerate a defeat of their ally, and intervene at the crucial time to prevent a total collapse. In any case, Bia Vuc would soon be flying the VC flag. The only other option would be to relocate, but the Council of Elders chose to remain, instead of leaving their homeland and assimilating with the Vietnamese far removed from the Highlands. Frenchy was designated as the clandestine liaison with the VC. For almost two years, he sustained the difficult tight-rope walking job of cooperating with both sides and not alienating either. In 1975, when the Central Highlands were overrun and many Montagnard camps demolished, Bia Vuc was left untouched.

It was business as usual when the new bosses set up shop. Frenchy was ready. He had obtained a Russian dictionary, learned about his new friends and their ways. The Vietnamese represented no new challenge, the faces changed but the longstanding distrust and animosity remained. Frenchy had done his homework well, and the people of Bia Vuc would be the benefactors. "Authority and power!" he would tell future leaders. "Let the other side believe he possesses both, and the Montagnards will prevail."

For the first time in anyone's memory, there was no war or side to choose. Military might and political expediency no longer dictated decision making. A little lip service was all that was required to maintain a status quo that preserved Montagnard integrity. Clearly, the mountain people at Bia Vuc were in control of their own destiny.

It is habit rather than a need to know, but Frenchy looks at his watch before retreating to the cemetery road. He is still amused with the Westerner's fascination with time, and quietly berates himself for having the same foible. To the Montagnard, time is the rhythm of nature, the ebb and flow of forces that governs existence and those of his ancestors: the rice fields rejuvenate yearly, seasonal rains come and go, the body is hungry when the stomach aches, a penis becomes erect when it is in need. How does a clock answer these questions?

"6:35," thinks Frenchy as he quickens the pace. His hand reaches into a large fatigue pocket to indulge in yet another form of decadence. He stops to light a Muscova cigarette near a small cluster of huts, bypassing fenced-in houses to a narrow path barely accommodating a single file, it is one road of many which winds its way around the mountain to the summit.

It is not an arduous journey, but Frenchy finds himself short of breath and perspiring heavily. Pride prevents him from taking a short rest, this trip had been a daily excursion for many years, in the days when this lookout point and command post was known as Mount Servin.

The concrete bunkers and sand bags of the outpost are enveloped by vegetation. Children play in the tunnels during the day, and young lovers seek its cool privacy at night. No longer are there any of the small dugouts that served as homes for the Montagnard sentries and their families. All that remains is a small patch of barren ground with a heap of broken bamboo poles, and metal debris, relics from a previous age, when angry men had come to Bia Vuc.

Frenchy, sitting atop the rubble on the peak of Mount Servin, his legs spread and hands on both knees, surveys his kingdom. The beauty of the valley never fails to tittilate: a cloud brushes against a mountain, a serpentine river divides the landscape, rice fields dot the hills, and there is Bia Vuc. Clusters of houses surround the compound, the air strip next to the river still remains as it did in the days of Mount Servin. Behind Frenchy, in the adjacent Moon valley northwest of Bia Vuc, is another scene of startling beauty. Only a keen eye can tell that the land had been punished; nature was willing to give man a second chance. The hillsides that had been sprayed with defoliants by the big birds now have abundant growth, bamboo flourishes, though it is untouched by the Montagnards who still regard the land as "cursed." In Moon valley, most of the pock marks from the B-52 raids have disappeared and blend into the surrounding greenery.

Frenchy's attention is now directed toward the most widely used and preserved trail on Mount Servin, ascending its southern exposure are two youths dressed solely in loin clothes, their mood is sullen as they climb the slope at a rapid pace.

The expected visitors are Za and Hui, two teenagers who have qualities the Elders perceive as promising. Training and education includes more than school and mundane village affairs. They are watched closely, their courage and judgment often tested, mistakes treated harshly and critically analyzed, the life of a future Montagnard leader is not easy.

Nor is it so for the instructor. He has to do more than teach and evaluate a prospective replacement, an emotional bond must also be shared. A leader must open his heart, and reveal secrets that lurk in the depths of the soul—it is the Montagnard way.

Za and Hui are now seated close to their mentor. It is time for Frenchy to call upon the hidden spirit of sorrow.

"It was early in 1967 when the Special Forces Commander, Captain Bixler, told me about an American Docteur at Da Nang who might be what Bia Vuc needed. Sergeant Flaherty was the medical man at the time, and did a good job with the skills he possessed. A few weeks later, an excited Bixler told me to prepare the village Council and get their approval. He handed me a carton of cigarettes—a sign that he considered the Docteur's presence very important.

"It was unnecessary. I knew the elders would approve and take a wait-and-see attitude. Only the Shaman had doubts about the Docteur, but he would never go against the wishes of the Council. We had nothing to lose, and the Captain was an honorable man who was well liked and trusted. His judgment was sound except when on a drinking binge.

"The Docteur came in an airplane with two buffalo who were cleansed and freed of evil spirits. I knew this was a good omen. Our people then believed in Docteur's medicine. I followed him from the moment the big bird arrived. The first time I saw his face, it looked hard. I guess it was the scar that made him appear angry but I was wrong, you could see he was the gentlest of men . . . in the compound, at the school, on Mount Servin . . . he reached out to Montagnard with sparkle in his eyes, like the stars in the sky on a clear night. He smiled at everyone and nod head—touched Montagnard on shoulder or shook hands and made people laugh. The pipe in his mouth smelled nice. I told our people the smoke drove away evil spirits.

"When Council met Docteur, Frenchy acted like a big man who was not impressed with American medicine man. I wanted him to feel he must do more to earn my friendship and loyalty. I visited him at his quarters in the evening and we talked many hours into the night.

"In the days that followed, we became very close. Each man's body and mind was open for the other to explore. Nothing was held back. There were no walls to climb over, or break down. We shared secrets just as I am doing now. We shared laughter and sadness, and yes, we even shared dreams. Spirits merged. Where there were two, there became one.

"He was my friend and my brother, but more importantly, the Docteur was a Montagnard. He was a part of our family. The people worshipped and adored him . . . I loved the man. When you possess the spirit of the man you love, it must be forever.

"Happiness had come to Bia Vuc. The sun of a new day brought with it the promise of hope—my brother made it possible. But then another man came to our village, and the light was replaced by darkness.

"His name was Chac Duo Trang. He was a Captain in the Viet Cong Army who had defected. He told a story nobody believed, no one that is, except me. I thought he was telling the truth, and that night I called an emergency meeting of the Council to inform the elders of my fears. A suicide attack, and the destruction of Bia Vuc and our people, was nothing to leave in the hands of others. The Montagnards have understood the dark side of those beyond the mountains, and their evil ways have cost us much blood.

"I was asked by the Council of Elders to confirm the defector's information, and strike a deal if necessary. That same night, contact was made with the Viet Cong through known sympathizers in the Valley—Montagnards who were permitted to live near us, for the very reason they could get in touch with the enemy in case of an emergency.

"The meeting with the Viet Cong did not go well. I felt time worked against us, and I was anxious for an agreement. Their representative did not deny Captain Chac's story, nor did he say it was a lie. His position was simple, if it was true, what would the Montagnards be willing to do to save their destruction? We agreed on a rough pact based on the approval of his superiors and the Council. He was afraid the Americans might bring in troops. I too had many questions and so we each had a way out if the situation became unacceptable.

"The original plan was diversionary, a probe and attack away from the compound. The Americans would leave, and the Viet Cong would be granted safe passage into the main compound to destroy supplies and steal equipment they considered important. They would kill Montagnards and Americans if they got in the way. Bia Vuc was to be an example of how the Americans could not count on the Montagnards. We knew many of our soldiers would not support the Council's decision and fight with the Americans. Only trusted troopers would be on guard the night of the attack. It all seemed so simple.

"I was concerned for my brother. The Green Berets were men who understood war and its risks. I tried to get him out of Bia Vuc by pretending he needed a rest for a Hawaiian meeting with his wife. I planted the idea in the minds of the officers, as well as his CIA friend who arrived in the early morning. All my efforts failed. I tried everything—prayed, grasped the magic Jew star necklace the Docteur gave me, hoping he would get the message to leave Bia Vuc! I even considered telling him about the attack, but I couldn't do it. I thought the very survival of Bia Vuc was at stake. I believed it, because I couldn't afford not to. The history of our people teaches us that man is not only capable of madness, but he needs the practice. Threats never satisfy his appetite. I couldn't take the chance. My brother might not have understood and would have told Bixler. We'd have been ruined!

The situation was deteriorating. There were troop movements that night, southeast of Bia Vuc heading in our direction . . . many porters . . . it looked like an attack was in the making. Our scouts never passed on the information to Captain Bixler, but the Council of Elders was informed and based their decisions on a situation that looked hopeless. Bia Vuc was going to be made an example of. Our women and children would be slaughtered. We believed the Viet Cong and the NVA were willing to pay any price for a victory. Even if the Americans were told, it would have been too late to save Bia Vuc. A reactionary team would have only prolonged the struggle. The original plan was replaced with another, and then another, until an agreement was made just a few hours before the attack of Bia Vuc. They had us. The Americans would have to die.

"That night, the light of the moon was strong, it glowed like gold. The earth had a softness. I could feel the ground give way with every step. The mountain air was heavier than I have ever known, it pressed against me. It was so hard to breathe.

"In the early nightfall, escorted by Montagnard troopers, 15 Viet Cong soldiers entered the military compound at Bia Vuc. They hid in an old French bunker used as a storage area. Another group of Viet Cong, probably no more than 25, were positioned at key spots around the camp for diversionary tactics. We provided the Viet Cong with five hostages, including two members of the Council. Speed and execution was to hopefully limit the number of casualties.

"The compound was guarded solely by sentries loyal to the Council. It had been an evening of song, good food at the Special Forces dining hall, and stories. The men were happy and relaxed. They were certian Bia Vuc was secure and in no danger.

"The Docteur left early. I knew where I could find him. There was a sick girl in the infirmary, and my brother was deeply concerned. I watched his every move in the darkness—so tender and giving. He kissed the little one, while an old woman chanted for family spirits to prepare for her coming. I was moved by the depth of his caring; it was beautiful to watch. I stepped out of the shadows and felt a desire to become part of the scene.

"After he left the infirmary, I too held the girl and kissed her on the same spots that had touched my brother's lips. We were, after all, of the same flesh. The old woman resumed her chants, but with greater vigor. She could only assume that the child's death was imminent, and that the Docteur and I had no right to be sad. Joining one's ancestors is a happy time—all life to a Montagnard, is in preparation for a more joyous and complete afterlife. But the little girl's body seemed so cold and lifeless, like a tree with no leaves. It was as though a part of her had already left this world to enter another. I was moved to hold her even more closely, as if to keep what remained of her spirit from escaping. I remember thinking, here is a little girl about to die who would not caress a rainstorm, embrace the mountain air, and love a hot blooded Montagnard seeking warmth and shelter for his seed.

"The attack went as planned. Two Viet Cong mortars blasted Mount Servin and the airfield, intentionally short of the mark. Machine gun fire ripped the air and pings of rifle fire were clear and loud. Grenades found their mark, explosions followed. A few of our own people rushed to the compound—it was Montagnard against Montagnard. The Special Forces fought valiantly, their fate a certainty. They, men of honor and great courage, died a soldier's death. The echoes of the battle still ring, loud screams of men at work . . . cries for a mother's breast . . . whispers of a new-found peace.

"I passed the Docteur's bunker with a few of my new Viet Cong comrades. I stopped and turned to the window opening. He was there, and though I could not see his face clearly, I am sure he saw mine. I grabbed my necklace with the Jew star. Did he understand my message? 'We are brothers . . . always, always.'

"A few minutes later, I stood at the bunker door, and tried to prevent the Viet Cong from entering. I joked with the Viet Cong Commander, 'Happiness is yours. What is it you wish?' I pleaded, 'he is not your enemy. A Docteur . . . a man of good will. He will help you and your friends.' There was no stopping them. They entered the bunker.

"He was sitting on a chair. No resistance was offered. The Docteur greeted me with a smile, not a big, happy one, but a slight partial opening of his lips which I interpreted as a sign of understanding. I am certain he understood the survival of Bia Vuc was at stake. He knew.

"I did what I had to do. The Council believed the danger was real and acted accordingly. It was only a few months later when the truth became known. There was no attack planned on our village. The orders had been cancelled even before Captain Chac had defected. The Council's caution and my meeting with the Viet Cong caught the Popular Liberation Front planners by surprise, but opened the door to another idea fueled by our distrust and hatred of the Vietnamese. There was a troop movement in the Southeast, but it was a false signal designed to attract our attention. The new plan worked perfectly, but with only one change. The Commander of the Viet Cong attack force had noted my attachment to the American Docteur. My loyalty to the People's cause would have to be tested. I would have to kill him.

"I told them I couldn't do it. I pleaded for his life in exchange for mine. My refusals only hardened them. They threatened to kill the hostages. Their guns were then pointed at me, and they were laughing. It was a joke, a big joke! My tears made them laugh harder.

"The Docteur's eyes were closed. I pointed the gun to his head and pulled the trigger . . . as gently as possible."

The sky is blue and the surrounding peaks invite inspection, a strong breeze sweeps over the summit. The man atop the heap nods, and then thrusts the head back to its vertical position; the cycle is repeated. A melody is hummed through tight lips as the rocking motion continues. Frenchy then sings an ancient Montagnard ballad.

There is a mountain beyond the next mountain, where my people dwell,

There is a mountain beyond the next mountain, where food is plenty,

There is a mountain beyond the next mountain, where trees are straight and tall, flowers are forever in bloom,

There is a mountain beyond the next mountain, where cold water, earth, and fire blend in perfect harmony,

There is a mountain beyond the next mountain, where man, animals, and gods live together in peace.

The teenage boys depart, neither has spoken a word. Tomorrow, the roles will be reversed. Za and Hui will return and critique the mentor's actions—it is the way of the Montagnards.

Their leader sits alone. The oppressive spirit of sorrow will not leave, it continues to haunt. He looks to the mountain, beyond the next mountain. "Hello, my brother! . . . Hello!" sobs Frenchy, holding the Star of David necklace, ever so tightly.

* * *

36

Virgil Cooper stood on the balcony of a second floor motel room, surveyed the Atlantic Ocean with his binoculars, selected a wave at a great distance, and followed its progress until it pounded the nearby surf. He found the roar of a giant breaker exhilarating; the quiet of tranquil waters rushing onto unexplored sands and then receding back into its own bowels, seemed like magic. Mesmerized by the ocean's ebb and flow, the black man's dark eyes searched for another distant wave. "C'mon ya mother-fucker. Give it to me!" he mumbled as he watched the curl of a tumultuous wave.

It was difficult to believe—Virgil always shook his head and laughed whenever he shared the secret—but the ocean first met his gaze at nineteen. The event occured in 1970, on a military transport flying over the Pacific in route to Vietnam.

Born and raised in Harlem, the second oldest in a fatherless household of six, he helped supplement his mother's welfare check by working the streets. There were no friends or lovers, only clients; 'makin' business' was the only game in town, it kept him in the fast lane. There were self-imposed laws; dollars were not made at the point of a gun, nor spent as a drug user. Glue sniffing and grass had been brief experiments, but junkies were lousy role models. They needed a lot of bread to sustain a habit and their minds and bodies listened to another voice. Virgil was always his own master. Dealing in drugs was the way to go. As a 12 year old runner, he followed his pusher boss with bags of heroin concealed under clothing, a single arrest of narcotics possession had marred an otherwise clean police record. The juvenile was punished with a stern judicial warning, and released after a few hours to the custody of his mother.

Virgil was beginning to make a name for himself in pharmaceuticals, when a war got in the way. The draftee's first excursion out of New York was a trip to Army boot camp.

Saigon for Private Cooper, was one big drugstore, akin to the renowned marketplace on 8th Avenue in uptown Harlem where he had received his on-job training. An administrative type, Virgil pushed paper in the day and heroin at night. South Vietnamese government officials and local police provided him with the protection, the supply was all that he could handle. A French Connection (Turkey-Marseilles-New York) had been replaced with the Asian Shuttle (Burma and Laos-Saigon). It was even rumored that the Viet Cong permitted clandestine laboratories for processing the opium poppy to operate on their turf, and gave safe passage to couriers for a heavy piece of the action. Pushing drugs in Nam was no different than the Harlem scene—to survive and flourish, you needed to know the right people and how much their friendship was worth.

Private Cooper's evening office hours were spent at the bars on Tuo Do Street in the company of grunts on R and R looking for a good time. The ladies were everywhere; a quick squirt into a warm snatch was a gimme. But all along Tuo Do were the hawkers on the private's payroll who whistled another tune.

"Need a fix? Virgil fix you up," smiled the B-girl.

"You wanna be cool? You want to go downtown? I know a fat cat," claimed a bartender.

"To stay nice . . . real nice . . . to stay nice," mouthed a soul-brother Army Sergeant in the know, "see this dude Virgil."

And many did. Shooting smack was an answer; goofing and taking in the stars at night a way of making the rice paddies bearable. But what about tomorrow?

It came. Thousands of GI's returned to the States with a habit, but a U.S.-Turkey pact had reduced the street flow of heroin to a trickle and the methadone rehabilitation programs prospered.

The early '70s were also not the best of times for the pushers, a quiet Harlem greeted Virgil after his Honorable Discharge. The marketplace was in a period of transition, a different clientele awaited his services.

The white middle-class flocked to uptown 8th Avenue with a new shopping list. Young people had turned to PCP; Angel Dust had become the number one Freak-out special in respectable suburban neighborhoods. Qualudes were a hot item, getting high on Sopors was the drug of choice for the downer set. Many of the affluent were attracted to cocaine, a fashionable stimulant often taken in combination with a depressant. Virgil worked the whole gamut of drugs, but it just wasn't like the old days. Narcs were everywhere and it was difficult to find one on the take, penalties were stiff for pushers, competition among the movers had intensified, and customers were lost because of poor quality merchandise.

Virg made his decision: it was time to get his shit together and change jobs, find a low-risk, high reward profession that was profitable and secure. Pimping met all the requirements. After all, with the problems America faced in the Vietnam era, prostitution was surely one of the more benign. And wouldn't it always be that way, reasoned the 'stay nice . . . real nice' merchant.

Living in style had depleted most of the profits from the Nam bonanza, but there was still enough money in the bank to move slowly and build a stable of high-class reliable whores. There was something else. The glitter of New York City was no longer appealing, Virgil's fascination with the ocean and the crashing breakers wouldn't go away. The combination of the sea and megabucks was made possible by the state of New Jersey, its citizens had passed a referendum legalizing games of chance.

Gambling was the cornerstone of Atlantic City's renaissance, but the ripple effect was everywhere. Casinos swept in the whores like the waves recover the sand back into the ocean's belly. Virgil's entourage of four foxes with finely honed skills that made them suitable companions for high rollers, were early entrants. The dream was to build an oceanfront mansion with all the amenities.

The Harlem transplant soon became the Kingpin, up and down the scale; street walker to call girl, straight to kinky, one-on-one or groupy—the man to see for your women was Virgil Cooper. The umbrella payroll included the police, the mob, and a host of casino employees. The ladies were loyal, they saw themselves as whores, members of an honorable society headed by a stern, but compassionate master. Virgil was their protector and father confessor, it was important to please him. In return, their needs were fulfilled. Makeup to dope needed the boss's approval, it all was part of the package. Drugs were tolerated, provided performance was not compromised. But a disturbing trend was developing. A few of the girls had not been turning their usual number of tricks, and they were the ones with the largest cocaine habits.

Snow had been a big winner in the Harlem marketplace. Virgil would get the pure coke salt and then cut it with sugar and local anesthetics. Only a little more than half of a typical sale was the real stuff. Cokers were a pleasure to handle, but the days of sniffing caine had been supplanted by another method which radically changed the way Virgil looked at the user. Freebase addicts were behaving like heroin junkies—their needs for a larger fix made them highly irritable, unreliable workers, and downright liars. He even saw a few show withdrawal symptoms, like heroin addicts with a monkey on their back.

The Boss Man leaned against the balcony barrier, the binoculars struck a metal railing. In the adjoining motel suite were the trouble-makers who needed to shape-up. "Maybe I ought to clean house. Get rid of my caine ladies. Maybe this will be the last time ol' Virgil gives a coke party . . . Yes 'mm . . . Yes 'mm," he thought as he trained his eyes on another approaching white cap. "I'm building that house on the beach. An' it's costin me a lotta bread. Do I really need this shit?"

It was not the roar of another giant breaker that caught his attention, but the sound of glass shattering, and the shrill scream of a woman. Virgil quickly opened the slider door and entered the motel room.

"It's Sugar," screamed Sheri, a shapely black girl with a striking long blond wig. "We were partyin, and havin a good time. Sugar was smokin up a storm an' real high. Suddenly she was makin no sense. Maybe she's takin one of them mind drugs on the side. I know she was heavy into LSD for a long time."

"I just put my arm on her shoulder to help, and she went whamo," Tracy, the other member of the caine ladies trio, offered defensively. "Sugar cracked, she walked around the room, threw things, grinded her teeth, and was talking to herself. What are we gonna do, Virgil? Maybe we oughta take her to the hospital," suggested the statuesque redhead.

"Now let me tell you all where I'm coming from. I've had it with all of ya. Ol' Virgil is not your man anymore. No way! You've all fucked me for the last time. Sugar! Sugar!" he yelled in a fit of rage. "Get your ass out of here and back on the street, but not in this town! You can sell your pussy to winos in the Bowery. You ain't big league anymore, you dig me?"

Sugar sat on the floor, one hand stroked the chin and the other hand moved through short silvery hair, sweat dribbled off the face onto a low-cut crimson frock, the white of her eyes were enlarged and the pupils widely dilated. The head remained motionless and her stare was fixed on the stark wall. In the silent pause it became clear that Sugar had been mumbling something in a droning voice. Even the irate Virgil listened.

". . . Grant Park is nice, but let's take a walk along Lake Michigan. The pigs are coming! The pigs are coming! Help me David, I'm stoned! Please don't club me officer! . . . Be in and be out. Tune in, turn on, tune out. I'm your chick, Robert. You know I love to trip. White lightning or purple passion? I'm wired. Rainbow time! . . . Jimi is coming! Jimi is coming! Jimi is coming! Outta sight. The guy blows my mind! . . . Who has the works? . . . Peace and love is the Swami's way. Put your house in order, brother. Let me help you. Flowers anyone? Flowers? How much money you make, Sarah. Let's get crashed. Are we shootin or going coast-to-coast? . . . "

"Spaced-out cunt! She must be speedballin or somethin," Virgil snapped. He reached into his pocket, and in one quick motion opened a switch-blade.

"Please, Virgil," begged Tracy. "We'll take care of her. She doesn't know what she's saying. Sugar won't give you any shit."

". . . I think commune life is great. The place gives me good vibes. San Francisco's a bummer, too many phonies. Farming's real groovy. And the stuff is the best. . ."

"Shut that fuckin stupid ass up, or I'll slice her pussy—and get her outta this town. No spaced-out scumbag is gonna work for me!"

"Sure Virgil. Sure thing," said Sheri, calmly.

". . . if that's the way you want it, I'll sleep with your friends, Samuel. . ."

The two prostitutes, fearful of Virgil's temper, sought to remove their friend, but the attempt only enraged Sugar. " . . . Don't hit me!" she started screaming. "Don't hit me! I'll go back to the strip. I love you, Luther. You're my man! Don't hit me! . . ."

"Oh, honey," moaned Tracy.

Sugar's eyes closed. The muscles of the face and extremities twitched. Jerky, unordered movements became violent as her body was propelled off the floor. She suddenly stopped trembling, blood trickled from the mouth, the skin had a marked pallor, urine now bathed her limp body.

"After all I did for Sugar, the lousy cunt OD's on me. Get rid of her, she's shark meat." Virgil wildly thrashed the knife in empty space to reinforce his order. "I don't know any of you. Nobody fucks with me.

Nobody! I'm too nice, that's my problem," cried the wizard of Saigon's Tuo Do Street.

The Seaside Hospital is small, old, dilapidated, and located in the worst neighborhood. Land speculators and realtors await its demise, convinced this area, so close to the ocean, will one day be the core of Atlantic City's next Casino building boom.

The Hospital remains a major stumbling block. Seaside is considered indispensable to the health needs of the community by a loyal patronage that cuts across class lines. Dr. Stanley Lagen is primarily responsible for that perception. He trained at San Francisco General Hospital, and then at the drug clinic at Haight-Ashbury. His 'Rock Medicine' section at Seaside Hospital attempted to mirror the West Coast model. In South Jersey, if you have a problem with your habit, Doc Lagen—the 'Rock Doc'—was the man to see.

Stan, dressed in blue jeans and Blue Oyster Cult T-shirt, had been chatting with a ward nurse when the loud speaker announced a Code Blue. He arrived in the Emergency Room in time to help the medical staff resuscitate a young woman experiencing a cardiorespiratory arrest. Afterwards, he joked about it over a victory soda.

"Hey, we were really jammin'."

"A million to one shot," said the hardened ER nurse who thought she had seen it all.

Not only had Sugar recovered from the ordeal, but there didn't seem to be any lasting effects. Two days later, on a bright sunny morning, Tracy stood behind Sugar and brushed her hair. Sugar looked intently into the small mirror over the dresser, unmindful, it seemed, of her friend. "Honey, Doc Lagen said everything's fine and you can go back to work real soon. He's a little afraid you won't be able to handle anything more than nine inches. But I told him not to worry. I would help out."

"What are friends for," said Sugar, ready to apply lipstick.

"Holy shit!" squealed Tracy, "your nails are terrible." She put aside the hair brush, and pulled a file out of her purse. "Virgil sends his love."

"Everything back to normal!"

"You know Virgil. He goes crazy, and the next day it's like nothing happened. The beach house makes him edgy all the time. Last night it was the size of the living room window, and the fireplace. . ."

"Tracy! I need a fix."

"Sugar, I can't! Virgil wants us all to cut down. He insists we see Doc Lagen. We're not turning as many tricks!"

"Fuck Virgil. Have you stopped?"

"You were dead! For Christ sake, girl, at least talk to the Doc. He said you have something called a Casey Jones Reaction. Remember that engineer who drove a locomotive head-first into another train? Even a small dose of coke can cause a repeat of what happened two days ago. A fix you handled easily in the past can lay you away."

Sugar never had a chance to respond. A smiling Dr. Lagen had opened the door, his stethoscope brushed lightly over his WHO T-shirt. "I know, I know," said the Doc raising his right hand. "You're feeling great and you want to go home this afternoon. But because I'm cool, you might consider going home tomorrow."

"That's about it, Dr. Lagen." nodded Sugar.

"Call me Stan. We can talk about your discharge this afternoon. There are also a few other things I'd like to discuss, but I gotta split. It's somebody else's turn right now. Tracy, can I see you in the hallway?"

A puzzled Sugar waved goodbye. As the doctor and Tracy left, a bearded man holding a bouquet of long-stemmed yellow roses appeared at the door. He walked in tentatively and smiled at Sugar. After a few seconds of embarassed silence, he cleared his throat.

"Hi Christie," he said.

"How are you Paul?" she replied.

Brother and sister sit in two huge wicker rocking chairs on an enclosed porch at the Seaside Hospital. On the back wall is a mural of an Atlantic City of long ago—a bustling boardwalk with strolling chairs and people walking in their Sunday finery; smiling faces absorbed in happy conversation, in their hair just a hint of the salty breeze coming in off the ocean. Christie has yet to look at the mural; Paul is having trouble taking his eye off it.

The rockers, close to a bannistered fence, face the beach and the ocean. The northern view highlights the ghetto: burnt out tenement shells, apartment houses with venetian blinds and wooden slats covering broken windows, open plots of ground once occupied by seaside cottages and now the site of community victory gardens, burned-out and abandoned junk cars with orange stickers on their windshields awaiting the tow truck, lots filled with old appliances and broken furniture—even the nearby beach is dotted with garbage.

Looming in the south are massive glass and concrete edifices; tall and erect, they abut the boardwalk. Like faceless power plants, the hotel casinos stand proud, ready to fuel the dreams of their patrons.

Paul surveys the scene, attuned to the sights and sounds of a discordant world. An elderly Hispanic woman peers over the window ledge of her room in a run down building. Two young girls wearing high heels, short pants, and blouses stand quietly on a street corner. "Just kids," he thinks. A sleek sports car cruises the street. A black man walks from an abandoned house, and the Porsche stops. "Right out in the open. The money those people make!"

Christie looks at her fingernails. The tip of the file removes the debris. The metal edge hones the cuticle at a feverish pace. Then she holds her hand up to inspect her handiwork. She opens a compact and smacks her lips. She wonders, "Can you see the stiches on my tongue when I open my mouth?" She uncrosses pajama clad legs and says angrily, "Shit! Tracy forgot the eyeshadow."

Paul grins—how else is he to acknowledge his sister's narcissism? Low key seems to be the best approach. In the old days, it was an unrelenting argument. They'd analyze the problems, dissect the components, arrive at logical answers: mistakes were the best teaching tools; his goal was to help her find her own way to an answer. As often as not, the argument got heated and ended with a 'stay out of my life' and a 'fuck off, Paul.' There were times when his patience was pushed to the limits, but he could not let go. The struggle continued, only the tactics changed.

In the beginning she would write, but when she thought he was moralizing and the battle lines were drawn, communication stopped. Any contact had to be initiated by him. The trail was never a mystery. Christie never bothered to cover her tracks, it never occurred to her to even try. Paul had backed off but he was never out of range. He always had spies—Tracy was his eyes and ears in Atlantic City.

Paul watches as Christie adroitly manipulates the nail file to its mark. The nose irritates and she sniffs, the throat tickles and a cough produces a white sputum of freebase cocaine residue into a tissue. The skin on the arm itches and an infected track mark is scratched.

"No shitass doctor is keeping me in this fuckin' hole. I'm getting out today. I know my rights. It's time to crank up the pussy, and get back to work."

"You saved her life, Stan," Paul thought, "and that's your thank-you for services rendered."

It was now time to leave. He removed a piece of paper with his new Chicago address and phone number, and placed it in her purse; Dr. Lagen, Tracy and a hospital secretary had been similarly notified. His lips touched her cheek, he tried an embrace but she squirmed out of his grasp.

His gentle expression remained unchanged, but inside Paul was churning. His stomach ached and his head pounded, but he could not utter the obvious. Instead, he mustered some conviction and said, "You really look great, Christie."

The lie gave him renewed strength, he felt better because of it. Paul had to prepare for the next crisis. Who else was there to help him fight the battle? Christie was a young woman, still in her thirties. Resurrection was not out of the question, nor would it ever be in his lifetime.

He stood alongside his sister, overwhelmed by guilt, distressed by the predictable turn of events, not satisfied with his performance, and unhappy that no new ground had been broken. His face became red, as if he were screaming at her inside, rehearsing the words that might break through. She barely noticed. He leaned over and clenched his fists at his side. If he was going to say something, it had better be now.

"Damn it, Christie," he fumed, "Damn you, Christie! He never would have wanted it this way. You know as well as I, Herb wouldn't have approved."

Her head remained bowed, the nail file continued its dance. All he could do was wait and hope. He looked for a sign of memory and recognition—or even anger over his breaking a promise made years ago never to mention his name. Perhaps this approach should have been used earlier, he thought. Without missing a beat and without looking up at him, she said, "Who's Herb?"

* * *

37

IN Philadelphia's Osler General Hospital is the surgical amphitheater which so captivated Christie during her lunchbreak. Its massive oak doors lead to a wide corridor connecting the Hospital and Medical School. The walls of this hallway are lined with portraits of the men who have shaped the Medical Center's dominant position in American medicine. From Sir William Osler to Ernest Cameron, a recent recipient of the Nobel Prize in medicine, the distinguished are given their due.

At one end of the hallway, on the Hospital side near the spiral stairway leading to the surgical ward, is a special section exalting Osler's WW I, WW II, and Korean War dead. Near the door, an astute observer can still see two small imperfections on the wall, the support nails of a missing painting and plaque. This had been the site of Herb's portrait, the only Osler physician killed in the Vietnam conflict.

A few weeks after his death, a painting was commissioned by the Wolfe Cohen Lodge, Ben's B'nai Brith Men's Club. The artist was Rosa Flaxer, a well known Philadelphia portrait painter. The actual dedication ceremony took place in November of 1968, Ben had died in the interim and Christie had started her odyssey, neither had ever seen the finished product.

The proceedings were brief. The Honorable Chadwick Beaumont, then President of the Osler Medical Center, said a few words in tribute. Rabbi Morris Wise, a hospital Chaplain, gave the benediction. Mrs. Flaxer removed a canvas cover and revealed her work; the plaque read VIETNAM WAR, HERBERT KLEIN, M.D.—CLASS of 1965.

The inspiration for the portrait was a photograph taken by Major Brad Frantz during Herb's first day at Bia Vuc. The style and technique were uniquely Rosa Flaxer's: multiple shades of light, brilliant and vibrant colors; sensibly woven shapes, richly textured and fine-tuned.

In the painting's background were mountains, conveying a feeling of depth as they curled into the bright blue sky. To the viewer's right, a river snaked through a valley; nearby a farmer and buffalo labored in a rice field. On the opposite side were two bamboo houses on stilts, nearby a woman breastfed a newborn and an old man stood at her side, he leaned on a makeshift cane and pointed in the direction of the good Doctor. Herb consumed the center, but he was not alone. Both arms cradled a young Montagnard girl, her coal black hair nestled against his shoulder. She was nude, covered by the ornaments of her people's heritage; the bronze skin glittered as it clashed with huge ochre circular earrings, the neck vanished under strands of multicolored beads and stones, white wristbands covered the forearms. Her dark sad eyes and tight lips signaled fear and melancholy. She looked to Herb for solace.

Herb met your stare and there was a surprise, no disfiguring scar on the cheek. Rosa's answer to the purists. "He left without one," she said, "and he's coming home the same way." Herb wore a green Air Force shirt with captain's bars, and his name in big block letters lay above the left pocket, a partially open shirt revealed his dog tags. The pants were severed by the bottom frame close to a blue belt and white buckle, the ear tips and tubing of a stethoscope protruded slightly from a front pocket. The lips were parted slightly upward at one angle of the mouth, Herb firmly grasped a Bulldog briar at the other corner. Perhaps it was the pipe which created the ambiguity, but his expression caused a controversy: What was the good Doctor trying to tell us? Rosa's response was always a shrug of the shoulders.

Osler Medical Center was not exempt from the turmoil which engulfed the nation in the late '60s and early '70s. In search of a symbol, the anti-war activists made Herb's portrait an issue and demanded its exclusion from the Hall of Honor. Supporters circulated a petition and it was presented to President Beaumont. The number of signatures, and whether or not there was a verification procedure, was never made public.

In December of 1969, the Board of Trustees, faculty, house staff, and student representatives met in a closed door session and debated the issue. Only the result of a secret ballot was announced: Petition Not Granted.

The battle was not over. A few weeks passed and there was a giant anti-war rally at Independence Square near the Liberty Bell. That same evening, Herb's portrait was smeared with feces and urine. A Viet Cong flag draped the canvas; the plaque was shattered into small pieces. And on the wall, inscribed with blood stolen from the Hospital's reservoir, the words: MURDERER, CHILD KILLER, PIG.

The painting was returned to Rosa's studio and meticulously restored by the artist at her own expense. Osler officials were relieved. The Wolfe Cohen Lodge didn't have the money available to pay Mrs. Flaxer, and the allocation of hospital funds, no matter how small, would have created another issue. But the process of reconciliation was far from over.

The invasion of Cambodia by American forces in May, 1970, set off another wave of demonstrations, including a protest by Hospital staff on the Osler lawn: proving once again that the Vietnam War had no safe house in America. The anti-war activists made their position clear, under no circumstances would Herb's portrait be permitted to return to the Hall of Honor.

Beleaguered Hospital officials sought a respite. Their hope was that future house staff would be less radical, and more amenable to dialogue than confrontation; they were trying to buy time, appease the Peace group, assume a neutral posture, and shift the battlefield somewhere else. The painting's future would be debated another day.

Herb's portrait resided in the darkness of a small storage room adjacent to the artist's studio. Mrs. Flaxer had attempted to work with administrative assistants, but a stalemate had developed. In the winter of 1971, she decided to take matters into her own hands. Rosa burst into the president's office, and demanded a hearing. Beaumont Chadwick told her what she didn't want to hear, the Hospital would not even consider the painting's disposition until the war was over. He also alluded to the strong anti-war sentiment, and suggested that another home outside of Osler would not be looked upon unfavorably by Hospital officials. The Wolfe Cohen Lodge was consulted, and they too, refused ownership of the painting. By default, Rosa had inherited an artwork.

The problem was resolved in the Spring of '72. A stranger knocked at her door and told his story. The artist happily relinquished the painting, convinced that Herb's portrait would have a worthy resting place.

The new owner's name was Duke. Herb Klein's portrait presently hangs above the fireplace mantle in his living room. Throughout the '70s, he endeavored to persuade Osler officials to return Herb to the Hall of Honor. Exhausted by endless meetings and sympathetic ears, he tries no more.

Duke shows homage to Herb's memory in yet another way. On a Sunday in early summer, he arises at the crack of dawn. The city streets and expressway are friendly at that hour, and the journey from his home is a little more than a half hour. His destination is a sprawling hilltop pastoral setting that overlooks the Schuylkill River. Beth El Jacob Cemetery has occupied this site for a hundred and fifty years, the Kleins not nearly as long.

At gate B, there is a foot path which leads to a small grove. The first grave on the row in front of the cluster of large maple trees is where Grandpop Jacob Klein rests, Uncle Otto Sachs is fifth in line, and a few yards away at the next highest level, Sophie and Ben share a single marble slab. Herb lies next to his mother.

Ben had provided for perpetual care for the family graves, but often a busy groundskeeper is not equal to the task. The Duke makes sure that Herb's burial place is properly maintained, he removes the weeds and debris and manicures the plot. A few years ago Herb's stone tilted, and his strong arms quickly remedied the problem.

Duke had been in Vietnam—that's also the place where he acquired his nickname. He served his time with the Marines in '69 and '70 in I Corp, mostly in Quang Tri province. One morning, he arose to find THE DUKE painted in bold capital letters on his helmet and flak jacket. The label has stuck, even his wife calls him Duke.

The first time he got to nearby Da Nang, he visited the Air Force Hospital and dispensary. It had been over two years since Herb's death, but maybe there was someone who could share a memory! "Do you know anything about Captain Klein?" he asked countless medical personnel. After the final tabulation, it was clear to the young Marine grunt, Herb's anonymity was assured.

The Duke knew Herb from his Osler days. They had spent many hours together, as many as Herb could spare. Duke's mother would often stand at the door before a meeting, hands on hips and eyes flashing, she would say in a firm and demanding voice: "Follow de Lord and listin to Doc Klein. You understan, boy?"

It was Amanda's way. Franklin Roosevelt Williams never questioned his mother's faith or Herb's wisdom, but he had strong reservations about his own ability. Franklin dreaded the tutorial sessions; they were difficult, sometimes impossible, and always embarrassing. But through it all, Herb exuded confidence, and never lost his enthusiasm or patience. When Franklin could not grasp basic principles presumably mastered in elementary school, the Doctor would only put his arm around the teenager's shoulders and together they would renew the struggle.

"Doc Klein's very happy with you Franklin . . . Thank you, Jesus," a proud Amanda would say excitedly, after another glowing report on his academic achievements. Nor was the fantasy to end with the devastating blow of his mother's death. The Reverend John Tucker helped provide foster parents, and the tutoring intensified. Franklin was never allowed to quit. Then came the day when he chose not to—enlightenment followed, and the charade was over.

Duke is now a senior partner in the law firm of Edwards, Brownstein and Williams. His wife, Alissa, teaches classical dance part time to disadvantaged youths, but most of her energies are devoted to their two children, Brenda and little Herb.

A visit to Beth El Jacob is never easy, but each year he makes the pilgrimage. The ritual starts with a sprucing up of Herb's grave. Duke then bends over, his arm draped over the tombstone. Penetrating eyes seek the earth's softness, and in a gentle voice, he whispers reverently: "Doc! . . . Doc Klein! It's Franklin. Do you remember? . . ."

* * *

Epilogue

THE neighborhood where Herb spent his youth is now a run down ghetto. The house on Wyal Street is gutted, a small porch has collapsed, glass windows have been replaced by boards, and a partially opened door invites entry and a clear view of the sky. This street of simple row houses has two day-care centers, and a corner residence advertises a daily $1.00 lunch special. A few of the houses are nicely maintained, but most are in terminal decay. Herb surely would have been depressed about the physical deterioration of his birthplace, but even more so for the poor souls who now reside within its boundaries.

Fairmount Park has retained its charm. Memorial Hall, the former Centennial Art Museum that dared to exhibit nude statues and paintings, is now the recording studio of the Philadelphia Orchestra. The 18th century mansions are still elegant; Herb's favorite, the stately Rebecca Morris House high above the Schuylkill River, looks particularly handsome in the evening when floodlights bathe its exterior. Horticultural Hall and the gardens have been revived and expanded to include an arboretum; not like the grandeur of old, but enough to have made Sophie, Ben and Herb renew their visits. Boathouse Row, a series of magnificent Victorian Crew houses is aglow in the evening's darkness by man-made light defining every turret, window, niche and corner. The bush where the vision was seen—it exists no more.

Society Hill is making a strong attempt to retain its Colonial flavor, but too often older homes are being radically modified or demolished. The Swenson House, a fine example of classical Georgian architecture, is gone. In the early '70s, student interest in fraternities declined, and Beta Sigma Tau was forced to disband. The property was sold to a real estate developer, and converted into condominiums.

Southwark manages to hold firm. An old seafaring community with strong family ties and a blue collar mentality, it continues to sustain the neighborhood integrity that so appealed to Christie and Herb. The old clapboard house where they lived on Kerr Street overlooking the Delaware has been painted the same color several times over the years, but the interior has been completely changed. The Flint's son, Thomas, and his family now occupy the Klein's apartment. The living room with the big bay window overlooking the river, is the master bedroom, the kitchen has been converted to an additional bedroom to accommodate the needs of their children. Molly is still alive, but old Horace passed away in 1969. The boys at the Southwark Tavern will tell you he never was quite the same after Herb was killed in Nam.

Dave Garret, a fraternity brother, is a General Practitioner in Southwark. His office is on Queen Street. He's been there since 1970, and can't picture himself anywhere else. Herb always used to tell everyone at the Hospital how great the people were in this old neighborhood by the river, and Dave always was a good listener. Dave says he sometimes looks at the big white shingle outside his front door and sees Herb's name right next to his. It's only natural to think about what could have been.

Joe Cinone has an active Internal Medicine practice in nearby Little Italy. He's happily married to Deborah Corso, a legal secretary, and they have four children. The nuns at the Saint Theresa Convent are enraptured with the man; they call Joe at the first hint of trouble. He likes to tell Debbie his popularity is due to the religious training he had as chairman of the Sisters of Mercy Proclamation committee at Beta Sig.

Sam Stein is now a Cardiologist at Mount Sinai Hospital in Northeast Philadelphia. He has three partners and is on the lookout for one more. Two years ago the medical corporation lost a great deal of money with a management financial team and Sam took over the books. Today he's doing more at the business end and less clinical work. His other partners are happy with the arrangement, as long as Sam continues to make acceptable profits. The former fraternity house Treasurer will tell you it's a shame the Medical schools don't offer courses in finance. Sam thinks doctors are unprepared to make intelligent investment decisions, regarding all the money they are raking in, and he's probably right. Sam's current wife, Sheila, like her two predecessors, continues to share the same concern.

The other frat officer at Swenson House, Vice President Larry Lewis, is a Urologist in a small Community hospital in Willis, New Hampshire. His wife, Janet, was a pediatric nurse at Osler General and worked with Christie. It was she who organized the gift fund among the floor nurses for Christie's Hawaiian trip. Whatever happened to that beautiful pipe lighter?

John McFadden is a cancer researcher at the Boss Biology Institute in Cleveland. He married Joan Bellet, a well known women's activist lawyer in the midwest. They are raising three sons with the help of a live-in housekeeper. John's a Little League Baseball coach and helps out with soccer, despite never having played the game. He's now a teetotaler, quite a change from his Beverage Chairman days.

Stu Levin finished an Obstetric-Gynecology residency and entered the Army on the Berry plan. He was stationed in Weisbaden, Germany, and then returned to Massachusetts General Hospital for a fellowship in Oncology. Stu was tight with an ER nurse named Sandy Travis, but it didn't work out. After they split, Stu left Boston and hasn't been heard from. Strange.

Peter James doesn't have a beard anymore, and is not the rebel of old. He stopped making a pitch for Christie after Herb's death and became a real womanizer; the protest crowd turned out to be easy pickins. He was a conscientious objector and served two years as a public service doctor. A psychiatric residency followed at the Meister Clinic in Atlanta. Pete returned to Philadelphia and in '79 married Stephanie Klews, a well known Main Line socialite. Their daughter, Heather, is now four. Peter has an office in Bryn Mawr and another at the Villanova Hospital where he is director and co-founder of the Executive Crisis Intervention Center. The James' are known for their theme dinner parties at Ravensnest, their Radnor estate.

Karl Werner is still a chef working at a University of Pennsylvania fraternity house. Old age has not changed his style. Der Feuhrer runs a tight ship, screams and curses when a rule is broken, threatens to quit at the slightest provocation, and is now about to start his twelfth year as the only untouchable in the eyes of the fraternity officers. Who doesn't like good food?

After 25 years in the Air Force, Master Sergeant Frank Lincoln retired to Rocono Beach, Florida, with his wife, Mary. He works part-time at a supermarket, spends many free hours fishing, but his greatest joy is telling Vietnam stories to wide-eyed grandchildren.

Captain David Wyatt, General Surgeon of Da Nang's 340th

Casualty Staging Unit, returned to Kansas City 20 pounds lighter. He was active in the Vietnam Veterans Against The War movement, but died in an automobile accident only a few months before the United States withdrawal in 1973.

The Commander of the Dispensary and Hospital, Lieutenant Colonel Stalley, returned to Phu Bai in the Fall of 1969 for a second tour of duty. He was promoted to full Colonel, and divorced his wife when he returned to Phoenix. An avid golfer, jogger, and duplicate bridge player, he currently lives in Scottsdale with a young woman 26 years his junior.

Sunny Watts served 20 years in the military and retired from the Air Force as a Master Sergeant. The loadmaster got his feet wet during the '73 air lift, mid-east crisis. After the Guyana massacre, a nationally distributed wire service photograph showed the Sarge removing a coffin at Dover Air Force Base, Delaware. Sunny lives with his parents in Omaha, Nebraska, and still enjoys a good trashy novel.

Major Brad Frantz left the military right after his Vietnam tour and entered commercial aviation. He is a pilot for TWA and resides in Los Angeles with his wife, Martha. Those in the know say that the Major's premature decision to leave the military was due in part to Herb Klein's death. It was he who introduced and helped persuade Herb to assist the Montagnards in the Special Forces camp at Bia Vuc.

Brad's co-pilot in the C-123 attached to the 341st Air Commando Squadron, was Captain Bob Pellham. The Gottcha Man remained in the military, and it was during a second tour of Vietnam in 1969 when he started taking drugs. A divorce followed on his return to the States, and the downspiral continued to '76. His body was found in a Houston motel room, a victim of a heroin overdose.

Lieutenant Wally Brooks recently received his CPA certificate. The pilot's miraculous recovery from the Gulf of Tonkin was followed by a long convalescence at a Naval Hospital, but the elbow and back were never properly rehabilitated. He was unable to return to the Marine Air Group–11 at Da Nang Air Force Base. Wally lives in Seattle with his wife, Carol, their son, Stuart, and a golden retriever, Scarface.

Major Bud Rich completed his second tour at Da Nang as a Spooky pilot without a hitch. The rape charge in the Lee affair was dropped by the Judge Advocate's Office because of insufficient evidence. He resides in Tacoma, Washington, with his wife, Helen, who after 27 years of marriage, continues to endure the hardships of living with an alcoholic. Bud, after a recent stay at the Conway Rehab Center, is presently dry and looking for employment.

Major Cal Richter is a stockbroker with the New York firm of Holidacker and Krimply. He is the company's resident consultant specialist on transportation issues.

The other officer exonerated of any wrong doing was Lieutenant Josh Trent. After Herb's death, he transferred from Major Rich's crew. A few weeks later his C47 Spooky gunship responded to an attack on a Special Forces camp in Tu Wat province near the Laotian border. Witnesses confirmed enemy fire caused a mid-air explosion. The plane was seen rapidly losing altitude in the direction of Laos, no parachutes were seen or crash site found. Though presumed dead, Josh Trent and the other members of his crew are classified as Missing In Action. Josh's wife, Deana, is employed as a social worker, remains active in the MIA Washington lobby, and has never remarried.

Sergeant David Milt's pimples are no longer a medical dilemma. The former Ranch Hand loadmaster has a confirmed diagnosis of chloracne, a direct result of Agent Orange exposure, which is why he receives a small medical disability check. David and his wife, Susan, live in Appleton, Missouri with their son, Richard. The boy was born with a hearing impairment, congenital heart defect and is dyslexic. Sue works as a waitress at Big Jon's Diner, her unemployed husband sits around the house and stares at the TV, complains of headaches, insomnia, impotency, depression, and many other symptoms his doctor has not been able to define. The entire medical history resides in a portfolio on Robert Weiner's desk. Judge Weiner anticipates presiding over a class-action suit that will be a landmark decision for men like David Milt. The chemical company's offer of a small monetary award has not weakened Susan's resolve for adequate compensation. Good luck, Sue.

Can a handsome, personable doctor with no big hangups still be single in his early forties? Captain Mark Jarden continues to look for Ms. Right at the Denver General Hospaital and its environs. Mark works in the Emergency Room, and has a great bachelor's pad near Mile High Stadium. He kept in touch with Christie for a little over a year before she stopped answering his letters. Mark still talks about Vietnam and non-existent war injuries to his dates; the boy in the man just won't go away.

After numerous telephone calls and letters to the Agency went unanswered, Representative Leonard Price was apprised of the problem of locating Mo Balen, and graciously offered his assistance. Congressman Price's request for information at the highest level brought forth the following response: "There is no Mr. Mo Balen presently in the service of the Central Intelligence Agency; nor have we employed in the past a man by that name, or anyone fitting the physical description submitted in your inquiry."

Herb would have liked that one.

*   *   *